THE LIKELY WORLD

The Urbana Free Library
To renew: call 217-367-4057
or go to **urbanafreelibrary.org**
and select **My Account**

THE LIKELY WORLD

A Novel

Melanie Conroy-Goldman

 Red Hen Press | *Pasadena, CA*

Book layout by Bryan Wong

This Must be the Place (Naive Melody)
Words and Music by David Byrne Chris Frantz, Jerry Harrison and Tina Weymouth
© 1983 WB Music Corp. and Index Music, Inc.
All rights administered by WB Music Corp.
All Rights Reserved
Used By Permission of Alfred Music

Library of Congress Cataloging-in-Publication Data

Names: Conroy-Goldman, Melanie, author.
Title: The likely world : a novel / Melanie Conroy-Goldman.
Description: First edition. | Pasadena, CA : Red Hen Press, [2020]
Identifiers: LCCN 2020010351 (print) | LCCN 2020010352 (ebook) | ISBN
    9781597098083 (trade paperback) | ISBN 9781597098113 (ebook)
Classification: LCC PS3603.O55769 L55 2020 (print) | LCC PS3603.O55769
    (ebook) | DDC 813/.6—dc23
LC record available at https://lccn.loc.gov/2020010351

The National Endowment for the Arts, the Los Angeles County Arts Commission, the Ahmanson Foundation, the Dwight Stuart Youth Fund, the Max Factor Family Foundation, the Pasadena Tournament of Roses Foundation, the Pasadena Arts & Culture Commission and the City of Pasadena Cultural Affairs Division, the City of Los Angeles Department of Cultural Affairs, the Audrey & Sydney Irmas Charitable Foundation, the Kinder Morgan Foundation, the Meta & George Rosenberg Foundation, the Albert and Elaine Borchard Foundation, the Adams Family Foundation, the Riordan Foundation, Amazon Literary Partnership, and the Mara W. Breech Foundation partially support Red Hen Press.

First Edition
Published by Red Hen Press
www.redhen.org

For Charles, all of the versions

THE LIKELY WORLD

part one:

in the eye

One

Roslindale & The Fenway
2010

The black SUV pulls into my driveway on the evening of my twenty-ninth day sober. Juni is downstairs, bouncing in the safari seat in front of her cartoons. Twilight has fallen, but I have been trying and failing to work all day, and I have yet to pause to turn on the lamp. Soon, my toddler will cry for her dinner. Everything is dim. Then, from deep within my labors, I perceive the scattering of gravel beneath car wheels, the noise of an engine shifting momentarily into idle, the brake-light red from below. I hear it, and in an instant, it's like I'm high.

Are you ready, SpongeBob?

My nerves spark, little signals pinging from knee to knuckle, from thigh to throat. Someone's here. Someone's come. I stand, move toward the window with the soundlessness of a midnight mother, staying within the shadowed interior until I can peer into the scant view of the driveway. California plates, white sticker on the rear bumper, rolled down window. Mud-spattered, it is a car that has been lived in, but the driver is only a nose and a forehead. From the cracked window, a wisp of cigarette smoke climbs, a whiff of campfire and molasses. Something sings in me. *It's you,* I think, and *who are you?*

I try, but I cannot make the link. Then, the driver's moment of indecision ends. The engine below revs, shifts into gear.

I'm in the hallway, on the landing, taking the stairs. The lights from Juni's bouncy seat scatter a pattern against the walls. *Go, SpongeBob, go! Go, SpongeBob, go!*

I reach the front door just as the car pulls out. The hand in the window flicks the cigarette (a gesture just a bit too girlish to be cool; a gesture I know I know) through the closing automatic window. I run.

"Don't you dare," I yell. I thump on the passenger door.

In the tinted window, my own mad face and shoeless feet regard me, the gaping door of my suburban home behind. The driver might be no one, a stranger making a U-turn or one of the bit player scumbags who accrue at the edges of lives like mine, but it doesn't feel like happenstance. Every flash and movement feels freighted with significance. *You are here. You have come for me. You're back.*

I focus in on the brightly reflective glass, the intangibly faint silhouette within. Man? Woman? A lighter flares inside just as the street lamps illuminate. The world shifts into a yellower palette, washes of detail. There is a hesitation, a hanging pause, as if the person inside has finally recognized me in return. *Do something*, I goad the shimmering glass. *Say something.*

The transmission shifts and then grinds as the driver throws the vehicle into reverse—I make out the image on the sticker I'd noticed upstairs: it is a pale green saguaro on a white oval field. The decal is familiar. Everything is familiar. The engine thrusts into drive, and wheels off into the night.

"Don't leave me," I call after it and then, for reasons I can't discern, I say, "I'm sorry," but the driver is gone. The taillights vanish and I am returned to the twilight of a few moments earlier. The suburban street is precisely the same as before—safe and bland, the sidewalks bathed in the glow of televisions. Only the still-smoldering cigarette butt in the gutter testifies to my visitor. I pick it up. It's an off-brand, a half-inch from the filter, but I drag in the old familiar flavor, and my chest throbs with loss, and—and unnamable shame and everything becomes ash.

You see, SpongeBob? Everything works out in the end.

Everything is as before, except I've been burned alive. I should, I must go inside, close up my computer, give my daughter her dinner, proceed with the script of my nights. I should, I must stay sober. But I am not going to do that. Instead, I am going to go score a shitload of cloud and get as high as I know how.

Juni doesn't fuss when I shut off the TV.

"Want to go for a drive with mama?" I say, bright as summer. Everything is OK. Everything is fine. It's just that I've fallen into the sewer of my own need, and everything stinks and I can't make it through another heartbeat in this filthy living room, this despicable life.

I hoist Juni from the bouncer and onto my hip. I put an applesauce and a tub of corn puffs into the diaper bag. She babbles brightly. She loves to go for a drive.

It might seem unthinkable, but you only have to cop once with a small child in tow before it becomes perfectly ordinary, before you find yourself handing over her car seat to your dealer's eight-year-old daughter so you can eat what you need. It's a junkie stutter in my love for her, the need for what I eat shorting the connection between my mother feeling and the care I owe her. First the drug, always, and then whatever is left over is for my daughter.

"Fern dorm," she gurgles as I strap her into the car seat. "Mend tie."

I am not singular in these routines. There is a small, elite sisterhood of users like me, buying our Gerber peas and testing formula on our wrists as we coast from high to high. For a while, occasionally for a long while, we can pull it off. Each day we make a thousand bad bargains, lie and say that we have insulated them. We say they do not notice the hungry wolf pacing the perimeter of our love. But my daughter knows my wolf. It is in the pitch of my voice, my shortened temper, in how suddenly everything must be done both quickly and perfectly. She knows, all right. I have not insulated her. She is late to talk and her language is strange, but I understand what her fist and her little cough are telling me: 'it's happening again,' she means, or 'don't let this happen again,' or 'this is doing me yet more harm.'

Look. I spent ten years, twenty, vowing to get sober. I'd wake up, today's the day. Sometimes I'd make it to noon. Sometimes I'd make it to breakfast. Each evening turned into a story about staying high enough not to hate myself for my own weakness. And then in the hospital, they showed me Juni's little beating heart on the monitor and I turned over a new leaf. Except, no, I didn't. Even a baby in my belly, even a baby three months old and crying did not get me clean. And then, two years later, in the senseless logic of addiction and recovery, my toddler got me sober where my baby did not. Twenty-nine days. It may not sound like much but it's the biggest, baddest thing I've ever done, and every second of it hurts like hell.

Did I eat cloud when she was inside me? Yes. Was she born damaged because of it? Yes. Yes. She has a regular brain and all the usual limbs but there are characteristic oddities in the size and shape of her fingernails, in the splay of her toes. There is a typical tendency toward respiratory infection that may turn to nothing or may kill her. Developmentally, there's real variation from child to child. Cloud use, in utero, is under-studied. For now, I can say that she's fine.

Stoplight: I root around for a pen on the floor. In the rearview, out the driver's window two SUVs slow and stop—one rides low to the ground as if weighted with an entire life. The only paper at hand is one of Juni's construction paper scribbles. Even though she's almost two, Juni still can't hold the crayon right, so her babysitter positions the paper, and pushes Juni's hand around so everyone can feel she's having a normal childhood. On three separate squares, I write *Prince Cigarettes* then *Saguaro* and *CA Plates*, proof against my fading memory, and lodge the blue scraps between the already-crammed pages of a paperback which has long served as my informal filing system. A Post-it wafts into my lap.

Fucking call Emily G-ddamn it.

Cloud users forget, like blackout drunks. We forget, and when we remember again, the familiar and the strange have swapped; things have gone missing entirely. Which is why, even though I've been waiting for it for two years, even though that flick of the cigarette pummeled my heart and that smoke woke me like the lifting of a curtain, I have no idea if the driver was a hookup or a husband, a savior or an enemy. But the return has cracked me open and now I need to get high.

The light changes. One of the SUVs peels off. The other—the low-riding one—sticks with me, and I take a hard left. My most reliable dealer is Billy in Brighton. He has a big screen TV in his living room, a girlfriend and a daughter, but I said some things to him last time I was there about getting clean, and now it's been weeks and so I'm going to the Village Fens instead. In my early memory, this was a hopeful little place where middle-income people might have lived well, but there were corrupt developers and zoning problems and building in a fenland is a bad idea from the start. These apartments became, by the time I was a teenager, the sort of place where people cooked cloud.

I pull into the parking lot, tires shuddering over the uneven paving, and no one follows. Juni coughs in the backseat.

"Good girl," I say as I hand her the corn puffs. "Good girl."

"Worm turn," says Juni. "Gemmed sky."

"Shh," I say to Juni now; I peel the foil back on the apple sauce, hand her the spoon, and ease myself out of the car.

Now, I think about the taste of cloud, harsh and acidic, and I listen to Juni's ragged breathing. She needs a real dinner, a real mother. The problem with children, with your own children, is that they aren't actual witnesses to your degradation. Since you are life to them, they do not hold you to account. And other than Juni, I am alone, unless you count Emily.

March in New England: everything is cold and brown, but you can smell the green shooting up through the layers of winter rot. You can already find the lunatic crocuses, the pale ones that come first and die soonest. In two weeks, there will be forsythia and tulips, then the last frost and the sudden green in the trees. I want to last until then. I do. I want to figure out how not to be the same shithead I've been for my whole life. I don't want to be some damaged person who cries when a stranger pulls into her driveway, but even more than I want to be better, I want to be high.

Cloud, when it first hits, bitter in the front of the mouth, harsh in the throat, bathes you in a momentary forgetting. The effects, over a lifetime of use, are known only anecdotally. After I bottomed out in California, after the bus trip cross-country, vomiting off some dirt road beneath the towering pines, after the hospital stay, I discovered I had accidentally traded luggage with a stranger. Unpacking my duffel bag, in the provisional room that was Juni's and my first home, I realized I did not recall any of the faces in the framed photographs. The suitcase belonged to some other woman, a woman like me to be sure, who had packed hastily, who wore my size and who balled underpants into the outer pockets of her luggage, but she was not me. Or I was no longer she.

Even the pines, the towering pines, by the lake shore somewhere, they now feel like visitations from a foreign mind. When I try to recall the gap between that moment and the hotel room, I slip into a red panic. Perhaps I was never there. Perhaps, in some other timeline, it is the place on which the whole of my fate pivots.

Now, I leave the car running to keep Juni warm, the doors unlocked because that seems safer. My footsteps crack the ice frozen into the mud tracks as I cross the parking lot. It's just a couple of steps from the car to the building. A few of the units are boarded up, abandoned. From one of the occupied buildings, I hear a father calling upstairs to a kid. The particulars are muffled, but I get the sense. *Come down and clear your plate* or *Finish your homework* or *You need to get in the shower*. I think of Emily, who at this time of night will be memorizing figures for her accountancy exam in the one bedroom of her Dorchester apartment, while her son Leo watches TV on his foldout in the parlor. Lemon-detergent steam, perhaps from a laundry vent, and perhaps from a cloud lab, pours from the basement of my dealer's unit. *Fucking call.*

G-d, I used to be so proud of my modest restraint, the three nights a week I didn't pass out. I thought I was so fucking exceptional. I thought I was barely an addict at all.

Fucking call Emily G-ddamit.

Details. The work I did in California, the reason I have a house and a paid-off car, was to embed hitchhiker programs in videos. My part was to convince people to download them, to split a narrative at the critical moment, to create a tiny drama which encouraged a cautious viewer to click through, even though they knew better, to agree to put our software in their hard drive. My boss, Lew, made the videos—dirty pictures, fetish stuff, copycats of popular extant porn. I waited for a tease, the fingertip at the neckline, the zipper parting, and then I offered fulfillment—*click yes to continue.* I remember how easy the work was on cloud, how it felt to scan the frames with the singing sensation of high in my skull. I was the best, the best damn technician in the field, and worth every check Lew wrote me, but every junkie turns unreliable in the end. Every junkie begins to lose details.

—I've reached the concrete landing before one of the lit units. Something about the details is bothering me. They all look alike, half-timbered, the fanciful tower, the stucco breaking off in chunks. From within, I hear the music of a singing competition. It's old-lady entertainment. The curtains are old-lady curtains, brown mushroom pattern faded from twenty years of sun. I cannot recall if it's the right place. Is this the right place? The house where I used to buy? Or is this a different house, the one where I came as a teenager and—what?—I ate grilled cheese and wore a skirt made out of men's ties and then the power went out. I fidget, shift, and then the lemon is in my mouth and I reach for the bell.

Cloud sucks away hesitation. High, details clarify. Sober, I get mired in the swamp of loneliness and need. For example, the job that had posted on the Seychelles server through which my boss routed his communications—I could not get it done. The project itself seemed to be only partial, contained a link to a truncated video clip, reference to a code I was supposed to drop in, an implied deadline. I owed Lew. When I bottomed out in California, it was Lew and his wife who had found me, had gotten me to the hospital. He'd given me this life. In return, for all that, I had made a promise when I had left. It wasn't something vague, like staying sober, though he might have asked that of me, too. There was a thing he counted on me to do, a specific project, and so secret or risky that at some point I believe I must have hidden it even from myself. I had waited for him to make contact for nine months. And when finally he did, I could not follow through. My sobriety was the problem. High, you don't deliberate. The answer comes like a taste in your mouth. High, you don't care who is driving the SUV idling by your house. You just climb in, before the chance has passed. The just not thinking, the not fucking worrying or trying anymore, the way you give yourself over to it, the way it absolves you of everything. I can taste that feeling too.

I lean on the bell again. *Come on. Come on.* Something stirs on the other side of the door and a shadow moves toward me.

You come to horse for release of pain, for the ease sighing in your joints. You come to weed for laughter. You come to coke for sharpness, to molly for pleasure, but you come to cloud to begin again. If cloud sometimes speaks to you from some other life, offers you recognitions which do not match your experience, then perhaps, in cloud, you can rewind to the moment just before it went bad; cloud promises you can start anew. Sober, I am stuck with myself, my own bad days. Sober, I cannot escape.

The dealer's door opens. The small figure within is backlit. Behind me, in the parking lot, there is movement, but I am too focused on the door, to turn and check.

The door answerer is an elderly lady, barelegged, dragging gray slippers. We look at each other, neither of us pleased. "Where's my delivery?" she demands.

I feel a sinking. An uncertainty. What if I'm doing it again? My dealer doesn't live here; my dealer lives in Brighton with his daughter. This is a different Mellie's dealer, a different timeline, a long ago cloud trip. All the details are wrong. The woman in front of me begins to shake her head, and then releases a volley of curses in a language I don't speak, though the gist is clear enough. *Junkie*, she's saying. *Get lost, you stupid.*

But she's not talking to me, is looking past me, over my shoulder. "You," she calls into the dark parking lot. "You. You junkie. Get away from there."

Now, I turn. The parking lot behind me is bathed in the headlights of a parked SUV. Someone lurches through plumes of exhaust toward another car. My car. It is still running. The figure moves with the spastic, disoriented energy of a user. *Juni.* I wheel, and catch my foot and trip, falling hard: chin to pavement, skull rattled. From my stunned position, I force myself up. My car door hangs open, the interior shadowed. I cannot locate the figure.

The old woman points. "You damn junkie. You want me to call cops?"

Then, there he is, by the door of a parked SUV, clutching a bundle. He tosses it inside. No cry. I lurch toward him. He slams the door and then, in the sudden flash of his headlights, my car is illuminated. I see Juni, still resting on the plastic seat, snoring and drooling, utterly undisturbed. It's only the diaper bag, the stupid diaper bag he's taken. My heart is in pieces. What have I done? What had I almost done?

The world wants to take her from me, this I know. Juni is nothing I've earned and no one I deserve. I've done the worst thing a mother can do to her child, and done it again and again. Someone will take her from me. Maybe someone should. I wrap my baby up in my arms, breathe in the milky funk of her smell. *Never*, I tell her. *Never again.*

The old woman staring down at me. "You people," she says. "You think can fool me. But I know fiend when I see fiend. I don't trust for a minute."

Come on. Someone is tugging at her from behind, the figure unidentifiable, a nurse or a son, a husband or an aide. *Someone* is at the old woman's shoulder. *Come watch your show*, the voice urges. She gives me a last glare, then nods and allows herself to be drawn back into the warm light of her apartment.

For a moment, the person remains in the doorway, a vague shadow. "Call Emily," I think I hear, but I don't trust me for a minute, either. And then the door closes.

Juni coughs in my arms, the cool air and the wake of panic. It's not the details I'm missing. It's the very heart. I hold her, gently, delicately, afraid, and then I begin to rock her, my grip tightening until she is secure in my arms. Her breathing eases, a warm patch spreading from where her mouth rests against my shirt. This is my daughter, I think. This is where I am.

I have not used, but how close I am, still and always. How close and easy is a return. I wrestle my phone from my pocket, balancing my stirring child as I do. *Fucking call. Fucking call. Fucking call. Fucking call.*

"Mellie," says Emily, my first and only sponsor, the woman who got me sober when nothing else would. She swallows exhaustion from her voice. "Where are you? Are you at a bar?"

Silence fills the phone line and Emily waits.

"I hate it here," I say, meaning a thousand other things, a thousand *here*s I hate.

"Great," says Emily. The bedclothes shift as she hoists herself up, the moisture of her mouth as she ungums her lips from sleep. "Oh, kid. You're doing so great. Now tell me where you are."

The light in the window in front of me blinks out. I hold the phone between my chin and my shoulder as I nestle Juni back into the seat.

"I'm just getting home," I slide in on the driver's side, shift, give the car a little gas. It rolls wetly from the parking lot. Juni, covered in applesauce, spoon lost in the seat cushions, releases a few gasping coughs. Emily delivers her platitudes, her one day at a times and her easy does its. The morning isn't far. Newspaper trucks rumble past me in the darkness and when I reach my street, I've made my first month clean.

Two

Brookline & The Fenway
1988

Since General Hospital has been preempted for coverage of Hurricane Gladys, Nancy and I decide to go to the crack house. We're taking the T. Out the window of our train, the sky looks weird and orange. Even though she has her license, Nancy is currently grounded for stealing a one-hitter from George's Folly. Grounding: whatever. We're sixteen. Nancy wouldn't put up with that shit, but then her folks removed the distributor cap from her Ford Escort to enforce the punishment. So, we're stuck with mass transit, heading to the crack house to meet Judah and Paul.

Three years ago, Nancy and Paul Greene, and Judah, the crack guy, we were all at Hebrew camp together—flag circle, flashlight wars and a Star of David on the outhouse doors. The following fall, Nancy and I started seventh grade together at the White School. We had the Jew thing behind us, plus we were the only two girls not to get picked up by housekeepers. Nancy's parents are geneticists and foreign so even though they are rich, they believe having a babysitter is a kind of spoiling. My mom is just too broke to pay someone to look after me. So, camp, and alone in the afternoons and General Hospital, me and Nancy ended up best friends. Even after she got kicked out and went back to Brookline, we kept hanging on Thursdays to watch soaps and argue about is Blackie cuter or is Frisco. The rest of the week, I'm building up my transcript with debate or yearbook, and Nancy is building up her tolerance, drinking and getting high with Paul Greene. Paul knows the tow truck guys, and they know Judah and that is how Nancy and I are cool to go to the crack house.

It might not even be crack, though. It might be something else he smokes.

"Actual crack?" I ask. "Like actual rock in actual pipe?"

Neither of us has personally talked to Judah since the days in Bunk ‫וו‬, but he has supposedly turned beautiful, and Nancy thinks the four of us will wax nostalgic about blue team in color wars, and somehow this ancient connection is going to help her get him into bed. It's a bad plan, at least my part. Even back at camp, Judah wasn't the kind of boy I talked to ever. He was a junior counselor, A, and B, his dad was a movie producer and had made some film called *Mack the Knife*. Meanwhile, I still slept with a unicorn pillow, and if I forgot my house key, I sometimes peed my pants before my mom came home. A baby.

To be factual, I still don't know a lot of boys. White School is all girls, and when I hang out with Nancy, it's just us. Nancy, the rest of the time, makes a point of boys. If a boy dropped out of the high school to get his tow truck license, or if he graduated and will buy gin for you, or will let you shoplift during his shift at Store 24, Nancy knows how to know him. Sometimes, at night, when we're supposed to be sleeping over, she'll take out the Escort and we'll do circuits of all the boys she knows. We drive by the pizza place, the gas station, the Section 8 housing units. Nancy has taken it upon herself to educate me.

"The thing you need to understand," Nancy tells me, "is that, for boys sex is an accomplishment, something that makes them better, and for girls, it's usually like an *un*-complishment."

I pay attention. Last weekend, after she and I had gone to bed, Paul Greene climbed in her window. He had been purposefully locked out of his dad's house, and it was one of those late spring nights that dip to the lower forties. He'd been on the street corner, pacing and smoking and waiting for his dad to relent, but he ran out of cigarettes, and so he'd come to Nancy's. His fingers were white with cold, scraped from hauling himself across the asphalt shingles of the porch roof.

Nancy could never be into someone like Paul, but sometimes when she gets bored, they'll fool around. With them, it's different; no one accomplishes anything or loses anything, because they don't have intercourse, and because Paul goes down on her the same amount she goes down on him. Plus, it's normal, in that they laugh at each other and complain about how each other taste—it's mostly a joke. Still: Nancy had held his hands, puckered with chill, in hers until they warmed. It reminded me in some weird way of the night when I first met Paul, when we'd been in seventh grade. It reminded me that boys I knew used to be kids.

Now, Nancy and I get off the train and cross the bridge that separates Brookline from Mission Hill. If you're driving, there's this one part of the Jamaicaway that goes suddenly up, just before you get to the medical area, but if you go to the right instead, you're on an access road that hooks around into the parking lot of the Village Fens Apartments.

My mom and I have lived in a lot of shitty places, so I'm not freaked out by how some people live. About half the units are occupied, cars in the parking spaces with Dukakis stickers, junk on the porches. No one has mown the lawns even though it's June, and grass sprouts from the pavement cracks. There's a weird burning odor in the air. We find the unit, but no one answers.

Around back, there's a patio and a sliding glass door. Nancy jumps the wrought-iron railing and presses her face to the glass. I peer past the mushroom curtains and see a thin woman in a blue bathrobe surrounded by stacks of padded mailers and cardboard boxes. She is watching the hurricane on TV.

"OK, Nancy? I think we should go," I say. "I seriously think we should leave."

Nancy shakes her head at me. "Can you please just for once not be a total freak?" Between us is the history of too-scary houses where we trick-or-treated, of girls who trash-talked us and grown-up men who leered when we were still twelve and skinny, is the history of Nancy holding ground and me running away. I follow Nancy; I try not to be a total freak.

Nancy taps on the glass, and the woman turns and squints. She shakes her head, harried, then mouths something obviously not-nice before she returns to her TV show.

"Crap."

"Could it maybe be a different one? They all look the same."

Nancy shakes her head. "That's the mom. She's, whatever, unhinged. Not in a like supervisory role."

Back around the side, Nancy tries the bulkhead. It opens easily and we descend into semidarkness. It's four o'clock on a school day, and we are walking into the crack house. The burning odor intensifies. A shirtless, barefoot man in a surgical mask and a pair of ripped blue jeans appears at the bottom of the stairs. His head is shaven and there's the partial script of a tattoo on his arm, *vain* or *pain*. He's very tall, and blond by his eyebrows. I have the junior-counselor feeling, which I now call the crack feeling. I don't see Paul.

"Hey." He yanks off the mask and smiles. "Little Nancy. Hey. What are you doing here? Come on in."

She clomps down the stairs to him, and he slings his naked arm around her and lifts her in a hug. I remain on the top stair, watching. It's not my feeling that he's handsome, but I am crap at telling, am always liking the one ugly guy in the band. Nancy says it's a self-esteem thing, that I don't think I'm good enough for the hot one even in imagination land, so I pick the keyboardist with the stupid jaw or the retarded hairstyle. Nancy goes for the blond front man. She's muscles and Mohawk, lead guitar and vocals. Judah is just her type.

The crack house basement is unfinished, but there are carpet samples on the floor, a trash-picked sofa and an electric bass in one corner. Steam filters around the edges of the curtain which divides the room, as if laundry is being boiled beyond.

"You remember my friend Mellie, right?" asks Nancy. "Come in, Mellie. Sit."

Judah's face does not like light up with recognition and since I see that Nancy's doing fine without it, I choose not to remind him of our athletic shorts days in back in Bunk *vv*.

"What's up?" I say, but of course it comes out all nervous-robot, like *what is up*.

Judah takes in my big black glasses and my Billy Bragg t-shirt and gives me the nod, then he pulls Nancy onto the sofa beside him, and he is done thinking about me.

The real truth of us isn't self-esteem. It's that Nancy has boobs, and I'm flat-chested. It's been that way since we met at the age of twelve and this one fact might explain all the differences between us. Boobs seem like some token she's earned which entitles her to other desirable things, to Judah-aged men and getting high and parents who don't care if she stays out. I think of birthrights, of Jacob and Esau, and I wonder if the treasures of her life are things I could some-how steal. But at the moment I'm the weird friend with the probably bad breath, hanging in the doorway of the crack house. I come inside.

"Paul's not here?" I take a seat in a tatty butterfly chair.

"Paul who? The twat Paul, or the other one?"

Nancy laughs, and taps a Prince out of her soft pack. "Paul Greene," she says.

Twat, I think, sounds like *twit* and means vagina and is a worse insult on a boy than on a girl. Girl, it just means extra bitchy. Boy, though—I think of Paul's cold hands steepled between Nancy's and I fiddle with the strap of my book bag and try to keep my face normal.

Nancy fixes her cigarette between her lips, then offers one to Judah.

"What is this brand?"

"They're on two-for-ones. Some new Congress thing where they have to rede-sign all the packages not to appeal to kids. They're pretty gross, though."

He inhales. I should say, Nancy's theoretically here to buy dope, but it's not like there aren't dealers at the high school, and I'm guessing Judah knows that the weed is an excuse.

"You guys gonna hang? I'm good until Andi. Or do you have to jet right away?"

"That depends," says Nancy. "I've been rolling shake since Memorial Day."

A timer goes off. "Hang on," Judah says. He hands Nancy his private stash and retreats to the secret drug land behind the curtain. Behind him I see a row of what look like plastic spoons hanging from a clip wire, their mouth ends covered in some kind of crust. To me, it's weird that no one is worried about the police.

"Because it's legal," says Nancy. "You can buy it in a head shop. Over the counter."

"I thought it was crack."

"That's a joke. Mostly. Probably."

Nancy begins pinching, separating the flower from the stem, the leaf. Even I know it's the good stuff, hairy buds which look more Muppet than plant. The organic smell of it escapes into the room. I glance at the ceiling. I can hear the faint noise of the television, and a thumping noise, like someone is pacing back and forth on a game leg.

"You're going to light up?"

"The mom's so out of it." She licks the rolling paper. "Four courses of electro-shock on top of unspeakable personal tragedy. She does not give a shit about are we smoking weed in the basement. It's the kid who freaks out if like one whiff escapes, and she's still in school."

"Andi?" I say.

"Yeah," says Nancy. "That's why Judah's always here. Which is gross, because wake up, she's like fourteen. That's seven years difference between them."

It is like this with Nancy, like watching General Hospital only once a week. Not much happens in between Thursdays, but you always feel like you've missed some of the flavor, one or two longing gazes that carry the show for the next month, and so the logic of Nancy's stories dangle without ending.

"She's his—girlfriend?"

"Right? No. Obviously not. It's like they can't sleep together because blah, blah, blah, but the attraction is undeniable, blah, blah," Nancy drags on her cigarette. "So he comes here just to cook, but then things transpire. Everyone says she's so hot. Listen to me on this: girls have the reputation for it, but it's boys who really get delusional about a tragic story. Also, redheads. Andi's not objectively that cute, but people always think redheads are prettier than they actually are because they're a rarity. The deal with her and Judah is a heartbreak, sure, but nothing anyone needs to slit a wrist over."

Behind the curtain, there is the sound of running water, glassware being knocked together, the whistle of gas escaping a valve.

Judah emerges in a wash of lemon steam, carrying Nancy's baggie and a cup holding four plastic spoons. Like the ones attached to the clip wire beyond the curtain, their mouth ends are coated in some substance, then covered in plastic wrap. Nancy brandishes the two flawless joints she's rolled and Judah taps her arm, and then somehow they've negotiated it so she's sitting on his lap, his arm threaded over her. She holds the tip of the joint in her mouth then flicks her lighter and inhales.

So much for Andi, is what I think, which demonstrates my being a total retard.

"You want?" Judah says, holding in the smoke and handing me the joint.

I shake my head, and Nancy leans back across him and pinches the tip.

"Mellie's going to be a politician," she says. "She's keeping an eye on her future career."

Judah, stoned, snorts. "What a joke. Think about our parents. Who, who's forty, has never smoked weed?" He and Nancy pause, rest the joint on the ashtray, and lock lips and then separate. Nancy takes the joint and Judah continues.

"Seriously? You live through the sixties *and* the seventies and you never smoked out?"

"It's a different standard," I say.

I know I seem like a complete hoser, not smoking, what Nancy said about politics, but I'm serious about my life. I was in New Hampshire for the presidential primaries; I knocked on 473 doors for Gary Hart. Politics, for me, isn't like wanting to be a ballerina. I'm going to Harvard, and then getting a congressional internship, and then I'll do grad work at the Kennedy School. I want to be a Speaker of the House. I'm going to wait until Tip O'Neill retires and then I'm going to run for his seat. Ballerina, incidentally, is what Nancy still wants to be. A couple of nights ago, she spent an hour on the phone, crying about her chest, about having too big tits now to play Clara in *The Nutcracker*. Sometimes I think this is why she wants me to smoke pot, so both our dreams will be screwed.

In my peripheral vision, I can see how things are progressing. The kissing is done. Nancy rests her non joint hand on Judah's genitals and is pumping his pelvis area through his pants.

"Guys," I say, but it's soft, and I'm facing away, and neither of them notices. On television, wind blows through the palm trees. Waves crash to shore. The reporter wears his studio face, as if none of it is happening.

I try not to be a total freak. I imagine I am driving around, like everything in this basement is passing by a car window, so I can watch and not watch at the same time. The scene on the sofa should be instructive, but also, it seems like Nancy must be doing it wrong. Sex stuff shouldn't look like flattening pizza.

I stand and fiddle with the rabbit ears. It's still the storm, how the tropical depression that has moved up the coast from Haiti seems to be reforming in the Atlantic. The weatherman is Puerto Rican, which my mom mentions about him every time he comes on. She is once again without a job, once again at home during the day, so there are many opportunities for her to promote tolerance by watching other cultures on TV.

I can't help it; I have to turn. Nancy is facing away from me, on his lap, skirt up around her waist. A thing I know about Nancy is that she has only had actual sex, like intercourse sex, seven times but it seems possible this is what she is doing, right here. With me in the room. She looks ugly, I think, her t-shirt rolling up over her back fat. He isn't even looking at her. He's looking at me. Has he been watching me the whole time? Staring at my hunched shoulders and my butt which is too big for the size of my waist? Or have his eyes only now focused on me, as he releases a shuddering sigh. His hand twitches like it wants to pull me into the sticky thing on the sofa. I'm ugly. I'm the ugly slut. He smiles, dopy, colluding, and not at all ashamed.

Someone is banging on the bulkhead. Nancy and Judah pull apart, guilty, hilarious, Nancy clown-mouthed with her own smeared lipstick.

Then it is Paul coming down the stairs. The light is behind him, wavery afternoon sunlight. He blinks, things flickering on his face as the scene below clarifies for him.

"Nice," he says, to the room.

"Hi, twat," says Nancy and she and Judah begin to laugh, the sound forced and still sticky with the thing that was in the room a second before.

"Nancy," he says. "Are you coming?"

"Why?" She slides off of Judah's lap. "What for?"

"The guys are ready to get your car." Paul is slimmer than Judah, a little darker. Like me, he's a half-Jew, but his other half is Chinese. He is not man-beautiful, his long skinniness, his fingers which go white in the cold, but if someone liked him, it wouldn't be bad self-esteem.

"What's up with your car?" Judah asks Nancy.

"We have to tow it to my garage so her parents won't fuck with it again," says Paul.

Nancy is still trying to stop laughing. "Sorry. I'm sorry. What do you want me to do?"

That's the thing about Nancy: she can be an asshole, but she's not a wuss.

"My dad will be home in like an hour," says Paul. "So, move it."

"Should I come?" I ask.

Nancy shakes her head as she yanks down her skirt. There's a stain on it by her right leg. "No room," she says. "Truck cab. But hang tight. I'll be back in like fifteen, cool?"

Paul fishes a roach from the ashtray and sparks it before they go. I guess that's the thing about Paul: it worries him to hide a car from his father, but he doesn't mind doing it high. Nancy catches me looking and gives me little smile as she smooths her hair. Her lip twitches, her eyebrow, something she thinks she knows about me. But I'm not the one having boredom sex, wearing a stain on my miniskirt.

Then the two of them are gone, and I'm alone with Judah Cohen in the crack house basement.

He looks at me. "You want to see the rest of the house? Andi's room is pretty cool."

"Are we allowed up there?" I ask him, but I am absolutely following him.

"Oh," he says. "Yeah. No one cares."

The galley kitchen and the TV room are on the first floor. The sofa where the mother was watching TV has been converted to a bed, and by the lump underneath the bright afghan, I assume she's sleeping. Her TV is still on, warning of storms, but muted.

"Is there anything to eat?" I ask.

"Here? Never. They have takeout or they starve. Mostly, starve."

On the second floor, it's like the family ran out of steam, a mattress plunked down in the hall. Milk crates full of dirty dishes and cosmetics. There is no place that might be Judah's, unless it's the basement, so maybe he doesn't live here after all. I find other people's living arrangements mystifying, even Nancy who's an only child in a large house. My mother and I live in three rooms just with each other. Every other permutation seems overwhelming.

I follow Judah up the last set of stairs into the tower room. It's round, with a window seat, which I guess is pretty cool, but otherwise it's a mess. There's a sewing machine, length of purple fabric spooling from it, runny lipsticks and stubby eye pencils scattered before a mirror on the carpet. There's a proper bed, unmade. I wish there weren't a bed.

"I'm going to sit," I say. From the window, I can see the edge of the hospital district, the nurses on their way to the second shift. The power plant belches black diesel fumes over the genteel mansions which remain from when this area was still remote from the city. Way beyond, I am now able to make out the White School. When Judah sits beside me, there is a half-inch's distance between us.

Campaigning in New Hampshire, a woman answered the door without a shirt. It was twenty-six degrees, the White Mountains visible in the distance, and this woman was standing there with not even her arms across her chest, just her stretch-marked breasts and her appendectomy scar and a pair of chinos. It is like that feeling now, like some stranger at any moment could open the door and see your secrets.

"Do you remember," I say. "At camp—"

"What camp? You were at camp?"

"I guess I was younger. In a younger cabin."

"What about it?"

"There was a girl who supposedly drowned herself?"

He gives me a quick glance, like am I fucking with him. "She didn't drown," he says.

It's like a skill with me, saying the wrong thing. It's like being a genius. "Never mind."

After a moment, I hear a small sigh escape his lips. "You ever try cloud?"

At first, I think I've misheard. "Cloud?"

"It's new, legal"—he smiles—"even for a politician. Although, someone got a bad batch, with weird additives. The FDA is reviewing it, I guess, but so far, no decision."

He takes from a cup beside the mattress several spoons with the mouth end covered in Saran Wrap. "But we cook this stuff right here. There's nothing bad in it. "

He hands two over to me. It is maybe the same thing as they were doing behind the curtain, making these spoons. The next generation will know the cloud of internet purchase, of Lucite boxes and stacks of lozenges separated by squares of Cyrillic newspaper. But the early users sucked cloud off the tip of a plastic spoon. One story will claim the method came from an immigrant way of making Korovka, a sweet, for lunch boxes, that cloud was first made in homes. Another story puts its origin to a lab in Ukraine which was situated next to a plastic cutlery plant. When I meet Judah again, much later in life, he will be interested in other origins, not in how cloud began, but in how it splits your life. But that's later. For now, I take two of the spoons from the cup and hold them carefully by the plastic end.

I think of Nancy squeezed into a tow truck cab with Paul and I ask what seems like the important question. "Does it get you high?"

He shrugs. "It's different for different people. But worry is part of it, stopping worrying. It's like this: you know how you do something dumb, some little thing, and you can't let go? Aren't there mistakes where years later, you still cringe when you remember? I saved her, you know. The girl who tried to drown herself, but I'm not sure it was the right kind of saving. That kind of thing. You know?"

I nod.

"Cloud makes you forget. Not forever. It comes back, but not as bad. Also—" he laughs—"sometimes a little out of order. For some people, forgetting is a kind of high."

"For you?"

Judah smiles. "I just like drugs. I'm not picky." He peels the plastic off his spoon. There is a toffee-colored gel underneath that he licks into his mouth and then holds for a few instances, and smiles over his half-clenched teeth. "It absorbs best through the membrane of cheeks. Some people rub it on the gums, but I think, just savoring it in the mouth is enough." He holds the cloud, and holds it and holds it. And then, he swallows—

—*pop*—

—he leans back, holding his spoon in his teeth, and drops his hand. Our fingers nearly touch on the seat cushion. I am thinking of the thing I witnessed on the sofa downstairs, and it's still disgusting to me, but also maybe something else too. I watch the distant lacrosse players in their red skirts running across the playing fields.

"So," he says, "taste?"

I look at Judah. I have a mother who cooks frozen pies and can't keep a job. I go to the White School and do my homework. I worry too much about too many things. I think: no one can stop this. I think: I am alone, and all I have to do is say yes.

A door slams below us, loud and pissed off. A book bag thunks on the linoleum and then a voice, high and urgent, calls out, "Mama? Mama? Wake up, Mama. Did you have your medicine?"

I am still holding the spoon. For a moment, I hesitate, and then I tuck the unlicked spoon into my bag, and I follow Judah downstairs.

What I'm thinking is that nothing would have happened, that I am a good girl, rich with junior wisdom and adept at responsible choices. But in the hours and days that follow, I will find myself returning to the image of the spoon, to Judah's lips closing over the gel. What if the afternoon had stretched out? It is as if his first offer primes me somehow, as if being in the room with cloud teaches my body to anticipate the drug's power, breaks down my resistance. I know a new kind of thirst. It is like how it happened when Nancy hooked up with a boy for the first time. She said, "I might not do it again." "Bullshit," I told her. "Now you know. It's harder to say no once you know what you are saying no to." I will remember the fog in Judah's eyes, the recognition returning, and I will want to give cloud my worry.

The woman Nancy and I had seen through the window before now stands in the hallway of the condominium, assessing a handful of blue pills. Andi, the daughter, is in the galley kitchen, smoking a clove. She's pretty, prettier than Nancy described, but small like a kid, like she's twelve years old. Still, if it was just her face, eyeliner and freckles, you'd think she was our age.

"Seriously, fucker," the girl is saying to Judah. "You want to have girls here? You want to get high?" She ignores us as we file past.

"I know," says Judah. "I really do."

There is the sound of a flush, a light flicking off, and Nancy emerges through the bathroom door with a bright smile and the eighth. I observe a wet patch on her skirt where's she's splashed water from the sink to blot out the stain. She grabs my hand. "Time to go. Get your stuff. It's time to go."

Judah spares us a glance, apology in it, but doesn't stir to see us out. "Later, little Nancy," Judah calls. Through it all, he's forgotten to zip up his pants.

"Definitely." Nancy delivers him her bullshit smile.

We reach the door. My own face is backlit, washed of detail like the early New England twilight framed behind us. Everything inside that house feels richer and more real than we are, like a soap opera without all the acting. I think of the spoon in my backpack, my fingers nearly touching Judah's on the sofa, and I feel like I've taken something of the afternoon with me. I walk into the evening, steady pace. No need to run anywhere.

"Paul didn't come back with you?" I ask. But Nancy is already ten paces ahead of me.

"Walk faster," Nancy calls over her shoulder. "I'm famished."

On the bridge that links the J-way to Route 9, I reach her side. She rubs the spot on her skirt, and I think of Judah's fingers on the window, the circuit between us. A confession moves into my mouth. And it's only because of that, because I can barely keep from telling her, that I ask her the dumb as dirt question instead.

"So, you and Judah? Are you like together now?" What do I know? I've never had a boyfriend, never made out, never kissed except truth or dare.

Nancy kicks a beer tab with her motorcycle boots. Mission Hill, on the other side of the Fens, is behind us, and twelve years earlier during the busing crisis, the riots spilled onto this bridge. Poor kids threw rocks as fancy cars fled toward the suburbs. It was 1975 by the time the North got around to integration and it's not like nationwide you had a bunch of awesome stories about how desegregation went down, but here, all the rich people had already left the city. Sending students from one shitty Boston school to another shitty Boston school, plus Irish, plus racism—we failed pretty spectacularly. And how it turned out, white guys waving the American flag, mobbing that black lawyer, my mom said, it made you think nothing could be fixed, ever.

We lived on the poorer side of the border before we got our rent-controlled place in Brookline, back up the Hill. We didn't have much money—but we got checks from my father's family. We could have lived in Watertown or Arlington. Maybe it was some kind of Irish penance, my mom's thing of living in a dangerous neighborhood, maybe she was trying to pay back something that had happened in those earlier years. My mom would walk me to my fancy private school, and point out the blocks where rioters had gathered. She has weird beliefs about the past, says that violence is a bloodstain, that its occurrence will always leave a ghost of itself in physical space. Most of that stuff is lunatic, but the imprints I believe in. Maybe the moment before I say that dumb thing to Nancy stays just behind us; maybe me and Nancy are back at the T stop, before she was kicked out of the White School. We're still twelve years old and waiting for the train to come. Maybe we could rewind to that. But, no. We remain in the here and now: Nancy, sixteen, and grounded from her car, flicks at the moist corner of her eye like I'm not supposed to notice she's crying. I want to take what I said back. I want to not be stupid, but I can't.

"I know when to put out, OK?" Nancy says. "It's a skill I've developed."

"Nancy. I'm sorry. I—G-d, duh—"

"What have you got? What makes you too magical to smoke weed or blow a boy or stay out past eleven? Why are you so fucking precious?"

What have I got? I excel at conjugating French verbs, at compare-and-contrast essays. I can write a killer lab report, but in my after-school existence, nothing of worth. No one is ever going to ask me to dance or kiss my lips or share their box of Entenmann's with me because I give good graph.

I am studying for a life that will be more like Nancy's. I am learning about stains that rub out and don't, how you need to arm yourself for basement rooms and no adults, and things behind curtains. Nancy has her tits, and the ability to ride in the cab of a tow truck, and to look mad when she's scared. What do I have? Panic, fear, thinking too much, hesitation and doubt. I think about the spoon still tucked in my bag, how the worry eased from Judah's face when he put it in his mouth. A drug like that, it could smooth you out. All the awkward moments, all the missteps, cloud could fix all the times you got it wrong.

Three

Brookline
2010

Emily meets me early for the Monday meeting. We stand with the others in little clumps behind the church. I can't help thinking this semicircle of paving was made for the hearses, to bring the corpses to their own funerals, but maybe this is where brides drive their horse and carriages, up to the door, away in a shower of rice. What do I know of church life on weekends? I'm just trying to make it through another day. It's fifty degrees with occasional gusts—still cold, but bright and sunny. Since this is Boston, weather like this, none of us have our jackets on. I'm about to get my thirty-day chip.

"You look like crap, though," says Emily by way of congratulations.

"I was up late. As you may recall."

"You want to do it how you've always done it. Hanging on by the skin. You think you can outsmart it. But willpower isn't how sober happens. You got to do everything the regular people do. Every damn thing. You understand?" She's perched on the stone retainer wall, huffing a cigarette.

"I do."

We've got fifteen minutes until the meeting starts, and I know Emily is think-ing about last night, whatever was underneath my late-night phone call. She wants to get her sponsoring in. Emily's taken me on, even though she already has too many sponsees, because of Juni. Emily got helped, when Leo was young, and she says there is something particular about having a baby in the program, how you can't throw your whole life after recovery, how a part of you needs to stay in reserve.

"You offering to babysit?"

"I've done my stitch in the romper room," she says. "Much as I love your kid. But if you could use a pair of hands, how about your mom? I know she's wherever, Costa Rica, but planes exist, people fly in—"

"It's Belize." I shake my head. "I'm fine, Emily. I've got the sitter forty-five hours a week. Juni's not the problem."

Emily sucks on her cigarette. "Not now, but you need a plan. I know you hate to talk about it, and I got my own asshole ex, but is it impossible, Juni's daddy? Or, how about his side, mother? Family?"

"There's no one," I say, but I think of the black SUV with white sticker and the Cali plates, the man trying my car door with Juni inside, and I know it's never clear who's a friend, who's a danger.

Emily reminds me that most people never make it this far, that even many of the people hovering by the church entrance won't be here in six months. Twenty years ago, when it was still legal, you could find people in front of some meetings rolling cloud. I'd see them when I walked past here on my way to the public library, spoons hanging out of their mouths like people drink the coffee now. It was a big thing in the recovery community when they made cloud illegal, a debate, and you'll still meet people who'll tell you a cloud addict never shot anyone, who will tell you you can work your program and still eat cloud, but the Monday noon meetings are a good place for people who've been through it to come. Once you have lived with cloud for five years, for ten, you learn that it is not benign, that just like any of the other monsters that drive people to church function rooms to tell their stories, cloud wants to eat your life. It wants to take your precious things and turn them into muck, to rot every good thing out of your brain. We've barely survived. We are all miraculous.

I hear the conversations around us, who's made it through the visit with Child Protective Services, with his parole officer, with her drunk mom. There's a new girl, teenaged with pink hair, picked acne and quick-bitten nails. She's here on court order, talking too fast to Jim, a sixteen-year-old favorite among the grandma junkies, sober since he was thirteen.

"—drop her at the mall with her eleven-year-old sister. She's supposed to look after the sister, and, whatever, eleven. I took the subways by myself at that age, but these parents are overprotective, the sister's sheltered, et cetera, so my friend is going to keep an eye. Anyway, an hour forty-five, the parents come to get them, and the sister is gone. The parents are like, where's Shana, and my friend is like, who? I don't know who you mean. Who is Shana? Panic, 911, the whole deal.

Eventually, they locate little Shana in the security office, eating starlight mints and watching people pick their nose on the video monitors. My friend had turned her in. Like a lost coat. She keeps following me, my friend said of her sister. She won't let me alone."

The boy shakes his head. "How many hits did the friend eat?"

The pink haired girl doesn't know. "Eventually, though, she comes down, *it was the drugs talking. I'm so sorry. Of course I love little Shana.* Everyone goes back to the country club and lives happily ever after."

"Except not really," says Jim.

"No," says the girl. "Not really."

Emily knocks a shoulder into me as she slides off the wall.

"How is job stuff going? I scanned the ads. There's some video stuff might be up your alley. You finding anything?" Emily steadies herself beside me, then taps another smoke from the soft pack.

I pull out my phone and open my browser. "Actually, something came through from my boss yesterday. Tell me what you think."

I turn my head away and watch Jim and the pink-haired girl while Emily opens the link.

"It's got a lot of traffic," she says. "You're not looking."

"Watch the video. Tell me what you see."

"It's a woman. In her underpants. She's in bathroom. I can't see her head, it's like cut off. What is this?"

"Fucked if I know. I couldn't watch it. I must have opened the link fifty times. Then, something happens. I'm in the bathroom, staring at my face in the mirror. No idea how I got there. I'm standing in front of the fridge."

Emily squints at the screen. "It's asking me do I want to download. Should I download?"

"G-d, no." I glance over. The video is blocked by a window. Beneath I can see the bare feet of the actress, the curve of her breasts. Even cut off, the image gives me vertigo. "It's weird. I mean, if the box pops, it means the embed's already there. That's what I did, when I did this work. So how's this a job?"

"He's messing with you? Sending you a message?" She taps the headless woman beneath the dialogue box. "That's not you, is it?"

"Not possible. She's got more—"

Emily glances at me. "Yeah. I see what you mean."

"Are you watching it again?" I ask.

"It—it stops right at the good part. Is there more to it?"

"Maybe. We did them sometimes in sections, you know. Like, you had to click through to get to the climax."

Emily shakes her head, then turns it off. "There's something weird about that video. It's not that porny, really. But I get it, how a person could become addicted."

A few feet away, the pink-haired girl rants at Jim, and we both watch them for a moment, then Emily hands me back my phone.

"This boss. He's from the old life, right? Did you guys have a thing?"

"Ew, gross. He's like seventy. It wasn't like that."

"But there was weirdness, right?"

"He wasn't a stellar human, but it's like, you know those people who are there for you at the bottom? If they've seen you then, and they stuck around, it doesn't really matter what kind of people they are."

"Here's my advice: It sounds like you're putting a lot on this one thing. You can find another job. You can't find another chance."

I haven't explained Lew right, but he's tricky to explain. Still, there's feeling there. We shared an ethic about our jobs, were both excellent at making shitty things where no one was ever going to hand us awards for what we did. It got into being friendly and personal, too. In the downtime between shoots, Lew would take me to the Philharmonic and minor league ball, and some nights, Trudi and he would have me over for starchy, un-Californian dinners. Lew's son was a junkie fuck-up, so it was about that too, all the niceness. Not many people those days bothered to be just nice to me, and I wasn't picky about motivations.

"So that's what set you off last night? This work thing?"

I hesitate, and then I nod.

"And how close did you get?"

I'm not a bad liar. I know you've got to focus on your own eyes, think about making your gaze shallow and blurred. I know it helps to think of the way in which your lie is almost true. "You know how it is. You do the drive-by at the old dealer's house. I was at the door, Emily."

"I've been there, you know, cruising in circles, then acting like it's providence when you happen to see your guy. God put the junk in your face. God wants you to get high." Emily shakes her head. "It's funny, though. My instinct said it was a man thing."

"I wish."

"More trouble than it's worth," Emily says. "Three-quarters of the time, it's not even any good. It's heartbreak and dirty sheets and you're still lonely as fuck after."

"What about the other quarter?"

She laughs. I laugh.

"You're not off the hook. We're going to talk about this again." Emily's a great sponsor. If I were crackable, she'd crack me, but I can't say about the driveway, the man in the driveway.

The Monday noon meeting isn't vast like the Tuesday night one, does not run to the hundreds. But on this particular blustery March day, there are probably forty people in the room. Cloud is a gradual drug. It took a very long time to wreck me. But also, I lost something small each time. From the very beginning, the slow catastrophe had begun.

The pink-haired girl is at the mike, one of those rehab enthusiasts for recovery who take to meetings like babies to the boob, but don't always have the staying power. She's still bitching about her roommate in the in-patient program, how spoiled she is, how crap her sobriety, but the pink-haired girl is no poverty-line case study herself. It takes insurance to get into those private programs. Even though the rich don't have it easier, the money boosts your percentage of success, oils the wheel of grace.

I watch the girl talk, but my attention wanders. Somewhere in the gathered group, the crowd of thirty-five or forty, there is someone I should be paying attention to. I feel it like the flicker of my old cloud sense, the thing that made me so good at videos when I was high, which is the same thing which woke me to the car in my driveway last night. I scan the crowd, but some people blur, or don't quite become people. It's a kind of face blindness that happens to us, cloud people. Anyone can turn into a stranger. Any person you meet might harbor your secrets and you'd never even know.

Then, they are calling for the thirty-day chips, and I raise my hand.

I don't do commitments. I don't tell my story. At my first meeting, when I asked Emily to be my sponsor, I told her the condition was I wasn't going to put on sentimental public displays of penitence. This was over coffee, at the Dunkies across the way, and not technically even a meeting. How it happened: in the mornings, when I was trying not to use, I would stroll Juni on these epic, like five mile walks. I always ended up in this neighborhood: nostalgia, probably. Then I'd stroll Juni around in circles, circle after circle, fists whitening on the plastic handles of the baby jogger. Emily saw me, a strung-out mom hovering by the meeting entrance, and started just walking beside me.

"What are you going to say to yourself, when you come to the end?" she asked me. It was the first damn thing she ever said, and she read me just like that. "Are you going to say, I got really close? I came to the door? But I just couldn't go inside?"

I told her to fuck off, mind her own business.

"Look at your baby," said Emily.

There was Juni sucking on her cracked pacifier and not complaining.

"She's watching you, already, you know. It's not like with an infant. She's learning how to be."

A cracked pacifier, Emily told me, provides no satisfaction to a toddler. The hole's too big. They're just getting air. It's out of habit, Emily said, if she's still sucking on it. Or maybe something else.

"Like what?"

"I got a kid," she says. "Big boy. Hormones, pimples, practically impossible to love, though, you know, I do. Even at her age—what is she? Fourteen months?"

"Eighteen," I say. "She's, whatever, a little late on the physical development."

Emily nodded—no judgment—though G-d knows I deserve to be judged. "Even at that age," she said. "They know how to fake it for you. That it's OK. Even when it's terrible."

So it was Juni, quiet, in the stroller, that made Emily willing to take me on, even on my crappy terms. And here I am. When they call out thirty days, I raise my hand, walk to the front, but I do not take the mike. Emily waits till they hand me the chip, then she slings her arm around my shoulder and pulls me in.

"Skin of your teeth," she says, which is Boston for 'congratulations.'

It's meaningful to hold the object in my hand. It has a certain weight, a certain thingness to it. I haven't lived a life of acquisition where I've gotten to keep much, accrued cabinets full of Lenox or Limoges, but there are one or two objects that matter to me. My paperback full of notes is among these treasures, its photographs and its ticket stubs, its glued pages and its fingerprinted corners and maybe now, this chunk of metal. On the West Coast, there'd be hugging and crying, but I'm back east and Emily's on lunch from work. She typically has Monday off from the courthouse, but the other girl is out with a repetitive stress injury, and there's a jury trial getting coverage in the papers. I get a quick squeeze on my shoulder and she's off.

Emily has told me that one of my deficits in recovery is that my world is under-populated. She's never been to California, to Houston or Mexico; she goes to New Hampshire to buy cheap cigarettes, and she spent two months in New Jersey training to be a court reporter, but otherwise, she's tethered to Boston like she's on permanent supervised release. Still, she's got people in her life, and mine is like a map without dots on it. "You need *folks*," she's said. "Old ladies with lots of patience, or girlfriends who you can owe favors. Whatever. Folks. People who can stand for you to screw up." I've used up all those people, I guess. Or maybe I never had them.

The only exception, possibly, is my boss Lew. The months of his silence had weighed on me like a rebuke. I wanted to be working. My bank account, fat when I'd arrived, was draining at an unsustainable rate. But those weren't the reasons I kept checking the server, even long after it was reasonable. What if I'd already failed him, I thought? What if the time for the thing I'd hidden away had already passed? When the file came through, I received it like a love letter from a married boyfriend, gratified, thrilled, even though I shouldn't have been. I received it like forgiveness. *At long last*, he'd written. *You have your part and I have mine. Complete as discussed according to timeline.* It wasn't the first time he'd given me a second chance, but each time, always, my debt had increased.

Case in point: 2007, when I was nearing the end of still being able to cope, I decided to go visit my mother in Belize. I should have known that I couldn't handle it, international travel and passport stamps, but my mother and a boyfriend I'd never met had bought a patch of jungle from a sketchy broker, and things were going bad. I still thought I was high school Mellie with the report card on the fridge. I still thought I could help, so I left without telling anyone to try to go fix things.

I booked a flight through Houston, but I dumped out on the connecting to score cloud. Out there, in the Texas summer, I had an attack of the sickness, and vanished. Meanwhile, back in LA, this home video—the one with the swimsuit model and the rock star—starts blowing up all over the internet. Lew sees the opportunity, but where am I? He hasn't made a picture without me since the '90s, since the market was in truck stop rentals. Trudi, his tech assistants, they're all like, so what? It's superstition, his attachment to me, sentiment. All right. Lew lets himself get convinced: he pulls the trigger, goes into production, gets the new project online before the traffic starts to fall off. Everything is as it should be, and yet. Nada. Nobody clicks. And so of course, none of the magical money things happened either. What it looked like was it was me who made the difference, my skill, and I was AWOL somewhere in the sweltering Southwest.

When I got back, Lew had his driver waiting for me. So maybe I was a lucky charm or a security blanket, but so what. Lew needed me, so I needed to get right and get to work. I was collected. Riding in the back of his car, I felt briefly like an errant child, or a precious, misguided tabloid star who would now be returned to the bosom of her pink bedroom. The driver was terrific behind the wheel, and I understood that that was what Lew liked about him. He admired excellence, in any field. So I leaned back, and felt the wheels almost lifting on the hairpin turns. Maybe that was my taste of grace, what it might feel like to have what Emily talks about, folks who can stand for you to mess up. But I was wrong. I was wrong in my feeling about Lew.

Instead of going to the studio, we drove into the hills. Lew was almost seventy, by then, but still wearing a cyanide pill necklace from his Laos days. Trudi had been a typist in the American embassy at Saigon, and the story went he single-handed rescued her before the helicopter airlift that would have left her behind. He was grotesquely overweight and on the stomach flesh that emerged from his shirttails, you could see the tattooed incision marks and instructions to would-be assassins for making a clean kill. Family dinners and ballgames aside, he was a guy who had a comfort level with violence. These were the things going through my mind as the car climbed above Los Angeles. No one was talking, not Lew, and not his driver. It didn't feel like forgive and forget.

"I'm sorry," I said, at last. Neither of them replied.

Eventually, we came to the bungalow where Lew and Trudi lived. It wasn't large, but there were outbuildings, a gray stone pool, and a view of the whole smoggy valley below. This was real estate worth a couple of oil wells. The driver took a gasoline canister from the back, pulled a cigarette from a pack, and Lew came around to hand him a book of matches. I couldn't make sense of what was happening, but I thought of the word *pyre*, of draped fabric igniting. I looked into the valley, and it was like I was already crashing against the rocks. Then the driver guy started to walk away from us, swinging the gasoline canister.

"Take the keys," said Lew to me. "You're driving."

I was still shaky when he directed me to park on a cliff overlooking his compound.

"What do you think of my chauffeur?" he asked. "I like that word, chauffeur, but I guess it's pretentious."

I shrugged. It felt like anything I said, a body might wind up broken.

"He fucked me," said Lew. "These new guys I unfortunately have to work with. The backers. Very tricky characters, making retire-to-an-island type money, and paying me like I'm some contractor. So how should I feel when I find my guy is on their payroll, making reports? Not good. But we worked it out, even that. My chauffeur and I figured out a deal."

"Sorry," I said again. "Shit, Lew. I'm so sorry."

He started to shake his head. "I love you, Mellie," he said. "Like my own kid almost. And what you do, I need you to keep doing. All these bankruptcies? These mortgage companies going south, that's going to hit us. Days, I'd like to hop on a plane to wherever, too. So, I get it. You need to get out? We can work that. But not without a word. Not without warning. There have to be terms."

That was when I heard the sirens. Below us, on the curving road leading up the canyon, fire trucks were snaking toward something. I made out a column of gray smoke. Then, I smelled the burning in the air.

"Is that your house?" I asked.

Lew shrugged. "I have insurance. Trudi's been wanting a remodel, anyway. Besides, they'll probably make it in time."

This, the conversation with Lew, has worn a bit over the intervening years, as things do for users. I know there was more to the discussion. For example, I know there was a more specific conversation about my leaving, how we needed our own retire-to-an-island plan. I agreed to take classes, to learn what we'd need. He was going to call on me, when the time was right. But the rest, I've lost. I do know what he said, before we started back down the hill.

"The whole business is going to be fucked, Mellie. But as long as I can hang on, I'm hanging on to you."

It's what was repeating in my head, yesterday, as I tried to watch the video.

It's not completely true what Emily says, that I don't have people. After the meeting, a group of us get a table at Pizzeria Uno. These are fragile and new connections, and I don't know if things like trust or loyalty or screwing up will be possible. Still, they're company, and that's a beginning. Among the people who used to get high, there are doctors and teachers and union carpenters, but the Uno's crew, we're the addicts with marginal or irregular jobs, with nothing on for the afternoon. We order the personal pizza, or if we're not on a restaurant budget, just a black coffee. Our waitress is a recovering meth head and so the refills are free.

"You're looking good," I tell her. She smiles, flashing us her new dental work.

When she retreats, Lucien whispers, "can't ever fix meth mouth."

Some of us laugh. Laura chucks him on the shoulder. It's a sin, in the sacred texts of recovery, to maintain a hierarchy of addictions, but we at this table are all cloud users, and we can't help it. We can't totally set aside our feeling that we've got a little something special. Not like the cokeheads and the drunks don't say the same about us, but still, we've got cloud sickness, with its unique lore and peculiar effects, and entre nous, we think we're a class apart.

Some people call cloud a memory drug. They call cloud sickness a memory sickness. There is a brief, euphoric amnesia, but what makes cloud different isn't the forgetting. It's what we learn in the interval between; what we hold onto when we return.

In popular representations of addiction, the thing that gets short shrift is the gifts of the altered mind. I don't mean in a Carlos Castaneda–hippie mystical sense. Fuck that. It's something else, at least on cloud. A secret we cloud users share.

Which we wouldn't say in meetings, but in these little gatherings, we indulge in rumors, in giddy gossip that doesn't quite fit the narrative of humility and regret we practice in church. Our talk about alternative therapies, for example, about shortcuts and quick fixes or the nasty way we describe all the people trying to kick it on their own—it's not nice, but you do get sick of being nice.

"Guy from my old crew shows up cloud sick, speaking the gibberish, whole thing. Has a stranger's cat in a box. Do I want the cat? Obviously, I know, it's his fucking cat. I take the thing in, give it Fancy Feast. Small enough favor. And two weeks later, he's back. *Where's Frodo? I missed him so much.* Tries to tell me he's sober now. Some magic meditation practice with these rocks, no side effects."

"That OneLife shit?" Noreen, the oldest woman among us, says. "My niece did that shit. There's supposedly—in real life—like sacred objects? Or places maybe? These magical stones help you target them and then you can walk away a changed person. Cost her five thousand bucks. What a scam."

"It didn't work?" asks Laura.

Noreen shrugs. "Something did. But you can't just yoga and boom, the need is gone. There's physiology. It lodges in your fat cells. Or in protein cells. One of them."

"Anyone who doesn't get cloud sick," I say, "didn't really use in the first place. Sure, you take a hit a week, get you through dinner with the in-laws, fine. But if you are a day-to-day addict, you are going to end up in an alley eventually, not recognizing your own hands."

"I don't know," says the bald man next to N. I can't remember his name, can't quite resolve his features into a readable face, but he seeks me out at meetings, whatever, like there's some long story behind us. Problem there, with a cloud history, is you don't know if you were flinging your panties around a party when you met, sucking scum from the gutter. Maybe this guy and I, we met in a museum, talking about a painting, or maybe it's just a mistake. Either way, he feels to me like the morning after a blackout, and so I've dodged his attempts to get friendly.

"I don't know," says the guy again. "Enversion? The OneLife therapy? We all have those things, blank spots. Enversion says that inside those, briefly, our minds can be susceptible, plastic, like in an original cloud state."

Noreen is unconvinced. "A rock is not going to fix you. Getting clean is brutal. People die along the way. Love does. You won't find a place where that's not a fact."

Age is one of the things that earns respect in these circles. Noreen gets props just for having lived long enough that she looks as old as she is. She's sixty, maybe, though looks can deceive. We all concede the point, even the bald guy who doesn't agree, and then the table breaks into smaller conversations.

Noreen takes my hand in her freckled one. I've ordered her favorite, sausage and onions, so she can nibble off my plate. She's on disability, and she's got the black coffee in front of her. "Hey, thirty days. That's a big one."

"Thanks." I say. "How goes it with you?"

"You know. I'm still looking at those internet sites, Birthmother.com, Adoption Reunion. I'm saving for the deposit for the private investigator, but nothing new."

I pat her warm, dry hand. What we're all talking around today is the shared experience of cloud. For each of us, something or someone has disappeared. It's no metaphor. Noreen has lost her son, a boy she can remember at two, at fifteen, but whom she cannot track. Lucien does not know where he was born, country or year. No one can place his accent. Laura is missing a hand. N has less than any of us, barely a personality. Here's our confession: inside the cloud, in that brief interval between forgetting and remembering, we have glimpsed possibility, a place of branching. The way we return is not the same way we entered. We come to believe we can 'go to the right cloud.' You'll get high, and the path you take back from the memoryless place between will bring you around again. You'll be the person you would have been without all the damage. And not just inside, abstractly: you'll have the cat, the car, the child, the wife you would have had. Even now, sober and wiser, we all still believe this possibility is actual. You'll eat cloud and—*pop*—you'll arrive at this ideal self. A man you never married appears in your driveway, takes out his briefcase, and walks through the front door. *Honey, I'm home.* You would be pure, unadulterated, unadulted, everything as it would have been if you never ate your first spoon. We haven't given up on the possibility. We've seen too much evidence, things flickering at the edges of our lives, little teasing promises idling outside our homes. But now, in recovery, we acknowledge that such chances were always lottery-small and that there are terrible risks in trying: your remaining hand, your name, whatever by getting sober you have managed to keep. Your baby daughter, even.

"We have to live in the likely world."

This is why we have learned to pray only for modest miracles, why we place our faith in magical rocks or weekly meetings or the kismet of a late-night search result that will bring us something, enough, to keep going. The man in the driveway, that's who I'm thinking of.

No one knows fuck all about what cloud does to a person after twenty years of getting high. N, at the end of the table, for example, is holding his fork up to the light and examining it closely. N is a freelance data analyst—intelligent, functional—but there is simply not enough there. Sometimes, I think I am like that with Juni, missing something. Where did it go, the proper feeling I ought to have had that would have made me get clean in time? It's not simply neurology, this missing part. Each bump of cloud is a branching. The people and things and knowledge we've lost at these choice points cease to exist. There are sisters, babies, skills, and even selves that evaporate in cloud. Our dim memories, our seemingly misplaced recognitions, are all that remain of what once was.

The man in my driveway. In some other narrative, maybe, he and I saved each other, or never got high in the first place. And so, I can barely resist the longing to have him, my missing person, return. That's my confession, what I could not tell Emily, what I can now barely admit to myself. But even if that's true, it doesn't mean he's a friend to me. He could be someone else entirely.

Now, the bald guy gently touches N's arm. "It's a fork," the man tells N. "A tool for spearing food and sticking it into your mouth."

N nods, gives a grateful little smile, replaces the fork on the napkin, and asks his companion to repeat what he was saying again. It's a project he's making, a kind of personal history of cloud.

"Topographical?" asks N.

The man shakes his head. "It's just parcel numbers, property lines. But I narrowed it down to a couple of places. Maybe there's nothing there; maybe the thing inside is the story of my life.

I get a box for the remaining half of my pizza and slide it to Noreen. We pay our meth head waitress, scrape and stack our plates for her, leave a giant tip. Outside, we each head off in our different directions, to day treatment or welfare or supervised work release. I'm thinking about the bank, the post office, how many errands I can get in before I have to get Juni, when someone falls into step beside me. It's the bald guy. He's has been waiting for his chance.

"Oh, hey," I say.

I side-eye him. I have a thing I can do, when I get the face blindness, where I look slant at someone, and then I can begin to assess. Truth to tell, he seems fairly non serial killer and even possibly kind of hot. But there's the maybe-knowing him thing, and the fact that you're not supposed to date in early sobriety. Besides, Emily tells me there's a rumor about him, about him and women, that makes him not necessarily sketchy, but still off limits. She's unclear, and either way, I'm not on the make. On the other hand, I am supposed to be making friends.

"I'm so sorry—" I say. "I don't remember your name?"

"That happens a lot," he says. He walks beside me, pacing his strides, not too close, correct, appropriate. Maybe he knows the gossip. Maybe he's working especially hard to telegraph good guy.

"I'm Mellie," I say, doling out doses.

"Yeah," he says, like I should know that he knows that. "You got your chip."

"And you'll be like, two years in July?"

"September. This isn't my first go, either. I had three years, once. And then I had a year."

"I'm a serial quitter, myself. Though, nothing like you. I think it's the beginning I'm bad at."

"Right?" he says. "But thirty days. It's good. It's not the beginning anymore."

"You can't just start from scratch, though. There are things that have to follow you into the new life."

He's nodding. "Listen. I'm sorry if it's too soon, but I have a question I'd like to ask you. It's this project I'm doing, an audio documentary—"

Suddenly, I get the bad feeling again, the history-between-us feeling. He takes a hand out of a pocket. It's a device—not a phone. Some kind of recording device, I think. Which weirds me out. And then it's worse than weird and I'm suddenly afraid.

"What I'd like to ask is—" he begins again, but what comes next is sucked away. The world stutters. I get the sense of time dropping out, a block or two where I've just gone blank. The storm clouds seem dramatically darker, but there's the man walking beside me like everything's still normal.

I pick him up at the edge of my field of vision, try to read his face. He's not bald, I think. It's—I don't know. His head is shaven, or maybe he's just got close-cropped hair. Maybe he has a normal haircut, and is just very blond—or maybe his hair is dark. I feel disoriented, like my vision is getting confused and maybe he's not the person I thought he was. Maybe he's been switched out.

He pauses. We have reached his car. And now, I am on my highest frequency. I suck myself inward, and inward, and deeper inward until I am a tiny dense point, a universe of energy focused on that narrow view. He drives a black SUV. Rain begins to fall, catching on my eyes and blurring my vision. The Brookline street, the dog-walkers and the parking meter, the two after-school children tossing a ball, everything recedes. I blink. The car is spattered with mud, has boxes pressed up against the windows as if it has been lived out of. On the rear bumper, there is an oval sticker. It's the same car, I think. It's not the same.

The man lights a cigarette, flame sputtering in the gathering downpour. I know the smell, the little Prince crown around the filter.

"You're him," I say. "You've come back."

———

If they made a war on it, and funded longitudinal research about it, and started granting PhDs in it; if they put it in a particle accelerator; if they froze it below absolute zero and pummeled it with lasers and derived formulae about it, they would never prove what we know about cloud. What we who have indentured ourselves to cloud's insight and greed know for sure. We know it in our bones and in our mouths. We whisper it to each other at the pizza shops and in the rehab centers and waiting to get our stomachs pumped in the emergency room.

There are other lives we've led, intertwined with this one, and we've shifted, again and again. Perhaps cloud writes those realities; perhaps they preexist the cloud use and cloud merely lets us move among them. Regardless, the evidence is there.

When you get clean, you're stuck where you land. Your flawed memory of the life that has brought you to that moment becomes fixed, yours for good. But might there not also be unexpected consolations? Might some refugee from your best life still be here, and now, in some form? The thing might be waiting there, around some corner; it might be walking toward you right now.

Four

Brookline & Belmont & Boston
1988

My mom earns some money doing past life regressions. When I was little, like four, she took me off to New Mexico. We slipped out in the night, without much luggage and it was a secret. The trip must have been a first pass at her trying to leave my father, some stage in that long project which was eventually made moot by his leaving her instead. So, anyway, New Mexico. The true part of the story she came to tell is that she got lost. We got lost from each other. I spent a couple of hours waiting on the porch of a reservation store. There was this old dude in a cowboy hat who mistook me for a boy. The whole time my mom was missing, he kept me entertained—roughhouse, football, bottle after glass bottle of grape soda. I was all right. My mom, though, came back messed up: her lips almost black with dehydration, raving and hallucinatory.

"I remember everything," she whispered to me when we were back in the car. "Everything that ever happened to anyone."

From my later vantage, it seems like a lot of damage to do in a few hours, and I have to wonder if she ate some bad cactus, but that's not the point. The point is something happened to her out there in the desert scrubland. She had some experience wandering among the red rock formations. It was more like maybe an encounter, and it was deep and it transformed her, so she says. It's hard totally to pin her down on the topic, but I've picked up over the years that out in the wilderness, she met a guide, a young woman, and that this woman had a way of opening you up, a kind of mind trick called the *On Elife*. My mom will get that far into the story, then she'll break off, like she fears she's betrayed something important, will lose what magic she was granted. Anyway, New Mexico is why my mother takes clients. When she is between jobs, and when the checks from my father's mother are late or get spent on my mother's manic extravagances, we live by the fees from the regressions. In addition to the checks, also, my Russian-Jewish grandmother pays directly for summer camp and my tuition at the White School. This was arranged at the level of the court system, without my input and long ago, but consequence being I have always had rich friends and lived in a dump where I was afraid to bring them home.

Nancy and me, it seems like an odd couple, but even when we were in seventh grade and obsessing over Guess? jeans and boy-girl birthday parties, Nancy didn't care that there were roaches under our sink and that all of our potato chips were generic. One time, she left her retainer on our kitchen counter and when we came back, there was a bug just twitching its antennae on top of it. My mom tried to fix it by dropping the retainer in a pot of boiling water and it melted. I've had girls in my class stop being friends with me because I accidentally spit milk on them, but Nancy's like, at a gut level, kind of fair about life and how it's different for different people. Tow truck drivers, roaches on your retainer, Nancy is fine with whatever.

At the moment, Nancy is standing in front of the fridge in our basement apartment. My grades are stuck up with a magnet. Nancy examines them, my straight As, with an A- in trig, before retreating into the bathroom. "Gross," she says about my fall semester, my dumb priorities. I am the only one we hang out with who pays attention to my GPA, but Nancy says that's just me giving adults power. Nancy's parents only care about her being a geneticist, but the closest Nancy gets to learning about science is how she studies the inside of her carburetor. She'll never, ever get her PhD and that's freed her somehow. My mother doesn't want anything specific from me, not a particular future or career, but she's greedy for my life in her own way.

"Can I use the bathroom?" Nancy asks my mom.

She's arranging frozen fish sticks on a cookie sheet and drinking Tab. "Sure, of course. You're always welcome."

I open the fridge. "I think we're out of tartar sauce," I tell my mom.

"Would Nancy eat fish sticks with ketchup, do you think?" She's whispering, like there's some nicety to frozen fish, like if Nancy hears from the bathroom, it'll be a catastrophe.

"I doubt it," I answer.

"Shit," says my mom. I can see she's on the edge of tears, which is how it goes when she's between jobs.

I hand her a tissue. "She eats only salad and cookies, mom. It's not personal."

My mom takes a breath. "OK. OK."

We're leaving for the dance, the Belmont dance, after my mom gets some protein in us, and in the meantime, Nancy's been trying to get my mom to read her past lives. Nancy is like that, serious about things like tarot that the rest of us do for a hobby. She used to spend her whole shifts at George's Folly trying to cast spells and divine for water under Brookline Village.

"So will you?" Nancy calls after my mom. "Will you do mine?"

I was kind of worried Nancy would ditch me tonight, after how things had gone down at Judah's, but she'd come to my place, just like she'd promised, smoked a little dope on my patio and everything seemed OK between us. Our apartment is small, so from the kitchen I can see through the cracked door to the bathroom, can watch Nancy pluck her arm hairs with the tweezers. She talks to us the whole time and even though she's used Visine, I can tell she's still stoned because she's insistent; she gets stubborn when she's high. She tells my mom, stop babying her; she can handle the truth about her past.

My mother leans against the stove. Normally, I'd tell Nancy just to shut up, not to provoke, but I'm still not sure she's forgiven me for being a dumbfuck about Judah so I'm trying to be low-key.

"Can I borrow this lipstick?" Nancy calls. "It's . . . Sweaty Salmon? I don't have my contacts in. No. Sweet Melon?"

"Sure," my mom says, bright as a bee. "And how about, when you're done, I'll read your energy. If it seems safe, I'll do a small session with you."

"Awesome," says Nancy. "My grandfather in Poland, whatever, but he was this famous rabbi? I sense this mission, like a real purpose waiting out there for me. Not like a love affair, like Paris or something, but leading, teaching. " She sticks her head out the bathroom door. Her arms are red and rashy from being plucked and she's got one eye done in cat eyes. I don't have the coordination for elaborate makeup. I always end up looking like someone from the women's shelter, everything runny like a bruise.

My mother closes the oven door. "You can make tartar sauce with mayonnaise and relish," she says. "Or, wait, no. Maybe that's for thousand island dressing."

My mother refuses to regress me. I 90 percent do not believe in it anyway. I 90 percent think her desert experience can be put up to sunstroke and amateur peyote-gathering. I found a notebook she keeps, pages of historical identities.

Power issues possible marital trouble. Lorena Barros "You were lucky to be alive. My gun jammed." ~~Nieves Fernandez~~ Agueda Esteban carried weapons and documents past American invaders. It could have been anything, some transcript of visions she was having, but what it read like, cross marks through certain words, was brainstorming, was her cooking up bullshit to feed the clients.

Some fancy people come to her, people with money. Our apartment is in a good zip code, in a nice brick front building between Coolidge Corner and Cleveland Circle. When my mom was in her protest phase, fighting against that diesel power plant they were trying to build in Mission Hill, she met a lot of liberals from this area, and it was one of them hooked her up with this place. It's rent-controlled, but in the basement, and has windows only in the back. When spring broke this year, hundreds of carpenter ants emerged to die on our kitchen floor. Still, it has the patio. I've been doing my astronomy homework out there, keeping a journal of the phases of the moon. This cracks Nancy up.

"Like, every day, you're out there? Like on your honor?" How she'd do it would be the night before it's due. The moon, she points out, you can pretty much extrapolate. It's not going to one night surprise you and be shaped like a heart. One night, instead of looking like a nail clipping, it's not going to have a hole punched through its center. I think of my mother in the desert, and I think maybe Nancy is wrong on that. The moon could surprise you if it felt like it.

Later, I munch tepid fish sticks and apply blush to my cheeks while my mother and Nancy sit across from each other at the kitchen table. The lights are dimmed and my mother is playing the Andreas Vollenweider tape, which is New Age harp played by an Austrian with a white man Afro. Harp and Austria and blond curls is a combination that makes my mother swoon and also possibly is evidence that human women evolve into another species after thirty-five.

"Tell me what you feel," my mom says to Nancy.

"It's dark," she goes. "I'm not alone."

"Not what you see; what you feel, on your skin."

"Yes," says Nancy. "It's very dry. Windy. It smells like—salt? There are two people with me but they're not—they're not able to reach each other."

"No," says my mother, very suddenly.

"Yes. A desert, but with the sea nearby."

"Somewhere oriental," says my mother authoritatively. "With camels maybe? There's a story about Scheherazade—"

"No," says Nancy. "Cactus, above the beach. I'm on a cliff. There's a pool, and then there's the ocean. I can read something. It says, like, Ne Lif?"

I close the bathroom door, and dip a Q-tip into the bottle of hydrogen peroxide. I am not allowed to bleach my hair, but my mother keeps peroxide because if you eat something poisonous, you can use it as an emetic. Slowly, as the weather warms, I am streaking my hair with it. I will be blonde by summer. If she notices—which I doubt—I'll blame the sun.

I'm transferring my makeup from my backpack to my purse when I come across the cloud spoon. It's collected weird dust, but I don't want to throw it away, so I toss it in with my makeup. I'll give it to Nancy later, or maybe to Paul.

There's a cry. I emerge to find my mother and Nancy standing, both of them suddenly awake and scared, looking across the table. And then they look at me.

"What is it?" I ask.

"Nothing," say my mother and Nancy at the same time, and then the lights come up, and they both are talking maniacally about something none of us care about, and I'm thinking perfect. Just what I need. A secret visionary conspiracy between Nancy and my crazy mother.

My mother drops us off in front of the Belmont School. Boys in polo shirts mill around by the entrance. This is how they do it at private school, like some hold-over from another century. You go to school with just girls or just boys, and then you have these occasional contrived social events where three blonde girls who already know the boys from Harvard Club or yachting near Yarmouth dance and the rest of us, the two Jews and the black girl from Randolph and the short chick with the terminal disease, we stand at the edge of the sweaty gym and eat ourselves alive.

Nancy and I find ourselves a side entrance from which we can watch the parking lot, the dance floor barely darkened and still empty behind us.

"When's he going to be here?" I ask Nancy.

She shrugs. "What do you care?"

Girls from my class are still arriving. Even the fat ones have beautiful legs, have perfect skin. Rich people are like that, great hair, good muscles, high-quality flab. There's an imbalance of course, because at private school, none of the boys hit puberty until they're like seventeen. I think it's tennis, too much tennis, or maybe they get it from alpine skiing. Nancy watches the polo shirts wandering over from study hall as she taps a Prince cigarette from a pack.

"Oh, my G-d," I say. "You can't just light up."

"It's not my school. What are they going to do, kick me out again?"

"Whitney's mom is chaperoning and she knows my mom from something. She will absolutely tell."

"So? Your mother hates me already. I thought it was going to be cool, the regression, but she was just spewing generic bullshit. She insisted I was some Christian imperialist, leading a crusade. As if. As if I would make Bedouins worship a guy who rose from the dead."

"Think of it like performance, maybe. She's got limited shticks. You're just not the intended audience."

"At least it was for a cause, something like a belief." Nancy inhales. "I could see myself in Lesotho. That I would have bought. But in the reading, the place I saw wasn't Africa, or the Middle East. To be honest, I don't think it was even the past."

"Possibly, was it a kitchen? In Brookline, Massachusetts?"

Nancy stubs her Prince. "Totally. Total horseshit. Are there like refreshments or anything?"

The DJ is playing INXS, which I like, and Nancy kind of dances on her way to food. There's a plastic bowl of potato chips, another one of cheese puffs and someone has fixed a punch. Private school boys watch her. Whatever she has that guys like Judah like, it works here, too.

"Douches," says Nancy through a mouthful of Lays. "Total fucking douches."

A horn honks and Paul pulls through the prep school gates in Nancy's Escort. He is a fantastically bad driver and can't handle stick, but he's been with the tow truck guys all afternoon and this makes him an automotive expert. He grinds the gears. I see alarm in the crowd of Lilly Pullitzer chaperones; ChapSticked lips purse; white loafers begin to march down the path toward the skinny half-Asian boy in the dented American compact.

Nancy and I jog, light in our pumps, miniskirts straining. Probably, Nancy tells me between huffed breaths, he rode the clutch the whole way here, but she's fine with it, fine with ruining her first car. Her parents deserve to buy her a new transmission, after what they've put her through. Paul shoves over when he sees us running. Among all the people we know, Nancy is indisputably the best driver, will always pilot her own getaway car.

A mom in a pair of pedal pushers with a perfect pageboy is hard on our heels.

"Girls? Excuse me? Can I see your permission form?"

I hop into the middle back seat and lean forward.

Nancy smiles gigantically and gives the chaperone the finger and Paul is packing a bowl, and the engine guns.

"Shit," I say, ducking down. "Shit, shit, shit."

We peel away from the Belmont School, away from the teachers with the Smith BAs and the boys with dermatology skin and the yacht club girls and we three head off into the June night.

"Shit," I say again.

"How about thank you," Nancy says. "How about I ate your fucked up fish sticks, and had to waste nine minutes of my beautiful life on these prep school twerps just to spring you for the night, my dear beloved friend."

"You ate the fish sticks?"

Between the mirror and my peripheral vision, I can see Paul in sharp detail, the razor nick where his neck meets his hairline, the faint gloss of pomade. He has particular coloring, not Caucasian, but not quite brown either. He wears a single, thick ring around his index finger. I lean between them, smell curry. Nancy doesn't like spice, so this must be Paul. I think of sitting on the window seat in Andi's room, of everything that felt like it could have happened with Judah. It feels like some credential I've gained, but there's no way to transmit it to the people in the front seat, and so instead I am a freak who is weirdly sniffing things.

It's an interesting question, are Paul and I friends. We hang out together all the time, but it's never been the two of us, never just the two of us alone. What you notice about Paul are the things you'd notice about a girl, wrists and ankles and knees and hipbones. His every gesture is both elegant and awkward, like a water bird unfolding its jointed leg. Dark hair, large generous features, golden eyes.

"Actually," continues Nancy, "in a weird way, I like your mom. I mean, she gives a shit, and she isn't fake, but she's also not at all normal. I don't care if she hates me, but for you, you need to stop letting her control you."

"She doesn't control me," I say. "You don't understand. My mom—it's just about what's easier. It's just about how much of a mess it is if I go against her."

"Whatever," says Nancy. "Sorry if I'm trying to save your life."

"My mother gets like that," says Paul. "Needy, needs me to make her feel OK."

"See?" I tell Nancy.

"Yeah, but he tells her to go fuck herself and leaves before the hysterics start."

He smiles. "You gotta be willing to tell your mom to fuck off."

A thing about Paul I know from Nancy: he still has his Bar Mitzvah money saved. He's going to use it to go to Europe and see the Globe Theater and real Commedia and Moliere in Paris. Another thing I know, even if he never told me:

Paul wasn't really out of cigarettes when he came to Nancy's window and it wasn't really about being cold.

The fight with his dad was about Hebrew School, Hebrew School versus Chinese School and which Paul should drop.

"Which do you like better?" Nancy asked.

"They both suck," he'd said. "Seriously, what's wrong with Spanish? Twenty-five percent of the people in this country speak Spanish."

Objectively, the father was the bigger asshole. The jokes Frank Greene made were usually about Paul, about how lazy he was, what a druggie, although Frank liked sex and race jokes, too, jokes with slurs no one used anymore. You'd laugh at the first two, Nancy said, and then keep laughing even though the jokes had crossed a line.

Paul's dad was smart, had almost gotten his PhD in geophysics, then ended up the slumlord of these fucked up brownstones. On all the deeds, in everything he ever signed, he listed himself as Dr. Greene, despite the fact that that was fraudulent. His tenants were always complaining about the heat being set at sixty-four, about the bare drywall and half-finished repairs.

Paul's mother was a lawyer, still filing briefs and challenges to the original custody agreement hammered out in the Mass courts in 1980. Everything was split evenly, but there was always something new to divide, always some perceived unfairness. This was why, Nancy explained to me later, Paul couldn't just go to his mom's when he was locked out. Even when Paul was high as Jesus, he remembered which house he was due at; he never messed that up.

Nancy shook her head. "We're all just waiting this out. Two years. That's the thing we have to get through."

Paul, now, from the passenger seat of Nancy's Escort, fills us in on the afternoon. The tow truck guys brought the repaired car to his place, and they'd showed him how to give it an oil change. Wiper fluid's topped off, too.

"Nice." Nancy runs her hand over the dash as if she can feel the mysterious engineering beneath, can appreciate the workmanship.

"You owe me," says Paul, and Nancy nods, and I know it's not about the oil or the fluid. Paul touches the bruise on his wrist, and I see that it has the shape of fingers, of someone's fingers trying to hold him or pull him.

We kick around. There's a rent party later, but before, there's just time.

"I hope he's not there," says Nancy.

"Who, Judah?" Paul asks.

"No. Nothing. No one," says Nancy.

Paul punches the lighter and lowers the volume on the radio as the weatherman comes on. The storm has made landfall in Florida. Here, it's still just a darker cast to the sky here, just what feels like an earlier and weirder coming of night. We're on Memorial Drive, windows cracked, Nancy and Paul barely audible over the rushing air. They gossip about people I barely know, the tow truck guys, and the girl who lives in the Fenway apartments.

"I heard it was an explosion, like some giant chemical explosion."

"Naw. It was a drug thing, a revenge thing from smugglers who were trying to get him into the country."

"What kind of drugs come from Russia? Drugs come from South America."

"Let's just go by the Fens," says Paul. "Let's just see if anyone over there has good ID."

Waiting for the light, Nancy stares at herself in the side view mirror. "I'm on a diet. Seriously, no more cookies."

We head back toward Cleveland Circle, and I watch the minute hand on my watch, trying to keep myself from falling silent for too long. Nancy makes us check the parking lot again for the tow trucks, then we head over to the one with a wife's house and do the whole circuit again.

"Man-slut," Nancy is saying. "A lot of guys are just man-sluts, and they'll just take anything they think they can get. They're not, like, discerning, and girls always think it means something."

It's eleven, and we're in Boston, somewhere between Chinatown and the South End. It's not a part of the city I know. Nancy stops at a payphone so I can check in with home.

"The dance was the usual," I tell my mom. "I'm not the type. Those boys aren't into me. This one guy, but whatever. Nothing's going to happen."

My mom tells me to thank Nancy's parents for driving me and putting me up, and reminds me not to eat too much of their food. I'm meant to be sleeping at Nancy's, but her parents go to bed early and never check up, so we're basically free after nine. Nancy puts on more eyeliner in the visor mirror and reglosses her lips. Paul prerolls a joint and stashes it in his box of Princes, tucks the rest of the weed and his pipe under the seat. He's been smoking all night, but Nancy tries to stay sober if she's driving.

There's a thing where we eye each other, where we each kind of look each other over, but no one says anything. We're a little out of our league, here. This party is a little too cool for us. Paul's the one of us who might know some of these people, and now he's walking ahead like he'd rather be seen with anyone else, as if he were in a band instead of beardless and girl-pretty and sixteen. We can hear the music as we enter the side door of the warehouse building. We follow the sound up the concrete stairs. There's a girl with a studded bomber jacket and a guy in a red Mohawk and a kid puking. We step over the vomit, the cigarettes mashed into the ground. I'm clutching my five-dollar cover. Then, suddenly, I'm like, I think it's going to be OK. I look skinny in my shadow, pointed in all the right ways and I recognize the song coming from the loft party. It's the Lemonheads, and Nancy takes my hand and pulls me and Paul up the stairs, and we're already dancing as we pay the bouncer, already inside with the noise and the pink lights and the crazy motion of so many bodies.

"I have to tell you something," I say to Nancy.

"Don't," she says. "Don't say anything. You've got to stop thinking it's boyfriend and girlfriend and over the rainbow. I'm saying this because you need to be educated, Mellie."

"Are you still pissed about this afternoon?"

"I don't even remember this afternoon. I'm saying, learn to do something with your face."

Paul gives us a look, like is anyone going to fill me in, and Nancy whispers to him, and my stomach plummets, but he still seems OK. It seems OK. Then, Nancy starts dancing backwards, cutting a path deeper into the throbbing dance floor. Of course, we follow.

I want to say this thing: when I was that age I didn't get high to dance. The music was enough, the smell of bodies. I want to say this about teenagers. That all of them are a hundred times more beautiful than the most beautiful adult. It's being uncorrupted by failure and gravity and entropy, but it's not just that, not just youth and innocence. Teenagers, the chubby ones pulling down their too-short dresses, the ones who aren't smiling because they are hiding their braces, teenagers are studies in vulnerability, have only the broadest cloth with which to cover themselves. Teenagers are lovely and when I see them now at the meetings, Jim from Mondays in Brookline, the pink-haired girl on day pass from the hospital, when I see them, I wish I had wings and breathed fire. I wish I could stand in front of them until they were good and ready to face the world. I wish I could go back, and stand in front of myself.

Still, how you consume danger as a kid, the way you eat it. The song is Dinosaur Jr. and Mudhoney and then it's Black Flag and the Misfits. It's getting harder as the night wears on. Nancy is fucked up and keeps leaning in to yell about this boy or that one against the wall, about were they watching our asses, or checking out our chests. Twice, I think I see Judah, but Nancy's all, *fuck it.* She thinks the DJ is unbelievably beautiful, and the guy who plays bass in the second band, and the one kid who is operating the keg. The key, she yells, is always to collect them, to collect as many as possible. That way you don't get bruised. Nancy shows me a girl in vinyl shorts, and she says that girl is a role model, is what we need to emulate. We dance near who we think we could love, and then away.

Someone bashes into me, shouldering my shoulder. I shudder, shocked, and then I bash back, and then we're this arrhythmic mob, this organic mass in five dimensions. I see Nancy swimming over the crowd and then Paul is at my back, the golden of his eyes almost invisible around his dilated pupils and he puts his hands on my shoulders and moves up close to me. He feels fragile standing so near me in the shuddering throng of bodies, his frame unprotected by muscle or bulk. I can sense, in the way he gives against the motion of the other dancers, that he's expert at absorbing blows; I know a story about him getting jumped by some Nazis in Kendall Square, but it's not just that. There are other things which make him harbor at Nancy's, other things he's sheltering from.

The crowd pushes us closer and pulls us apart, closer and apart.

Long sleepy afternoons with Nancy, pulling off her stolen one-hitter and watching *Quantum Leap*: I could see how that might be a world someone like Paul needed to burrow into. I sense his need to fall into things, to hide inside someone. Paul's hand slips into my pocket and I put my hand in on top of his. I can feel the welt on his bruised wrist like a swollen bracelet. There is a breath between us, still, but our touching is what the crowd wants, a geometrical figure in which the distance that separates us becomes smaller and smaller until it disappears entirely.

I have no choice. My body chooses, and I shift my weight, my whole length pressing into him, the bones and the bulges. I feel some bright spot at the center of him, a hot wound enclosed by his delicate shell. I want to armor him against the elbows and knees and occasional fists that thrust into us, the dance's crazy brutality. I want to be armor.

Paul is touching me, his whole body touching me, and then, someone, deliberate, pushes into us. Above the crowd, I hear Nancy's voice. "Do something, Mellie. Do something with your face." The instant I break the connection, Paul is sucked back into the crowd. He mouths something, *Don't go* or *Too slow* and then he's gone.

It's probably two in the morning when someone finally tells me Nancy's already gone. Outside, I hear the distant sound of sirens. The mosh pit is disintegrating. I see a kid go past me cupping a bloody nose in his hand; limpers limp by; when I look up, I find Paul. He is up against a wall, the vinyl shorts girl grinding him against the brick. I'm too stupid for words, standing there. The look on his face is bewildered, as if he's found himself in this candy funhouse by complete and total accident. It doesn't feel like an accident, vinyl shorts and Paul. It doesn't feel like a coincidence. It feels like a caution.

When Paul looks up, he still has those pupils, the giant vacant blackness set into the gold rings of his irises. Like a total hoser, I say his name.

After a fuzzy instant or two, he registers me, smiles, like isn't it insane that he's getting dry humped by this spectacular specimen of a girl?

I can feel hot tears gathering, heat in my cheeks. *Man-slut*, I think. *Stupid man-slut.*

I do what I do: flee. I zigzag across the loft and into the hall, then vault myself down the stairs. As I reach the basement landing, I catch my heel on the final step and the contents of my purse go scattering. Here I am, sucking beyond belief at everything, a stupid baby. I slide to the ground. Then, I see the cloud spoon.

Grow up, I tell myself. It's a command. *Grow up.* Then, it's a wish, an incantation. *Grow up. Grow up. Grow up.* I peel off the wrapping, and lean against the clammy wall. I recall Paul's lips, closing over the spoon, the circuit. I flick the tip of my tongue to taste. It is less a taste than a sensation, like accidentally swallowing laundry detergent. It burns, like the acidic medium that carries the charge. I push the spoon toward the back of my throat. My tongue parches and then waters and then there is only the faint after-flavor of burnt lemon zest and soap.

—pop—

—the candy-look, the shorts, it all recedes and disappears. Everything gets sucked backward. I am momentarily a pure, blank mind, an amnesiac or a baby and then I'm walking through the boiler room and past the dumpster. I am easy. I am the coolest fucking shit in the world. The night is awake with red flashers, and the first fat drops of the promised rain. Drunken party-goers stumble from the main entrance into a line of police. I pull my coat over my head, and somehow this gesture makes me invisible. I stroll, unconcerned, past the paddy wagon, past the beat cops and into the night. I am taller, older, more beautiful, and nothing worries me at all.

———

Obviously, I'll never be the woman for the job, am not going to be the frank adult volunteering in the high school health class, but someone capable should find a way to talk about adolescent desire to girls. The focus is on predators, on protection, which I get, which is important. The thing is, here the thing is, also harm is done by not talking about the other, by not talking about the impulses that come from ourselves, from the things we invite. Teenaged boys, that's easy. You say how irrational they are made by the throbbing in their pants. But what I needed was for someone to tell me about my own throbbing. I felt it and did not even know what it was, did not know how to call it desire. I remember, swear to G-d, thinking my tampon was in wrong. That was how desire got power over me, by being unacknowledged.

———

My mother is asleep on the fold-out in the living room. I am exhausted, soaked through from the miles-long walk along the T tracks home. I have the bedroom behind the kitchen. Because of the carpenter ants, I cannot remove my shoes, and my mother is in a phase where she is not taking her sleeping pills, and so when I get home, inevitably, she wakes. I hear the tin beat of a pot collecting rainwater in the bathroom. Drip *dripdrip* Drip *dripdrip*.

"Amelia? What time is it? Are you all right?"

"It's OK, mom. Don't worry." I am poised between footsteps. I imagine dying ants beneath my soles, mildew water through the sagging plaster.

"Why aren't you at Nancy's?"

"We had a fight."

My mother rises on her elbow. "What about?"

"Drugs," I say. "Nancy tried drugs."

My mom doesn't reply for a few moments. I think she is trying to see me in the dark, but we are far from the windows and there is only the line of the hall light under the apartment door and the single eye of the smoke detector indicator on the ceiling. The moon is not in phase for us.

"You know, I think you're old enough to drink coffee," my mother tells me.

I nod, and crunch my footsteps over the insect carcasses until I reach the carpet of my room. I am lying in bed, clothes on, my thoughts swimming gently in cloud's current when I hear my mother again.

"That girl," says my mom. "I never thought she was loyal. I never thought you could trust her with your secrets."

"Is that why you didn't want to regress her?"

My mom makes an unconvincing noise, as if she's fallen back to sleep. I burrow under the comforter, my own familiar smell of powder fresh and girlsweat mingling with the new sharp smell of lemon. Outside, the wind is picking up. Hurricane Gladys is centered somewhere in the ocean between Virginia Beach and Delaware. At its heart, it has winds of eighty miles per hour. The weather forecasters marvel at how slow moving it is, at how broad the bands of rain are that surround it. People have been filling their tubs with bathwater and panic-buying cans of tuna since yesterday, and still we only have this, this accumulation of rain, this waiting for the disaster to hit.

Five

Brookline
2010

It is late afternoon, cold rain sleeting down, the vista awash in gray, but the man before me is Technicolor, the driver of the SUV.

(things stir between my vertebrae, long-stilled sensations: fistanger sobloss teethrage musclerejection waterloneliness stomachguilt sugarshame tonguedesire scratchviolence and other nameless creatures that have lived in my knotted muscles these long years)

My vision sharpens, the details revealed like the distance closing in a tracking shot. His hand, a familiar curve to his lip, the new grays in his hair. The man resolves, becomes meatier. His muscles transform into unlikely patches of fat where no man should bulge (the finger pads, the palms). I recognize a peculiar gray beneath his skin which is a pallor particular to longtime substance users. I know him, not just from the smell of his cigarette, or the outline through the reflective window glass. I know him from way back. We've met before. But now I see he's not here for some sweet reunion. I sense the coiled danger in him, but I can't make myself run. It's him. It's him.

"Get in," he says, nodding at his ride. He grips my arm, but I try to resist. It is like moving my actual body in a dream state.

"No?" he says. It's so simple. This is so simple for him. G-d. Of course it is. He's still getting high.

"My car." I push the word from me. "I drive."

He holds my forearm like a gun and we begin to weave through traffic. I feel the approach of cars like a collision already happened, flinch into myself. This is what it is to panic, the brain throbbing, lungs constricting. Then we are at my car. I halt without warning, use the momentum to pull him in. Now we are facing each other. The rain stops, suddenly. There is that instant clarity that can follow a New England rainstorm, the shivering brightness. Something shifts in his muscles—confusion, to mirror my own, a dawning and then a glimmer of something: recognition. He is close enough that I can smell the scent on him, the chemical burn of recent use. The smell is tinged with the familiar lemon, but there is something else in there, too. An exotic variety, I think. The drops of water on his skin are gold. He smiles at me, and now, we are in a different film entirely. The fear from a moment earlier does not leave me, but it slips into the background, like a parent's advice you never intended to follow anyway. Openmouthed, I smile back at him.

"That's what I've been waiting for," I tell him.

"You sure?"

Am I sure? I know him, I know I know him. It is ludicrous, that I've been alone, that we've suffered apart, when I've been right here, just waiting, ever since he disappeared. Uncertainties remain, of course. Does he look like how I expect? Do I remember those exact eyes? Can I call up, precisely, with total confidence, his exact name? Continents recede; mountains swell up; every interval between every breath is another epoch passing. Yes, I am motherfucking sure.

"Too long," I say. "Too g-ddamned long."

I open the door, and he slides in a duffel bag I had not realized he was carrying, then climbs in beside me. I start the engine, the vibrations joining the hum already in my body. He, the man I have been waiting for, tunes in the college station from back in our pimple days. It's the Talking Heads, playing their naïve melody, the drums beating just under Tina's guitar. *Home—is where I want to be.*

I pull out and just start driving.

I forgive you totally, I want to say, but that's not a fraction of it. *I'll never forgive you,* and *why are you here?* and *where the fuck have you been?* But cloud makes it hard to hold onto resentment. Hey, you should say, Hey, you did some really bad stuff to me and you hurt me in terrible ways, but all the details have been sanded off the story, and it's tricky to sustain intensity around an abstraction. Or this is just pushover girl stuff, just classic dumb bitch. I'm lonely, and he feels right and I'll take whatever I can get.

I shift gears, pick up speed, then drop my hand onto his. He startles, physically, but I don't take it personally. In the life, in cloud, intimacy is always a bit proximal.

"Is this how it's supposed to be?" he asks. He's shaky, an hour in on a double hit, or maybe the nerves come with the new variety, but I won't let him off too easy.

"It's like this until you fuck it up again," I say. And then I'm just laughing with the pleasure of his company. G-d. Not being lonely. Just not having to hold myself in. It's amazing. Now, he laughs, too, and my shoulders relax, and I begin to bounce to the music. *Home—is where I want to be. Pick me up and turn me around.*

We're going to drive through the old streets with the windows down and the radio up playing all the old songs. The sun is out: maybe we'll go to a drive-through. He'll order for me, or I'll order for him, and wipe the hot sauce off his lip and we'll throw the wrappers over our shoulders, and pretend to bang our heads when the metal tunes come on, or he will let loose his beautiful voice, singing the girl parts in all the duets. *Make it up as we go along.*

The story of where he has been is one I'll have to hear eventually. He's gotten by somehow, made his own bad compromises, and I won't like everything he has to say. For example, he has been following me for some days, and with some peculiar purpose in mind. Something pressing and desperate. I'll have to hear about that thing he thought he was after. Too, I have my own urgent news about our time apart. Behind him is Juni's car seat. In a moment, he'll turn his head, and then I will tell him. Hey, I'll say—we can have all this, just as before, but there's just this one thing first. She's a girl, a beautiful baby girl. What the experts say about them, about cloud babies, doesn't tell her story. Her words may not have ordinary meaning, but Juni's baby talk is song, has magic in it, sometimes even messages. I know I sound crazy, I'll say to the man beside me, but I am her mother, the mother of someone so miraculous she could survive even me. Listen, I'll say, listen to my confession, my outsize pride.

But he doesn't turn his head, and so I don't say any of it. Memories, in cloud, return sometimes slowly, in mosaic. Give it time. First the recognition, I think, and then the reckoning.

My phone buzzes on the seat beside me. He looks interested and not very interested at the same time.

"Go ahead," I say, tapping in the code and handing it to him. "I've got nothing to hide."

He navigates through the windows. I hear a snippet of dialogue from the headless woman video. I reach over to grab for the phone, and he pulls it out of reach.

He scrolls through "Guess I'm not the only one coming back around."

"That's nothing," I say. "Just work."

"Nothing yet, lady honey. This is still preview season." With his free hand, he unzips his duffel. I have a brief glimpse of what's inside. There are dirty clothes and a frayed toothbrush, half-eaten sleeves of crackers and an archive of paper. He's been living out of this bag. Now, he makes a note, and then zips the bag closed. He punches some buttons on my phone. "How they do, right? Get you suckered with the promo, feed you the reruns, so you're hungry when the ratings kick in?"

"That's West Coast time. Out East, we call this March. But it's the same, stuff you thought was dead crawling back to the surface."

"What you could maybe explain is, why the delay? Have we been waiting on something? Someone? Not that I'm in a rush. I'm in the exact opposite of a rush."

Also, me. I'm taking my time. I turn onto Beacon Street, cruise slowly past significant parking lots and convenience stores and T stops. His face registers things, but I cannot read the meaning. I loop greater Brookline on a silent tour of everywhere I've ever been, George's Folly, the Golden Temple, Dunkin Donuts. A stately side street that stretches to almost Route 9. We pass massive houses, old but not necessarily beautiful, set closer to the street than rich people elsewhere in America like to live. We slow as we come abreast of a blue three-story house. The oaks hang heavy over the street. There are children shouting from the nearby schoolyard. See it, I think, the rusting Escort in the driveway, the ancient cat sunning itself on the roof of the porch. Everything is as it was: Mr. and Mrs. Dussel still live here, refusing to retire from their medical labs. All of it's the same, I say to him. Whatever purpose has brought you to me, whatever you think you're doing, this is what matters. I wait for the one word which will connect these streets to the hole in my chest to the man at my side.

"Something's missing," he says. "That's what we're waiting on."

"I've got time," I say.

My passenger rests his cigarette hand on the window, gazing at the schoolyard kids. I inhale the familiar scent. It's not an original Prince, is some Indonesian knockoff, but it smells just the same. He smells almost the same. Nancy's fled, of course, absconded, expatriated—everyone has an opinion, but no one can say for sure. Still, in her attic room, the old artifacts remain, the blackened incense burner, the collar-cut t-shirts. Remember, I think at the man beside me. Remember her and remember me. Instead, he just flicks his cigarette onto the Dussels' lawn, and motions for me to drive on. Fact: he always was a bit of an asshole. Always thought he was too cool. Obviously, I don't hold it against him. Obviously.

He breaks his gaze, leaving a patch of breath on the passenger-side window. "So," he says. "Are we done seeing the sights? You want to keep on the great suburban tour? Or could we possibly consider dealing with this thing?"

"You have a better plan?"

"Yeah," he says. He's rifling through the duffel again. I spy the fruits of a search, checklists of addresses, a survey map with careful annotations. *See? You have been looking for me. You just didn't realize it.* I have a vision of us, this evening perhaps, after dinner, reading aloud from our respective records, mine in my paperback, his in his duffel. You saved that one, too, I'll say, and he'll spread out his map, and retrace his journey, then we'll finish our lives together. Now, he locates what he's looking for, a pad of paper with a couple of items penned in and crossed off. He squints. From this angle, the lettering is illegible to me, so whatever talisman he holds has to wait.

"Up there. Stay to the left."

"You think you're so smart."

He shakes his head. "I don't. I'm just a grunt. You're the smart one, apparently."

I take it as a compliment, though it feels off. He isn't a grunt, never was. Like *lady honey*. Not his kind of endearment. Still, we change; people change, so I go where he points. He knows his way around, seemingly. Nods me down Longwood Avenue, and then to Chapel Street. I anticipate what we'll see before we turn, though it's been years, decades since I used to wait at this subway stop at the end of the school day.

"Pull over." He points to a spot across from where I used to get the T; there's an immense structure set above us, on some irregular rise the sun is caught behind, and so all I see is the enormous shadow. Or perhaps it is like the face blindness, something about this location that I can no longer see.

"What is this place?" It calls up no particular feeling, but for some reason, I can conjure an aristocratic hush, the red of high-end carpeting, as if I've been inside.

"It's an extended stay hotel, now," says my man. "Dignitaries recovering from vein surgery, awaiting hearts for implantation. But, some of the old residents are there, still, too, at least going by the deed. So? What do you have for me?"

My passenger has taken out a pad of paper, the kind you steal from the dentist's office or the insurance agency. The tops sheets are crowded with handwritten notes. He pages through until he gets to a blank one and begins to write. I know these gestures, the fake phone number, the easy smile. I'm about to get the brush off. My stomach clenches. That's when I realize, he's been testing back. I've been being observed the same way I've been observing him.

"You ever get sick of the repeats?" he says. "Tired old shit made like it's new? You remember where you know me from yet?"

"Of course," I fib. "Did you?"

"We—" A kind of confusion washes over his expression, shadows of softer things flickering beneath. We've held each other, I want to say, skin to skin. I can sit here and tell you what you taste like. You must remember. "Maybe once we—Maybe, but—*we* aren't the issue here, Amelia."

From his throat, the name spikes into me. He does know me, but it's wrong. "No one calls me that."

"But it's your name, right? For *work*?"

"Listen, you," I say. "You found me. It wasn't easy, right? You drove to my house. You waited in my driveway. You were thinking about something, there on my street. I think you followed me last night. You watched, but you kept second-guessing. You needed time to think it through. Why? Today, you came again. You got into my car. What does that sound like to you?"

He considers me, then leans in very close. "It sounds like you have something I need. So where is it?"

"There's no *it*. There's only us, you and me." I want to shake him, wake him up. He's caught in some stupid loop, and here I am. Right here. Why can't he see me?

"I wish I could trust you on that," he says. "No *it*. You took care of it. It's already gone. But what about the buildup? The come-on? The coming ha ha attractions. They want to see how it turns out so bad, they let you reach inside them and put it there. The whole world, they let you use them. But I think we agree, you and I, that is not a great plan."

"I don't care about the whole world," I say.

"Good girl. So, I guess that means it's your season to wake up, too. Look around. Anything you recognize? No? OK, you've got your little sober thing: good for you. But that cannot interfere with the bigger picture here. Human to human, I get how you want this to go. You move into the bright big future, all the old mistakes fixed. Believe me, that's what I want, too. But there are things outstanding, Apollo. What do you call it? Dormant. Stuff inside is sleeping, right. You know this, because you put it there. Then it wakes up again, blue. That is what we're waiting on. It's not the ending. We've been to the ending. It's the middle that's gone, and the middle is the alarm. That is why I'm going to need it. In my hand, not on some promise. Because rerun season is over." His speech is muddled, contains ellipses and insertions, but I can't decipher it the way I can with a cloud user. He's high. I know that, but it's not a high I recognize. The smell is strange, powdery and mineral, and yet, just a touch of lemon licks into the air.

He thumbs back through the written pages. "Kif-Vesely'e? That do anything for you? Still no?"

I want to give him whatever he wants, but it's like trying to do the work, my old familiar work. I can't. I can't conjure from my mind the thing he wants from me.

"You have it, or you know how to get it, lady honey. You just need to dig a little deeper."

Then he makes a gesture. The gesture is so known to me, so familiar, it's like we share a skin. He lifts his weight of the seat, slides his hand into his pocket, and extracts a tiny thing. Square of paper. Nub of cloud. He's on something else, but he knows what I like.

"Get right, Mellie." He lifts the door handle. "You know how to find it. They're not waiting for nothing, and they're not waiting for long."

In his palm, where there was paper a moment before, he now holds a handful of confetti. The one square of cloud has multiplied in a magic trick.

"No," I say. I am going to hold onto him bodily. This isn't how this ends.

Then he tilts his hand, and tiny scraps of paper waft to the seat between us—a banquet of cloud, a feast. I am mesmerized by the bounty.

My senses fire wildly. A D-line train pulls into the station and disgorges a few dozen passengers. In that instant, my passenger and his duffel disappear.

Things blur and brighten, a waitress and a telephone pole, a McDonald's bag and a bicycle wheel, a handbag and baby, all the little pieces of paper on the seat where he once was, ashes or evidence or my only consolation. If this were one of Lew's films, if I could see things the way I used to when I was high, the critical details would coalesce, the contrail of his path, and I could follow. But though the evening seems to strobe with significance, nowhere amid its shadows is the man who used to be my man.

Six

The Fenway & Brookline
1988

They are dismissing us early from the White School because of Hurricane Gladys. Outside, the limousines and Mercedes and humble Volvo wagons are lining up with the buses. After school, I usually go to Children's Hospital, where I file patient records in the physical therapy department, but my supervisor has left a message that they're sending nonessentials home. You can tell by looking out the window already that this isn't a regular rainstorm. The trees lift the whites of their leaves to the sky; the rain cuts toward the earth at an acute angle. I watch as I wait my turn with the payphone. We're supposed to call our emergency contacts, let them know of the early release.

All day, I've been full of manic energy, trying to climb out of my own skin.

I'd been stranded with my mother during a flood last year. Washington Square was under a foot of water, power lines down, T cars garaged. Beacon Street was one big electric lake, and none of us able to leave our apartments. Four days of electricity sparking across the water and my mother's cabin fever set in. "I'm just so lonely, Mellie. It's just so hard to be unmarried and still want things." But, in truth, it's not so much what I want to avoid that makes me call Nancy.

When she picks up, I tell her about the dismissal. "So can you? I need a ride."

There's an interval of silence. Mrs. Gordon, who is waiting to call her husband, taps on the glass.

"I thought you were pissed at me."

"I thought you were."

I can hear something in the background, like an animal or a baby.

"Is someone there?" I ask.

"No one. Just Paul," Nancy says. "We're going to watch the hurricane with Judah." She's not inviting me. She's uninviting me. But it's Friday, and I feel like I'm halfway through something that needs to be finished, or like I'm hungry for some specific food.

Mrs. Gordon taps the glass again, eager to leave the school, to go home to her professor husband in Cambridge and play Trivial Pursuits by candlelight.

"Perfect," I say.

By the front door, they're checking kids off a permission list, but it's Mr. Peters with the clipboard, and I'm a junior with straight As. I wave myself past the line of kids, and barrel out into the slow-moving storm. The drops spatter, sting my exposed skin and fog my glasses, but I'm impervious, the heat coming off me as I bend into the wind. The Village Fens is a full half-mile away, but that's not where I'm going. Across the Jamaicaway, on the other side of the T stop is a place called Longwood Towers and this is where Judah apparently resides. I can't shake the feeling that a few days ago, he lived in the crack house, and that something has changed, and now he lives in a fancy condominium, that this change has something to do with cloud. Too, I have a free-floating hunger, something I want, that I cannot attach to anything. Cloud is where it used to be.

This is my second time crossing the Riverway today. I have off-campus privileges at the White School, and at lunch, I'd been too boiled up to sit with my classmates, so I'd walked the twenty minutes to George's Folly, the head shop where Nancy worked until she stole the one-hitter. George, a hippie with grossly long fingernails, was behind the counter.

Massachusetts state law prohibits the sale of drug paraphernalia, but what falls into that category is a negotiable list, and George always had things like tobacco pipes and screens and lined tins, things which technically could be used for other purposes. He also sold herbal mixes and beedies and spoons of cloud. I didn't want to eat it, obviously. I would never eat cloud in school. Still. I thought of cloud's lemon taste and some faint ghost of its relief floated back to me. Just in case I couldn't shake this mood, just to have, I decided I'd walk over during free period.

I wandered around looking at the Indian comic books and imported wooden elephants, the ceramic ashtrays and batik tapestries for a few minutes. It seemed impossible that I was the kind of person who could walk into a store and just ask for drugs, even if they were legal, but when George took a phone call, I ducked behind the eighteen-plus curtain, where the dirty magazines and erotic statuary were kept. Between the dildos and the sheesha, there was a single wrapped spoon in an otherwise empty case.

Pursuant to local code 380.49.3, "cloud" will no longer be legal for sale in Massachusetts.

George came in behind me. "You eighteen?" he asked.

Teenagers were George's customer base, but not his favorite people, because we stole and we hassled and we loitered and distracted his employees. Being wheedled by an adolescent was nothing new for George. I thought of flight, but just behind the impulse to run came a wash of calm, of strange confidence, like I could conjure back cloud's blankness. I lied by two years. But he shrugged, and unlatched the ring of keys from his belt, and opened the case.

There's just a little sheen of pleasure that comes from knowing I've got the spoon now, that oils my skin against the rain, and what I'm doing is something still unfolding in my mind. I think of myself as I walked home through the deserted midnight streets, everything glossy, everything blurred. I feel meaner. Like a person who can be mean on purpose.

Now, the light changes; the uniformed nurses cross opposite me, back toward the hospital towers. Beneath the bridge is the same waterway that peters into the swampland of the crack house apartments and an unmaintained section of the Emerald Necklace, a park that rings the area. My mother has stories, deep lore, of the Fens below and we'll stop here when she occasionally comes to a soccer game or to walk me to the pediatrician so she can point out certain features. Even in summer, the growth below is tangled brown among the green, the tall reeds weeping over the slow-moving and narrow waterway. We never go in. Hidden from the road, it is rumored to be the lurking place of perverts. But it is also the location of more benign mysteries, like bamboo. Bamboo is invasive, grows and adapts like a dandelion or a zebra mussel, but it does look tropical there beside the Yankee cattails. My mother tells me that during the triangle trade era of New England, bamboo was used as packing material in the bottom of spice crates. After the crates had been emptied, sailors dumped the bamboo here and it grew. The lesson, like the past lives, may be half-invention, but it's interlaced with my sense of my world.

It's funny, Longwood Towers. It's just across from the T station closest to my school. I pass it every day, but the way it sits on a rise, something about the angle from the street, or just that it's not significant to my personal geography—even as I approach it, I can't quite see it until I am already in its shadow. Longwood Towers: crenelated and turreted, it rises like a kid's version of where rich people live. The lobby is hushed, the carpeting not new, and elderly white ladies push their walkers slowly around the chintz sofas while their attendants trail behind.

How Judah lives here is by his father and how his father affords it is by soft-core pornography.

The doorman is older than the Boston dames circumnavigating the lobby. I approach him, shivering and dripping rain. I'm in a man's white t-shirt that mysteriously appeared in our laundry, and my mother denied knowledge of. It's a small apartment, ours, but I'm often out for the night, so whatever. Gross. I clear my throat and try to see through my rain-speckled glasses.

"My friend is having some of us over," I begin. But I'm blanking on his last name. "I'm here to see Judah—" I know it. It's Cohen. I think. I'm nearly positive.

The doorman squints through his smudged reading glasses, takes me in, and nods. "Tower C," he says. "Elevator on the left. Second floor. Apartment F."

Tower C, 2f. I write it in the pages of a paperback. It's this dimness, lately. Up too late, sleeping too little, so I've been trying this trick of writing things down. I tuck the paperback away and press the up button.

In the brass elevator doors, I am a watercolor girl: white skin, purple lips, and the very first streaks of platinum lightening my hair: total soft-core. Soft-core is how Nancy has described what Judah's father makes, as if there is some critical difference between the real stuff and what Mr. Cohen does. Maybe soft-core means not fully nude, or naked but no actual like insertion—naked and just rubbing. Or maybe it includes sex, but just nothing super pervy, nothing horrible like hurting someone or putting objects into people. Oral sex is probably soft-core, but through a Vaseline lens, in blurry focus, so everything looks like the cover of a religious greeting card.

Nancy thinks I still sound fake when I use foul language. *Blow. Suck off. Go down.* Nancy has a theory that most girls can't perform good oral sex, particularly to a bigger penis, and that if you can just keep the penis in your throat for longer than thirty seconds, you will addict them. You can make the boy into an addict of you. I look at my smeared reflection, think of the taste of cloud under my tongue.

The elevator opens on a silent hallway. The smell is of something odorless, some odorlessness, or it is the smell of dust in the cooling air, the smell of carpet fibers. Apartment 2f is at the far end, awkwardly angled in the curve of the tower. Outside, the storm is still just a rainy day; I could make it home, before the winds rise, but the crawling feeling in my throat goads me and I knock. The door swings, opening, and I step inside the apartment of the soft-core pornographer.

"Hello?" I look for Nancy, for Paul. For any sign that this is the right place. The thing gripping my throat, which is like thirst or need, tightens. "Hello?"

No one answers. I zip open the inner pocket of my backpack. Tucked next to my wallet is the last legal cloud in Massachusetts. I unstick the Saran Wrap from the spoon and suck the clear gel from the plastic.

Something stirs, a body part under covers in the back bedroom, nude limbs untangling from sheets.

"Who's that?" a male voice calls out. The person in the bedroom stands. I swallow, pulling the grainy gel into my parched mouth.

—pop—

I feel the bitterness slide into my belly. It metabolizes into something perfect and hard—everything retreats for an instant, and then—the blond shaven head, the glimpse of blue tattoo script. It's Judah, only Judah, pulling on a flannel over his bare chest. He points his chin in my direction and I'm fine and I keep smiling and he smiles back.

"Hey, you," says Judah. "You happen to know what time it is?"

The jitters ease. It has something to do with cloud, but also something to do with Judah. When Nancy is not sitting on his lap, he seems more regular.

"Coming on four," I say. "You guys were going to watch the storm? It's OK if I join?"

"Sure," he says. "I'm going to make some coffee, and then go dumpster dive while we wait for it to build up. You cool with that?"

I'm amazingly cool, alone with Judah. "Do you have cream?"

"Some that might be expired in the fridge," says Judah and steps into the kitchenette.

In Judah's living room, all of the furniture matches. The picture frames, the entertainment center and the coffee table, each of them is made of the same plasticky reflective material. My friends are generally richer than I am, because I know them from the White School or through Nancy and Brookline. One thing I have learned is that rich people do not necessarily have matching furniture. What they have is old furniture. Nancy has a secretary, which is a kind of a desk, which is worth a hundred thousand dollars. Her grandfather had it stolen by the Nazis and then it was returned through some complicated process that involved Israel and an auction house. Now, her dad pays the electric bill on it, grumbling. Through Nancy, I know the term *nouveau riche*. I decide Judah's father must be nouveau riche. That you don't make old money from shooting porn is an idea which makes sense. I'm collecting data.

Judah's hips are level with the countertop pass-through that separates us, his flannel mostly unbuttoned. I try to think of how you'd describe his body if he were a piece of art; my art history teacher might say, hyperreal, but that is when it is a painting, when it is a statue in a museum in Rome. Ropy, perhaps. Long-muscled. He turns suddenly and catches me watching him. He has a more of a man's body than Paul.

"Something wrong?"

I shake my head, unembarrassed, cloud smoothing everything over, and step away from the kitchenette.

On one of the living room shelves, there is a red glass bulb which is either a way to smoke drugs, an art object, or a piece of soft-core pornography. Everything here is like that—impossible to tell is it is filthy, or clean as Mr. Bubble. For example, there's a wall-sized art silhouette of a man and a woman touching. They have too many arms between them, an extra leg. On the sofa, there is a naked girl doll, plastic and smooth. Or, also, there are film canisters labeled in permanent marker *Audition (Probe), Dayan Roza, Niagara Falls '84*.

A haze has descended over the space, like Vaseline on my lenses, but certain things tug at me, seem sharper. Is it cloud making me see this way? I try to recall if I'd had these same sensations on the walk home from the loft party. What it feels like when I think back is that there was something left dangling in the evening, and that I'm meant to find it, and pluck it.

On the bookshelf, there is a cabin photograph from Jew camp, the matching t-shirts emblazoned with the words *fun-fun*. The boys grin. Judah is there, and Paul. It's only a couple years ago, but I can see the difference between now-Judah and his high school-senior self. The ears sticking out, the rutted skin. I imagine how sad it would be, the only child of an old, bad man, roaming these soft-carpeted halls on school vacations.

Judah reappears with two cups of coffee and the creamer under his arm. He sets down the cups, opens the carton, and makes a face.

"Black is fine," I say replacing the photo.

I have been in the apartment twenty minutes and still Paul and Nancy are not here. Gladys is hovering over the coastline, is growing tired of moving so slow. Soon it will be crazy to go outside. I am alone with Judah Cohen at the edge of a hurricane, and maybe that could be fun.

You have to suit up for dumpster diving. Judah hands me a pair of plastic grocery bags and shows me how to wrap them around my hands like gloves. He's brought elastic bands to secure them—they are girls' hair elastics, the kind with the pink plastic bobs you loop over each other to hold the tie in place. Nancy wears that kind sometimes, to be funny.

He holds my wrist while he loops the hair ties over the plastic bag. I crinkle as he leads me down the silent hall to the garbage room. I see there are no actual dumpsters in this episode of dumpster diving, that like everything in Longwood Towers, trash picking here is going to be genteel. Judah removes each of the lids, peers inside, and then motions me over. What is in our garbage at home? Egg shells, the foil wrappers from my mother's birth control pills, half-burnt smudge sticks which failed to chase away the ghosts. Or else, it is SpaghettiO cans and Van de Kamp's frozen fish sticks and paper wrappers from Arby's.

Judah shakes each of the two garbage cans and then digs in.

Here is what is strange about the garbage of the rich: it includes no food. There are coffee grounds and tea bags and reams of discarded typing paper, but there are no half-eaten toaster waffles, no apple cores. The rich probably eat oranges peel and all. The rich probably do not eat.

"What are you looking for?" I ask.

I'm still seeing hazy, but the sense of a tug I'd felt in Judah's living room has sharpened. There's a thing I must locate. Claim. I need to find it.

"Someone threw out their Christmas wreath before Christmas even. This perfectly good doll. Yesterday, I found a griddle and an alarm clock. People just get a new one if the littlest thing is wrong, but you can fix almost everything."

"That's the best thing you've ever found?" I ask. "A waffle iron? A wreath?"

Judah shakes his head. "The best stuff in probably in the penthouses."

"We should look."

"I wish. You need a key for those elevators."

"I didn't know penthouses were real things," I say, pushing. "I mean, actual."

Judah considers me, then strips the bags off his hands and stands up. "You scared of heights? I have an idea."

The highest point in the building is in Tower A. All four towers have the same number of floors, but because of an anomaly in the foundation, in the bedrock, tower A is in fact taller. Judah explains this while leading me down to the lobby. It's a separate elevator for each of the towers, a key to get off at the penthouse. To get to Tower A, we'll need to cross the roof from Tower B, and to get to Tower B, we need to go through the lobby.

Judah buttons and tucks his flannel before the elevator opens. I notice the way the ladies and the nurses smile at him, as if he were still a ten-year-old in corduroys instead of a tattooed dealer. The doorman looks up as we cross.

"Getting pretty hairy out there," he says to Judah.

I look through the revolving doors. The rain cuts across the glass front of the buildings; something big and bright—an escaped Frisbee or a part of a lawn chair—clatters past.

"True enough," says Judah.

Where is Nancy? A normal person you'd say the storm held them up, the downed wires, but Nancy's not a normal person. She once walked three miles to buy a pack of Princes. One of the seven times she had sex was with her boyfriend in his hospital bed. Things like storms do not stop her.

Tower B is the only tower without a penthouse. On the top floor, there's no key access because it's just regular apartments, but that means you can swing out the window onto the fire escape and walk along a wrought-iron platform until you reach the ladder to the roof. Judah goes first, into the pelting rain and rising wind. My turn. I let loose a whoop as I lean out the window. I reach for the platform with my toe. The iron railing is slick. I let go with my left foot and for an instant, I'm dangling, loose in the wind. Below, the trees thrash; the pavement glistens. Then Judah's got a grip on my arm, on my other arm. My feet find the ladder. My lip is banged up, my palms scraped, but Judah tugs and I haul and we land on the roof. We're on solid matter.

Below the lip of the building, there's a temporary shelter from the wind. We lie still for a few breaths, me trying to catalogue which sensations are cold, which wet and which pain. In the far distance, the sun still pierces the sky, but above our heads, purple clouds lower and lightning slices the gathering darkness. It's pretty majestic. Judah touches me on the shoulder, shoots me a grin, and then points off across the tar expanse.

"You ready?"

I smile back at Judah. He hitches up his pants and I follow him over the rain-slickened rooftop. The door to Tower A is wedged open with a cigarette-filled pineapple juice can. A cinderblock configuration near the door looks like a makeshift room or sitting place. Someone, obviously someone young, spends a great deal of time up here. We duck into the stairwell. Whatever I'm after, I feel I'm nearing it.

Judah salvages a barely smoked butt from the landing, shelters in the doorway. He examines the filter, which like the others, is imprinted with lipstick marks, and then lights it up. "Interesting." The cinderblocks, which are scrawled with sharpie, bear poetic, but not necessarily meaningful messages: *make the thing matter. All heart experiment. Nothing and no one and never.*

"The whole towers," says Judah, "the whole time I'm growing up? There's only one other kid. Penthouse, just the girl and these two maiden aunts. It happens that we're both in the courtyard. Or she's by the fountain or in the lobby asking has her aunt's paper arrived. Never, she never says word one to me; maybe ten years, riding the same elevator sometimes, and she never makes eye contact."

"She's pretty?"

"Sure, in a snotty way. I haven't seen her in a couple of years. I guess I figured she went to college or moved to Switzerland. Something. Anyway— " he stubs the cigarette, and I let the rooftop door swing closed. In the sliver of light through door crack, we feel our way deeper into the building. "When I was a kid, the roof was her space. She staked her claim. And unless her two old aunts write graffiti and smoke French cigarettes, I'm guessing she's back."

The stairwell gives onto a hallway. At one end of the corridor is a door which is ajar. Music leaks from the room, the smell of cigarette smoke.

I nod in the other direction. "This way," I say. I sense my nerves returning, the cloud wearing off, but still the thing beckons.

Judah follows me across the carpet until we reach an incinerator room. We open the door. In front of an empty blue bin is the thing we've come for: a penguin wearing a lampshade on its head. The penguin has a lampshade on its head because it is a lamp. An old blue-and-white pattered cord emerges from the bird's rear. Both Judah and I consider it, and then we look at each other to see if what we are observing can possibly be true, but it seems it is. The penguin lamp is beautiful. Also, I think immediately, it is known to me.

Never, in all the years I rely on it, will the sense become specific. It tugs on me; it pushes me away. *Here*, it says of a video clip and *not here*. I can place an image in a window; I can select a typescript, but always, it's this sense of knowing, which comes from elsewhere, from beyond the bounds of my experience, as if it's borrowed from some other mind. From the beginning, though, in the penthouse incinerator room, I know to trust the sense.

I step forward at the same moment Judah does, but his stride is longer than mine and he seizes it before I have a chance. My foot nicks the garbage can and there's a shallow, echoey crash.

We listen. A moment passes without any other noise and we nod at one another and retrace our steps back to the stairwell. That is when I realize the problem. There are no stairs down. The staircase ends here, on the penthouse floor at a concrete landing without egress. Judah thinks I'm going back to the roof. Above us, debris clatters in the wind. I think of the slick ladder to the fire escape, of the double risk of climbing down, feet finding rungs by feel. We whisper heatedly, me pointing to the elevator, him shrugging and shaking his head. The record reaches the end of the track. "I can just meet you down there," says Judah, but when I dart back into the hallway, he follows.

I press the elevator button, and then there is an attenuated pause. We wait, in a stranger's hallway. The needle lifts from the record. Judah watches the apartment door, listens to the movement within. The elevator is taking an absurdly long time, the movement of pulleys slowly becoming audible. *Ding.* It arrives with a shuddering halt, the creaking of chains. Judah and I look at each other in the moment before the elevator door opens.

"Aunt Beatrice? Aunt Delilah?" a voice calls from within the apartment. "Sidwell? Is that you?"

We step into the elevator as we hear the sound of heels crossing a large and cavernous apartment.

"Aunt Delilah?"

A very thin woman, college-aged, appears in the door to the apartment. She is beautiful, a slash of black bangs across her forehead, and her cheekbones and chin sharp. In one hand, she dangles a burning cigarette. In the other she holds a tool of some kind, a chisel perhaps. She smiles, in a way less friendly than confused, and then she sees the penguin and her face contorts. "That's mine," she says.

Judah and I freeze.

"Give that back to me. I made that." She steps forward, just as the elevator door closes. Behind it, we sink into the falling floor.

"Fuck," says Judah. "Fuuuuuck."

"I know," I go. "Fuck."

And then we are laughing, and for the night, at least, I know something's clicked for us. Judah's a man-slut, and a crackhead, and he's twenty-something years old, but he's something else, too. I think: even Nancy doesn't know this thing about him, the little-boy-in-an-empty-tower thing. And, anyway, if she's so concerned, where is she? When is she even coming? Meanwhile, I've come down from my cloud high, and George's Folly is a bust, and I'm glad I have someone like Judah who could hook me up.

Seven

Brookline & The Fenway
1988

An eerie light is breaking through the hall window when we arrive at the door to Judah's apartment. I think: maybe Nancy and Paul have made a dash for it, but no one is waiting for us when we come in. Judah plays his messages: two hang-ups, and then a girl I don't know's voice.

"Hi," she says. She pauses for a long time, audibly swallowing. "So. Same deal as always. I don't know. She went to go send in an order form, and now the storm is breaking, and I'm not sure—I don't even know why I'm calling, but—"

Andi. It has to be Andi. She sounds like she's never heard of lying, like her heart looks the same inside and out.

"Listen, forget it," says the girl on the machine. "Everything's fine. I'm just being stupid."

Judah presses the reset button and the tape spools back. "She gets pissed off when I help her. And then she calls me for help."

"Why?"

"Excuse me, but girls. It's a thing of a certain kind of girl who needs to be thought of as badass, and then can't deal with how it goes down." He glances at the doll on the sofa, which disconcerts me. "It's old business. She wants to be a kid when it's convenient and an adult when it suits her."

I nod; there is information here, important things; the thing with the doll.

"Not that I'm not an asshole, too. I'm a total fucking asshole."

I shrug. "So, does that mean you're going to go? Or not go?"

Judah peers at the window, points. Outside, the evening is sharp and calm.

There's a tree down across the train tracks and the air is dead still, but in the distance, heavy clouds still threaten.

"Is the storm over already?" I ask. "The TV said it was so slow-moving."

"Must be the eye," says Judah.

"How long does an eye last? Could we make a run for it?"

"Half an hour? Five minutes? Probably varies." He shrugs. "We could sit tight, smoke a little weed, relax. We could chance it."

I feel the clamping of my throat, the creeping worry and hunger. And also thrill, dashing through the attenuated sunshine. I lay out the situation to Judah with my cloud supply, but he's not holding. It's all at the crack house. So we've both got our reasons.

"We could make it," says Judah. "The Fens is close—"

I think of leaving a note for Nancy. My feeling from earlier, the thing trying to climb out of me, resurfaces. Say whatever is lingering from the loft, there's also me, heading out into the storm with the guy Nancy likes. You could say, it's me having the better night.

Anyway, I don't end up leaving a note, but Judah flips the bolt so it stays open, so they can get in if they ever show. I can see it's a practiced gesture, that he's often leaving his door ajar for a girl, that he often comes home to find some teenager in his bed.

Judah doesn't exactly have a real parking space. His dad, who is in LA on a film shoot, leaves behind his Brougham in the apartment's designated spot. But it's next to a pillar and there's a gap big enough for a compact if the driver pulls the mirror in and backs up super slow. Judah's '74 Saab is the shittiest car I've ever been in.

"My dad wants me to buy something American," says Judah. "Something new. A Jeep."

The fabric interior has peeled away from the ceiling and passengers have carved various things into the crumbling foam beneath. I settle my book bag in the seat well in front of me and read the writing: I see kids' names I recognize, *Armand* and *Josh* and *Dina*. Judah is like an ambassador from the world of grown-ups to our teenaged kingdom, trafficking in drugs and dirty acts and adult concerns.

The front seats have safety sensors to tell if there's actual ass on the cushion, and if there is, the car won't start unless the seatbelt sensor is also triggered. Judah explains, though, that the belt sensors are broken, so the car knows you're there, but it thinks you aren't wearing your seatbelt and won't fire the ignition. I have to boost my pelvis into the air at the precise moment Judah turns the key. Judah's brought the penguin, and once the car is started and I return to my seat, he gingerly places the lamp in my lap. I want to keep it, to not give it back, but I know I won't be able to argue. It does calm the unsettled feeling the object gives me, to hold it in my lap, to examine it.

"What is this made out of?" I ask him. The penguin is crafted of some familiar-unfamiliar material. Judah pulls out from the underground garage. Now we're on the street, you can see the wind damage that's been done, telephone wires bowing toward the ground, lawn furniture in trees. The lights are dead at the intersections. There is no wind, not a single other car on the roads. We raise arcs of rainwater as we turn onto the J-way.

The paint is flaking off the penguin; the black has gone white about the eyes and feet, making what might have been cute a little ghostly. It floats above itself, is hollow-eyed.

Judah digs a fingernail into it. "So, this is weird. It's wax." There is something about his inordinately long fingers. I do understand why girls go for him.

"No," I say. "You don't make a lamp out of wax. That doesn't follow."

"Yeah," said Judah. "Yeah, I know. She works in weird materials."

"Who?"

"Valerie Weston. The girl who wouldn't talk to me. The artist who lives with her aunts on the two top floors."

I shake my head. I want to explain to Judah that he's wrong, that no art school girl made this penguin. Why we went across the roof for it is its history, its finger grease of time and use. But even if it's old, that doesn't explain the material, why anyone at any time would make a lamp of wax.

We are waiting at the next intersection, but the lights just blink yellow. "Is this crazy, or what? We're the only ones out here."

"It makes me want to loot or something," I say.

He laughs. "Would you pack me a bowl?" He fishes a bit of soft felt from his front pocket. It's a Crown Royal bag and inside there's a baggie of weed, and a little wooden box which opens up to be a cleverly contrived pipe.

I've been around it; I've absorbed some drug skills osmotically. As we swerve around the tree limbs, I manage to pick out a few buds without scattering the drugs all over the floor. He, on the other hand, is an expert smoker. I admire everything about how he does it, the way he cracks the window, the way his feet continue to work the pedals, the seconds his lungs can hold the smoke.

"There was a storm like this one night at camp, do you remember?"

"Camp?" I can see a bit of Judah's tattoo script at the collar of his shirt. *She* or *Shall.* —*Broken heart____Sh (e) (all)____Live in vain*

"Sure. We took the canoes out in the middle of the lightning storm. It was freezing, idiocy. They were all watching something, some big international news event we kids didn't care about, and we took advantage. Camp director flipped, later. We all got sent home. But, just drifting there, watching the lightning crack against the sky, thinking it could never come for us."

"Was that the night it happened?"

"Yeah," he says. "Yeah. You know it was Andi?"

"I don't remember," I say. There is a strange sense about this whole episode, that it's been removed from me, carved off, that I will not recall it in years to come. "There's a picture of you from then in your living room."

"God, yeah."

I laugh. "You look different."

"I know this sounds arrogant, or whatever, but it was better. It was easier before I grew into myself. A lot of girls are available to me, now."

I laugh. "Sorry. You do sound arrogant."

He laughs, too. "I know. But, isn't it easier to be good when you don't have the opportunity to be a shit? I'd like to live with myself for a while, but I'm such a hungry fucker. I can't even behave for a few days. Do you get that?"

I shake my head. "Myself, I'm trying to be more of a shit," I tell him. But, I know there's an intersection between what he's trying not to do, and what I'd like to do more of. It's about appetites, about starving versus gorging, but I can't make the idea into something I can say.

He smiles, pats my leg in a not-sexy way. "Is that why you're friends with Nancy?"

"She's not a shit," I say, but I'm not sure I mean it.

"Maybe not," he says. "I get a sense she's trying to look out for you."

"Sometimes," I say. "I think when she seems like a bitch, it's because she's trying to protect me."

"Protecting people is a mess," says Judah.

As we pull into the Village Fens, I hear the wind beginning to pick up. The sky is growing dark again. We angle into the parking spot in front of the crack house. Garbage cans lids rattle. It's hard to open the door against the force of the returning storm. Leaves sail through the air.

The crack house is bright, lights blazing, the black paper over the basement dormers pierced with lamp glow. We knock hard. A person is facing off against us as the doors opens, arms crossed. My first impression is that it's a little kid, some younger sibling I'd missed on my first visit. She wears an adult's pajamas, rolled up at the ankles and sleeves, but then, my eyes adjust for scale and I realize it's only Andi. She allows the door to fall open. Judah smiles. I'm a part of the backdrop, not really relevant here.

"Do you want some tea?" Andi asks Judah. Her voice is high, manic. "I'm making tea." The kettle sings in the background. "But we don't have honey, and we don't have sugar, and the tea is kind of gross."

"Come on," he says. "Put that down. Let's go out and look for her."

Andi shakes her head. "I've checked all the usual places. Post office is closed. Donut shop. Periodicals at the library."

"Still," he says.

"I shouldn't have asked you," Andi says with her clenched jaw. Even in those pajama pants, even with that expression, she is truly lovely. "You shouldn't have come."

Judah gives me the barest of glances—*see? Women, right?* And I thrill.

"Anyway, she's probably been picked up already. Or she's sitting in some Samaritan's kitchen, eating their cake, and sobbing." She moves around the kitchen carefully so as not to step on the cuffs of her pants, pouring water from the kettle into the teapot, and then lighting her cigarette off the burner to smoke while the tea steeps. The set is beautiful, china, pink and filigree, with delicate fluting.

"Who would pick her up? Ambulance?"

"Yeah. It's kind of fascist. They can nab you for looking weird. Actually like wearing a winter coat in summer or something." Her voice remains high, tense, but maybe this is just how she speaks. "Plus, non-English speakers."

Andi begins to transfer the tea things to a red plastic cafeteria tray, the cups clattering together, then she picks her way toward the TV room. Judah watches her closely. In the hallway, we step around the mailers and packages which are so thickly collected on the carpet, it's hard to navigate.

Truth? I am thinking of cloud, of the segue that will allow me to get my mouth on a spoon.

Between the television room and the entryway, something thrown or dropped has left a violent brown spatter. It's recent, since two days ago. Andi and Judah glance at it, some shared understanding passing between them, and then he's taking the tea things from her and she sidles into his arms.

I back away from the pair and locate the telephone. There's a vague need to call my mother, to let her know how I'm weathering the storm. I hear Judah murmuring to Andi.

Nancy's stories often light on Andi and her mother and I collate some of these half-ignored bits of gossip now with the details the home reveals, the china and the mailers and the tea-drinking. The mom is a chronic catalogue shopper, no defenses against capitalist urges. It's a communist country they immigrated from, Eastern Bloc. There's something horrific about the dad, too, a failed refugee escape or a bomb, something with a shade of historical import. Anyway, he's dead. Cloud, crack, whatever they cook down there: it's a piece of how they make ends meet now. Judah's mixed in there, too, drops in with cash for groceries or to deal with the landlord, whatever. Part of how they hold it together, and part of the problem, too. There's a kinship, Andi and her mom, me and mine, but it still feels alien to me.

I get a long, low drone on the phone, though whether it's from delinquent payments or the storm, I don't know. I think what Nancy will say, if my mom calls looking for me, whether she'll cover. I can picture her and Paul laughing, like it's an alliance, them against me. That's what has had me feeling unfinished all day. I want to eat cloud, make the feelings slink off.

A terrific crack from outside brightens the living room before me. The eye has passed, and the storm has returned in force. Andi stands apart from Judah, staring at the black square of the sliding door, the drops crawling sideways across the glass. Andi's X'd tape across the pane, but it's the wrong kind of tape, nothing that will hold against the impact of debris. Judah touches her.

"It's OK," he says. "This isn't your fault."

"Yeah," she says. "But it's my fucking problem."

Judah is holding their coats.

"I don't know. What if she comes back, and I'm not here?"

"Mellie can stay," Judah says.

"You don't mind?" Andi asks. This is the first she's acknowledged my existence this evening. She and Judah are putting on their coats.

"I'll keep an eye."

The sky splits behind them as they open the door, splits again as Judah throws his arm around her and they step out into the rain.

I feel a nonspecific yearning, to be with a person who would face wind like that with me, or it's Paul and Nancy who by now, facing facts, have obviously ditched me to be together. It's something like that that has been eating me all day. Like that I'm Nancy's second-best friend. My mother, last night, something about her not being loyal. And, there's a sense of something red and shiny, lipstick colored, a wall, thumping music. Of train tracks, and rain drizzle, and wrists flicking beneath too-short sleeves. I want to be the first choice.

G-d, I think. I suck. It seems obvious to me that no one will ever like me that way, that I'm unlikeable, that I'm detestable, and then it becomes more urgent for me to find some cloud, and I wonder if this is why Judah has left me here, so I can score without having to count my grubby bills and be someone who is buying drugs from a girl who can't pay her phone bill, whose mother is missing in the rain. I listen. The silence deepens, though it is textured with an electric sizzle at the back of it.

I try the basement door, but it's locked. I am in the kitchen. Nothing's on the stove, no cooking, but the room still smells of gas leaks and the carbon monoxide of chemical fire. I remember the bulkhead door.

The air outside cuts, little slivers of sleet mixed in, and I have to push back against the wind as I make my way over the boggy ground of the unfinished compound. I shoulder into the weather until my shoe finds the basement door.

In the makeshift sitting area before the TV, there is evidence of work. There are stacks and stacks of bills from catalogue companies, neatly slit open, and on a piece of binder paper beside, dollar amounts written into sums. A shoebox of Xeroxed letters, *I am writing kindly remove from your list.* There is evidence of trying to help out, trying to fix things. The divider curtain is pulled aside and by the blue light of a gas burner, I make out the armature of photographic clips strung on wire between the insulated pipes, two ice-filled Rubber Maid bins, and about four dozen spoons cooling in metal utensil trays. There's the cloud, cloud enough to soothe ten of me through the slowest of hurricanes.

At that moment, there is a loud crackle, a burst of light, and then the house goes dark.

The flame is about ten feet in front of me, but the darkness between is complete. It feels as though there might be deep holes, or the walls might have collapsed, like I might be in the midst of nothing. I take a tentative step, and then another, and I'm too scared to walk, and I drop to the floor.

I see my future. All the filthy carpets I'll find myself on, all the times I'll crawl, just to get cloud. My scraped hands drag through filth and decayed spider web as I move toward the blue burner light. Someone should come. My mother, or Nancy, a policeman or a teacher. Someone should pick me up, and get me straight before it's too late. But I keep crawling, and then I've got my hand on the spoon, and—

—pop—

I am sucked in like a breath and exhaled. Everything turns easy. When Andi and Judah arrive home, rain slick and raw-faced from the pelting wind, I am in the living room babbling with Mrs. Auslander. She's speaking Estonian or whatever, and I'm not making much sense either, but she's got a towel wrapped around her, and I have eight spoons of cloud in my pocket. Andi's coat drops from her shoulders; the still-open front door closes behind her and she rushes forward to hug us both.

"Slow goblin," I say, aware that cloud is gumming my speech, but Andi's too grateful to care, and I have a hero feeling, like it's all been fixed. I'm the person who fixes things. Judah collects Andi's coat off the floor, and holds it up, shaking off the rain, while Andi fetches her mother's medication.

I think, I will write this all down, before it slips off. It's becoming a habit.

Twenty minutes later, Andi and Judah stand in the hallway, not touching. He tries to pass her the wax penguin, but she's putting him off.

"I want to think about whether I want it. I'll try to come by your place after if she looks like she's sleeping OK."

"I know," says Judah. "It's been a long day."

"Aren't they all, always?"

Judah is a full foot taller than she is, but he slouches and she straightens her spine, and you could easily ignore their differences. The fact of a kiss is a possibility that hangs in the small space between their bodies. Unacted upon, it is nonetheless material, exists like a charge in the air. That's how I feel, too, like something about to ignite.

The secret knowledge rests next to my awareness of my eight spoons of cloud. I could eat them all tonight, or parcel them out to myself over months or save them for some unpredicted, unbearable pain. No one can tell me what to do with any of it.

In the car, penguin perched on my lap, I listen to Judah's breath.

"Do you think she's really going to come? Did it sound like she meant it?"

"Could go either way," I say.

"Yeah, but what's your instinct?"

"Sure," I lie. I'm sorry for him, which is not what I expected.

"Girls," he says. "The whole coquette thing. No offense. But just for once, I'd like someone to just tell me to fuck off. If that's what they want."

He turns his blinker on and looks over at me while we idle at a blinking stoplight. "Hey, are you OK? You look, like, pale or something."

"No," I say, cloud sloshing over me. "I'm great." And I am. The streets are empty, the traffic lights dead, the asphalt glistening with rainwater. Dead leaves and filth rush in the gutter, but the wind has stilled. The moon is out, the stars. The storm has moved out to sea or inland to New York. Still, the night is empty.

"You always wear those glasses," says Judah. "Can you really not see?" It is after midnight and I feel relaxed. I slip my oversized frames off my face and stash them in my book bag.

"It's like being blind," I tell him. Everything becomes a corona of its own colors, a halo of light on the surface of the dark.

"You look transformed," he says. "Like a new person." We roll the windows down and turn up the volume and drive home through the blurred and flooded world.

Eight

Brookline & Roslindale
2010

For a long time, I sit across from the Longwood T Station gazing at the scattered scraps of paper on the car seat beside me. When I look up, the clock on the dash reads six thirty.

For a moment, I can't credit the numbers on the display. Because six thirty would be an hour and a half past my daughter's pick-up time from the sitter. But then I add the evidence of the sunset, my phone's notifications. My texts are full and the ringer is on silent and the battery is almost dead. I'm late for Juni. Then, an explosion of mother-panic startles me into motion.

This is how it goes on my reality show, for a mother in meltdown; the apocalypse in intervals between the appointments, the crisis rerouted by the sudden cry.

The caregiver is sitting on the porch with Juni coughing beside her. As soon as the woman sees me, she hoists the pink shopping sack which is serving as Juni's diaper bag, tucks Juni under her free arm, and waddles toward me. "Your emergency contact number is in a *foreign country*. They speak Spanish."

I had given her my mother's number in Belize. There hadn't been anyone else.

I take the pink sack in one arm, and Juni in the other. My daughter buries her face in my sweaty armpit and releases a raspy breath.

"I had tickets," says the sitter. "We had *Sox* tickets. Get it? The game starts at seven ten."

I see that her boyfriend and son are already in the truck, the engine running.

She taps her sandaled foot while I write her a final check, then climbs in the back, and leans her head out the window. "Don't be calling thinking I'm going to change my mind. You know she's brain damaged, right? Not just anyone would take her. I'm serious. Most moms would be grateful to me."

In my arms, Juni begins her beautiful cloud song. "Apple. Peach. Potato heart."

The sitter peels out of the driveway, eyes averted. She'll make the second inning, maybe even the first. But my daughter, in my arms, is on the edge of crying. It feels as though there is a long, dark fall beneath me, jagged rocks and frozen waters. Wyle E. Coyote time. Time for the plummet. I nuzzle my little girl, who smells of sour diaper and missed dinner. I am in my body, still. I have not used yet. I can make it until bedtime.

But just. The bits of paper on the seat beside me lift as the air leaks through the cracked window, as I lurch over train tracks. To distract myself, at the stoplights, to keep myself from licking the leather interior of my car, I write what I remember of the afternoon in my paperback, the driveway man's nonsense talk. *Old residents. Going by the deed. West Coast time. The buildup. The come on. The coming ha ha attractions. They want to see how it turns out. There are things outstanding, Apollo. It's the middle that's gone and the middle is the alarm. Kefeselyay. Wakes up again, blue. Bright big future. You know how to find it.* Then a horn honks, and I am driving again.

Home, I put a hot dog to heat in the microwave. I open a can of baked beans and roll some whitish baby carrots onto the high chair tray. I count to 506 while I feed her, her mouth opening obediently, her incomplete set of teeth gnawing through the bite-sized food. I wipe my daughter's face clean and dump the tray in the sink and get her upstairs. I count to 216 while I balance her on the changing table. She's good when I take off her diaper, and even though there's already a touch of rash, she doesn't complain when she feels the chilly wipes or the cold Desitin. I bundle her in her sleeper, and begin to count again as I rock her and rock her and rock her to sleep. Seven hundred eight. Nine hundred forty-two. Just past a thousand, my daughter's eyes close and her breathing steadies and then, like a blessing, she is asleep.

I descend into the adult sanctuary of after bedtime, famished. My phone complains in my pocket, message after urgent message, but I am beyond its reach now, concentrating on stepping lightly, on stirring as little as possible that might steer me from where I'm going.

No one sells cloud by the spoon anymore—today, dealers package it between paper, like fruit rollups, only in small, stamp-sized squares. I am quiet, deliberate as I move through the house. My mouth waters. It is urgent that Juni not wake, that nothing be disturbed as I open the door that connects the garage to the house, stealthily unlock the door, and climb inside. Then it's me, ass in the air, dome light on, combing the gritty floor mats for every scrap of paper that might yield me a high. I can call up the moment of the scraps' falling like a crime scene. Some bits had descended weightily, shimmering with the gloss of dried cloud gel. Others had wafted benignly, disappointingly, to the seat. I collect every single one.

How many are there? Fifteen? Some are clearly useless, have bits of writing on them, blue ink. But, actually, maybe. The dealers are always getting new ideas, shapes to press the cloud goo into, hearts and clovers and bitty Taj Mahals. Maybe this is some new branding scheme, jokes like in bubble gum, or fortunes from cookies.

Your future will be as blank as cloud paper.

I lift the first scrap to my lips and dab my tongue at it. It tastes of soggy cracker. There is no acidic charge of cloud. I spit it out and I squint in garage light. Always, this has been my refuge, the place of my squalid desperation. In this, I am like parents across America, stashing their Camels, their love letters, their secret vices between the coiled garden hose and the gasoline canister. Here, thirty days ago, I scoured each shelf, lifted watering can and power drill, until I was sure I had nothing left. And here I am again, scrounging my filthy car mat for secondhand cloud; licking someone's sloppy spittle seconds, hoping for a high. I knew it wouldn't last. I knew I couldn't do it. I was stupid, an idiot, to even try. One by one, I place the pieces of paper in my mouth, and wait to be released.

One after another, they yield nothing, wood pulp and watermark. *Fuckfuckfuckfuckfuck.*

The final one has a promising sheen to it. I tongue it delicately; there's something; a hint of detergent, a trace of citrus and then—

—*pop?*

I am seized again by my desire for the man in the car. The man had known me—*Amelia*—he had said my name, but he had said it wrong. I had recognized him, but I had not known him. I wanted to be right, for my side of the story to be right, but perhaps we both have parts that have to be puzzled together.

I open my paperback. I take notes, have always done this, to fight against slippage and confusion, but also to find significance. Pages are glued together, things sunken into other things. The binding has been taped and retaped. Things fall out. As a record, it is haphazard and incomplete, but occasionally, a penciled word, an old photograph, has restored something to me after cloud has taken it away.

CA Plates. Perhaps that had been the error. I draw a line beneath the *CA* and flip through the book until I find today's notes. *West Coast time.* What if the confusion came from that? Perhaps us, we, our time of knowing each other tracks not here, to this place, but back to my later time in Los Angeles? In which case, my tour of Brookline would not have elicited any particular memories. My hand shakes but I struggle to keep rooted here, in myself. I left California two years ago, not entirely voluntarily. I had been sent, for a reason. What was it? In the interval, there were tall pines, by a lake shore, a red wall and then I was home again. *It's the middle that's gone.* Two years would make the man's timeline and Juni's coincide. I pick up my phone. The screen still shows a string of messages from the sitter, increasingly angry, and a handful from Emily, plus one from a burner phone with a string of question marks. I swipe them clear and then I open a browser and tap in the searchable terms.

I try combinations. *Bright Big Future*: A marketing firm. *Apollo Blue*: Greek mythology. I scroll down.

It's shameful, humiliating to want something so bad on such slim evidence. But I do. And now I'll admit what's obvious, what in particular shames me. The solution I want, the thing I hope I can read in these faded pages, is the thing that will compensate for all my failings. I know I'm admitting something that obvious here. I wish my baby had a daddy.

Apollo Blue. An industry pseudonym, for a film you don't want to be credited on. I have the impression that everything is about to snap into place, link up, reveal itself. I just have to reach. The paper in my mouth tastes like nothing more than glue, than Elmer's glue, a little milky stickiness. Any cloud has been licked clean. Or it was never cloud paper at all. I extract it from my tongue, and in the faint light, I see that this is one of the ones with marks. *OD TO.* A scrap of monogram, a tiny curling portion of a design, and below a couple of handwritten characters. *2f.* It's piece of something, a note to self, like one you'd pull from a duffel bag of your life, is the kind of note you'd write if you were afraid you'd forget where to go. *You know how to find it.*

OD TO 2f OD TO.

I cling to the syllables, waiting for the revelation.

Now, my baby is coughing, inhumanly, cough after cough. She has been coughing for some time. I take note of headlights in the window, of a beat-up Ford observing me from the street, a person shape through the dusty glass of my garage door, banging to be let in. Emily. I stand, preparing my excuses, but we are way past that point. My sponsor has already seen the paper on my stuck-out junkie tongue, and now we turn, both of us.

Through the open door between my living room and garage, I see my daughter. Juni is standing at the top of the stairs. Her face is going purple, her mouth open, but emitting no breath. The baby has escaped her crib. She gasps for air, reaching into the space of the stairs, and then she plummets. The leap is not in me, the saving leap.

She falls into the empty place left by my tardy and inadequate love.

Nine

Brookline
1988

When we return from Andi's, Judah stands in the hallway for a moment, fiddling with the lock. In the apartment, Nancy and Paul are cuddled on Judah's sofa eating Entenmann's and drinking General Foods International Coffee. On TV is *Fantasy Island,* one of the pop star episodes. I fall still in the doorway. Paul. His hairless cheek rests on Nancy's shoulder, his long legs tucked up on the couch. I can read tracks on his cheeks, from tears or hysterics. Between Paul and Nancy, the naked doll rests like their child.

Nancy looks up, red-eyed. "Do you like coffee?"

Paul chimes in, "Do you like chocolate?"

Together, they chant, "Then you'll love mocha."

Paul gulps, laughing, in a way that sounds like a sob.

My body twitches, galvanic, toward the square of sofa cushion between them, the space occupied by the doll. There is a kind of vapor from the two of them, comfort and secrets being exchanged like viruses.

"Where have you been?" I say to Nancy.

"Where have I been? I told you where I was."

"No," I say. "You didn't."

Now, Judah enters the apartment, and gently nudges me. I see Nancy's gaze sharpen.

"Elsewhere," I say. Because of cloud, my voice is perfection, arch but unhurt. *Bitch,* I think, *cunt. Slut.* I feel something akin to angry, but there's cloud buffeting it, softening the landing.

"Hey," says Paul. "What's up with your face?"

I touch my cheeks, expecting some rash, or eruption.

Nancy stands unsteadily, pulling her tight shirt over her pouched belly, and sidles toward me, slings an arm around my shoulder. "I've been reading tarot," she says. "Do you want to know what I found out?"

I start shaking my head. "Don't."

"Wouldn't you rather know?"

"You're wasted," I tell her.

"Mellie, listen. You don't want what you think you want," says Nancy, following my gaze.

Paul peers at me. "You look so much nicer. Like a nicer person."

Judah gently nudges me, on his way to the kitchen to make coffee. "I think, because of your glasses."

"Damn it." I touch my hands to my eyes. "I left them in the car. They cost a hundred and fifty dollars."

"That's how I do it," says Nancy. "Be clear-eyed. Look it in the face."

She's never going to be a ballerina. Not in Cleveland. Not with some lesser company. "I have to get my glasses, OK?"

Judah hands me his keys. "You remember where I parked?"

I flee into the hall, Nancy watching me go through her carefully drawn cat eyes. She's never going to get Judah. She doesn't know anything I don't know. As I wait for the elevator, I think of Andi, her quality of not one thing or the other, kid or grown-up, sexy or naïve, strong or weak. That's what gives you power, even if you're thirteen years old and can't afford new clothes and have to behave for the social workers. No one really wants the truth. Judah, in the car, asking me if she'd really come tonight. They want mysterious, the neither one nor the other. My problem is I'm obvious. So it's my actual feeling I have to change, if I want to be liked. The trick is figure out how to feel in-between things, love and not love, without inhabiting one particular state, how to stop wanting what I want so badly.

The elevator door slides open. I squint. It's a thin woman with bangs and then I recognize the artist from upstairs, the penguin woman. She is crying. My myopic gaze must contort my face into something mean, because the girl sneers back at me.

I let out a sound, *oh*, and draw back.

"Fuck. You," says the penguin artist. "Fuck. You. You. Stupid. Little. Twat." She shoves past me, elbow hard to my ribs, and stumbles into the hallway. This cannot be her floor. Is not even her tower. I step toward my own reflection in the elevator's brass. Stupid twat. My heart thumps. I'm the twat. And it doesn't mean bitchy. It's something else—small and obvious and hideous. My best friend is a whore and I'm a twat and I should never have taken off my glasses. Because my face is a twat face, obvious and ugly. The door opens on the parking lot, and I force myself into the underground air, the odor of garbage and exhaust. Judah's Saab is where I remember: wedged into the half-spot beside the Brougham. I let myself in and then I sit. Stupid twat.

I want to go home, but that would be a mistake. If I go sulking back to my mom's, I might never go to another loft party or hang out in a building shaped like a castle or figure out what it is that makes boys walk through rainstorms for you. Whatever happened at the loft, the red shiny thing, is like a deepening wound. I need to learn to feel differently. Besides, I think, I deserve it. After the week I've had, of course I need a little help. It's too late to go home, too late to do homework, and you can always extrapolate the phase of the moon. I put on my glasses and stick a spoon in my mouth and—

—pop—

—I am messing with the glove box in somebody's ancient Saab. The ceiling fabric has peeled away. In the foam, glyphs have been etched but they are illegible in the dim light of the parking garage. Someone's weed is in there, paraphernalia, some condoms, and a photograph of little girl and an older teenaged boy. I know the photograph isn't recent, is worn, has been studied. The boy, a blond, has a look of uneasy authority, both pleased and bewildered to be trusted by this little child. The girl is redheaded, is tiny, is wearing sopping wet clothes. It looks cold in the picture, the light dusk or dawn. The leaves are not yet on the trees in the background. You hope for adults, urging sweaters and blankets from beyond the frame, but even if they are there, it's clear that the child will under no circumstances let go of this hand, not to loop her arm through a sweater, not for anything. I turn the sheet over and there are their names. *Kif-Vesely'e.* The strange words roll easily on my tongue, and I know them, the people and the place where they are standing, *Kif-Vesely'e,* but I can't quite. Can't quite.

The square of photographic paper is irresistibly bright and sharp, as if it were colorized. It reminds me of something else, a penguin, a glass bulb. I stare at the image, the adult-acting boy, the sopping wet girl who will not let go his hand. The photograph has thingness, a weight like history or significance. I recognize it, even though I have never seen it before. I take a paperback from my book bag and slip the picture between its pages.

In the elevator, staring at my spectacled reflection, I return to myself, floor by floor.

The apartment is dark and quiet when I reach it. The pop star is gone, and Judah has threaded a reel of film into a projector. We are watching *Niagara Falls '84*, which turns out, in fact, to be soft-core porn. I don't know what hard-core entails, but there's everything on this video that I imagined there wouldn't be, penises, close-ups, penetration.

Judah is standing behind me. "S'fucked up, right? I mean, right?"

I shrug. Cloud blesses me with its cool, but this still is the most vagina I've ever seen. Up to and including my own. So, yeah, s'fucked up is correct.

"I've met that woman," he says of the girl blowing the penis on screen. "She's not that nice in real life, but still, she's a person. That's what my father does, he makes real people into that."

"Where are Paul and Nancy?" I ask.

Judah points a thumb through the door to his father's bedroom. I listen, and can hear athletics within, muffled animal sounds. Paul, at camp, did this thing for me once. It's blurry, physically blurry, My vision was already so bad, that in the memory, I can see myself but nothing beyond the perimeter of my wingspan. Paul didn't know me. He's a year older, was in the boy's cabin, but for some reason, he helped me. I was in the forest, alone, and lost and everyone was gone, and he came for me.

At the back of my throat, there is lemon. From the bedroom, Nancy howls, and Paul shushes, and I'm grateful to cloud for its rescue.

"Are they an item?" Judah asks.

I shake my head. "I don't even know why they do it. It's like, an activity for them. Like TV or cards."

Judah turns off *Niagara Falls*. "I don't believe in that, sex for something to do."

The penguin, which is to the left of the television, near the wall, is bothering me. It needs adjustment, is misaligned.

"It can't be wax," he says, following my gaze. He's standing much closer to me than I realized.

"Let's plug it in," I say.

Judah shrugs and then shifts some stuff until he finds a socket. The lamp works, the penguin's whitened eyes glowing brighter than the rest of it. The light through its surface is red, as if there is a real heart and actual organs inside. I'm on drugs. But still, there's something incredibly alive about it. That penguin could hoist itself onto the window sill and ride the eaves down to the Fenway below. It wouldn't surprise me.

"What is it?" I say. "If it's not boredom?"

Judah's mouth is the surprise, his hand on my nipple.

"Oh," I say, and I open to meet him. He prizes apart my lips with his lips which are harder than lips I recall, harder than the spin-the-bottle lips of my recent memory. These lips are drinking from me and I am not sure what my own mouth is doing because it will not listen to me. Vividly, I am thinking of Paul against me on the dance floor, of the spot in the small of my back where I felt his hot empty place. I am stealing back the kiss that was taken from me.

Judah and I wake to fire. The armature of the lamp stands in a puddle of its own wax, and the thing is aflame. The fire alarm is sounding. Paul and Nancy emerge wrapped in sheets and still laughing. I am aware that I am wearing bloody underpants, that I still have not called my mother. There's a fire for Christ's sake, every reason to run, but I resist the instinct because I want to watch. I want to understand what happens between Judah and Andi when she walks through the door. She is wearing clothes too large for her, and carrying a broken fan in her left hand. Judah is naked, untangling himself from me. The fire is leaping up the curtains. There is smoke and heat, but the two of them stand still in the flames and stare at each other, like they are inviting the meltdown to come.

On cloud, people say, pain passes through you. Or glances off you. Suffering can be released. The question is, then what? What becomes of those experiences which we have not experienced? In the apartment of the soft-core pornographer, the boy I love grunting in the next room, my body underneath Judah's surprisingly heavy body, I anticipate the way the night will disappear. In the early morning, I will walk back to Nancy's house in time to call my mother. She will never know; Dr. and Dr. Dussel will never know. The night will have been erased. But once the moment is upon me, I understand this formulation of erasure isn't entirely accurate. Somewhere, in some way, the aching self still exists. She remains entangled with my current self; I could collide with her at any time. It is me I've put through this night, even if the cloud allows me to deny it. Elsewhere, in some dimension that has as much reality as this one, I end the night cradling myself, shaking and sobbing, disgusted and ashamed.

Ten

Roslindale & Dorchester
2010

Juni lands, surprised, halfway down the stairs. Her mouth opens, draws in a great breath, and then she begins to wail. I open the front door.

"Christ," says Emily. She pushes past me and launches herself toward my child. The room for me clarifies and I see it as Emily sees it: the shriveled and burnt hot dogs, the rotten carrots I had tried to feed my child.

"Go back to the car, Leo," Emily commands her son. He glowers from the doorway over his stack of three-ring binders and index cards. A cloud of sneaker musk hangs about him.

"It's OK," I say. "He can come in."

"Are you high?" Emily asks. She is descending the stairs, my daughter coughing in her arms. There is a visible welt on Juni's forehead.

"Actually," I say. "I know it looks—"

"You know what? Shut up. And you—" she nods at her son. "Just, whatever. Find somewhere to finish your social studies."

I know I am blinking stupidly.

"Is Juni OK?" Leo asks.

Emily holds a hand in front of my daughter's mouth and nods. Her expression is hooded.

Leo lopes past us, watching the baby who continues to wheeze.

"How long has she been like this?" Emily hands the baby over to me. The touch of her, her mucousy skin wakes up my mother feeling again, and I hold her to me.

"It's just a cold," I say.

"You know kids like ours can get respiratory sickness. Leo had it, when he was little. Still uses an inhaler."

"It didn't seem like anything," I say.

"You should get some ice," says Emily. "That thing on her head is going to bruise."

Eventually, Juni's breathing calms to a slightly raspy normal. Reluctant and pissed at first, Emily bounces Juni and just her regular sleepy baby things eventually soothe my sponsor. My daughter curls her fist around a hank of Emily's bleached-blonde hair, and rests her baby head on Emily's breast. Juni's eyes begin to flutter.

Emily sends me to put Juni down again, and when I return to the ground floor, my sponsor is grunting her approval at Leo's binder. He settles in with the remote, a bag of Cheetos, and a sleeping bag.

"No point in going home now, anyway," says Emily.

Leo casts me a suspicious glance as I pass the doorway. The band on his t-shirt, *Smoking Ruin,* is nothing I've heard of but I know his joggers probably cost more than Emily's weekly salary. They have their own problems, Emily and Leo. The dad that used to hit them is up for parole and in the meantime, he's using his phone privileges to chat with Leo before Emily gets home from work. He's like, *does little man miss his pops?* You'd think you wouldn't have to explain to a child, Emily has told me, that a man who beat them isn't any kind of a father, but for Leo, it's not just one conversation. She keeps having to tell Leo, over and over.

"It's really fine," I say. In my mind, of course, is concern for them, Emily and Leo, but also, I want to be alone with my paperback, to sort through the scraps, and see what I can uncover *OD TO 2f.* I can solve the puzzle of his life, figure out *where to find* him, and bring him back to me.

"We're spending the night," says Emily.

"OK," I say. "Thanks."

"It's not a favor," says Emily, pouring herself a Diet Coke. "If a baby gets the respiratory thing, their breathing can fully stop. Just so you know the level we're at."

I pop myself a soda, to keep her company. She is contemplating the tray of food leftover from dinner, the bloody entrails of ketchup and char and compost.

"Also, you should have a baby gate. A fall like that—if she gets a concussion. Even if you don't care, if DSS ends up here, that's cause."

"Emily, I care about Juni."

"Obviously, I've made mistakes." She sounds really angry. "With you, I mean. I let myself make exceptions."

All of a sudden, I know where this is going. I'm too much work, too much risk, too stubborn. Emily is going to dump me. She'll be direct, and she'll be thoughtful, and she'll offer me the name of some environmental lawyer or children's librarian. Which will not be OK. Which is not going to be OK, because I can't do it without her. I don't want someone who is going to talk about school board elections and Weekend Edition on NPR. It has to be Emily.

"You're my first sponsee with a little kid, and I let you convince me things had to go down differently in this case, but I was wrong."

I meet her eyes. "I swear to G-d. I did not get high."

In the next room, gunfire is exchanged on the television.

"A guy from the Monday meetings saw you by your old dealer's house yesterday. Did you buy? And then lie to me?"

I shake my head. "I mean, I did go there. But I didn't buy."

"And yet, today, you are sitting with a bounty of junk in your garage while your baby has respiratory failure. You got the cloud by accident? And you didn't use? Keeping secrets is what an addict does. Even if they seem harmless, it's part of that web of deception."

"I'm not trying to lie to you."

"You're embarrassed? You want your privacy? Get over it. You don't get dignity in this process. All you get is clean."

"I know," I say. "I know."

"Let's try the story from the beginning. With no details left out."

"All right," I say. "OK."

Leo falls asleep during the late show and snores lightly at the muted screen. I pull up a chair, and I tell Emily everything: the way it felt to hear those wheels in the driveway; the man who turned into another man in the rain, who, as much as I could say, that I believed he was; the high I could not decipher; the confetti of cloud. Apollo Blue, the little sheen on the cloud paper.

"So what happened," she asks, "when you licked the paper? You get a little something? Did the world turn on is axis, and angels start to sing?"

I shake my head. "There wasn't anything left. I felt, for an instant, a pinprick, something, but then it was gone."

"That is how it always is, Mellie. That's what cloud is like. It giveth nothing, and it taketh everything the fuck away."

"Not everything," I say. "That's what's so difficult. When we were there, in my car, it was so close. I think maybe I knew him from California—maybe that was what I had wrong. There's a pseudonym, and a thing he's looking for. If I could figure it out for him—"

"Drop it," says Emily. "Guy could be Muhammed Ali with a rose in his teeth, and you still wouldn't get to have him. People from the life, Mellie, they want you to fail at this. How come? Because that way, they don't have to change a thing themselves. Whoever he is, your ex, some dealer, some fucking criminal-ass motherfucker, he's a junkie and that means he wants you to get high."

"I know, but what if—"

"Oh, my God, Mellie. This isn't complicated. There aren't extenuating circumstances. You need to stay away. No contact. No seeking him out or hanging at places he might happen to be or stalking him online. If he comes after you—and I know how this goes. He'll come after you—you call me first thing. Can you do that for me?"

"So," I say, letting out a sigh I've been holding for what feels like an hour. "You do believe me?"

"God help me, Mellie. I'm not saying I'm not a sucker, but yeah. Whatever. I've been there. For the time being, I'm sticking this out, but things have to change."

I know there's a program line about addicts, how special we all think our pain is, how different and unique the shape of our dependencies. I know Emily has to tell me to humble myself. But. Part of what I think Emily gets about me is that my experience is not actually standard and I don't mean because of Juni. I don't mean, either, some entitled crap about the house, the job, having made good money for a while. I've met people in meetings who have fewer advantages and make more of their lives than I could ever hope to. I know that. But still. Why I trust Emily, why it has to be her, and not some cokehead from Marblehead or some meth addict from Methuen, is that she has seen what I have seen on cloud. She keeps a wedding ring in a drawer that makes her cry, and it's from a husband she never had. I have a baby whose father never existed. The edges of our lives are haunted by things we can't reach. There are good lives for me—and probably for her—waiting one cloud over, and it's not just dignity we have to sacrifice to get clean, but also happiness, also not being alone forever, also being loved by someone who loves us back. Every addict struggles, but I think our path, Emily's and mine, is particular. How many people know what it is to walk away from the beautiful life ghosting your own?

Before I lie down, I allow myself a visit to my study. From yesterday, the link to Lew's video remains open, the woman in underpants frozen where I left her. When I tap a key, the screen shivers, and the counter in the corner registers traffic. *5062. 5063. 5067. The buildup. The come on. They want to see how it turns out.* Then the video unfreezes, and the woman begins to pace. *Don't talk to me like I'm some animal*, she says. The thing happens again, a shudder of sickness, and the next thing I know I'm lying in my bed. I don't have an explanation. I try to hold the image of her, of the woman, in my mind, but it keeps vanishing. Then I am listening to the wind, and to Juni's raspy breathing, and the acoustic strangeness of guests in the house, a slightly altered white noise form the presence of Emily and Leo.

In my dream, I am back in the car with the man from the SUV. I can see his face clearly. I remember everything about him, but only in a dream way. *I'm him*, he says. *I'm Apollo.* He is my man, but not my man, and I understand precisely what this means: it means I'm in danger. There is a thing I have hidden even from myself. *You're so close*, the man tells me. *It doesn't have to be this hard*, and then he is handing me a spoon, and I am putting it in my mouth, and the thing dissolving on my tongue becomes the thing I've forgotten. I am beneath the towering pines. In my hand is the paperback. It's right here. Slowly, I turn the page and suddenly I'm terrified.

The buzz of the message indicator on my phone wakes me the next morning. I am already sitting up, the dream fear still clenching my throat. There are more question-mark texts from the burner phone and below, the sound of movement, the smell of food cooking. For the moment, I ignore these things. Emily, last night: *This isn't complicated. You need to stay away.* Yes, yes. But what if the danger comes after me? What if it comes after Juni? If I understood it better, I tell myself, if I could prepare, perhaps I would not weaken in the face of it. Perhaps I could resist.

I rise and go to my desk, guiding my eyes away from the woman in underpants (just her torso; her head and feet cut out of the frame) until a fresh window replaces the video. The counter registers more traffic. *10,872. 10,872. 10,873.* What compels, about this woman in her underwear? Why does the window appear, as if someone has already embedded the program?

There is time to attend to this later. For now, I turn my attention to the tiny scrap of licked paper. *OD TO 2f.* The number is handwritten, in faded blue ink, the larger letters torn from a sheet of printed stationery. I examine the nervous scrawl of the characters, scratch marks of partial letters at the torn edges. I make out an image, it might be a wall, a game board. The search window yields ten results. *Od* is an archaic unit of measurement. *OD TO 2f* appears in an 1838 Australian newspaper archive, is an index number in an annual report, is nothing but nonsense. I try another. *Kefeselyay.* Some near-cognate calls up a Spanish-language page about cannabis, an old survey map, five sites in Russian. More nothing.

I try again last night's searches.

Apollo Blue: three hundred thousand hits.

Bright Big Future: two thousand.

Together: one hit. I click the link, and I'm again watching the headless woman video. *Apollo Blue*: a pseudonym in the film industry, used on a project for which you'd prefer not to be credited. *CA Plates, West Coast time.* There's some connection there, between the man and my video. And yet—there is a thing here which feels older. I have memories, deep brain stem responses to the smell of cheap tobacco mingled with spring, to the feeling I had dragging on that butt I'd found smoking in my gutter—Prince Rounded Flavor. Some tertiary tobacco company had marketed them to kids with a cartoon frog in the '80s. There were congressional hearings, bad press and the line was discontinued. I would have been sixteen, when they were first selling them as two-for-ones.

I make notes, am always making notes. What I transcribe is not happenstance, I have come to believe, but fragments that can occasionally coalesce. There is meaning here, I know, and the fear, which is not dream fear but real, urges me on. I page through my paperback, an old library book still with its lending card in the front pocket, until I find a photograph stuck face down. I peel up the image, the photo paper cracking. Young man—a blur around him. I try to look at him slantwise. Is he someone I recall? But the age of the photograph, the business of time and memory or my own broken brain resist me. The girl is clearer. She looks as though she has been swimming, and she gazes up at the older man with perfect trust. They are at a lake shore, surrounded by towering pines. The girl is not me, but I have been there, by the side of the road. I turn the photograph over, read the lettering on the back. *Kif-Vesely'e. Kefeselyay.*

We go back, I think, this man and I. We go back before California, whatever he thinks. But the news feels like a flicker from the interrogator's side of a one-way mirror. Something is over there, studying, assessing, but from my side of the glass, it remains a looming shadow, the nature of the threat only made more mysterious by the occasional strobe of light.

In my paperback: illegible text, leaves glued together, paper always spilling from between the pages. I run my finger over the photograph. *Kif-Vesely'e*, the girl wet and the boy blurred. I am turning the pages, beneath the towering pines. I am going to find something I have hidden even from myself. Now, my fingers trace a shape, hard and small, the size of a penny, but with right-angle edges. The pages are thicker here, the yellow glisten of old glue at the edges. I slip a fingernail between the two leaves and hear the almost-inaudible crackle of adhesive releasing.

"Mellie!" Emily calls. "Mellie! You awake?"

She is coming up the stairs. I startle, pocket a handful of scraps into the jeans I am still wearing, have slept in, and close the paperback. Emily, in the doorway, looks me over, then grunts.

"Stop it," she says. "Whatever you're doing. Put it away. We have to get going."

By the time I have pulled myself together and descended to the kitchen, Leo is gone, already picked up by some Dorchester lady on her way somewhere. Juni is eating Cheerios and cubes of cheese, neither of which I had in the house last night. Her breathing is still rough, but it isn't stopping her from shoveling the nutrients in.

Emily's on the phone with another reporter, getting a sub for the morning court session. It's like a super power, her ability to call a whole team of bossy brassy blonds into action at a moment's notice. I envy her her collection of big-haired Our Lady ladies with tight pants and sun-spotted cleavage. But, this morning, at least, I have Emily. We do.

"I think I need to go somewhere," I say. "Away for a while."

Emily looks unexpectedly relieved. "I've been thinking the same thing."

Florida, I'm about to tell her, can be cheap in the off season. I have a vision of myself and Juni, my pale skin, her slightly more olive tones, in the shade of a beach umbrella. Then, I notice my purse has been opened, its contents rifled through.

"I thought you believed me," I say.

She hands me a plate of cold eggs and a cup of coffee. "I wasn't checking for cloud. I needed your insurance info," she says. "And also this."

She slides my OneLife card across the table, the little green cactus graphic in the corner.

It's my VIP pass. I start to explain how this particular item ended up in my possession. It was pressed on me, you might say, back when the whole concern was new, which is why I wasn't going to chime in at Uno's yesterday. Obviously, I'm not the type to meditate with a rock, or pay a premium to have some yoga body tell me how to live my life, but I have some personal experience with them, the rock people, their cures. Emily isn't interested in the long version.

"It's going to be your ticket." She's been calling all morning, but there are no beds anywhere. Until she tried the flakes.

"Come again?"

"Pack your bag," says Emily. "You need to check in thirty minutes or they give the spot away. I've got Juni's stuff already set."

"This is what? Rehab?"

"Fact: you are not pulling this off," she says. "You're a handful, and I don't have the hands. Thirty-day detox would be my first choice, but you've got Juni. Your mom's in Belize, you've got no friends you trust, and I know, we talked about the father being out of the question."

OneLife runs this place, she tells me. Quincy Independence House for Women in Transition. It's a public-private partnership, so not as much weird shit. It's supposed to be pretty nice. You get your own efficiency. And it's one of the few places in Massachusetts that does addiction counseling for people with kids.

"Transition?" I say. "Is it a shelter?"

"Actually, it's focused on former inmates."

"I was going to sublet a timeshare," I say. "Gulf coast, maybe."

"They have cloud in Florida, Mellie. This place, it won't be a vacation; all the monitoring will make your head pop off. And given who runs it, there's bound to be some hippie stuff: guided visualization. Art consciousness, clay therapy, you know. Plus, the state mandates parenting classes, checkbook balancing, how to boil spaghetti. You might hate it, but, you'll stay sober, and Juni will stay safe."

Emily looks at Juni. The bruise has come in on her forehead, rich with blues and greens. At the back of her breath, I can hear the lingering catch.

"Be clear with me: this is a condition? For you sticking with me? Or, it's a suggestion? Because I feel like the beach would work, too."

Emily takes my phone, punches in a number, and puts it on speaker. I hear hold music from the local light station.

"My ex," Emily says. "He did so much cloud, a certain thing happened to him. I could see it when he was hitting us, me or Leo. It was like, we weren't quite alive to him. We weren't people. He was always an asshole, Mellie. He was always violent, but the hitting and pushing, it was real to him. With cloud, it was different. It was like he was doing a chore, when he hurt us, like he was kicking the shit out of a bag of trash."

I nod. The staticky soft rock plays through the phone.

"When I got here, last night, that was you, Mellie. Your own kid is upstairs. She's not breathing. What does she do? She comes for you, her mom. And you're not there. You're busy licking someone else's secondhand cloud off their dirty paper. I've had sponsees relapse, and I had one die. I can take it. But a kid, a little baby. I'm not having that on my conscience."

"Hello?" says a voice on the speaker phone.

Emily grasps my hand as I reach for it.

"If you're half-assed, tell me now," Emily whispers. "Put Juni out to foster till you get your shit together instead."

"Hello?" says the voice again.

"I'm not half-assed," I say. And I'm not. Now that I've made my decision, relief floods me.

I'm still spelling my name into the receiver when I finish packing, and Emily leads me around the house, flicking off lights, unplugging appliances. Even with insurance, it's going to be very expensive. I have enough savings in the bank to get me through a couple of weeks, but then I run out, unless I can somehow manage to do the underpants job.

"You worry about that when you get there," says Emily. "Even a couple of weeks, it's worth it."

I nod, take my keys off the counter, but my sponsor shakes her head, and I hand them over to her. I'm in no position to mother, no position to drive. Then I follow her out the door.

I don't want to go, obviously. I don't want to be in a room full of convicts having fake epiphanies. I don't want to eat communal meals and have chores and learn fucking life skills. I'm an adult; I own a house and drive a car, and I want to be able to have a stupid relapse if I feel like it. I'm going anyway.

We exit through the garage. There, on the car seat, are all the licked and discarded scraps of paper. I think of the man, the *OD TO* man from my dream. I think of the lemon-burn of a lick of cloud, of Kif-Vesely'e, the feeling of being observed through a one-way mirror. Emily is right: I need to stay away.

Emily presses the button on the garage door. For a moment, it sticks, as if offering me an out, a second option, but then, it is closing, and we are walking across the lawn to Emily's car. Before I can draw a next thought, they've transferred me to the next agent, and I begin my recitation of symptoms. Paranoia, I read from the card Emily's prepared. Delusion. Manic acting-out.

"You going on vacation?" shouts my neighbor.

"Aruba," says Emily.

"I hope you arranged someone to take in your garbage cans this time."

By the time I hang up with the agent, we're halfway to Quincy. There is an intake number, a preauthorization code, and I reach for my paperback and—it's not there. The feeling is like forgetting your head, or the briefcase with the bomb inside.

"We have to go back," I say.

Emily shakes her head. "You're due there in fifteen minutes."

"It's important," I say. Something the size of a penny, lodged between two pages.

"You know what your face looks like? A liar's face. I don't care what the lie is right now, what scheme you're still working, but I want you to think about what this would be like if you were on Medicaid, how it would go down if you were homeless or HIV positive, or a hooker."

"OK," I say. "OK."

"No going home. Not for tampons, or some stalker in your driveway, or some asshole boss whose approval you need. I don't care if you left the stove on and your house is going to burn."

"I said OK." Still. It does feel like the house is on fire, like I've left something there which will burn. I remind myself that I'm impossibly lucky. I have someone like Emily, and I have Juni. I've made it to the program; I have my thirty-one days. But, it's almost like I'm on the cloud, that kind of splintering. I can sit here with her, I can let her lose pay and spend a personal day, I can make it all the way to Quincy, but some sliver of me is thinking about the little object inside my paperback. I had hidden something even from myself. *It. You'll know where to find it.*

part two:

abroad

One

New York City
1993

This is the tail end of a certain New York City. This version is the city of sirens and crack vials and cherry bombs going off beneath alarmed cars. This is the New York City of squats in the Lower East Side, and people you know still living in Manhattan. I am aware, downtown, of several places where I can get a meal for under four dollars. More often, and at the moment, I am in my boyfriend's apartment uptown. I'm supposed to be here studying for finals, away from the distractions of the dorms. But he's paged me to say that he's on his way, that there's a thing we need to talk about.

Now, I have about thirty minutes to prepare.

It is twilight; in Morningside Park, a blue peculiar to this region of Manhattan descends. For a moment or an hour, the light of dusk and the light of the city are in equilibrium, and everything appears washed of detail. There are no angles, no edges. At my best, I am like this hour, blurred. I love the feeling during sex, when I am high on cloud, that I have deputized my body to tend to Mr. Boyfriend, that my mind is roaming elsewhere. These twilit moments, I am bodiless, adrift in the murky blue. I have no hunger for things I cannot have, no worry over the weight of my mistakes.

Which evidence of my crimes, I wonder now, has Mr. Boyfriend uncovered? I perch on the windowsill, make a small note in my paperback, and feed myself a dose of cloud. His apartment is huge and empty. He has the first-generation anxiety about the quality of his decorating taste, like is it gauche or tacky. In order not to get the colors wrong, he's relied on a palette of black and white.

Black sofa, zebra rug, white chair, gray ottoman. On the walls, a couple of WPA-era prints of poor people and some lithographs from nineteenth century artists. One of them is on cream paper with gold trim, and I catch Mr. Boyfriend staring at the image uncertainly from time to time. I know he isn't puzzling about the subject—a set of sketchy figures under the weight of what are either wings or a bundle of firewood—rather, he is grilling himself about the cream and the gold, whether these are errors.

I could help him. At my internship with a small production company run by two perpetually warring brothers, one of the ADs has begun to have me look over the sets. We run on a slim budget, and have to make do on a single take, so the directors commonly have their work checked and double checked. I catch things no one else does, the clock hands set to the wrong time or the reflective surface that will mirror back the camera operator. I am said to have a good eye, but it's more than this. It's a perceptual ability I link back to my dumpster-diving days; I know in advance if a take will make the cut. I can see the failure before it comes.

Incidentally? This whole apartment, Mr. Boyfriend's whole apartment, is off. Despite his caution, despite his monochromatic approach, he's got irredeemably shitty taste. If I were in charge of continuity for my mediocre lover's life, I would clear these seven rooms of everything but the zebra rug. It arrived in a shipping container from Russia, which is what his family does, ship things hidden in other things. The rug just appeared, Mr. Boyfriend says—he is always playing naïve about the actual nature of his family's business—along with crates of outlet strips. Perhaps he knows that it was once a real zebra, but I look at it and sense an extraordinary path, its heat-soaked birth on the veldt, the poacher's bullet, the traveling caravan, the vast container ship, and its arrival at this Manhattan apartment. I couldn't see that rug thrown away. We would make love on top of it, the one tragic object, if I were having a different kind of relationship.

Passion's not the point for me. That is to say, my boyfriend is worth a lot to me regardless of passion. I mean, financially. And now he needs to talk. Earlier this evening, when I returned his page with a phone call, I asked him, could he just stop off at Bello's for the penne? I was stalling him. I needed the interval to mount a defense.

Before I met Mr. Boyfriend, I was racking up debt in the financial aid office at a rate of a $124.67 per day. I'd cancelled my dining plan, and was feeding myself, buying books and subway tokens off the $150.00 a month I made at Yankee Muffin. I could have pulled it off, ramen dinners and library texts, except I was also simultaneously running a hefty tab downtown, where my Alphabet City dealer charges a buck twenty for a two-fer of cloud. I'd gone ten straight days eating only mixed-berry and white chocolate chip muffins which, because they are disgusting, go unsold at the end of the Yankee Muffin workday. February, and I still hadn't bought half the books for my classes. The night I met Mr. Boyfriend, I was living on muffins and cloud.

I took the train to midtown to meet my father's mother. Her doctors had sent her to Sloan-Kettering about a lump for which help was already too late. She took me out to dinner at one of those places that serve prime rib and seem fancy to rich people who never went to college. It was a darkened restaurant, red carpet and walnut banquettes. In a corner booth was my grandmother, this sick woman who didn't feel dressed up without a brooch, clasping and unclasping her purse. I was thirty-five minutes late, underdressed, unshowered. The purpose of the dinner, though it would not be mentioned directly, was the fact of my grades, which had slipped from *A*s to *B*s and then to low *C*s. I ordered a bourbon while she picked at the olive dish. When my eyes adjusted, I could see the growth on her neck. It was just below the jaw, and she'd styled her wispy hair to try to cover it.

"So, are you getting the checks?" she asked.

I wasn't. My mother forgot, cashed them, intending to give me the proceeds, and then needing unexpected car repairs or a new dress for a date with a man from the personals. Also, she considered maintaining her apartment a parenting expense, even though I'd spent the previous two summers with Nancy in Western Mass.

"Of course," I told my grandmother, white chocolate muffins churning in my stomach. "Yes."

"You should write me more often," said my grandmother, who would be dead two months later, the trust checks permanently diverted. I gulped the bourbon, my grandmother frowning. "Nobody in our family ever drank," she said. "Do they drink on your other side?"

After her nurse came to fetch her, I found the nearest bar. It was bland, with TVs and only six or so patrons, but Mr. Boyfriend was among them. I wanted to get drunk, and I didn't have any cash, and he was buying. Maybe it matters and maybe it doesn't that my glasses were broken, tucked in my pocket with the tape around the eyepiece, and so I looked prettier than usual. Also, I'd learned in the interim some basic things about how to dress for my body type and shape my eyebrows which knowledge improved the quality of boy I was able to attract by about 40 percent. Still, 140 percent of what I'd drawn before doesn't equal sex god. Mr. Boyfriend was short and had a bad haircut, but I don't think we were about how I looked or he looked. Probably, it was my familiar thing of sad guys who think I can improve their stock, might make them look more responsible at holiday dinners. You get that about Mr. Boyfriend, that the extended family see him as unequal to his inheritance, that they all think they could handle things better. That night last winter, I went home with him and my financial prospects improved. Is he in love? Do I owe him something in return? These kinds of questions don't rise to the level. I need the money more than I need to be good.

—*pop*—

The tab hits, swallows whatever worry I'd been harboring, cleans it out, and returns the better part of the evening to me. Mr. Boyfriend. Something to talk about. Penne from Bello's. I look around the apartment, hone in on a sense of glimmering significance in Mr. Boyfriend's study. He has a desk in there, book shelves, the usual shit, but mainly he uses the room as a place to toss the mail. It mostly hits the desk, but as the months wear on, some of it cascades onto the floor, the Publisher's Clearinghouse, the bill from the chiropractor's office, and all the revenue checks. He's the sole heir to the shipping business, but, he tells me, it's not the picnic it might seem. There's a network of immigrant cousins and associates who are always onto some riskier scheme, whose foolhardiness he endorses by his inattention to the family business. There's a chemical factory in Pripyat, in the actual Chernobyl exclusion zone. Lunacy like that. He is forever after himself to take things in hand. "Call a meeting, tour the warehouse." Meanwhile, it's me he should be worried about. I've learned the look and character of the payment envelopes; I know which checks are small enough that they won't be missed. I keep a glue stick in my pocketbook, have a technique with a moistened Q-tip and a nail file. There are check cashing places that don't care what my ID says.

Tonight, the study is transformed, the teetering stacks of correspondence now in neat piles, slit envelopes in the waste bin. Mr. Boyfriend has been investigating me. I call Yankee Muffin and ask to speak to my assistant manager. He's a familiar variety of pervert, is constantly trying to lean up against the counter girls when he's instructing us on hygienic practices. My whole life, I'll never meet a girl who hasn't put up with the same. Not in retail, or service or entertainment or media, not in New York, or Los Angeles where I spend my twenties, nor in Boston where I eventually wash up, will I ever meet a woman who hasn't been groped or humiliated or otherwise had to deal with it. Sometimes, at Yankee Muffin,

I'll puke, but that's as much to get the muffin out as it is because of the assistant manager's erections. Plus, I have cloud, so I can always just get past it.

"Hey," I say, phone perched on my shoulder so I can peel out of my uniform orange polo and khakis. Mr. Boyfriend is always on me to wear tighter clothes, but I tell him this isn't New Jersey. "Did you tell me someone called earlier?"

"*Jah,*" says the pervert manager. He is not German or anything. He just thinks this is funny. Just like it's funny to rub up against the female employees when he passes us behind the counter.

"Can you elaborate?"

"A guy was checking your references. Were you generally on time—I said no. Did you handle money or bank deposits? I said, yes. Did you ever steal—I said no. Did you dress appropriately at work? You looking for a new gig, Mellie? You leaving us?"

"*Jah,*" I say and hang up the phone.

An instant before the click, my pager begins to buzz. The number isn't one I recognize. It is evening. The ambulances approaching St. Luke's have begun their nightly wailing. I'll admit it's a bit of a chronic problem with me, underestimating people. I think: if they're not quite as smart as I am, they must be dumb, but that doesn't always follow. Mr. Boyfriend, for example, isn't stupid; he's just lazy and insecure. And I don't have a good instinct of what he'll do if crossed. I'm not convinced he's scary, but there's the shady import stuff, a tendency to punch walls that can be disconcerting. Probably, it's a good idea for me to come up with some sort of plan, but cloud makes such action feel urgent at the level of penne from Bello's, as the question of whether he'll buy me an appetizer. I write the seven-digit number from my beeper into the paperback and then dial it with 718, 917 and 212. Individuals associated with the Avenue D Bodega occasionally contact me. I'm thinking also it could be my uptown delivery guy with a new beeper number. My cloud connections put me in the practice of returning calls. But, for the moment, I can't make sense of who's paging me.

I scrape deodorant under my arms, spritz perfume, and reline my eyes. I can at least look decent for the confrontation. Cloud sometimes takes too much edge off. The beeper pings again, and I find a black dress on the floor of the bedroom, then flip the pager display over, like it might read as words—how you can type *help* with upside down digits. Something about the last four numbers sparks my circuitry. 7285. 7285. 7285.

Nancy, who's three and a half hours away, has been paging me from this spiritual retreat. She'd lost her housing in the aftermath of a campus building takeover.

The suspension wasn't permanent, but Nancy wasn't going to write some crap apology and promise never again to et cetera, because she still believed in the cause, obviously.

"Although, college activism is complete bullshit. Overeducated kids yelling at overeducated adults, and meanwhile, people out there are suffering."

On short notice, housing options had been limited. Anyway, this girl Andi we used to know showed up in a crisis, and both of them found work at this health farm in the Pioneer Valley.

Now, I try the unknown pager number with her Berkshire area codes. It rings.

Nancy had gotten political second semester of sophomore year. This anthro professor from *Unmaking the Western Mind* turned her on to Paolo Freire and Althusser and meanwhile, the protest crowd was throwing these outrageous all-night dance-a-thons. Eventually, the activist students had occupied a building—two whole weeks in there, this one dean's office—until admin had cut off the sewage and cops had come to lead them away. The stink, after they'd left, had been what was covered in the press. Gone to shit, said Nancy, literally. She wasn't done with politics after that, but she had to regroup.

The health farm was kind of a commune, kind of a self-help retreat. Rich people would come and pay, mostly to lose weight but also sometimes because they were having nervous breakdowns or had crashed their cars drunk. The kitchen staff had some hot guys, Nancy said, and two job openings. Andi turned up in Western MA, sick on drugs and running from a bad boyfriend and so the two of them, Nancy and Andi, ended up making granola and being healthy and sleeping in a hayloft. Mostly healthy, Nancy qualified.

"Tell me about you," she said, during our most recent phone call.

"Not much to tell," I said.

"Obviously the stuff they do here, the guided meditations and the vision sessions: whatever. Still, Mellie, in my readings, you keep coming up."

"Me?"

"It's probably groupthink. How you get sucked in. I know, but, whatever, stay in touch. Speaking of which, guess who's flying in from Russia this week?"

Anyway, this time, whoever's trying to reach me isn't Nancy. The number rings at a Greek restaurant. I replace the receiver and check myself in the mirror. Eyeliner blurry beneath my lids, and thicker on the left side to make up for my one smaller eye. I've gotten good at it, finally.

And just in time. Beyond the locked door of Mr. Boyfriend's apartment, the elevator door sighs open. I hear the laden tread of Mr. Boyfriend with his cardboard containers of supper. He jingles the key in the lock, decides he can't manage it one-handed, sets down the bags and then tries the key again. In the mirror, I look good. Obviously, he's in love with me. He obviously still loves me, even and despite what he's figured out about the missing checks. There's room for forgiveness, in those take-out containers. I rehearse my smile.

My beeper crawls across the coffee table. *7285*. Almost *suck*. Almost *salt*, s*aul*. And then, I see the whole thing. 487 7285. I-T-S-P-A-U-L. The second lock turns; Mr. Boyfriend's keys slide into the pocket of his 501s; he opens the door with a bottle of wine, my favorite dinner, and a sucker-punched face. He wants to look enraged. He is trying to make his mouth about not accepting apologies, trying to be all business, but he's missed me, and his lips love me before he can make them behave.

"I can't stay," I say, grabbing the beeper. "It's an emergency." I have told him I am a volunteer EMT; this is where I am to him when I'm downtown. I make up all kinds of shit about arteries and anaphylaxis.

"Tell them no," he says. "Mellie, this is important."

I peck him. I take my glasses off. Mr. Boyfriend likes me this way, but also it's easier to lie when I can't see the details of his face.

"Mellie," he says. "This isn't like every other time. This is a big deal. I need you to tell them no."

I give him a longer kiss, curve my hip into his with the suggestion of nasty things I can make available and I imagine I am drifting through the blue twilight.

"I promise I'll be back," I say sliding my lenses back over my eyes. "Someone's stomach just needs to be pumped."

"It'll be midnight," he says, sighing. "At least take your dinner."

I will eat the penne on the 1/9, the salad on the F. But I will not be back by midnight.

Two

New York City
1993

St. Mark's Place—panhandlers and gutter punks and up too late and cigarette butts and iron grates and tattoo shop and forty ounce and photo shoot. I weave between obstacles, trying entrances on the building without luck. The directions I have to meet Paul are vague. From a pay phone, I dial Paul's dad in Brookline, but Mr. Greene doesn't answer. I scroll through my pager, looking for Nancy's most recent call. "Hello?" Over the voice of the woman who picks up the line, I hear the clatter of dishes, the easy laughter of dinner crew. "Sorry. Can I have her call you back?"

A man turns onto the block, coal end of a joint burning between his lips, pauses, spits on his fingers and carefully extinguishes the ember. He draws my eyes, the way details do on a film set. The man is handsome, not tall but muscled like a dancer. He wears a bandana over his longish hair. He mounts the steps, fishes a lanyard from under his shirt and opens the door to the building.

The place is a theater, a three-story venue with dormitory space for resident troupes and just whoever lucks out and is invited to crash there. I pocket my pager.

"Hey," I call to the man in the bandana. "Hey, hold that."

The dancer-type turns around. I have banked for most of my life on looking wholesome, but lately—my darker eyeliner, my blackberry lipstick, the honor roll fat melting off me—I've lost that thing that made strangers want me to take their picture with their hundred-dollar cameras.

But the man in the bandana decides to chance it or is too high to judge, and holds the door open until I get in.

Paul had been in Russia on a college theater program trip, a sort-of theater program trip which was also somehow a professional production. He'd gotten onto IRC from a computer room at Lemonsov Moscow State University, and Nancy and I logged on from our college computer labs, and we could chat to each other with barely any delay. Moscow was shitty. The food was shitty. They'd been fed a meal that consisted entirely of turnips. He had been to Siberia and fallen off a train and no one would X-ray his broken arm.

[22:48:45] <PaulMoscow> I can't believe it!!!! It's really you!!!!! I'm puchy
[22:49:03] <PaulMoscow> Punchy
[22:49:23] <NancyHatesYou> USSR failed because not true form of socialism
[22:50:01] <Mellie123> Is it winter there? Is that a dumb question?

I'd given him the pager number during the chat, but I hadn't expected he'd actually get in touch. I chalked his desire to connect up to the exuberance of homesickness.

The visiting troupes of actors at the St. Mark's theater are housed in the attic dormitory. No elevator. I climb the one-hundred-year-old stone stairs. They shine in the center, are worn into a form of smile from so many heavy feet. I should exercise more. I should eat less cloud. Near the top story, the silence of the lower floor falls away. Someone is playing music; people are laughing. I recognize the singer as Tom Waits. He's singing about home, how you won't go home. I walk between racks of clothing with bright plumes and sequins and bustles. A dozen carnival masks with long, villainous noses and sharp leather teeth hang from a papier-mâché tree. The place smells of body odor and glue.

A naked woman runs by me, halts, and retraces her steps. She has a luxuriant growth of pubic hair, enormous bare breasts.

"Do you have any pizza?" She strokes my sleeve and offers a hazy smile. When I don't reply, she trips off into the forest of hanging clothes.

The next room is kitted out as a dressing room, mirrors and bulbs and grease paint. A blond boy is curled up on a tutu. I step over him into the next room, which is where Paul's group has been sleeping. There are two dozen metal cots arranged along the eaves. A man with brightly fresh tattoos is dancing to the Tom Waits tune. He's also naked, his half-erect penis jumping as he frog steps to the music.

A young woman, clothed, sits cross-legged on one of the cots writing in a journal. She gives me the nod, the orderlies-in-the-nuthouse nod. "You must be Mellie," she says.

"That's right."

"I'm the stage manager," she says, waving her hand around the room. "All these guys have been together for ten weeks. It's full-on mass hysteria."

"The wooden palace," says the naked man. "The spring festival."

"Night and day," says the stage manager. "And our most important set piece has been lost in some former flipping socialist republic. Everyone's pretty rational, considering."

"Georgistan," says the naked man. "Turkekraine."

I locate Paul among the rumpled bedclothes. He is asleep on a cot beneath a parade float dog with wild red eyes. Paul's broken arm is in a sling, resting on a dirty pillow. He's changed, sharpened in the lines of his face, but he's still as hairless as a girl, still as pretty despite the black exhaustion under his eyes.

"Hey," I say. "Hey."

He startles in sleep and cries out. I touch his shoulder, on the uninjured side. He blinks. He rubs his eyes. Then, finally, he recognizes me and the panic fades from his expression.

"You came."

"Of course. You doing OK?"

"I can't sleep here," he says. "That last half hour is the most rest I've had in like—"

"Jet lag," says the girl with the journal.

"Amphetamines," says the dancing man.

The boy with the tutu snores and the naked girl farts as she runs by.

"You could crash at my dorm," I tell Paul.

"God, seriously?" he says. "That sounds like. God. Yes. Let's go."

They are doing a play, have been touring a play across Siberia. They are the first Western theater troupe to visit that region, but this turns out to be something like being the first Western theater troupe to Mars: the journey as interminable; the audience when you get there just as lively. The tundra had not exactly nurtured a love of experimental arts in its people with the result that the troupe had played to unheated concert halls in former prison colonies, two rows of senile women smoking cheroot and nodding off. The actors have various theories as to what went wrong, kickbacks or an underdeveloped travel industry or an outright scam perpetrated on Davos, their director. At last, they are home for their New York run, but they all have weird diseases from travel, have all been secretly sleeping with each other's girlfriends, and the play, they suspect, is not very good.

The travel has maybe wrought other traumas, as well. There's an obsession with the missing set piece that seems misplaced and a too-deep silence around the train journey through Siberia which ended with Paul's falling from the train. Paul is wide-eyed and manic on the subway trip uptown, packing and repacking his Prince Rounded Flavors, flicking his Zippo. "Was it always lit like this on the subway? How long have they had that ambulance-chaser ad? Does it seem hot in here?"

Maybe I should not be so surprised that Paul has gotten in touch. By senior year, Paul and I had basically turned into normal friends. How it happened was Paul was living on his own, in a two-bedroom apartment with like four other guys. Mice were leaping from the trashcan. Once every three weeks, they assembly lined dishes in the bathtub. Eventually, the landlord gave notice. It didn't seem abnormal when Nancy suggested he crash with me. Meantime, my mom had found a boyfriend and so she was sleeping out of the house, and leaving me like a hundred guilt dollars a week for take-out. "They hit him, at home," I told her, to get her on board. It pleased her, when one of my Brookline friends' parents did something horrible. It meant even though we lived in an apartment with bugs, we were still as good as them.

For my part, I'd had two actual boyfriends in the intervening years, so it seemed reasonable to assume I was over whatever sixteen-year-old business there had been between me and Paul. Factor in, it was winter, and the bugs didn't appear until spring, and we all agreed it made sense.

For a while after that, Paul living in my house and leaving fingernail clippings in the bathroom and me eating take-out Greek salad, I thought I'd figured something out. I found a way of listening to him that was less about gobbling things up, and more about just learning which made the thing of us feel more regular. Regular, except I would sometimes go into these cloud comas and wear one of my mom's aprons and stir fry rice and clean the toilet and I would imagine I was in my own future and that Paul and I had ended up married with a brood of half-Jew, quarter Chinese, quarter Irish babies. So I guess I was still hung up after all.

The last night he stayed with me, he smoked weed on the back patio and I took a spoonful of cloud. I never wanted anyone to know I was a user. Even Nancy, she knew I had a spoon now and again, but not how much. But with Paul, I stopped privately licking spoons behind the shower curtain. I don't know. It seemed like a step, like a part of how we were making something outside of Nancy.

Anyway, that last night, it was near Christmas, and there was frost on the ground, but it wasn't really cold yet. A client of my mom's had dropped off a bottle of red wine which I knew she'd never miss and we poured it into juice glasses and sat out there where I used to keep my moon journal. I thought about saying something to him about used-to liking him, but I instead I just listened and let my lips turn purple and looked at the sky. Waxing. Gibbous. Nancy was right. It stayed more or less the same. You didn't need to watch it to be sure.

Paul was waiting on college acceptances. He wanted to go to conservatory, for acting, instead of small liberal arts, but his parents were too wrapped up in which one of them would pay, and how much, for him to even get this conversation on the agenda. Nancy meanwhile had a whole plan for embezzling the tuition; he could go to Europe like he wanted to; she could get her parents to pay her way by blackmailing them about what shits they were. Fuck college. School of life, motherfucker.

"It might have worked," said Paul, "except my mom is a lawyer."

That last night was the first time I heard him talk about her, the mom. I had seen her once, an unhealthily large Chinese woman with a stack of silver bracelets digging into her skin. She'd been the only Asian woman all four of her years at Wellesley and now she worked for the state. It was, Paul said, because she didn't make as much as a regular lawyer, as one from one of those downtown firms with all the windows, that she had trouble paying her bills. In her opinion, Paul said, networks of prejudice conspired against her, to keep her from what was righteously hers. Was that true? I asked him. Partially, he said. You always are who you are, and then the world starts getting in its licks because of who they think you are.

He sucked on his one-hitter, repacked it. There had been, he told me, a whole drama when he was fifteen; her mailbox became crammed with dire letters from credit agencies. She couldn't bear to open them. Her car was repo'd and the con-do foreclosed and a bunch of other shit. He thought: she'll turn it around now. But instead, she just had the mail forwarded to an old address, and the whole cycle started again. I thought about it. He was the only kid I knew, my entire time of growing up, who was also a renter. The places he and his mom lived were nicer than our apartment, but maybe there was some connection forged, being the only two people we knew who had actual money worries.

In the end, Paul's parents scraped enough together for a year of Colgate, and there Paul was, summer of his eighteenth year, still going back and forth between houses on the court-ordered schedule. I guess neither Nancy or I was surprised when he left upstate New York to travel with this director. I guess we both kind of thought that for Paul, it was probably better to be an experimental actor in Eastern Bloc countries than to continue to flunk out of private college.

"You've changed," Paul says as the N train carries us uptown. "You're less— you're more—"

"Tell me about the play," I say.

The lights in the train flicker off and on again. Paul rambles. It's a fairy tale, Nordic, ancient, about a fortunate man who has an only daughter. This girl is so beautiful, the clan becomes convinced she's divine. They begin to leave offerings for her rather than the troll people who live in the forest surrounding their settlement. You see the trolls from the first rise of the curtain, in the shadows, moving in and out of the wings, but you don't know what they are at first, whether set piece or character. Talking, Paul loses the thread, gets distracted.

"These ads for genital warts, it's some kind of entrapment. You can't help but look at them, but then because it's public looking at them implicates you, suggests that warts are relevant to your life, that you need their help with warts."

"The play," I remind him. His neck leans, his head almost touching my shoulder. The train speeds. Rickety rack rickety rack rickety rack.

It is lonely, Paul tells me, being a rich man's daughter, being treated like a goddess. Being worshipped is different from being loved, and being beautiful can hurt like wind hurts, like cold. When winter comes, the beautiful daughter fashions herself an ice brother. There's a song, and snow falls, an effect they manage with buckets of ivory flakes and then these soft silent brooms. Then, inevitably, the spring. For the first time in the production, the trolls enter into the light, and the makeup, the costuming, they transform out of the shadows. They are not what we expected, the trolls. The beautiful daughter begs them. She begs and begs for them to bring her ice brother to life so the sun cannot destroy him. The trolls agree, although we know like all magical bargains, this one will turn out poorly. Paul's eyes close for a moment, in the telling.

"Time to transfer." I shake him gently. I notice a smell, an odor of an old man, which is nonetheless his own, as if the smell of his future is already upon him.

We navigate 114th Street, Paul making wide arcs around the musicians and the homeless. He's nervous like a tourist, but he does not stop talking.

"I'm trying to think how many times I've actually been to the city. My father won't come. It's like it's still the seventies or Central Park jogger but I tell him it's cleaned up. Is it cleaned up?"

"Not really. Not yet. Who'd want it to be?"

With the old ladies, he takes a bench on the 1/9 platform. I am close enough to touch. The train comes, and it's running express and that's fine by me, fine, because he leans against my arm while he talks and it seems like he thinks it's natural that I should lead him, that I should tell him where to sit.

So much for friends, I tell myself.

The rich man's daughter, Paul continues, keeps him secret, her ice brother. He's not a brother, maybe. That's one thing the play leaves open, the possibility that he's a lover or another self. It's summer, and they meet at twilight and there's a song where they're happy and it's just them, an hour just for them. But then it switches to harvest music and everything is flushed in an orange glow, and the villagers appear carrying sheaves of wheat and buckets of red berries. The villagers dry fish over fires, and the rich daughter presides, taking their offerings, and the trolls, back in the shadows, gnash their teeth and complain of hunger. A hush falls, the industry of the villagers continuing in pantomime, and then it is twilight and the ice boy appears.

I have to prod Paul at Columbus Circle so we can get the local. My internship is around here, the main office where the production company rents out equipment to student filmmakers and industrial film productions to finance the art film and documentary side of the business. I listen to Paul as we head uptown and watch out the window for rats on the tracks. Even in Boston, where they were more rare, I've always made this a transit pastime. Rats remind me of science fiction, those novels about when everything has broken down. Rats are time travelers from Armageddon. Near Yankee Muffin on Forty-Second Street, there is a place we call rat rock. It's just what it sounds like and at the same time evil and mysterious. In the middle of this normal city block, there's a massive, jagged boulder. It's like some ancient glacial deposit that proved too expensive or time consuming to move, so even though that fifteen feet of real estate is worth about five mil, the developers left it and rats moved in. I suspect Yankee Muffin exacerbates the problem by filling the dumpster with leftover raspberry white chocolate chip muffins. At night, when you pass the rock, it is alive with their furry bodies; it is a rock of whiskers and bright black eyes and long hairless tails. It is not the only rat rock in New York City.

The train stops at 116th and we follow the crowd of students returning from Zen Palate and Super Bob Flanagan and the Angelika toward the night, toward the fluorescent glow of West Side Market. Paul is still talking as we wander the aisles collecting an unlikely basket of sundries, melba toast and Doritos and crème fraiche and grape juice.

The ice boy, Paul says, is more beautiful than his human sister and he enthralls the villagers, enraptures them. Their wheat rots; their berries ferment; their drying fish burns. The harvest is abandoned and the village is going to starve. The girl looks on at what she's wrought, as the brooms and buckets of soap flakes emerge and winter approaches. They'll have neither wood nor meat not wood not meat, sings the fortunate daughter. The villagers begin to freeze in attitudes of prostration around the boy, bowing and stilled with wonder. The trolls beckon the girl: *you can fix this.*

There's a deal, of course: cut off the ice-brother's nose and plant it, and enough food will grow for the winter. She has no choice. She takes a glistening, sharp blade and swipes at her own brother. He bends, cradling his wounded self and remains on the still and darkened stage, as the villagers stir and awaken. After the audience is sure the play has ended, even beginning hesitant applause, the boy at last reveals what is left of him. He is hideous, hideous, so hideous that even his sister cannot bear to look at him.

In the final scene, the ice boy takes refuge among the trolls and as the curtain falls sings a broken song about losing love when you lose your beauty.

"The knife's one part of the play which doesn't make sense," Paul tells me as we take our place in the checkout line, "because it is made of ice and it cuts ice. Something's not good in the logic. Right?"

"Oh," I say. "Absolutely. Definitely."

The checker smiles at Paul, even though he is four people down the line and I realize: I'm not the only one who can see the thing about Paul anymore. He is still on the thin side, but his twenties have begun to sculpt his face into something angular and arresting. His lips are full; his skin is a lovely color which people call olive or describe in terms of kinds of nuts—cashew skin, macadamia skin, skin which is edible. Even now with the yellow of travel and illness beneath the surface, with sleeplessness visible below his eyes, lady checkers and the boys in tight pants buying condoms behind us and the fashionable downtown women smile at him. He wasn't Boston beautiful, is not Midwest or bland, but this is New York, and beauty has a richer palette in this town. Paul doesn't respond to the attention, but if it's from obliviousness or disinterest or cool, I can't say.

"I wrote you from Siberia. Did you get the card?"

I shake my head.

"Yeah, I think maybe I didn't have your address with me."

Paul is the ice boy. The blond boy in the tutu had originally been cast in the role, and then whatever happened on the three-day train ride from Novosibirsk, whatever had broken Paul's arm and now the ice boy is Paul. He'd been in a train car alone with the director; he'd thrown himself off the moving platform; he'd been recast. This is what I gather. The tutu boy now plays a troll-villager-tree.

"It's still kind of probational. My look, you know, isn't what most people associate with an ice boy," Paul says, clearly mimicking someone. Paul's father is darkly Sephardic, his mother palely Chinese, and the lineage predicts nothing about his looks. It is not a cherubic beauty, not blond or rosy. I cannot look at him. I cannot help looking at him.

Before the checker totals our food, I throw in a stupid bouquet of Gerbera daisies. I have Mr. Boyfriend's money in my wallet, but I'm feeling extravagant anyway, regardless. For the record, I am actively on purpose trying to be normal, but I keep doing random fucked up shit like staring down pretty checkers or buying flowers. Paul isn't aware. He's gawking at the magazine, which shows a bikini-clad starlet, or maybe he's simply gone slack-jawed with his face pointed in that direction. The tight pants guy watches him, the checker and the pretty woman from downtown.

"Time to go," I tell Paul.

"I'm frayed, Mellie. I feel like little threads of me are coming loose."

"A string walks into a bar," I say, stopping him until the light on Broadway changes.

"What?"

"It's a dumb joke. *I'm a frayed knot.* You need to sleep."

"Yeah, but how? How am I fucking going to sleep?" His leg is a blur; his foot taps up and down, up and down. As soon as the signal changes, he takes off.

"We should try to call Nancy. When we get back to the dorm. Do you have a good number for her?"

"Is she still with Andi?"

I shrug. "Working in the kitchen at that retreat center, last I heard."

"You know it's not a real rehab," Paul says.

"Rehab? Nancy doesn't need rehab," I say.

"Andi, I meant," says Paul. "I don't know. That's what I heard."

"Nancy will take care of her," I tell him.

I flash my badge for the security guy at the dorm, and he makes Paul sign in.

My freshman year, this girl's Mercedes was stolen as her parents were unloading her suitcases onto the sidewalk. People get jumped. It's not fucking Princeton New Jersey up here. It's not Hanover New Hampshire. Pretty preppy kids get one-hundred-thousand-dollar degrees, but it's still an actual city. So, security at the dorms.

As I open the door to my darkened room, I hear the phone ringing, see the pulse of the message indicator. I think, Nancy and then, Mr. Boyfriend. Indeed, later, I'll listen to seven messages from my Russian admirer, but at this moment, it's someone else. It's my other stalker.

"Amelia," says the breathless voice. "Amelia, this Zarah. I'm still trying to reach you."

I've got a single this year, and the room smells faintly of plant matter, of something tropical and thick. I flick on the light, and hand the receiver over to Paul. He puts it on speaker. The source of the plant smell is a giant, overgrown ficus which I'd left by the half-open window some weeks earlier. It ought to have died, but it's been raining, and there's a drainpipe at just the correct angle, and enough light through the airshaft that instead it's been photosynthesizing like the tropics. It can't have been three whole weeks since I've been here, but then also I think three weeks seems right.

Through the speaker, Zarah prognosticates. "We're worried about the signs. The readings aren't clear, but I see a cliff. Arid, dry land. You are being drawn over the edge against your will." Zarah is a psychic. She'd called me first after my grandmother's funeral. I assumed that my mom had put her up to it. There'd be some scam, eventually, some need to pay more to find out the ultimate answer. But now it's been weeks, and still, she contacts me at intervals without explanation or request for payment. It's like some plot I'm entangled in where I have to see it through to the end, even if it's only an accident, even if it's all been meant for some other Mellie with some other fate.

Paul flops on my mattress. There is laundry everywhere, not all of it unembarrassing. Balled-up Kleenex spill from my trash basket. Last I'd been here, I now recall, had been to convalesce in the dorm during a bout of bronchitis. Mr. Boyfriend had offered to nurse me, but he had a frustratingly undemanding schedule, wanted to hold my hand and spoon-feed me ginger ale. After about twelve hours, he left me for his twenty minutes on the treadmill in the basement gym and I pinched a check and escaped. Next to my computer, there are still several plastic cups encrusted with orange DayQuil powder from my illness. The combination of fever and cloud and the fuzzy high of pseudoephedrine had been a pretty lovely place, and the fact that I was missing classes seemed to matter less there.

"Someone close to you is very worried," says Zarah. "The numbers are clear—you must maintain contact with this person, or there will be consequences that stretch ten or twenty years into the future. The second thing is your diet. My readings suggest you are eating too much red meat, too much color in your diet."

Paul has cracked open the Doritos and is dunking them into the crème fraiche and at the same time smoking his third Prince. I drink the grape juice from the bottle.

"There's an ancient story," says Zarah. "A man comes to the base of a mountain . . ."

"Listen," says Paul, cupping his hand over the mouth piece. "You know what's still legal in Russia? They sell it in these packs, from a cart on the fucking train. They call it Oblako. They're like, Tea? Cigarette? Chips? Oblako? The train was eighty hours. That's more than three days. I wouldn't have made it through, Mellie. I swear, something was trying to make me go crazy."

"Oblak?"

"It's their cloud. No one in Siberia gave a shit. How about you? Are you still into it, at all?" He sets his cigarette butt delicately across an empty mug and shrugs out of his jacket. He has changed, set building and carrying packs across Russia, and just the final adjustments of his early adulthood. He is muscled, is what I notice. He has gained a little of the right kind of weight. He picks up his cigarette again. "It's just so I can sleep. So, would you? Know anyone who could hook us up?"

Through the speaker, Zarah says: "Which means the decision point is approaching, the place between your best possible future and your worst—"

I click the receiver into place and lift it again. What Zarah wants is unclear, but I expect, if she's been sent by my mom, it'll continue until I call home. I'm not technically out of touch with my mother. I leave her messages when I know she has clients, and I even wrote a letter, but I let the holidays come and go; I haven't told her what I plan for this summer. In ten days, I'll be kicked out of the dorms. And, I know I should be trying harder. This weekend, for example, I'd promised myself I'd study for finals, but I hadn't reckoned on Paul's arrival.

"I have a number," I say. "People use it for parties, whatever. I still roll a little cloud."

"Parties," says Paul, looking at me. "Rolling cloud. Look what's become of you, Mellie."

I patch in the phone number, enter my code, and wait for the callback. What's become of me gazes back from the reflection in the half-open window; I remember falling asleep a few weeks ago on my way back uptown. I'd woken in the Bronx, staring at the morning-after party girl across the aisle until I realized she was me. I can clean up, even in a reflection. I can rub away the circles of eye make-up and smooth my hair and I still look like someone you'd give the internship to. But I can see it might not always be this way. That on my worst days, my own future might be upon me like Paul's seems to have come over him. The phone rings; it's my delivery guy; I place my order and he gives me his time frame.

"What should we do while we're waiting?" I ask Paul.

We are sitting next to one another on my bed, listening for the phone. I look coy, in the mirror. The light is not unflattering. I look thin.

"I don't know," says Paul, stretching out his long legs. "What do you want to do?"

And then I decide. I'm tired of holding myself in, or it's the way time has reshaped him, or it's cloud, the courage cloud has loaned me. I reach across his body with my far arm and place my hand on the bed beside his, my cheek grazing his, our lips close. I shift my weight and I lift my body. He turns toward me, and it's enough.

"No talking," I say.

We are good at hips, he and I. We are good at mouth. We speak tongue, and skin, and slipping from clothes. I like the way I have to pull at his jeans, how he bucks his still-slim and hairless legs out of them, like a creature momentarily roped, and then free. My things tear, are left in shreds. I swim closer. I've got to be closer, I've got to get inside. I remind myself to open my eyes so I can see his face and the lines of his muscles, so I can grip in my teeth the evidence that this is real. He is better without clothes, the unexpected curves and dips of him. What I think, I keep thinking as we move with each other, is that I want to clench him inside of me, to hold him forever. How has it taken so long for this thing I have wanted, and what, G-d what, will I ever do now?

We fall apart by stages. We are slick, and cold with our own sweat. It is probably four in the morning. We lie under my small blankets, trying to keep all our parts covered. I know I cannot say anything about the sex. From Judah on, men have taught me this. I know what is urgent now is that I say nothing of the sparks which are showering my skin, of the light breaking from me. I hold my lips together. It crosses my mind to think of Nancy. Of what she'd tell me. I had stayed with her, the previous summer. In the evenings, people would just kind of wash up at her place, the protest crowd, townies, the meditation flakes. They collected around her. Andi, the high school friend with the bad boyfriend who was trying to get clean. People thought Nancy had something to offer. I asked her, one night, what they thought she could give.

She shrugged. "For most people, you know, girls our age, being a slut is about getting approval. But I never slept around to like acquire love. Which is good, obviously, because sex is a crap way to get anything but crabs. No, I went home with people so I could hear their answering machine messages, see what was in their medicine cabinets, check out their nightstands. I think it's the same now. Only I don't do it by sucking cock. People want you to know them, you know? It's stronger if you're not putting out."

I wasn't sure that covered it, entirely. She was a last resort kind of person. Andi had had two sweaters, and the address of the health farm, when she'd arrived at Nancy's dorm. They hadn't even been friends, really. That was what people came to her for—not to be known, but to be saved.

Paul lies shirtless against the one pillow, smoking his Prince, quiet, but nowhere near sleep.

"Where you at?" I ask.

He rolls over to face me, cigarette hand perched on a hip. "Davos, our director, invented this game, or like not a game, but a kind of theater exercise on the train through Siberia. I mean it was so fucking boring. It was a transcontinental flight times four. Beautiful blue, the purest blue, but the same, the same damn thing mile after mile. Like how you always imagine heaven will be, how sick of angels you'll become. He called the game *brutal honesty*. What you'd do, whoever's turn it was, they'd sit in the middle, on this mini suitcase. Everyone else is crammed into the compartment, perched on laps, squeezed on the bunks, asses hanging out of the windows, whatever. But whoever's turn it was would sit there in the middle and get the honesty treatment." The idea was to say something you truly thought about the other person, that they didn't know. Those were the rules. It couldn't be a compliment, and it had to be true.

"In theater, you know, people who don't do it think it might be cathartic or therapeutic. No. It's the opposite of that. Most people bury pain, or deal with it, you know. Move on. For an actor, he has to court it, to nurture it, to make it like a pet, so it will come when he calls."

"Or she," I say.

"Or she. Or happiness, or anger, or loneliness. It's material; you've got to hold onto it. Hold it in. I'm making it all sound more coherent and like explicit than it was. The game on the train evolved kind of organically and of course, people hesitated at first. No one wants to be the first person to say something mean. So it starts out, easy shit, like, 'In the third scene, you're flat on the song,' or like 'you can be kind of arrogant.' Not fun, but nothing that's going to fuck up your life. And then it becomes, 'Your ass is fat' and then it's like, 'everyone knows you are fucking Paul behind Ned's back.'"

"Who were you fucking behind Ned's back?"

"That's a for instance," says Paul. "It got so the competition was all in how deeply you could devastate, how mortal the stab could be. The turn ended when someone cried or called uncle. Then, whoever had set the victim off would buy everyone a round of Oblako, and we'd all eat it and then *pop*, we'd be friends again; once again everyone could take a joke."

"Your director plays this game or whatever, exercise?"

"Have you met him yet?"

I start to shake my head, and then I pause. "Short guy? Wears a bandana?"

"He's not that short."

"But he was with you in the train car, the whole time?"

"By my turn, 48 hours into the journey, it was just the two of us. Everyone had dropped out to sleep or have diarrhea from the cart food or screw in the baggage compartment."

"And Davos is the—the one being honest or whatever? Is he doing the talking?"

Paul smiles a smile which is perfectly, naturally blank, as if he is recalling some bland amusement. It is a church picnic smile, a smile for a win at croquet. Still, I see the shimmer of some other expression, something not nice before it evaporates. "Fucked if I know."

"The whole thing sounds awful."

"Maybe. I got thrown off the train after," he rubs his sling. "Fracture. I'll get over it. But also, the point is, the exercise worked, did something besides idle damage. The horror was momentary. We stayed friends. And the play, after performing for all those shit audiences, it was getting stale. Davos said whatever thing was wrong with me, I jumped off the moving train, and then the play was—if not fixed, then better, fresher again. The one Moscow performance was amazing. From the game, what stayed with you wasn't the cruelties, but this knowledge about people, about the other people in the cast, that we are all full of judgment, that we are all making each other crazy all the time, and that none of us is special or weird."

"Explain the part about jumping off the train?"

Paul shakes his head. "Thrown off. Jumped. I have an image left of the ground coming toward me. I guess we were pretty close to a station or the train got stopped or something because I was put back on. But it was painful and we were still a full day's travel from medical care. I do remember that, lying on the bunk chewing someone's Tylenol and willing time and the pain to pass." Paul pulls on one of my sweaters. It's a feminine cut, blue, and it looks terrific on him. Jesus Christ. Paul in a blue sweater. I'm done for.

Paul leans back against my two propped pillows. "Davos says you have to rip things open and see the guts before you know what you're dealing with. Theater is about being willing to expose yourself at the level of organs. We showed him ourselves on the train, and he made the play new and I guess I believe a little pain and forgetting is worth it."

I want to tell Paul that that might be so for the stage manager, for the tutu boy Ned whose role Paul took, or for Nadine with the boobs and the bush, but that Paul needs protecting. I see the line of dirt along his shoulder blade where the sling has rubbed away. He can't reach it, with his fractured arm, to keep it clean. He needs someone looking after him.

"Plus," says Paul, "I got the lead."

The dorm phone rings. My dealer has arrived. Paul reaches for a towel and I tell the doorman to sign our cloud in. I buy a one-off, trying to look like less of a junkie, and act surprised at the price. The dealer, who knows me, gives me a benevolent smile. He's never seen me buy with someone else in the room, and you know, your dealer is sometimes happy for you, sometimes spares you an idly generous thought.

I hand Paul his spoon, and he slowly unsticks the paper. I watch. Maybe Paul and me couldn't have happened before. Maybe I needed to toughen or he needed to soften or we both needed cloud to sand the past into something more finished. Maybe, I think, Paul and me hasn't happened at all and this is just some night, like the nights he spent with Nancy, that we'll all ignore tomorrow.

"Stop it," Paul says, laying his spoon on his tongue. "Don't get emotional, Mellie."

Oblako is the perfect name for cloud, better than *cloud* in fact because of the way it recalls *obliterate* and *blacken* and *blotto*. I watch Paul's eyes, his beautiful eyes which are ringed with the black-green color of an old bruise. What is inside them? For the moment, he still retains the memory of what has occurred between us. I intuit a little regret, a little involuntary lingering heat. He shows some kindness and some disdain and a mess of things that don't have names in English. Friendship is there. There is surprise.

"Admit something," I say. I see the cloud washing through him, rising in the blood. I see it in a fading or flattening of his gaze.

"What?"

"I'm pretty good in bed, right?"

Paul shakes his head. It's a friend move, the restraining hand on the shoulder of your homey, wingman gesture when your bro is about to make a fool of himself. "Mellie," he says, confidentially. "You're not still at the library researching for your opening arguments. Things evolve out here in the world. We don't always get the thesis statement in the introduction."

I want to ask him, because I'm still a baby inside, because I still have my babyfat belly, because I'm an itty bitty crybaby, I want to ask what Nancy's thesis statement was. But Nancy is high school, Nancy is in another state, group encountering and extreme fasting; I make myself understand that I've already gotten what Paul's going to offer before the cloud begins to take it all back, take back the good and the bad, before his eyes become oblako.

At last, Paul sleeps. It is four thirty-five and soon the morning will begin and the muezzin at the mosque will let forth the adhan.

Allahu akbar.

I open an email from Nancy. The time stamp is an hour earlier.

It's mostly a rant. The retreat lady has decided rather than pay them, she is going to make them apprentices and put them through a training. Andi feels like it's worth it, a fair trade, that she's already made progress, spiritually. Maybe, says Nancy. But if you're not getting a paycheck, it's still exploitation, still basically indentured servitude. Plus, she suspects that Andi's idea of fixing herself involves continuing to get high, that someone in whose interest it is has been smuggling dope onto the health farm.

I was working in the greenhouse yesterday. There's all this lead in the soil, from the paint on the barn, so we have to get the perennials out of the ground, and try to grow them in potting soil. Most of them die, and even the ones that live, the lead is still in them. I can smell it, like a handful of old pennies buried in the new dirt. Andi's like that, is what I'm trying to say, with leaving her boyfriend.

There's a thing here that reminds me of how we were during the building take- over. You're like actually sitting in just some low-level bureaucrat's office, like looking at his stupid honorary certificates and his awards of excellence, whatever, and eating the last mints from his mint tin and you convince yourself that by so doing you are saving actual lives. Actually, it ends up clogged toilets and everyone who was going to die dies anyway.

Mellie, we're at this juncture—you, me, Andi, Paul. Remember that, like, sense I had? Of a danger? Picture you think you're in a big room, but really it's a little tiny one and it's getting smaller. I know it's not clear. It's the best I can do.

I write back: *Would you want me to tell you if you started getting weird? Here, too, for the record.*

I look at the five remaining spoons, resting on my desk. Paul snores lightly. After the train through Siberia, after the fracture, he'd picked up a respiratory infection in the Russian clinic which had worsened on the Aeroflot plane home. I tuck the stash of spoons in Paul's messenger bag and then I begin to meticulously clean the room. Here and there, under the shelf paper lining my bureau, taped to the top panel of my desk drawer & etc., I find spoons. Cloud doesn't age well. After about three weeks, it hardens and cracks, and lots of people say that the chemical changes which occur as it ages render the substance toxic, or at least that it loses its potency. Old cloud certainly doesn't taste good, but it still takes the edge off. You insure yourself against famine, when you use.

And what is cloud for, in my life? I am not on any train; no one is telling me things I can't bear to hear. It's just for something inside me, that comes when I don't recognize my own reflection anymore. It comes when I climb into bed with someone whose money I need but whose kiss does not stir me. It's for bad grades and the room I can't clean and my sick grandmother and forgetting to call my mother. Once you know what cloud can do, it's easy to keep passing your little sufferings along to it, the small failures and the enormous shames. Cloud helps, helps everything but for the moment, an ocean stirring in me, I think that cloud might not be as good a fix as the man snoring on my dorm room mattress.

I trim the ficus, and train its errant tendrils. I arrange my textbooks into neat stacks, and even think a little bit about my finals. I've written myself a study schedule, like I have every semester. It's more desperate this time, the chances that my study will save me from the classes I've cut and the books I haven't read more doubtful. According to my schedule, I should be getting up in an hour to finish up my take-home for Professor Mackin. Why wait? I collect four trash bags, two duffels full of laundry and nine spoonfuls of desiccated cloud. I think hard before I drop the last of them down the garbage chute, but I do it. Awake, exhausted, I perch beside Paul on my dorm mattress and make notes in my textbook. Next to him, I wait for dawn, refusing to let the night fade.

Three

Quincy, MA
2010

Tonight, at the Quincy Independence House for Women and Families in Transition, we are celebrating the return of Marisa's son, Rafael. We have coffee and Hawaiian Punch and a supermarket cake that says "Welcome Home." It's home enough, here. The son, an eleven-year-old who already wears size ten sneakers, has just cracked his first smile.

"That's right," says one of the Independence women. "He's a little man now."

I'm late to the celebration—Marisa's legal aide lawyer has been fighting the courts for two months to get Rafael released into his mom's custody. I'm late, but I catch some of the joy. Marisa's younger daughter is an overweight kindergartener, who through the absurdities of the social service system, had never been taken away. The younger child has been ridiculously sweet with Juni, teaching her simple clapping games which Juni can approximate in a clumsy way. I am, for this reason, a pretty big fan of Marisa, her raunchy tattoos, and her Irish-decibel style of parenting.

"Oh, no he ain't," says Marisa, smothering her enormous middle schooler in a hug. "He's my tiny baby."

The OneLife staff monitors us from the edge of the common room, listening for a dirty lyric to come over the boom box speakers, for one of us to let slip a curse. They watch for touching: any form of physical contact, a fist bump, a chuck on the shoulder, we get written up. Three write-ups, we are kicked out. Even as a child, I never had to contend with this level of regulation, and there have been days, since I've been here, when I thought: it wouldn't be so bad to order myself a

Starbucks again, to buy some decongestant without a signed permission slip. In the next second, though, I'll find myself sniffing the lemon-scented Dawn dish liquid, just to get an echo of a fix, and I'll know I'm not ready for freedom.

Juni wriggles in my arms, "gong food Mama bawd flower," and I let her squirm onto the floor, where she scoots over the tile to the toy basket in the corner.

"Come on," Marisa says to me. "Have some friggin' cake."

I smile, sip my black coffee. The being watched, the rules, it's a different story for the other residents, most of whom are on supervised release from MCI Framingham, are just excited to be able to wear an underwire bra and use a flat iron again.

"Where'd you say you're from?" Marisa had asked, watching me clean the toilet earlier. "Wellesley, some shit?"

"We have a house in Roslindale."

"Bet you moved there recent. Not like when Roslindale was Roslindale. But where'd you grow up, right?"

"Brookline," I admit. You don't get points with these women for basement apartments or infestations. There was the White School, and the checks from my grandmother. I had advantages.

"Brookline, huh?" She nods, like she knew it all along. Marisa's the nicest of them. Some of the other residents lean on the *R*s when they talk to me to parody my White School accent, my stubborn habit of scrawling down anything I want to remember. Here, it's the counselors who take notes, who make decisions about whether you get to have a visitor pass or can move into a room with a window.

Still, the worst of Independence women, the dumbest and the meanest, still they knock me flat on the daily. The street hungers for these women's return, sends them news of fatal overdoses and cousins locked up and little sisters pregnant, and all of it leads back to getting high; each day, these women lower to their knees their two hundred and fifty pounds (or ninety-five pounds or a hundred and eighty) and beg for strength and are granted it because they all love their kids more than anyone on the planet. It's a love that's been tested, that's been brutally tested, and that's what I'm trying to make rub off on me. I am lucky to celebrate among them.

The supervisor is looking at me now, giving me merits or demerits. It's all couched in self-help language about growth and truth, but it gets down to a Pavlovian game of behavior and reward. There are a million tiny privileges here, window privileges and refrigerator privileges and hair drier privileges and porch privileges and telecom privileges and guest privileges. If I lose the drier time, I feel like a fuck-up, like I'm a shitty person who doesn't even deserve to have dry hair.

I care if I get to pick the cereal or open my window seven inches. I am suckered in by Juni, who is babbling more, making more word-like sounds, who is always in someone's lap, or getting passed a piece of candy from a leopard-print purse. When she toddles off the rug and toward an open door, there is someone to yank her back. Emily was right: I need the help, still.

So now I watch the staff watch me and I do the stupid things for which I will get treats. I paste a smile on my face, and step into the tight circle around the refreshments, and have some friggin' cake. It's good, too, moist with preservatives, sharp with salt and sweet with frosting that is pure anhydrous dextrose and Crisco. I scoop Juni up from the scuffed tile and even dance a little bit to the music. None of these gestures feel organic to me, but I'm trying to do this properly, not to take shortcuts. Fake it till you make it, Emily would say, and I do. I fake my laughter and my small talk and my dance step until Juni saves me by being a kid. She starts to fuss, and then I can make my excuses, and allow myself to slip off to the one-room efficiency that Juni and I are living out of, the tiny space that has been for the last three weeks, our home.

It's lonely, this life. My terrible secret is how lonely I am, even in the midst of so many people. Half the nights, I am so miserable, I wake myself up with the heartache. It is these hours, three in the morning, in a sterile room with only the sound of my sleeping toddler's raspy breath, that I am most vulnerable to relapse. My longing isn't general. In these moments, in the middle of the night, I can almost recall the person I desire. He is like the hard shape of something glued between two ancient pages. I slip my fingernail between them and then the desire slips into terror, the lemon lick of cloud. I want him back, and I am afraid to have him back. I cannot be trusted.

Night after night, this is where I arrive. The door to the facility is alarmed; the street outside dark and far from transit. But if these barriers were not in place, Wednesday, Sunday, any night would be reason enough. As it is, I clutch myself into a ball and I rock and I rock and I rock until morning comes and the baby begins to cough herself awake.

My particular therapist is a woman in her twenties who looks as though she's gained and lost dramatic amounts of weight in her life, the folds of loose skin beneath her chin aging her. She wears a small, inexpensive diamond on her right hand. She does not have well cared-for teeth. In this morning's session, I present her with the therapeutic drawings from my OneLife workbook and she flips through them attentively. I have complained to her about how twitchy I feel without my memory book, but she thinks it's for the best. She hasn't counseled many cloud users, and she's been reading up. We have, she tells me, disjointed memories. But scribbling things down doesn't provide healing. There are even data that suggest record-keeping can actually stall recovery, etch deeper the broken pathways of the brain. She wants me to rely on internal processes more to retain things.

"How's it going with that?" she asks.

"I feel like my brain is going to fall out of my head."

"It won't," she says.

"We'll see."

"Memory, encoding, storage, retrieval," says my therapist, "these functions are enormously complex, but we're now fairly confident that in cloud users, the connection between social processing that happens in the amygdala and the retention of imagery that occurs in the temporal lobe is blocked. In a healthy brain, a familiar image—say, a face—triggers an associated set of social responses. In the cloud user, a stimulus can spark the emotions and senses, but the recognition function fails. On the one hand, a stranger may appear meaningful and beloved; on the other, an intimate can be completely recognizable, but the feelings that belong with that recognition simply do not trigger. Either one—recognition *or* meaning—can be cued, but something interferes with the link."

"There's no good data on cloud," I tell her. "There haven't been any longitudinal studies."

"You keep saying that," she tells me. "The science on cloud is terrific these days. The results are very solid."

"Since when?"

"Since the NIH, the Hopkins study, the one just last summer out of Brigham and Women's. Do you want to read the papers?"

I shake my head. I still can't concentrate for more than twenty minutes on anything deeper than *Goosebumps*.

"There's the face blindness, selective, which you've experienced, yes?"

I nod.

"The language muddle, obviously, word substitution, which lay people call cloud sickness. What else have you felt?"

"There's this constant sense that I am just at the cusp, that I am on the verge of some revelation which never comes."

"These are all consequences of faulty encoding. You take cloud, initially, to wash away a bad experience, correct? What we now think is that this erasure is actually singular, an area of the brain which operates like a stutter or a skip into which new experiences get tracked and retracked. The experience you may have, of having connected to different lives, is an after image of this trough of forgetting. I don't need you to accept this, just now. But memory is really always rememory. It's always ground gone over, and over. So each time you pencil in some severed thing, you may in fact be deepening this area of detachment. Can you imagine that your record-keeping might in fact be inscribing your memory troubles?"

"I can understand what you're saying, but the truth is, it doesn't really seem to describe what happens."

"This may sound counter-intuitive, but some of these severed memories may have to be released. We need to start to track around this function, which is going to mean letting some of the things, those things you typically return to, go, so we can build in new pathways."

"So, I'm remembering too much? That's supposed to be the problem?"

The therapist considers, then tips her head to the side, her flesh folds wagging at me. "Think of it more as—you've carved these memories too deeply in. They're easy to slip into. New things want to connect to them. Perhaps you've already guessed what I'm getting at, though. The reverse of misplaced meaning. That's what I think we need to consider. Some long-term users have reported a dulled sense of attachment. Trouble bonding with a supposed intimate. Historically, can this describe you? Are there people you ought to love that you can't feel anything for? Have you ever surprised yourself with your capacity to hurt someone else?"

I am listening. I have tried, since the night Juni fell down the stairs, not to think too much about the meaning of what happened, that she couldn't breathe, that she came for me, and that instead of helping, I watched her tumble. Everyone has bad nights. But it haunts me, what Emily said about her ex. What if I've been that woman all along? What if Juni has survived two years of that night, and it's only just now I can see it? And not just Juni. Even if I cannot call up the deeds, I know I have done things a normal woman with a normal mind would be repelled by. It is true, there's a slowness to my heart. My love does feel a beat behind.

"Mellie," she says. "What's going on? Tell me what is happening in your head at this moment? I'm getting the feeling something is there."

"Oblako," I say.

"I'm sorry," says the therapist. "I'm not familiar with that term."

I shrug. It is a word which has surfaced from some point in the past, but which I cannot now place. I would write it down, but instead I roll it on my tongue, searching for the link. "Stupid slang. Junkie code word."

"I know that you are skeptical of the OneLife teachings, but the program has been successful with people like you. Not cloud addicts, necessarily, but people with memory gaps. We call it a curriculum, and its outcome, in successful cases, has been to *identify the faultline* and to *navigate new pathways* and eventually, hopefully, over time to *build in new tracks* in place of the broken one. We use a series of targeted activities, and self-study, which you've already begun with the workbooks. The method has been very successful with soldiers, with disaster survivors."

"Cloud sickness isn't PTSD."

"There are parallels though, with dissociative episodes, with blackouts, with the sudden onset of attacks."

I'm being difficult, but I've read enough about trauma to follow what she's saying: her process helps you locate the blank left by years of cloud use, and then you do these deliberate, forced activities which are supposed to kind of compensate for the half your life you missed in a fog. Early in film, I did some editing. This is back when you worked with splicers and glue. Sometimes, if a take went bad, you could cut out a part of it and put another in. That's what she wants me to try.

"Isn't it, though, going to make me into a fake person?"

"If it works, it might make you into a functional person. A functional mother. I know that's important to you."

The drawing on the page open between us shows a staircase, a little tumbling blur falling.

"It's obvious," she says, "if you think of it in terms of addiction. The drug puts itself first, last, and in the middle. It is always the cause, and the effect, everything else slides into it. You go another way, and eventually, other things will have room to grow."

The therapist turns the page. In today's exercise, I've drawn my secret identity. I know what the point is—to locate the underdeveloped parts of yourself. I know it because yesterday I made a spiritual pie chart and the day before that I was supposed to write a letter to myself at five. *Dear Young Me: You will spend the next thirty years screwing everything up. Love, Old Me.* I have begun to run out of fascinating insights, but then the secret identity concept made me think of cartoons, and cartoons reminded me of a jest I'd once made to Emily about Adequate Woman, a single mom who has to change a diaper before she can save the passengers on a speeding train, so this was the figure I drew.

The therapist does not like it.

"I can do it over," I said. "I was also thinking of snakes, of that Cretan goddess with snakes."

"N-noo. No. This is—well—" she turns it around on her desk so I can see it more clearly. "This is what you made. There are no right answers, but take another look. What do you notice here?"

It's me. Big glasses, full lips, baggy under-eyes and decent bone structure. I'm wearing a cape with a sort of logo on it.

"What do most people draw?"

The therapist laughs, the folds of her skin quivering. "Someone better looking."

"I'm not much of an artist."

"That's fine. Fine. But, it's a hero, yes? This is a cape, and that's an *A W*? Not the root beer?"

"It's Adequate Woman. Her superpower is to pull everything off, but just barely. Just adequately."

"Adequacy is a super power? That's a new one."

"Some days," I say, "it feels like it."

"But do you know," says my therapist, "how many times you have referred to cloud as a 'power,' a 'skill' or a 'talent'?"

"Oh," I say, "Now wait. I didn't say *cloud* was a talent, I said it *enhanced*—" I pause. "Crap."

"It is very common," she says. "It is utterly unexceptional for an addict to consider herself to be somehow gifted, or for that relationship to the substance to be qualitatively different from others' relationships with the substance."

I fix my jaw. I know where this is going now. Because of a stupid drawing. "So, you're not going to approve my day pass?"

"You earn privileges here. How would it look to the other residents, some of whom have been here three times as long as you, if we gave you an early pass because you need a faster internet connection?"

"It's just one file," I say. "Your system won't let me access it."

"I am aware," says the therapist. "You have made me aware."

I have, of course, been thinking about the object between the pages of my paperback since I arrived here, but I'd been able to talk myself down. I could wait. My house felt like I'd left it burning, but that wasn't real. Then, something happened a few nights ago that made it feel as if the fire were actual. It was late, and I had wandered down to the communal kitchen, past the computer terminal, for a snack. We surrender our phones on check-in and we're not allowed personal electronics, but we're allotted time to job hunt, whatever, during the day. I had promised Emily not to go after the *OD TO* man, and I had stuck to it, mostly. Mostly, I had been using my computer time to gawk at my dwindling bank balance. A check to Independence House had nearly bounced. The next one wouldn't clear. I'd also portaled over to the Seychelles server, and linked to the headless woman video. In the back of my mind, I thought of Apollo Blue, of the missing middle, but I told myself that wasn't why I was idly surfing the widening web of conversation about the headless woman. I reread Lew's instructions. *You have your part and I have mine,* he'd written. The site's visit count was over a hundred thousand now, some portion of those people presumably clicking through the dialogue box, the malicious program burrowing in. Under our old model, this was already a finished job. Yet there was more to it. *Complete as discussed according to timeline.* He was waiting on me for something; Emily had said, it stopped right at the good part. *Rerun season is over,* the *OD TO* man had said. *The middle is missing and the middle is the alarm.*

Lew, I should say, did not believe in telephones. When I'd worked for him, it would always be an assistant who called, Lew barking in the background. The days of his having assistants, however, was over. I might have tried his wife, or the landline at his bungalow, but those numbers were in the pages of my paperback. And, anyway, I felt a growing caution about this thing, which I had hidden even from myself, which was perhaps the same thing as the *OD TO* man was seeking, and perhaps not. I felt a need to understand what it was which was driving me.

The thing in my paperback. In my mind, I traced its edges, reconsidered its shape and size.

Sitting there, in the late-night hush of the Independence Common area, I cheated on my promise to Emily in a small way and ran the search again—*Bright Big Future Apollo Blue.* People had been talking. The results now yielded eight more terms, and I derived that the filmmaker-actor in the background of the clip was using that pseudonym: Apollo Blue, and that the project itself was called *Bright Big Future.* Of the rest of the results, two were from message boards in the sicko corners of the internet, but others were from an exchange on a Leeds University discussion group called *Avant GBarde.* Buzz was building, I understood, a sense of something more coming. *They want to see how it turns out.*

Something else I had tried, once or twice, was to test myself. Ten seconds. Stop. Fifteen. Stop. A little clip at a time. It hadn't escaped me that my reaction to the video bore something in common with what my therapist had been saying about cloud research. There was nothing in the clip I recognized, and yet I reacted as if I knew it. Cloud slippage, I would have said, if I'd been talking in Uno's, the reflection of some branching left behind. At home, I'd fallen into a trough of forgetting, come back with the sense I had almost seen something, that in that place I knew more. So, say I tried it the new way. Then, it followed that I could assign myself a bit of a curriculum, lay in new tracks around the blank place. I could build up a tolerance. Two nights ago, cars occasionally passing outside, the Independence women sleeping above, I thought I might try for thirty seconds.

From the point of view of the industry, the adult film industry, the video was inexplicable. The woman put on makeup and made inane small talk with the cameraman. Apollo Blue was, I gathered, the husband as well as the cinematographer. You couldn't see the subject's head or feet, but her body was young under the lights and makeup and her smoke-spoiled voice incongruous. You could see how it might be addictive, Emily had said.

This was what I was mulling as I sat at the terminal that night. I don't know. Juni was upstairs, and I shouldn't have left her alone. What if she'd woken up? A handful of cereal rested in the well of my lap as I linked to the video. While I waited for the little spiraling counter to launch, I linked through the new search results. A couple years out of the business, and you can't be surprised if all the hubs and aggregator sites have changed, but the meta tags on the feeder sites for my video included descriptions like *experimental video* and *museum studies*, instead of the more familiar *young girls live nude hott cam*. Message boards theorized about another video upload. It would be snuff film in which the girl in the underwear was knifed on camera. It was part of a viral plot to take over the US banking system, launched by the Azerbaijanis. It was a marketing ploy by a defunct porn company.

On one techie site, there was a brief discussion of the program that implanted if you responded to the dialogue box. *Russian origin? Sleeper virus? Harmless, unless activated.*

Seconds ticked by, as I shoveled the last of the supermarket-brand oatios into my mouth. The video began to play. I hastily lowered the volume to a murmur and I half-listened to the trite dialogue begin. I watched the ticker measure traffic. 106,432. 106,665. A hundred thousand views. I couldn't see it, but my reaction was no good measure. High, perhaps, I would have understood.

Don't talk to me like I'm some animal. As the video reached the thirty-second mark, I switched windows and watched intently. The filmmaker spoke. *Show me your—you have such a pretty little—* At his voice, my old queasiness rose in my throat, but I swallowed against it. He reached for the waistband of the actress's panties, and then—

A dialogue box opened. *Click yes to continue?*

The finger at the pantyline, the static stutter in the clip, the benign little question in the plain black box. It wasn't just that the program was already embedded. I recognized the handiwork, knew it like I knew my own mind. *Rerun season.* This was my work, I who had done it and so, of course, even though I knew better, I clicked. A counter appeared—a countdown: sixteen days, three hours, twenty-nine minutes. Beneath were the words *Bright Big Future Part II: Found Footage.* The whole world. They were waiting on something, and they weren't going to wait forever.

Everything shivered, the room, the screen. I stood, oatios spilling from my lap. Before I could write it down, be sure, whatever file it was began to worm into our server, and the system booted me. Moments later, I heard the sound of the night staff making his rounds, and I hastened back to Juni, her openmouthed snore. You can believe I've tried again, but the site is inaccessible now, whatever malicious thing I'd downloaded having been tagged in the interim. But now I understand the timeline, and something of what I am meant to do.

There are pieces of the puzzle I still can't solve, the fancy traffic from the high-end sites, what Lew could have meant by *his part* and *my part*, but since that night, I have been going back over the conversation with the SUV man. *Why the delay,* he'd asked. *Something's missing,* he'd said. Something dormant would be woken up. I think he'd said these things, but without my paperback, I cannot be sure. If the middle is what's missing, then where is the end? And what of Kif-Vesely'e? What about way back?

Even if the thing in my paperback (the size of a penny, but with hard edges) is not what he is looking for, even if it's unrelated to Lew, whether they are the same or not, it feels like a house on fire, and I cannot tell whether to race in and save it, or watch it burn.

Now, my therapist leans back and closes the workbook. "What is it you people say? You have to live in the likely world? That's not enough. There's still magic in that idea, mumbo-jumbo. There's one world. Right here. This is the actual world, and you already live in it. Slog along in the muck the rest of us are slogging through. You know I lost 150 pounds? Wanted to do it for years, but I kept looking for the 'periodic fasting diet' or the 'three simple tricks' or the laxative herbal supplement or the metabolism boosting pill. These are like your memory trough—I kept throwing everything into to this one place. And it all disappeared. Then, I did the OneLife program, no promises, just a little bit of progress, every day. It was there that I saw: losing the weight was going to be hard, and depressing, and I was going to miss bingeing on mountains of cake. I gave up on magic, and then I started to drop pounds."

I get ready to argue; the OneLife I recall is all about magic and promises, but I draw in my breath instead. I'm trying. I really am trying. And I get that it has the stink of cloud, the man in my driveway and the missing video clip, my old boss. "I understand," I say. "I'll wait. I'll try again."

"You're doing great, Mellie. The worst thing we could do is send you out into the world before you're ready. It could put your entire recovery at risk. When you qualify for a pass, you can go back to your house, or to the library or to whatever hip café in JP and sip kombucha lattes and watch performance art. But for now, we take it at the pace we take it."

She has turned the page again, found a doodle I've made on the endnotes. There is what appears to be a castle of some kind, a room in one of the towers spouting flames. *OD TO 2f* it says in the margins, *TO DO DO OT TO OD.*

"What's this picture?" she asks.

I shrug. "It came to me. I don't know."

She frowns. "According to the literature, initial memory repair can feel to the user like a cloud high, coincidence, kismet. This because the experience of a richly linked memory is so unfamiliar to you. You need to guard against mystifying it. The research tells us that this is how the brain incorporates new pathways. Like the way leaves can sometimes fall in a beautiful pattern. You don't then say the tree intended the design. Eventually, I think, leave off the writing, do the work, and you'll find you begin to respond more organically to things, but in the short term, the process can be confusing. It's important to prepare for this."

"But what do I do with actual coincidence? When things in the world really do connect?"

"Twenty years of scraps in a book, Mellie. The entire internet. It's easy to find links after the fact." She taps the page—*OD TO 2f.* "It's not even a word, Mellie. This feels like brain detritus to me."

She gives me a pity smile, and tries to pat my hand. "Listen: you've started week four. That calls for a structured outing. When your sponsor comes this afternoon, the three of us can talk about a proposal; I have an idea that fits a two-hour time-frame. If it goes well, the open pass will follow next week. And did you hear what I said before, about doing great?"

"Yeah," I say. I try to let it sink in. "Yeah."

It is mid-April. Days will go up to sixty, but the mud freezes into tread marks overnight. Emily and I stand on the smoking porch, she in a puffer vest and me in a shapeless wool sweater. On a patch of still-brown grass, the older Independence House children have shed their coats in a giant pile. Juni has been deposited with the non walking babies on a blanket where they flop about like caught fish, but my child will not stay in her spot. Every time the caregiver steps off to break up a fight or wipe a preschooler nose, Juni will toddle after, suction her baby self to the woman's support stockings and hang on. After the nose wipe or whatever, the caregiver detaches Juni and deposits her back in the baby blanket. Juni rises again, stumbles again. I watch her little bow lips purse and release bubbles of air. I like that there are no other toddlers. I don't think I could stand to compare.

"Mama pow Dudley hour flow Mama pawn bower Body low Mama fawn flood shower."

"Did you hear that?" I said to Emily. "She said 'mama.'"

"She like nineteen months now?"

Just this morning, Mrs. Support Stockings told me she was referring Juni for medical and speech. She said it with a studied face, one meant not to convey judgment. "Most of them, they outgrow it," she says. "But Quincy kids, we're extra careful. These babies have had hard little lives."

Sometimes, my counselor had said, there can be a dulled sense of attachment. I have to do the math to answer Emily's question. "Twenty."

"She's getting what she needs here, I think," says Emily.

It takes me a few beats to make my voice cooperate. "Yes. Yes, I think this is a place where she can grow."

"Both of you," says Emily. "I see how hard you're working. It's in you, Mellie. Give it time to take root."

The facility here is new, and it has to be noted that OneLife has poured money into what can't be a profitable operation. Each suite has its own balcony, two separate bedrooms and a common area/kitchenette. The furnishings are mid-price hotel, lots of ivory and beige. I think it pissed Emily off, when I showed her the in-room washer-dryer. They live pretty minimally at her place in Dorchester; Emily's still working out her credit six years after getting sober, and her CPA tuition is something she has to pay outright. I can see how Quincy House might feel luxe. Between the OneLife card, whatever it conveys, and Emily's pleading, I've jumped a ten-month waiting list. The other women who are here have fought like hell for their spot.

Not surprisingly, Nancy is the one who pushed the card on me and it's through her that I know the rough outlines of what they do at the high-end centers. There are these headsets, with rocks fixed into them which are supposed to focus you on an inversion point, a place of branching possibility. A bit, they pass off the flake factor like it's just a more specific practice of mindfulness—the stones are soothing, are more or less placebo. What the representatives say on Oprah, on their websites, it's all about cross-references in reputable journals, about outcomes-assessment and best practices. But once you get more deeply into it, the preferred client services, the higher levels of work, the promises OneLife makes become more exaggerated. Money in your pocket! Lovers at your doorstep! All your dreams fulfilled!

There are no rocks at Independence House. A OneLife person comes in weekly and leads us in guided meditations—emptiness is an opening, that sort of nonsense. Most of us sleep. I think about what I know about the yoga centers, the rich people going on these retreats, eating macrobiotic diets. Maybe it's because of this public partnership that this place pushes science instead of séance. Maybe someone thought women who've done time aren't going to be susceptible to scams. Maybe it's shittier than that, an assumption about poor people and what they need. It's around the edges, though, the mystical aspect, in the workbooks and the curriculum. I've seen a headset on my counselor's desk.

But either way, the curriculum or the rocks, they're more the same than you'd suspect. The fact is, there are only a few things anyone can offer that a junkie wants: the possibility of transformation, a certain means to get there. And whether it's a stone or a workbook, they all pretend you that eventually, you'll be whole again.

Now, on the porch, Emily shakes her head. "Is it a load of bullshit? Of course it's a load of bullshit. If cloud sickness were a memory problem, it wouldn't bring insight. We know, you and I, what we've seen in the cloud. But that doesn't mean this therapy doesn't work. Let's call it a difference at the level of interpretation. There's a just inherent value in sucking it up. I know, for example, you don't pray. You know how I started praying? Sank down on my actual knees and said the actual words. I didn't believe any of it. My heart was full of ash, but I did it, and I got saved."

"I'm a Jew, Emily. We don't do saving and we sure as fuck don't do knees."

"Junkies need structure, Mellie. You need structure." She flips through the notebook and can't help a snicker here and there. But I wouldn't love her, I wouldn't trust her if she took every little thing in earnest. I tell her something along these lines, without the love part.

"Precisely," says Emily. "You don't have to take it in earnest. You just have to do it. Life, one thing after another."

"What if I don't like life?"

"You won't," says Emily, "not always, but if drugs worked to fix that, we'd both be high right now."

In the curriculum, as my therapist has explained, you use the workbook to *identify the faultline* and during guided meditation you *navigate new pathways* and then you go on these contrived little outings to *build in new tracks*. For the activities, they encourage you to do something which is relevant to, but not a repetition of your old life. So, if you were homeless, you volunteer in a soup kitchen. If you shot up, you distribute clean needles. But I've been trying to explain that there aren't like volunteer gigs in my industry; I can't make a pinch pot about it.

"Well," says Emily, "OK, but how about, your shrink's idea is it might make sense for you to *be in* a production? You know, instead of making the thing?"

"No," I say. "Let me think about it. No. No way. No."

Emily smokes her cigarette and watches me flounder.

"I can't act. I don't act. I mean, what evidence do you need besides I've been around cameras for fifteen years and I never once stepped in front of one?"

"Really?" she says. "I thought you did a turn like that."

"Must be your other sponsee," I say.

"Anyway, no camera. No acting. That program guy—Isaiah? Some weird name like that—is making an audio documentary? Is that a thing, like an audiobook? Anyway, you know him from Monday meeting."

"The bald guy? He has some kind of a rep, right?"

Emily shrugs. "Nothing super creepy. There was an injury, I guess, or maybe like a mental thing, result being he does not date. Anyway, he's been looking for people who used in the early days, in the eighties. He wants to illustrate cloud before the big Clinton bubble; before they came out with all those prescription anti-depressants. I mentioned you—or maybe he asked about you."

"Why don't you volunteer?"

"Me? Are you kidding? With my ex's hearing next week, and his family making noise about custody? I can't put my voice on the internet saying how much I loved getting high. Plus, my court job, and maybe fingers crossed, having an accounting gig someday. It's only this year my arrest got officially expunged."

She exhales over the railing.

"I can't take the risk," Emily says.

"But it's fine for me?"

"Have you Googled yourself recently?"

I shake my head, but I know what kinds of projects I'm credited on. Plus, it's not like anyone's going to sue for custody of Juni.

"It doesn't really matter if we think it's stupid. It is stupid. So's a thirty-day medallion. So's the serenity prayer. Your shrink thinks being interviewed by some guy will map your brain right? Give the interview."

"Emily," I say. "One thing we've always understood about each other is that down here, in this world, practical stuff intervenes. You can be in recovery, but you still need to take out the garbage and show up at the appointment. I need to get home. I'm on a deadline. A kind of a deadline."

"This thing with your boss? You figured it out?"

"Almost. If I do this thing, this interview, will you smooth it with my therapist?"

"I don't make bargains, Mellie. But, it would incline me more, which yes, would incline your counselor."

There is one other matter on which I have not been entirely straight with Emily or my therapist. It's a small thing. But when I'd arrived here, that first day, and gone upstairs to change, a handful of scraps had fallen out of the pocket where I'd shoved them when Emily interrupted me at my desk. I've been keeping them folded in my wallet. *OD TO 2f,* the blurry photograph with the message—*Kif-Vesely'e* on the back. I haven't been entirely straight with myself. Those nighttime spells, when I am aching, I trace the letters, repeat them like an incantation. What to make of the old photograph, of a place I know I've been, with the words from the driveway man written on the back? How to square that with California? And what if it is keeping them, these little objects, the rememory and rememory, which is burning the broken tracks in my mind? If I let them go, would I launch on some long and virtuous path toward a better future? The video clip, the object in my paperback, there are habits of mind which lead only backwards. And urgently, urgently, I need to go in a different direction now.

Juni is wrapped around the caregiver again, and this time, the woman caves to her tenderer self and hoists Juni onto her hip. You want your child only ever to be looked after by those who love her, and it is the thing which breaks my heart most in the world that I am all she has. I don't believe a kid needs a dad, per se, but it's only by the narrowest margin that someone like me could ever become enough for a child with her needs.

The caregiver said it was the irregular breathing that alerted her, that there is a hitch in my baby's breath she has seen before. And the thing with the nonsense.

"It's not nonsense," I said. Again.

"It can be hard for parents to distinguish between vocalizations and actual language," she said. "How long has it been going on? Has she ever had an episode where she couldn't get a breath? There's a correlation between the symptoms, the speech problems, the breathing irregularities and full-blown CBS. That's what the experts need to determine."

Now, Emily taps the cigarette on the railing and her ash falls and breaks on a holly bush still bright with winter berries. It feels like spring is coming late this year. There are the pale yellow stalks of daffodils, the green shoots of tulips, but the snap of winter lingers in the air.

In Cloud Baby Syndrome, not enough oxygen reaches the brain. Early intervention, to some extent, can correct for the damage. To some extent. I will air into her lungs. And, as if in answer, she speaks. Her words to me are so lovely, carry so much in them, I cannot accept that they are signs of deficiency. It feels like an incantation, like she's calling something down for me. I know I cannot risk it.

"Good tow Mama pod low Mama flower."

OD TO: I must repeat it out loud sometimes. I know that occasionally I'll roll it around in my mouth like a dwindling piece of butterscotch. Which must be how she picked it up, my Juni. *OD TO.*

"Shod fruit mama would tong Mama fraud glow."

Emily stubs the cigarette, and tucks the butt in her pocket. "This audio thing. You don't need to commit. Take the meeting. The guy, Isaiah, Immanuel, he makes it nice. He's booked a conference room near the Monday meeting. The one with the towers? What's it called? Like the tennis tournament? Wimbledon? Lawn something? Green Lawn?"

"Longwood," I say. "Longwood Towers." There's a flash of heat, a melting sensation, a starburst of light behind an enormous building.

"Right," says Emily. "Fun. I'll sign off, and then your counselor will make the appointment. What's that you're writing?"

OD TO, I write, *Would tong. Fraud glow.* LongwoOD TOwers. *OD TO.*

Four

New York City
1993

Paul has slept in my dorm room for six straight nights, though it seems wrong to measure time now in the same units as before his arrival. Nights with him pass like time borrowed from another physics. An hour lasts an afternoon, an evening six minutes. We lie in the park, watching darkness thicken; we eat ice cream at breakfast time. We sit in my dorm room and it fills with smoke and the smoke dissipates and it is late afternoon and Paul is still downtown at rehearsal. We are not even in the same universe as before. I have a secret I am keeping from him. Christ. I can barely hold it inside my mouth.

When I call Nancy at the retreat center, a man picks up.

I can't place how long it's been since we've actually talked but there's a conversation I've been having with her. It's in my head, but I can't help feeling like she is listening, even despite the distractions. I am distracted, too.

"I'm calling for Nancy?" I say. "Or Andi?"

The man grunts and then sets down the receiver, presumably to find my friend. In the background, I make out a high, uneven sound which might be a kitten's cry or a woman's wail.

There have been developments, I gather from Nancy's collection of emails and voice messages. It was a kitchen guy who identified Andi's source. He'd witnessed some exchange in the goat barn, apparently, and so now it was pretty clear who had been getting Andi loaded. Nancy got in the leader lady's face. This was not how you taper someone down, she'd said. This was fucking all-you-can-eat and no amount of lentil fasting was going to make up for that. Now, the problem was Andi, that Andi was still defending the woman, still seemingly getting high. Nancy has an idea to fix things, and it's definitely a bad one, but she'll probably go through with it anyway.

"Nancy?" I say when someone picks up.

The voice on the phone is Nancy's, I'm almost sure, but she is whispering. "Listen," she says. "Someone needs to get her out of here and I don't think there's anyone else who can convince her."

Then the sound of the kitten becomes the sound of the wailing, and the line goes dead.

Paul appears at odd hours, swallows the world, then evaporates again. It is easy to lose track of things like Saturday, like exams and the closing of the dorms. At Yankee Muffin, I am somewhere between probation and fired. I have been here forever, always listening to the dial tone, always waiting for Paul while he rehearses downtown. Each episode is without sequence or precedent.

I decide: I can't wait another second. I hang up and catch the downtown train. In the standard way of reckoning, six days has been long enough for me to establish myself as a presence at the St. Mark's Theater. I've made myself into something of a mascot. Today, I bring a tray of Yankee Muffins, one of which I hand off to the girl at the ticket office as she waves me through to the fifty-seat black box. Nadine, the actress with the tits and the bush, is onstage, making her way through an impossible snowstorm to go and plead with the trolls in their forest homeland to save her people. The other members of the company, Paul included, stay half wreathed in shadow, moving in and out of the ambient light. In production, they'll have the soap flakes which will catch the stage lights and produce what Paul assures me is a magical effect, but for now, they don't want to waste material, so they rehearse with empty buckets. The actors hold them limply, seem to have forgotten they are meant to be sprinkling pixie snow. In the ecosystem of New York, Paul's play is small potatoes, is the upstairs cabaret at a downtown theater, but it's also not amateur, has attracted some unlikely halo of interest. At the previous night's preview, some people of significance had shown. One woman in particular, according to Davos, is relevant, is a young and talented critic for *The Voice*. Now the cast are all trying to float on mustered faith. She'll write a review. It will be positive. The audience will come. I can't help watching the buckets, which make this look like a play about janitors instead of magical beautiful children.

"We are not creatures who can winter over," says Nadine to Paul the ice boy, to the empty chairs. "We cannot hibernate or still ourselves. The hunger will persist even after everything else of us is gone."

Plays like this, the story of them, isn't really what the audience watches. A lot of the plot, you have to feel, exists only in the mind of the writer; maybe, in the mind of the actors and director, too. The events, the cause-and-effect, they aren't the point, Paul tells me. So, what is? Paul shakes his head like I've just demanded evidence of G-d. In Europe, Davos was known for his explorations of Observational Dramatics, of Direct Theater, his assertion that raw and fragmentary aesthetic of reality-based art could be deployed around fantastical plots. He'd done a Snow White with methadone patients and mounted a Midsummer at a defunct nuclear reactor. He wanted things to be jagged and surreal, dreamy and harsh.

I work with artists at my internship and one thing I have discovered about them is that they never provide complete explanations. A filmmaker can pitch you a three-hour film in thirty seconds, but ask him what it means and he'll become incoherent, or list the ideas of others. Fear, obviously, that someone will expose how little they understand themselves, that the questioning will unmask some sentimental platitude at the heart of their avant-garde work. You break them down, these experimental pieces, and there will be something like: things are more complicated than they appear on the surface! Or: it's important to be kind! Or: you can hurt people, even when you have good intentions! This is what I hear when Paul mimics Davos. Beauty is a burden. Beauty is necessary; beauty is fickle. Something like that.

And who cares about beauty, about the difference between the blond boy's universal attractions and Paul's cigarette-smoking loveliness? I do. I look at Paul, and I wish he were uglier and I know I wouldn't have my secret if he were.

"Stop," says the director. "Stop. Stop. Stop. First of all, you walk like a bunch of bankers. Move your hips into it, give me a little ass. Feel it. Don't carry yourself as if you were in line to pay a parking ticket."

Nadine heaves herself across the stage, waggling her behind.

Davos is young, charismatic in that dick way that college boys seem susceptible to. He's handsome, standardly, strong jaw bone, though not tall. Apparently it is taboo to observe this. Davos is handsome, but short. He smokes constantly, constantly wears a bandana. If, on the journey across Siberia, the troupe had gone collectively crazy, it is Davos who ushered the lunacy in. Paul said it was a game, or an experiment, but I watch the director order the cast about, and I wonder how calculated it all was, if he was trying to extract a performance, or simply amusing himself on a long, slow journey at the expense of these young and vulnerable people.

"What's happening to you, to all of you?" he says. "What happened to the energy you had in Moscow? Come, come."

The actors emerge from the shadows. Their eyes are ringed with makeup or sleep. They carry their buckets and, I see now, are in dress-up mode. They have scavenged various bits of costume, a headdress, a boa, a suede vest. Paul, in lederhosen and black glasses, his sling set aside for the scene, occasionally winces from pain.

Davos steps into the light. "You fuck around constantly. You are unserious. We try it again. Nadine, tiptoes. The entire time. Boys, you switch buckets. Back and forth. Good. Back and forth. Everyone?"

The boys in their dress-ups flex and release.

"Do not think about what your face is doing," says the director. "It is cold. You are freezing and have no food, but you are in ecstasy. An ecstasy of starvation. But control! Do not pretend! Be!"

Nadine tiptoes. The boys starve and swing. They hang between preview and opening night. Paul says they sometimes nail it at the last minute, find the magic the exact moment the first audience files in. Paul says, they still haven't found the missing set piece; it is a black stone archway that marks the transition point between the troll kingdom and the village and without it the play goes incoherent. They are superstitious. None of them believes they can fix the play, recapture the Siberian magic, unless they find the stone gate. Paul watches the pretty boy whom he replaced stump around woodenly. Nadine flirts with the blond, with Paul, with the director. Everybody's faking it.

Paul says, "We're interested in real, not in real*ism*. We don't want to make a copy. The theatrical experience is itself a real experience."

"No," Davos tells them. "Erase. Erase whole scene."

When they break for dinner, I prepare to slip off. I have a paper to turn in; my internship is filming uptown and the AD's just paged me. Besides, the experience of watching the play isn't mostly pleasant. The experience of being near Paul, the same. It is not easy. It is like an ecstasy of starvation.

The brothers who run the studio where I intern make documentaries, but before they shoot in a house or a subway station, they like to enact small, fussy changes. Tear at a billboard poster, get one of the PAs to write graffiti. Move the clock from the mantelpiece. I can always tell what they've altered. This is my gift, and the higher I am, the sharper I become. Though, even though I haven't eaten cloud in almost a week, when I look at Paul's play, everything seems like it's been staged after the fact, like it's been grafted on.

"What do you think?" asks Paul, as I kiss him goodbye.

"Extraordinary," I tell him. In my head, to pass my own lie detector test, I separate out the syllables. Extra. Ordinary.

I make my face do regular as I turn onto St. Mark's Place. I think about what tattoo I would get, a pair of lips stitched closed, an organ bound in black twine, a full-body image of Paul on my skin. *Hello, New York.* I pass the towering queens with their lady ankles and their football shoulders, the septum punks decked in needle punctures. *New York, I have a secret. My secret is a word that I can't say. New York, I'm done with myself. So what if he hates me? So what? Even if I repel him, disgust him, I would still slide over in my bed at night, just out of hope. I will still come sniffing around his feet, begging like a starved coyote. No matter what, no matter what, no matter what.* I keep the conversation going in the rhythm of the train's motion, all the way uptown. Obviously, New York has heard this all before. To New York, I'm just another boring version of the same story. New York, it's true, isn't sorry for me, but still, New York understands.

It is early evening; I cross campus and duck into Schemerhorn. Beyond the propped classroom doors, students scrawl in blue books with sharpened pencils. I've got mostly papers this spring, and I'm writing them badly and late. In high school, I never knew how to get a C, but in college I've learned how little it takes. Turn something in, anything, and these Ivy professors will pass you. Lately, however, even that small effort has become difficult. Witness, the manuscript in my hand, speckled with Wite-Out, the footnotes written in blue pen during Paul's rehearsal. I try to slip it under the lit office door, but it sticks, and when I apply a little pressure the door swings open and there's Professor Mackin. She looks up from her grading and frowns.

"What do you have there?"

"It's my paper."

"What paper?"

"The one on Soviet-era immigration."

She is a very attractive bottle redhead in her early forties. She wears leather miniskirts to class to show off her terrific legs and has a husband not handsome enough for her. She is meant to be a genius, academically famous, attributes we repeat but do not understand. Plus, she writes about sexy things, bondage and communism, leather and authority. Two months ago, on the strength of a previous class performance, and a paper I'd stayed up three days to write, she offered to mentor me through the application for a Marshall Scholarship. I remember the feeling, when she said it. Of course, I hadn't heard of the Marshall scholarship, but it had the ring of White School things, of those kind of Longwood Tower old money secrets to which I'd always had only slanting access. It was February, sunny but with snow, when I left her office. Everything had a beautiful, thin light. I thought of all the things I could do next, all the knuckling down and cleaning up, and then I ate some cloud in the bathroom of the dining commons. Now, the deadline has come and gone, along with several others.

"Listen," I say.

Mackin holds up a hand. "Save it."

"No," I say, "but listen."

Mackin sets down the stack of paper in her hands. Gestures a chair. She is pretty, but I see in her face that forty isn't young, that it might be hard to have an unhandsome husband and a stack of late papers and still wear a leather skirt to class.

"You hear ever of the New School of the University of South Florida? That's where I went to college. Early seventies. Everyone was listening to progressive rock, and dropping a lot of acid." She traces a hairline scar on her cheek. "One night, tripping my brains out, I walked through a plate glass window. A hundred and seventy stitches, skin grafts, ten months of surgeries. What I think about now, is all the time that led up to that night. Freshman year, sophomore year. Why is no one concerned? My parents are happy. My professors. My friends. Everyone is thrilled, because I'm delivering the As. As long as I do the basics, no one calls me on anything. Right? No one is worried."

I nod. I'm not dropping acid, I want to tell her.

"And afterward, what do you think? Maybe two people. Maybe two people, the whole time I'm walking around with surgical gauze on my face, ever told me I was fucking up something that mattered. So, listen, you don't try to bullshit me."

"No, Professor," I say.

"Are you interested in getting clean? Do you want to fix your life?"

"It's not drugs," I say.

My professor, she holds an MBA from Harvard, and made—before she went to get her PhD in political science, before she was lecturing on Iron Curtain/Iron Maiden—five million dollars in a single day.

I tell her, "I'm in love with someone, but he doesn't love me."

The disdain on her face is naked, and I think of the light through the snow in winter, and I think, I deserve this.

"My point is, it's a matter of conserving resources. I can't care about all of you." Her mouth becomes a flatline, neither disappointed nor cruel.

I hesitate. It seems like there must be a rule that I'm violating, like I might get sent to the principal's office, but Mackin's point, I see, is that help is a precious commodity which should be reserved for people who have nothing to start with; that for people like me, all my wasted advantages, Mackin believes we earn the outcomes of our own bad decisions.

"It's ten points off for each day late and another five for being sloppy. Shall we call it a flat *C* and save ourselves both some time?"

I nod. "I'll see you."

Mackin nods and returns her eyes to her stack of tidier, worthier essays. "Sure," she says.

Walking through the twilight to my internship, I recall a dream. The phone is ringing and ringing; someone is pounding angrily on my door. *Sir*, says a voice like that of my RA. *Sir, you can't be in here. Sir, I'm going to have to call the authorities*. The phone continues to ring.

I write it down in my paperback, *something tracking me*. There's no need for a psychotherapist to locate the thing I sense at my heels, to name the entity that is knocking at my door. Since I have stopped eating cloud, I have not slept well. Three days from now, my contract with the dorm ends and I will be kicked out. My summer plan of living rent-free with Mr. Boyfriend is no longer possible. I've skipped two shifts in a row at work. I pull a tab off a sublet sign as I make the twil-it walk to the film studio on 125th. The sense of being pursued is as palpable as footsteps even when I am awake. There is so much I've put aside, exam schedules crumpled, summer plans undone. I don't ask what's tailing me, but which, which of the many things that might want me is following in this moment, today.

Five

New York City
1993

The production company I intern with also rents out equipment to student films and commercial productions, and they have me dropping some lighting gear in Murray Hill before I'm due on set at 125th. I have a couple hours' dead time. It's a beautiful late afternoon, but I'm jumpy, cloud-hungry, and so I decide to walk the eighty blocks. It's a day when I need to walk eighty blocks. Thirty-Fourth and First Avenue, bad shoes on my feet, I head uptown.

The director, this sculptor Westie, is shooting the production out of her studio. She's not a film person, but she did this one arty short about two kids and a hanging, and the brothers who head my studio are obsessed. They are enormously nervous people to begin with, the brothers, the kinds who call you in the middle of the night to change the number of sesame bagels or rethink the gels on the lights. On top of this you have Westie, whose process, the Assistant Director tells me, is very improvisational, very informal. The collaboration has not been easy. Each hour of production time costs, and the brothers never have an adequate budget. I call the AD from a pay phone to let him log the delivery, and he tells me that it's chaos uptown. They haven't cast the supporting role, and suddenly Westie has been called home to Boston, aunt in the hospital, something. Now, says the AD, you have both brothers running around the set like mad leprechauns, throwing blame like confetti.

He likes to talk, the assistant director. "It's a nuclear meltdown, here. Westie is against *casting*. Her idea is that actors should magically I guess intersect roles."

We're friends, kinda, me and the AD. He might have a crush. Any case, Westie hadn't wanted to hire a casting director and now in her absence, the brothers can't agree on a choice.

"I should go," I tell him.

I pick up a voicemail from Nancy.

"So, yeah. We're both out of there. Which is good. Is absolutely a good thing, even with who got us gone. I'm waiting, now, to make sure Andi gets on that train," says Nancy. "I'll breathe easier when she's on the train."

She is calling from somewhere public and busy. There's a PA system in the background, barking announcements. *Smoking is permitted only in designated outdoor smoking areas.*

Meanwhile, Paul has been having his own dialogue with her. From him, I know that Andi's escape had been facilitated by the bad boyfriend. Months ago, when she'd left Boston initially, it had been to get away from him. It was too sick, with him, too old and twisted. If she was ever going to be well, it had to be on her own. She'd made him swear he wouldn't follow her. But on the farm, Andi had not gotten well. She wasn't OK. And now the new kind of stuck felt worse than what she'd left behind. So, she'd snuck out in the middle of the night, shoeless, wearing only a nightgown. From a payphone two miles from the retreat center, she'd called. Would he come for her, she asked on the phone. Would he please?

Now, as Nancy speaks the final lines of the message, I can hear her shaking her head.

"It's one of those things, like how it would be to be God. You can't just make decisions for someone else. It's like trying to design a leaf. Like trying to invent photosynthesis if all you have is a molecule."

It is dusk when I reach the park. I pass women joggers with mace in their waistbands, and men, spaced out to their headsets. Am I scared, alone sometimes on the streets of New York? Am I scared when it is dark? Do I sometimes walk faster or glance behind me or cross the street? I do, but that's not the whole story. There's something you earn, by taking the risk, by walking anyway. And I haven't been mugged yet.

Uptown, student territory, and then the empty blocks between the college and 125th. Westie's studio is in an old industrial building, high ceilings, no AC, which is honestly better digs than usual. The brothers' production company never has even half the budget to do what we need, is always stealing from its commercial division to support its experimental and documentary branches. I've met the accountant, doing a messenger run. He is thirty-one, completely bald, and has three ulcers, but for us, it is still a plum internship. This is why we'll pick up the phone for a bagel order in the middle of the night or lug cameras from Harlem to Washington Square. We loan the production our subway passes, our parents' apartments, our cats. We cook for the crafts services table in our dorm kitchens, we roll pennies, we plead parking tickets. Regularly, we are required to ditch classes, to spend twenty straight hours on set. The brothers are geniuses, have two Academy Awards, and have never spent more than fifty *K* on a production. It's incredible to watch them work.

Tonight, the fat brother, Albert, is running auditions in the sawdust-strewn studio. This is the mnemonic we all use, *fat Albert, thin Ansel.* The brothers are twins and otherwise alike. The studio door isn't a door. It's like someone built the wall, and forgot about an entrance, and then just hacksawed into the drywall. The cut-out square is fixed on a set of brass hinges and hangs insecurely in the frame. The effect is as if some mad prisoner forced their way out—or in. The AD stops me at the entrance.

Ansel begins to shout. "Collaboration *is* emotional, fuckface."

Albert is glowering darkly. An actor stands between them clutching the script. I'm surprised there's a script. A script is kind of conventional for Albert and Ansel.

"I'm not reading lines," says Ansel. "Get the girl to read lines."

The AD is a decent fellow in that he's the only crew member who doesn't shit all over the PAs, doesn't practice trickle-down exploitation on his subordinates. He tries to insulate the interns, or at least the me-intern, which returns to the crush possibility. Internships. My freshman year roommate was rich—not trust fund rich, but two-psychologist-parents-in-Connecticut rich—and she sort of got off on being abused by literary agents and MTV Productions. She felt like her suffering was buying her future success. She'd spend like eight solid hours comparison shopping padded bras for her employer, and then she'd take herself out for dinner at Bouley in consolation. Me, I think about the fact of having a job that costs me money constantly. Especially now that my boyfriend-revenue has been cut off, I do the bad math all the time.

But for the moment, I'm the girl. Beyond the AD, in the loft, a silence falls. Ansel and Albert beckon. The AD drops his arm and allows me to pass through. Things begin to spark for me as soon as I am inside. The feeling is of a bad recognition, is like opening a box of hurtful letters you thought you'd thrown away. I've never been in this room before.

"Mellie," hisses the AD. "Mellie, go on."

I keep walking, but the room, the studio, the stuff throbs at me. Floor to ceiling, the walls are lined with shelves, each shelf divided into irregular nooks, each nook stashed with some item. Many of the objects do not require explanation. A five-pound bag of flour, for instance, a teddy bear, a bent spoon: fine. But interspersed with this ordinary inventory are elements of a collection which disturb. A jar of pink pickled egg with the words *Rat Poison* written in marker. An umbrella lined with human molars. No one else seems sensitive to it; no one else seems out of sorts.

OK? I go downtown. I have seen a man drive a nail through his penis. I can handle weird art, even if it's not exactly my bag. The way this room sparks my heart rate is like the onset of cloud need. Is like the feeling of something I almost remember. I want to write, but there's not time to write now, no room. There is in the organization into cubbies, a dark logic I understand.

"She the actress?" Albert asks.

"No, sir," I say. I'm not being modest. I can't act.

Ansel whispers something to Albert. Albert catches his upper lip in his teeth and considers me.

"Fine, whatever. Let her read."

The actor, A, is hot. He's tall and built and I remember thinking he was nice to look at on the big screen at the Angelica. B, he's like what the fuck? Some nobody girl in giant glasses, with a sheen of grease in her T-zone, and I'm supposed to audition at that? Plus, the script isn't a script. It's more like a series of interview questions with the answers left blank. The actor is meant to improv, Ansel tells him. Is meant to answer in ways which are honest or at least honest-seeming.

He's a pro, squares his shoulders, looks in my eyes like he's not facing a piece of wood, and becomes something. "When were you last afraid?" I ask him. "Who do you find attractive? Are you yourself attractive?"

The AD thanks the actor, says the requisite words of dismissal. Obviously, they'll be in touch with his agent. Obviously.

"So?" says Ansel to Albert.

Albert, who can pass for one iota nicer than Ansel, but probably taxidermies babies for a hobby, looks at me. I shrug. The brothers scare the crap out of me, and I'm not going to voice an opinion, but they read it on me anyway.

"He's not the guy," says Ansel. "You wanna go kiss some indie film actor ass, be my guest. But you wanna make this picture, we need to keep looking."

Albert squints at me. The brothers are careful about all of their choices. In all the articles about them, this is what the critics say, that they get second, and third opinions, that they run through scenarios ten, fifteen times. That they do laborious post, rather than do reshoots, and that they are incredible technicians, because how they do what they do is by not wasting resources. And so whatever, to getting my opinion, but the AD points out later that they aren't asking any of the other PAs.

"You agree?" Albert asks me.

I nod yes, just a little nod. The brothers have begun to distinguish me from Melissa and Ari, the other Ivy assistants. They don't want it to go to my head, but they might have learned my name.

Ansel says, "how long does a funeral have to take, anyway?"

"You were the one who said she could be counted on," says Albert.

They have been known to get physical with each other, two men in their fifties in not especially good shape. We exit the studio, and once I'm in the hall, I relax somewhat. The AD closes the makeshift door on the studio, and the voices become muffled.

On my way here earlier, before I'd reached 125th, I had stopped by the post office hoping for a check from my mom. Instead, I found a letter from Nancy. Now, while we wait for the brothers to decide what to do, I try to decipher the handwriting.

It's postmarked Pittsfield and it's written on an Amtrak napkin. Look, writes Nancy: New England. We like our stories to end on a farm in the country, a kitchen; the heroine is scrubbing pots and eating dry meals, and probably praying. That's where we think this is going. He's the bad guy and she's his victim, but she's learned some valuable lesson, feeding goats and making yoghurt.

But it's her begging him on the train platform, and it's him saying no. No. It's gotten too bad, and it's too late. They've managed to scrounge enough for one ticket to California. He'd dropped a muffler and popped a tire on his way to the farm, but Nancy still thinks it's fifty-fifty he'll go after her eventually. It's fifty-fifty for a wedding on the beach.

Around me, the crew are gathering their belongings, slinging their bags onto their backs.

The AD taps my shoulder. "We're calling it a night. Do you need me to walk you?"

There are seven dark and empty blocks between 125th and 118th, where the foot traffic begins to pick up again. They aren't easy blocks to travel alone, but I'm already calculating how fast I can run, how soon I can be back in my dorm to my man. Above me, the train hurtles past. I am thinking of the Amtrak, on its way West, whether the boyfriend will drive after her. Paul has paged me, which means they are leaving Blue and Gold, that there's every chance he's already lying in my bed. The night is summery, still in the high seventies. The streetlights have haloes of humidity around them. I too feel I hang above the city. I begin to run the blocks, fearless and hungry.

After rehearsal breaks up at the St. Mark's Theater, Davos and Ned and Paul and Nadine go out to the bar. Paul gets drunk on well gin and tonics, on Happy Hour specials, and then he rides the 1/9 to me. I take off my clothes as soon as I get through the door and we don't mind how sweaty it is, how slick our skin is in the gathering summer. Now it is night. He is sitting by the fan in my dormitory, looking down at the street, ashing into the whirring blades. I kiss him. He tastes of Prince Rounded Flavors and his own sour breath and a giant slice of Coronet pizza. He tastes of cloud. He is tired but he is twenty-three and I pull off his shorts, and I kick out of my panties and slide him into me. Our mouths are bone hard, are open, are yearning into each other.

We fall asleep under the cool sheet on my twin bed, one of us dangling over the side. Early, still raw with exhaustion, I wake up in a room without oxygen. I am like a beach before tsunami, the tremble of the lake before the sinkhole swallows. This is me trying to stay still; this is my body before I give in. My legs and my spine and my eyeballs want cloud. They want it, but they will take Paul, will accept Paul as substitute. I know it's too much, but I have to wake him, too. With my hands, I have to do it. I have no choice.

"Jesus, Mellie," he says, four hours into a gin sleep. "What's wrong with you?"

Paul is twenty-three years old and, including me, he has slept with twenty-four women. Paul says that none of them, not one of the two dozen lovers, has ever acted like I do, constantly after him, waking him to make him have sex with me. It's too much, is what I understand. It's abnormal. But, I am trying to fix something. A quality of numbness that keeps interceding between our two skins. There is a thing in my mind, red, blurry, and if I focus on it, if I hold onto it, I can find him in there. I can break through the skin of cloud between us. We meet at midnight, at dawn; we fuck and we sleep and that is how I am holding us together.

Later, in full light, I wake again. The bed beside me is empty. Paul sits a few feet away with *The Voice*. "Mellie, listen."

I haul myself upright and prop a pillow between my back and the wall. He's gotten me a coffee from the cart and he is squatting on his long legs with the folded newspaper in front of him. My phone is ringing but we are used to ignoring it.

"So," says Paul. "Remember how I was telling you we saw Vera Woczalski at the previews?"

I nod, but I am still groggy, have no idea who this is.

"The critic. The theater critic from the Voice. She's like twenty-two or something, but she was there. And she published a review of the play."

"So?"

Paul gives me an involuntary smile that contains no pleasure.

"I can't read it. You read it."

He hands it to me, and I anticipate what it will say, because I have known all along. The play is a disaster, is an insult to the audience, is crude and amateur and derivative. Woczalski writes:

> Davos Kruck has developed something of a reputation in the downtown scene, but this play casts a backwards shadow over the director's early works, which after all only come to us in translation. Having seen The Magic Knife, one wonders whether earlier faults might have been overlooked, whether it is time for a reappraisal of the director's reputation.

But then she says:

> Newcomer Paul Greene is seemingly as artificial as the others onstage, but his artifice transcends to become the thing the play promises . . .

It's just that line, but when I look up, I realize that Paul has already read it, and that it accounts for his agitated euphoria. He wants me to help him know how to react.

"It's always better to be bad in a good production than good in a bad production," he says.

"Still," I say. "It's talent. You get to know that from the newspaper. That you have talent."

"Not that I even necessarily agree. Who is Vera Woczalski? She's twenty-two. There are a hundred drama school girls she could be."

Suddenly, I'm seized with something fierce for him, a righteousness on his behalf. "She's right, though. She's completely right. You are good. It's the rest of them that are full of shit."

He holds the paper, eyes boring into it. He waits for the words to gain some incantatory power, to manifest themselves as true or false.

I think about what was said to him on the train through Siberia. It would have been an assessment, a judgment about his native gifts. He boards the train as a supporting player. Davos pronounces. Paul jumps off the train into the unbearable blue. The thing is forgotten. Paul gets the lead.

What Professor Mackin said to me, when I missed the Marshall deadline. "You are used to being the smartest student in your literature seminar. Fine. That's fine. But we're talking about the smartest people in the country now. It's not something you can bullshit in a one-day marathon."

New York tells us: *you're playing my game now.*

"In the script," I say to Paul. "How does it describe the ice boy?"

"It just says, beautiful."

Yes, I think. G-d, yes. Lean, hard bones, skin that is both pale and brown. And his beauty is more intense with the worry written there now. He puts down the paper, sips his coffee cart coffee. I want Vera Woczalski's words to have power to match whatever Davos told Paul while he was sitting on that square suitcase in that freezing train compartment; I want him to listen to *me*. It should be enough that I say it. You're talented, beautiful. I have a secret.

Nancy calls us, drunk. "I'm reacquainting myself with tequila," she says. She is at her parents' house in Brookline. No one can reach Andi.

"Is she with the bad boyfriend?"

"It's the same boyfriend as always," says Paul. "It's that same guy Judah." He's been having his own conversations with Nancy. I wonder if he has a secret, too.

"Is there still going to be a wedding?" I ask.

"I've got my dress," she says. "Is it tacky to wear red when someone gets married?"

"Maybe it's for the best," I say.

"You should come for opening night," says Paul. "On your way."

Nancy says, "I've got to puke now. Love you. See you."

Paul is looking at the review again, scrutinizing it as if it's a message from Zarah, full of hidden warnings and signs of the future.

"I think I should go easy on the cloud tonight," says Paul, lighting up a Prince. "I think I need to cut back." He gives me an absent squeeze, wraps himself in my pink robe and pads down the hall to the floor's shower. Kids screw in there, all the time. I want to follow him in with a bar of soap and I am beginning not to know whether my impulses are sweet or creepy, sexy or sick.

Instead, I go through his things. I open his messenger bag, and thumb past his annotated script and his Swiss Army knife and the Gumby pencil case in which he's taken to carrying his cloud. I hold it up to my face and inhale, inhale, inhale the sharp lemon scent, then I open it. Inside are two spoons and a torn leather cuff with three letters tooled in. *D A V.* It is a memento, a mystery, and it carries with it a sense of violence. The phone rings, but I don't pick it up. The only person I want to talk to is right down the hall and once he goes, he'll never call. Downtown, dress rehearsal, it's an entirely other world.

Six

Longwood Towers
2010

I stand, for a moment, just out of view of Longwood Towers. My pulse beats at my neck as I come into sight of the dark façade. The sun is in my favor, or less plausibly, the therapy is working, because this time, I have no trouble making out the fountain, the looping drive, and the several towers.

The countdown to *Found Footage* is at nine days. The video of the headless woman has two hundred thousand hits. Something is stuck in the pages of my paperback. Now, I stand in the exact spot where Mr. *OD TO* had vanished. *No seeking him out,* Emily had made me promise. *No hanging at places he might happen to be.* I think of what I know of the SUV man, his twitchy hunger, the confusion, his urgency. This is not a person who would sit around a lobby for weeks, just on some hope I'd return. Still, I'm looking for him in the shadows. Of course I am. But it had also been Emily who told me to come, that I didn't need to be in earnest. Everyone has bad motivations. You just have to do life, one thing after another.

So, now here I am, Longwood Towers. As I make my way toward the entrance, I conjure back my conversation with the bald man after pizza, the rain coming in. There was something he'd wanted to ask me, a little device coming out of his pocket. He'd mentioned the project. And then he'd become someone else. Someone smoking a Prince cigarette beside a black SUV. He'd vanished into these shadows. Two men? One man? Cloud tries to make connections, wants things to relate. My boss, the man in my driveway, and now the man from the Monday meeting. As if there is some kind of polarity in operation, disconnected episodes try to connect, to intersect, but perhaps it may be impression only, merely brain detritus, the afterimage of a high I am suffering rather than perceiving.

Still: it feels real, like pieces, logical connections are looping in. Things spark and flare in the periphery, notes of meaning which refuse to coalesce. The itch to write, to get it on paper, is almost impossible to resist. I step through the doors.

I recall, vague, red carpeting, a sense of hush, but the lobby is chiefly beige now. There is a coffee bar in the corner, a sundries shop. An older man snoozes beneath a newspaper, in a shaft of light. A doctor-type mutters into his phone. A teenaged girl collects mail from the clerk behind the desk. And what of Mr. *OD TO*? I scan the room, for some indentation in a cushion, some cigarette butt in a planter, but everything is mute.

Then, someone is striding toward me from the direction of the elevator. His face is vague. I look slant at him, trying to make him come into focus, the juice of adrenaline rising. Shaven head. The documentary man, the SUV man. They want to swap. But the faceless man is smiling, and the smile shows no menace. Now, he calls my name, my right name.

"Mellie?" His voice is benign, no smoker's rumble at the back, none of the gummy muddle. "Hey, you OK?"

I know him, but not from my driveway or the car ride. He's just the man from the Monday meeting. My clenched muscles begin to loosen. I am relieved, which surprises me, which is maybe some kind of progress.

"You're—Isaiah?"

He laughs. He has a nice laugh. "That's a new one on me."

"Sorry. Emily couldn't remember."

He hands me his card and I slip it in my wallet next to the *OD TO* paper and the photograph, then I follow him toward the elevator. I glance again, sideways. He looks back.

"I'm so glad you've agreed. You kind of took off, last time we spoke. I thought I'd spooked you."

"As I recall it," I say, "you were the one who vanished."

"Could be," he says, and we leave it at that. He's cloud people, and so am I. I'm not done with my suspicion, the sense that there's some unrevealed history there, but he doesn't call forth in me longing or desire and perhaps among our kind, it isn't always necessary to square these things. For now, I try to trust that he won't transform into some bad other version, reveal some hidden face.

"You haven't been around," he said. "I thought you—" He was going to say relapsed, but he's stopped himself.

"Checked myself in," I say. "I guess I kind of had to."

"Well, you look great," he says.

I want to cut myself down, but instead the compliment just hangs there for a moment, awkward but not entirely unpleasant. As the brass doors close, I catch my own face in one of the mirrors. I've weathered my cloud use OK—I don't have the blank look of N; I don't resemble the junkiest girls, with their rut marks and their chin blooms of color. Since I've quit, my hands are more typical, less puffed, but still. I don't look twenty-five.

"I used to steal stuff from the garbage rooms at this place," I say, the thing becoming true as I tell him. "As a kid, I mean. Not like last year."

He nods, gives me a look as if I've told him something he already knows.

"I'm curious, though. These apartments. How'd you end up doing interviews here?"

He shrugs. "It's a little sterile, huh?" The elevator door opens, and we step into a large, light-filled room. A guy in the corner reads a newspaper in Arabic. The big-screen television shows captioned coverage of a tornado, up-ended trailers. We take a table by the window.

"It's fine," I say. "Nice. I just, I meant Longwood. Is there a reason you picked this place, in particular?"

"You know a little bit about my project?"

"Emily said you were after origins, the origins of cloud. Like Cold War? Mad Doctor Strangeloves smuggling it in caviar tins?"

"There's actually some evidence for film canisters, in the early case law. They raided this warehouse in Sullivan County, in the Poconos, pornographic materials coming in from Ukraine, and that's the very first cloud seizure on record. Anyway, my father—you know my father?"

"I wouldn't, I don't think," I say.

He nods, does the thing again like he's considering correcting me, like we've been over this ground before. "Personally, my father was involved. Is connected with that first cloud property. That's what I mean. Origins is close, but it's more personal. Interpersonal, even. The term we use is root place."

"This is a OneLife thing? A point of branching?"

"Let's have coffee before we get into the mystical stuff, huh?" He stands, and fusses at the coffee station, turns over his shoulder to address me. "Cream? Milk?"

"Extra," I say. "Either."

Here's an entertaining fact: I haven't talked to a man like this, like in a pair, over beverages and without being high, since I was a teenager and it feels a little bit like touching the frayed end of a hacked-off electric cord. Emily claims she doesn't have sex anymore. Her ex that she used with is the guy in prison. No way, she says, not even if he were clean and got Jesus. Still, she tells me, when you go for a long time without, sometimes you can have weird spells. Emily says, she gets to be like those starving cartoon rabbits who see every umbrella as a carrot stick, every pencil. *Only it's not carrot sticks I'm seeing.* For me, as he hands me the coffee, there is a kind of echo, as is we've both long ago made this same gesture. I try to smile and talk like a normal person to the guy. It would help if I could remember his name. Not Isaiah, but like it, holy and homeschool, Jedediah, Ezekial.

He takes a seat at one of the tables and shifts his bag to make room. It doesn't look big enough to hold much equipment. "So, yeah. The audio project. It's about this idea of root places. Users, you know how they short out, come up blank against certain things?"

"Or people, even. Sure. It's—unpleasant."

"Then, some addicts get the blindness around objects. Locations, commonly, can be triggering, too."

"So, this place? Is it like that for you?"

"This room, no. The opposite. Initially, I was doing the interviews in my apartment, but I guess I got high a lot back in the day. When I was young. I thought, that could be good. It might set the stage, get me into the mind frame, link me as the documentarian to the experience. But that was a mistake. It's also possible for something to be too rich in experience, in memory. Think of it like a point on a map, which you've routed through repeatedly, traveling again and again, always different routes, until eventually, that spot becomes illegible. A root place is like that, territory revisited and revisited until it starts to record as a blank."

I sip my coffee. "My therapist says something like that, but for her it's neurological. We keep tracking things into this blank trough."

"Sure, that squares," he says, "It fits, mostly. But certain phenomena, I think, point us to another explanation. If the blank is merely perceptual, what do we do with the intersections that happen there, the experience of linking with another? Why do others, sometimes, seem to share these precise memory gaps? Doesn't it seem, sometimes, that blank places also belong to others?"

"Delusion? That's the line I'm supposed to buy right now. Our brains are malfunctioning, and some like executive function or the superego or whatever, stitches it together into a kind of weird conspiracy. The links, the coincidences, they're after the fact. So I'm told."

The man reading Arabic folds his paper and stands, passing through a shaft of the afternoon sun, and then exits the room. I am alone with the man. Isaac, I think, Abraham.

"The founder of OneLife, you know, she was a user herself? She came to think of the cloud as a space of possibility. You get high, and there's a kind of roulette. You enter the emptiness, ricochet out into some unpredictable point. Something is lost, something found. High, we're passive recipients of the process. But what, the founder asked, if we could harness it? Control, even, what we gain in the process? Sacrifice willingly, what we are able—or even what we need—to lose." Until now, his voice has remained conversational, casual, but an edge has begun to creep in.

"By getting high again?"

"No, no. Certainly not."

"You said you were doing interviews in your apartment."

"Sure. So, what I think the likely world gets right," he says, "is that cloud is mapped into our lives. Certain places or objects or people are like the—what did you call them? Troughs of forgetting?"

I nod.

"This particular root place I'm interested in, it's been a lot of things. Old bungalow colony—you know?"

"Catskills? Middle-class Jews having summer vacation?"

"And then it appears to have had a life as a holding place for recent refugees, as an informal resettlement camp before the Soviet Union began to open up immigration. After that, as I mentioned, it warehoused imported films, and probably cloud was smuggled in at the same time. For two summers in the eighties, it was home to a children's summer camp. Cloud places are like that. Like a trough. Many lives route through these places. OneLife calls them inversion points. If we can penetrate into the blank space, sacred object, see the face, we have a brief period of opening where certain lost tracks may be accessible to us. The likely world, but in this one."

"I think I follow. This place—Longwood—why I was asking how you chose it—has something of that quality for me."

"That's what was going on in the lobby? You seemed disoriented, briefly. I wondered."

"Could be," I say. "Possibly."

Abraham places a small device on the table. I recognize it from outside of Uno's. He pauses before he continues. "Listen. I almost never record the first interview.

Even with the best subject, you have to establish rapport. People get awkward, start performing or clam up. But, do you mind?"

Subject. I try to decide if that's sexy or creepy or creepy-sexy. "Yeah, OK." The request weirdly flatters me, as if I've passed some test. I am aware of the distance between us under the table, which feels precise and deliberate. How he is, his care with his physical presence, seems somewhat to have the reverse effect from the one he intends. It makes me pay attention. I look at him, try to make out the details of his face. Bone structure. Brown eyes, but it's not just that I can't see him. There's something that makes me hold back.

"Let us say that these inversion points function as attractants."

"I was thinking about magnets, earlier. Polarity."

"I like that," he says. "I can fall into yours, perhaps. You can fall into mine. We go inside, we get muddled." He pulls the lid off his coffee and drinks. "So, that's what seemed to happen with this project. I was meeting with interviewees in my apartment, and then I had a break-in. There was this map, lakes and trees, a real rural place, which I'd annotated. It means a lot to me, represents maybe six months of work. But to a stranger, it shouldn't be anything."

"An annotated map," I say. The phrase calls up an image, vivid and recent, but I can't place it. The prickle of discomfort returns.

"Yeah. I've got gear in there. Computer, audio equipment. Even some decent art. But all the guy takes is this map, Sullivan County. To me, it's childhood, long ago. Why would someone else care about it? It's important to me, but is it also possible that my place belongs to others? Draws them? Do we share our inversion points? So you see why I moved the conversation to somewhere more neutral. My project is about root places, but I didn't want to operate out of one."

"But my—disorientation. When I got here? Maybe this place isn't so bland after all."

"Do you feel it up here? In this room, too?"

I shake my head. "I can't say yet."

He shifts the recorder slightly, perhaps the better to catch my words, perhaps just a tic. "I think of it like the internet," he says. "Some weird video everyone gets obsessed with. Objectively, it's not that funny or interesting, but all of sudden, all the searches are routing through this point. People are inexplicably riveted."

The discomfort shifts toward vertigo, but I remind myself that this is how the brain incorporates repair, the feeling of significance—

"This place, this building," he says. "Longwood. The thing you said about trash cans, as a kid. Does it have some kind of significance for you?"

"Oh, G-d. Can we skip this question?"

"Sure. Of course. Let's get at it another way. Why did you come here today?"

"You're right, you know. The tape recorder does make me self-conscious."

He smiles. It's a practiced smile, reassuring. "Here's what I've seen. For a couple months, maybe. You've been dodging me. And today, for some reason, you've changed your mind."

"Wait," I say. "I thought you were just looking for folks who'd been through it. But it's me in particular?"

"It's fine. I get it," he says. "But what I think, maybe something changed."

"Is that a question?" I ask.

"What happened, Mellie? That's my question. I think, since we last spoke, you entered a blank and it brought you here. To me. I would like to know about it."

I shake my head. The coffee in the cup has gone cold, and I've barely had any of it. "I've been staying away from all that," I tell him. "It's part of getting clean. Route around, they say. Avoid falling into the same old trap."

"At the higher levels," he says, "and I get if you're not ready—but as you progress, when you're strong enough—you will have to go inside."

"Inside? You used that word before, but I'm not sure I know what it means."

"I'd like to tell you something, Mellie. It's about you."

"I'd rather you didn't."

"This is a couple of months ago. Right after I started OneLife, this one day, I was low. Just kind of wandering around, trying to keep myself focused. I'd been sober for almost two years, but this was a day when I wasn't sure of myself. There are things I have to live with that I sometimes don't think I can. And they eat at me, acid, on the inside."

"This is about me?"

"I know I did things, and that forgetting doesn't absolve me. Times like that, the only thing that feels like it will is a mouthful of cloud. So it's one of those days, I'm grinding through it. 2:05 p.m. 2:10 p.m. Every minute, it's impossible—and then there you are. You're walking beside Emily, pushing a stroller, but it's you. It's Mellie."

"That was a bad day," I say.

He shakes his head. "That's not what I'm getting at. I hadn't thought of you in years; maybe, to me, you no longer existed, and then there you were. At my next inversion session, I saw my place, the place on the map that got stolen. This place, that place. You, on the sidewalk. Geographically, they're separate, but there are lines running through them in the cloud. It may not make sense yet, but whatever you're looking for, why you came here today, I think it's possible it links to my place."

I know it's a bad idea. Look, I do. But I reach into my wallet and pull out the *OD TO* scrap, unstick it from the photograph I've been storing it with, and slide the paper across the table. His eyes flicker, brighten. The photograph I keep beneath my palm.

"Listen," I say. "I'm newer at this process than you are, but there's another thing you should consider. We are sometimes wrong, when we attach significance. Sometimes, those attachments are misplaced."

"What is this?" he asks, tapping the paper.

"It's not related to your project. It's not a root place. There was this guy—I thought he was someone, but I might have wrong. We got into it. He dropped this in my car. That's what brought me here, why I agreed. I thought, on the strength of four letters, that it was all magically connected. He'd still be here, or there'd be some clue, something I would discover that would clarify things."

His fingers, on the table, seem to be inching toward mine. What disconcerts me is that he seems unaware of it, that a part of his body is about to escape the perimeter he's built around himself, that it's me who's making him do it.

"Exactly," he says. "Precisely. Today, when you walked in here. You were disoriented. What was it? Things being drawn in. You, this man. The feeling like there are branches, things reaching out—"

"But not necessarily in the same direction," I say. "Right?"

"I know. I admit that. It makes sense," he says. "But the links feel so vivid to me. The lines between you, and me, and this place I saw. The water in front of me. I'm a kid—not a kid, but not an adult either. I tried to save this girl from drowning but—it was my fault—when it happened, I think you were there."

I see the details are meant to draw me out, but they don't call up anything in me. "Coincidence," I say. "Correlation."

"No," he shakes his head. "Mellie. I've been back. Not long ago. I drive to the place on the map. No roads, but whatever, I circle the property. Nothing. I circle again; still nothing. So, I get out of the car. I've got a trek compass. I enter the coordinates, and start walking. It's the same deal. I keep finding myself back at the road. I'm like a person looking at a gorilla. I can't see the damn gorilla, even though it's right in front of me."

"You know," I say. "I could have been exactly there, in the exact same place, but it might not help you at all. That's maybe the point. Memories deceive even normal folks. For people like us, they're the same as fiction. Stick to the facts."

"Here's a fact," he says, and he is sliding something across the table to me. It's some kind of ticket, faded, muddied over. "This is what I found. The only thing I could find."

The object is a bus ticket, origin: Los Angeles. End point: Sullivan County, New York. The date is about two years prior, and the name of the person it has been issued to is now illegible, but it is a particularly long name, with an *l* in it, a *z* and a hyphen.

"I think that's yours, Mellie. I think you've been to my place, too, to Kif-Vesely'e."

I know this isn't right. "Say that again."

"Kif-Vesely'e," he says. He considers my scrap of paper, then he hands me a key card. "And there's this." There's a monogram, a curling design of a tower. *OD TO.* "That's my apartment number. 2f."

"No," I say. "You're not him."

"Not who, Mellie?"

The sparks return, things at the edge, pushing in. *Old residents. Judging by the deed.* A map in a duffel bag. I push back.

"Kif-Vesely'e? Those were the words? And they were on the map?"

The man nods.

"How did he find you? Any idea?"

He shrugs. "There was monitor footage. I might have recognized him."

"From where?"

He hesitates again. "We're connected." His fingers are still moving across the table. There's a part of me that wants to follow him over whatever bridge we've reached, but I've been through that kind of hippie stuff before. My mother, with her past life regressions, and Nancy with her gurus and meditation.

"What did he look like?"

"Big," says Abraham. "Gym type. Twitchy."

I sit back, let it come to me. *Kif-Vesely'e. You know how to find it. Former residents.* "He was after something; someone who used to live here. He knows you? He wanted something from you? Tell me your name again. Your full name."

He says his name, but it is as if it's spoken in my high school French. There is a bursting of flame, a sense of melting. I reach into my wallet and pull out his card. It takes a minute for my vision to clear. I'm aware of actively fighting off a certain haze. *Cohen Audio. Judah Cohen.* "You're Lew Cohen's son."

He shakes his head. "This isn't about my father, Mellie. It's not him. It's not Mondays. We've run into each other again, and again. "

"You said you hadn't seen me in years," I say. "Is it because I worked for Lew? Is that how you know me?"

"Not only," he says. "Not just."

"And this place, on the map. You said your father was connected to it, too? Lew Cohen? You mentioned a video. You said, there was traffic to a video."

"It was an analogy."

"Tell me about the video."

His eyes fix on my hands. "I don't speak to my father. I haven't seen him since I got clean."

"But there is a video? One of his?"

"After the break in. When I returned. There was something on my monitor."

"A woman walking back and forth?"

"Your name is linked to it. My father's, too. This woman, Valerie Weston. That's all I know."

"Listen—" I know his name; I want to say it, but it won't quite come out of my mouth. "Listen, guy. You know what I did for your father? I took these videos, and I hijacked them. Someone's just trying to watch a little skin, and then they click on my program, and all of a sudden, their machine is doing our work. This particular video, it's missing a part. This is what your thief was looking for, why he came to me. Kif-Vesely'e. It's just another place on his list, a location to cross off. You want something. You want to fix something in your life. I understand that. But we're not all going in the same direction. You, me, the thief, your father, we're hijacking each other. You might end up where you want to go, but it's not going to happen through me."

I collect things off the table, my purse, the *OD TO* scrap, the bus ticket, but when I reach for the photograph, I realize he has it pinned under a finger. It wasn't my hand he was reaching for, but this.

"I have this book," I say. "I keep scraps. Not everything in it leads to something."

"*Kif-Vesely'e*, my place, the name of the camp. It's written here too."

"Take it," I say. "I have nothing to do with it."

Now, he picks up the photograph. "It's me," he says. He tilts the warped photo paper, cocks his head. "Is that you? Are you with me there? Were we together?"

I can watch the cloud sickness fog over his features, even if I cannot quite make them out. He remains a blur to me—a blank place. But I am not the same for him. I've never had any impression that he has trouble seeing me.

"It's someone else," I say. "You confused me for someone else."

"No. You come to me, too. That night, at the Fens. I was staying at that exact unit. With that old woman. The big guy was there with you. I was worried, and I—it was me who told Emily."

His words click for me, then. *The Fens.* Emily said someone had seen me at my dealer's house. I remember myself, pathetic and hungering. My baby in the running car and me so hungry for cloud I left her there with some strange man lurking just to score a one-off. And he knew Emily, and so he had been the person who told her I'd been visiting my old dealer. Am I supposed to owe him for that?

He's just one more person trying to reach into the depths of my crappy life and make it into something he can use. That's why I like Emily. And the women at Independence. And even my formerly fat counselor. I can't give anything to them. They aren't watching me through a one-way mirror. And so I can trust what they say. I had escaped, that night, but barely. And everything this man is offering is about drawing me back.

I don't know what kind of threat he represents, but I see clearly that I am like him. A zealot, following my own mad trail, *OD TO*, a couple of slips of paper I think will give me a better life. How you end up, if you follow things like this: begging some stranger to know you. I see him, clearly for an instant, and he wears a mania I recognize, a willingness to trust people who might not mean him well.

"It's happening, Mellie. Right now. I'm inside of it. I can see it, all the possibilities. You were there, at Kif-Vesely'e. Please stay with me. I want to make sure I come back the right way. I want to travel on the right path. I need your help to return."

"Sorry, Israel—" there's more meanness in my voice than I intend. "I was only at the Fens because I thought you could get me high."

He shakes his head. "Israel. Good one."

From without, bells are chiming. It's four o'clock. I'm due back at five oh five for checkbook balancing in Life Skills. Fifty minutes on the T to Wollaston, with an eight-minute walk.

A train is just pulling away as I exit. Fuck the T. I may be a junkie who lives in a halfway house with her bastard child, but I'm still middle class. A taxi waits in front of the Towers and I climb in like I'm the one who called it. The cabbie doesn't know me from a doctor's wife; I give him the address, and he pulls into traffic. Four ten. My cloud sense is awake, everything sparking. On my phone, visitors so riveted by the woman in her underwear click yes and yes and invite her sleeper program into their hard drives. Goggle-eyed, they wait for completion, for the countdown, for *Found Footage* to upload, unaware that the sleeping thing may wake when they do. Somewhere, the man in the SUV is searching for the missing middle. Lew, too, is waiting for the right moment. *His part, my part.* Something is hidden in the pages of my paperback. Still, there are things I can't explain. A journey from Los Angeles, a bus ticket from two years ago, why I hid the thing I hid. I want to write this all down in my paperback. I want to tear the pages open and find out what's inside. I want it to tell me why, when I drew in the driveway man's smoke, he felt like mine.

I close my eyes, and I remember this woman from my Parenting without Partners class. She'd been a cook, in one of those chain restaurants, had a four-year-old, a baby daddy that was dead. Even in shitty kitchens, there's a lot of skill involved, a lot of pressure. There are fryolator hazards and sous-chef drama and bus boys fucking each other on their alley cigarette breaks. Naturally, also, there's a ton of drugs. Anyway, this woman, she lives at home with the four-year-old, her moms and a brother, and it's her thing with them, within the family, to make Salisbury steak. She's high, of course, goes absent like junkies do, but then she'll come back prodigal and make these feasts. This she can do, her one gift to them, even when she's useless. She gets arrested, does sixty days, and on visitation, in Rehab, it's all the fam can talk about, how much they miss her Salisbury steaks. But once she's actually back, it's like *poof!* She's fucking it up, burning, undercooking, forgetting ingredients.

"I can't even remember: is it a steak? Is it a hamburger? Is it even actual meat?" It's like someone stole her ability while she was high, like it went to some other woman. "So finally, I go to my family. I'm crying. This thing matters so much to me. It's all I ever gave them. And I just say, I think I'm done. I have to make you something else, and they're like quiet for a second, and then they go—you know what they say? They're like, thank God. We always hated the Salisbury steak."

You don't get to just be done with one way of thinking in an instant. You don't just wake up clear-eyed one beautiful sober day. Things come back in pieces, and you reassemble yourself. I reach into my purse. The key card, the business card, the scrap. I'm collecting again. It's nothing, brain detritus, Salisbury steak. It's so clear to me now; whatever I'm looking for; Isaiah, Lew's video, even the SUV man, they're on their own paths, chasing their own longings. But the life I want to step inside is already here. It's the one with Juni in it. I have to stay focused. I consider the scrap: *OD TO. 2f.* Then, I roll down the window. For a moment, the paper sticks to my fingers, but then the wind gets it, and it floats out into the actual world.

Seven

New York City
1993

I find Paul at Blue and Gold Bar. It's three o'clock in the afternoon, the place empty but for Paul, a couple of men from the construction site down the street and a drunk Ukrainian guy. Paul's got the dregs of a beer and an empty shot glass in front of him, and he's rattling his knees against the countertop, drumming his fingertips. It's not a good mood, and I imagine myself as some older, wiser version of myself, who would turn her back now, who would know how to walk away from whatever I'm about to intersect.

"What's up?" I ask. My will is a thing in my mouth and it falls out whenever I open up.

He pushes aside the shot glass, downs the rest of his beer. "Come on. You coming?" He's red-eyed, a little stage makeup gumming his eyelids. I can tell he hasn't been crying, but close, like one more thing could make it spill over.

"Where are we going?"

"To your connection, Mellie"—he slings his gas station jacket over his shoulder—"your guy on Avenue D."

"Are you already done with the—" I start to ask, but he has slapped down his money and is mounting the stairs, two at a time, into the sunlight. On the street, Paul walks fast, steering around dog walkers, between couples. He's become a New Yorker so quickly. I have to skip stride, to use the pauses at the street corners to catch up. He's on his third agitated cigarette by the time I figure out how to stay beside him. "What's going on? Did something happen at rehearsal?"

"It's so fucking stupid. It's just so fucking idiotic."

"I thought you guys were doing tech? All the new lighting cues?"

"Davos told us today. He's delaying the opening by two weeks. Ellen finalized it with him last night."

I am in my own head. I am thinking about how this relates to me, what it means for a plus mark between our names and a heart around, but his mood doesn't have anything to do with sex, or with does Paul like me back. What's in his mind is all about Vera Woczalski, the review in The Village Voice.

"Come on, now. Really? They have to know that's not your fault."

"*I* don't even agree with her." He keeps lengthening his stride. "She's one critic."

We are nearing the border between the East Village and Alphabet City. Three high school girls, lovely in long legs and platform sneakers, in knee-high rainbow socks, gaggle at a shop window full of useless Japanese cuterie, cat pencils and pig lanterns and lip balm inside a jeweled ring.

"Let's stop for a minute," I say. "Maybe we should slow down."

Paul wheels. "I've been waiting for your ass for three hours, Mellie. I don't want to slow down. Do you understand?" He punches the walk button, then strides into the traffic before the signal has a chance to change.

"I was at my internship." I lope along behind. "There's no phone at the studio."

"I know," says Paul. "I know, I'm sorry. I just need a little cloud, OK? Can we get a little cloud before I have to be *thoughtful* and *sensitive*?"

We reach the curb, the park, Avenue D. The streets are emptier than in the Village. There are more vacant lots, piles of weather-bleached construction debris, bright fresh tags spray-painted on the boarded windows. The smell is different, too: dry and smoky, with a volatile gaseous edge, like something about to blow. We're almost there, at my bodega.

I put a hand on Paul's shoulder. "Better stay outside."

"You can't introduce me to your connection? Am I like not badass enough to buy my own drugs?"

"Shh. Christ. They're just cautious. Next time, OK? I'll mention it today, and then next time."

"Sure. Whatever. This is your territory."

I wonder sometimes about the organizational behavior of my bodega. There are cans on the shelves—Chunky Soup, Dinty Moore Chili, a stick or two of Sure Fine deodorant. But the freezer cases are dark and empty. You can pick up a bag of chips, Utz or some other off-brand. You can get a pack of cigarettes or a forty of Colt 45. But no one's going to walk in here for sandwich fixings without getting a pretty good idea of what drives the transactions behind the ceiling-high bulletproof glass.

"Hey, Alek," I say to the guy with an eyepatch on the other side of the counter.

"Mellie," he says. No smile, no customer service. "What do you need?"

"A twofer will do me." A twofer is a dozen; six is a one-off. The lexicon is familiar to me now, but I still take the aficionado's pleasure in my specialized knowledge.

Alek nods and his cousin or son or whatever disappears into the back. I shift. We listen to the tidy shuffling sound of the bill counting machine, and the boy returns with a rolled-up *Post*. I have to pay for the paper, even though it's often two or three days out of date. The boy smiles and I imagine him momentarily in math class with the rainbow socks girls. Before I go, I mention I might bring a friend some time.

Alek shakes his head. "No, don't do that. We are trying to keep it in the family, limit our reach."

"Understood," I tell him, and I rejoin Paul on the street.

"Wait," I say to Paul's ravenous expression. "Seriously, wait."

Afternoon is deepening, and I get Paul as far as the park before he insists. He sinks onto a bench. Street kids with mutts on rope are gathering in circles to play music now. The drums pound; a guitar twangs. Paul leans back against the bench with a spoon hanging from his full lips.

"Oh, Mellie," he says. "There's no point now. No one's going to come see the play after this."

I put my arm around him.

He sinks into my embrace. "I thought Davos was going to rip my throat out. And the rest of them, seriously, delighted to see me on the outs, Davos reminding me the Ice Boy role was only ever a trial, everyone else so fucking pleased it was like celebratory in there. Like we were on the verge of that scene from *The Bacchae* when all the moms are ripping off Pentheus's limbs. I don't even *agree* with her."

He takes another spoon, and I touch his hair. It isn't clean, but the day-old pomade and the light smell of sweat are intimately mine. I don't care what he says, as long as he keeps talking, as long as he lets me hold onto him.

"That feels good," he says. "Keep doing that."

"She's one critic," I agree. "But that doesn't actually mean she's wrong. You probably are more talented than the rest of them. That's why it pisses them off."

"I know what you mean," he says. "I know that. But—"

"Shhh," I say.

"Jesus, you're good for me."

"Remember that," I tell him. "Try to remember."

But then I see the *pop* flare in his eyes, the moment being swallowed, the perfect blankness taking over. He smiles, slips his arm from the sling and stretches it. It's stiff, and a bit atrophied from four weeks of lack of use, but soon the damage will be invisible, the little line of dirt between his cast and his skin washed away. He turns his attention to a knot of street performers and I watch his afternoon, stripped of feeling, return to him. The Blue and Gold, the rehearsal, the bland girl in glasses who is always at his elbow, always peering at his face as if expecting something.

The beeper vibrates in my pocket. I rise and locate the phone booth at the corner of the park. It's the AD wanting me uptown. Westie's back from Boston, he tells me, but it's an even bigger disaster now. The artist has sided with Ansel at Columbus Circle, while Fat Albert is laying in for siege on 125th. It's factional warfare. The AD says he needs my help, which is more than I can say of Paul. Under the canopy of elms, he dangles his healed arm from its socket and watches, mouth slightly agape, as a shoeless performer eats fire from a stick. I tap him on the shoulder for goodbye; I know better than to try for a kiss.

Eight

Quincy

2010

The women of Independence House are in the van on our way to the commitment at MCI Framingham. The van smells of hair relaxer and Juicy perfume and the orange Tic Tacs someone's passing around, but we keep the windows closed because we all took so long doing our 'dos and don't want the wind to mess them up. A hot van, on my way to prison: I can't think of a way I'd rather spend my Friday night.

I'm squashed into the second row between two women, Niani and Althea, both of whom still have the hips of their recent pregnancies. Althea, like several other Independence residents, has done time at Framingham and she's entertaining us on the two-hour drive with stories about some of the long-term inmates. I can't stop laughing.

"So this new cellie turns out to be the one that held me up."

"Serious? You recognize her?"

"Naw, I couldn't a picked her out of a lineup five minutes after, but she remembers me. Because the minute I saw that gun, I started calling her *Madam*. Madam. What the fuck? Who says Madam even in normal circumstances? But I see that nine-mil, and it's like we're in *Gone with the Wind*. I start offering helpful suggestions, too."

"You're being robbed and you're trying to be useful," I say.

"Yeah, I point out the pricey necklace, I'm suggesting other places on the block she could hit, showing her the safe."

Marisa shakes her head. "You don't know who you are until you got a gun in your face."

"Now I know," says Althea, "I'm a class-A suck-up."

"I take it back," says Marisa, "we knew that all along."

I'm almost a month in at Quincy. No one thinks I'm part of the club, but it's like a baby in a famine zone. Now that they think I might last, they're willing to invest a little love in me. It's equalizing, desperation and degradation, and how hard it is to climb back out, and you can't be in this place long without recognizing that. I don't have what Emily has, not a full bench, but I'm beginning to catch a hint of what it would be like, having people.

"What about you, Wellesley?" Niani asks me. "You ever done time?"

"She has a friend on the inside," says Marisa. "That's why she's gracing us with her ladyship, but she's never visited. Right?"

"Oh, honey," says Althea. "You got to visit."

I hedge. "We're not really friends."

"What your friend do," Marisa asks, "to get in Framingham? Rob Bloomingdale's?"

Niani laughs. "What do they call it when rich people steal? Embezzlement?"

"Hey," says Althea, "that's what I got sent up for. Worked for a visiting nurse outfit, and I embezzled. I'm high-end for low-end."

"Seriously, Mellie," says Marisa. "What'd your friend do?"

I'm sucking on one of the Tic Tacs, so it takes me a minute to respond. "It was an art crime."

"That can't be past a misdemeanor."

"She white?" says Niani. "You white, you have to murder a granny."

"Naw, it was a painting, yeah? She stole like a Picasso or some shit."

"We're not really friends," I say again. "But, it was forgery."

Marisa laughs. "Now that, you deserve a bid. You got skills; you can do insurance, loans, real estate, and you do a painting?"

Niani shakes her head. "There's one I'd take a copy of. It's got a little white dog in it, this dead bird. I always liked that one. Could your friend copy me that?"

"I saw one once with these little girls? I would hang that on my wall. It's good to look at shit like that. I think, for your brain."

Three of us have phone privileges, and so somehow, for most of the rest of the trip to MCI Framingham, we're passing around images of our favorite paintings and discussing art. Conversation falls off as we come into sight of the gates, then Marisa picks up an earlier thread.

"It seems obvious to say it, Wellesley, but prepare yourself. It can feel normal in there, for a few minutes. Just you talking to another human. But watch out, because something's about to whack you in the gut with a wooden baton."

"Got it," I say, but I'm certain that I don't, that I can't imagine.

"Check it here, see? This scar? That's what they do to you in there."

"Bitch, those are stretch marks."

"Fuck you. This is brutality."

"Well, I got brutality on my thighs, on my ass, and all around where I carried my baby."

They continue, giving each other a hard time, working off the nerves that come from returning, the inevitable anxiety that somehow you'll get stuck inside.

After the encounter with the documentarian, I had squeaked in with two minutes to spare. The taxi hit traffic on 93 and for the next twenty-three minutes, I was sure I'd get discharged. People show up sometimes, moms with trash bags and two-year-olds wedged into doll strollers, just hoping we have room. I am aware, constantly, of the women on the waiting list, of the children for whom our little efficiencies with the in-room laundry unit would be heaven.

Someone had called for me, in the days following, a man, on the Independence payphone, but I was in session.

"This guy's your ex?"

"I don't think so."

"Well, he was sorry like he wants you back. He's all: tell her she was right. I shouldn't have involved her. If he's letting you go, I asked, why's he still calling? You get right, and they start to smell the money on you. Who wouldn't want it? Someone to cook the meals and pay the bills?"

"He's got that, maybe. This old woman he's staying with."

"He says, he's figured it all out. He has something to tell you. But that's a familiar tune. What he's figured out maybe is that he can trade up from this old lady, get a little, along with the meal ticket." says Marisa, "If he's from the life, it's nine out of ten he ain't changed."

Anyway, there are plenty of other things to worry about: Juni's test results from the medical check, for example. My finances, which I know aren't good. In quiet moments, I'll look down at my lap and catch my fingers twitching like they're scribbling on the pages of a book. My thoughts will drift toward the SUV man; where is he searching now? Or I will wonder about the thing in my paperback, whether it's what he wants and what it would mean if he had it; I will think of

Lew, and the sleeper program that perhaps I have promised to awaken—but, only once have I sneaked down in the middle of the night to gaze at the woman pacing back and forth. The documentarian hadn't been lying. I found the link which led me to my name, to Lew's and Valerie Weston's. There were more videos there, art films of Valerie's, but I didn't click through. The view count had reached almost three hundred thousand. Still, when I watched, I could only feel sickness, could not understand what compelled about a woman in her underwear.

In the morning, I told my therapist to lean on the night staff to lock us out of the computers. I didn't want to fall into the hole.

"This is good, I think," she said. "Watching these videos feels like a brain trough for you. You go back, and you go back, but there's not really anything new. At the same time, I'm observing something else here, which is that you are actively avoiding certain lines of inquiry."

"What do you mean?"

"For example, the man who followed you. You were very moved by the fact that he knew your name. It was a kind of proof to you. But, obviously, he could have found your name via this video, correct? As you did, eventually and as this documentarian did as well? You were invested, were you not, in your sense of connection to him, so you avoided that discovery. Now, you have questions about this video. But instead of looking for answers, you just keep watching the clip. Why? Because you answer those questions, and it may prove what you seem already to know: that your feelings about this man may be projections. That his connection to you may be based in your professional, rather than in your personal life. There's an opportunity for remapping here."

"I won't watch," I said.

"Right, I agree. But why not call your boss? Ask him."

I tried to explain about Lew and phones, the landline number in my book, but my therapist laughed at me. "So, try this other woman, the artist. Or track him down. You work in computers. It ought to be easy."

It had not been. Lew's number was unlisted, but I knew his address and was able to back channel to the line, but it had been disconnected. I was somewhat more successful in reaching Valerie, was able to get a message through to her current whereabouts. I didn't know how that worked for inmates, whether she'd receive it, but when we were discussing commitments, where we should go, I cast the deciding vote for MCI Framingham.

There are ways of thinking that are habit for me, circles, back into the trough. But, there might be other ways to pursue my questions such that if I follow them, eventually, the noise in my head will stop repeating. Emily and my therapist think so. They've decided to approve my day pass to go home, but I'm no longer sure that I want it. Or, what I wanted was to open the pages of my paperback and find my man in there, but now it seems clear that whatever is lodged in those pages, whatever secret, it belongs to someone else. To Lew, or to the man in the SUV. I suppose that's a piece of progress. And there are other signs. The drawings in my workbooks, my therapist pointed out, are mostly of Juni these days.

"You know what that says to me?" she asked.

"Please don't say it. Don't say it out loud."

"You might end up one heck of a mother," she said, and she was smiling all the way down to her chin wattles.

Emily is meeting us at the prison. I tried to tell her not to, but she insisted. She's due for one of these anyway, she said. It occurs to me, something in her voice, or maybe just emerging from my own fog of self-pity, to wonder what Emily's actual story is; what drove her to follow me, when I was a pushing a stroller around and around the block, too much of a mess to even go into a meeting, or to show up in my driveway with her teenaged son on a weeknight, what makes her travel two hours to meet me at a prison. I believe it of her—honestly, I do—but it still feels implausible that anyone could be that kind to me without some hidden motive or damage at the base of it.

At the entrance, the guards run you through the metal detector. We leave our handbags in the van, our wallets, but still, I set off the alarm. They have me walk sideways, with my hands over my metal fly. Yet again, the detector pings. Each pass through, I expect they'll wave me on. I'm Mellie, from Wellesley or Brookline or wherever. I've been to college. I'm harmless. But, the guard has me take off my necklace, and then my hair clip, and then go through a fourth time. The sensor trips.

"You got underwire?" Niani asks.

I think. I furtively feel beneath my breasts. "Shit," I say.

"I got you," she tells me, and returns from the desk with a paper bag, nods toward a restroom. We're not prisoners, but most of us once were, and there's a blurry line. As far as the guards care, we're on the wrong side of a crucial divide. I hand over my bagged bra and sidle through the detector once again. This time, I read as clean.

We wait at and then pass through four sets of steel mesh gates, the clicking and the sighing of locks, before we reach the Programs wing. Marisa is trying to explain how meetings operate on the inside, that it's not exactly the same as what I'm used to. Recovery is popular with inmates, regardless of their relationship to sobriety, and they are ecumenical about it so whether we are peddling twelve-step or OneLife, they're on board. There are guards just outside of the room where we'll meet, but there's a diminished level of supervision, the chance to communicate with inmates from other blocks, and coffee. We walk on the left side of the yellow line, and nod as we pass the guards.

"That one," says Althea. "That one is fucking whore."

"Be nice," says Niani. "Make nice."

Emily is already sitting in the front row when we enter Programs. The room serves as a remedial classroom during the day, and has optimistic exhortations stenciled onto poster board on the walls. *Success is the sum of small efforts, repeated day after day. Do it now. Sometimes later becomes never.* The light is not good, or Emily has not been sleeping, because she wears the five years she has on me heavily today. The first group of inmates files in and take seats at the back. Marisa hugs a woman with a white raised scar running from her ear to her chin. Other Independence moms exchange news with neighborhood girls under their breath.

"Her cousin? Naw."

"For real. And the auntie too."

When Emily sees me, she stands, and gives me a small smile, and sits again before I've made it to her side.

"Everything OK?" I sit beside her. The muttering continues behind us.

She musters a better face. "Same old crap. My motherfucker ex sent his sister around to my house, when I was out. She was going on to Leo about how he wants back with me, how it's me won't talk to him."

"Shit," I say.

"Yeah, right? And I have to decide about the hearing. I don't want to testify, but I don't want him out, either. Change addresses, get a new phone number? It's all too close to the bone, waking up in a bed that doesn't feel like yours. I've been through that too many times."

"Maybe he'll mess it up on his own. Someone told me they never give you parole on your first try."

"This is his third."

"See?" I say. "Shows he's no good at it."

She shakes her head. "How are you? No. Let me look." She gives me the once over, nods. "You still could use a haircut, but you look a little more human."

"Stop it," I tell her. "You'll give me a big head."

"How'd it go with—whatever that guy's name was? The audio guy."

"I don't think he's really making a documentary."

"He want to sign you up for the first level of enlightenment?"

"Not exactly; not just." I tell her, about the interview, the documentarian's idea about my stalker and the thief, how he thinks meeting me was a result of his en-version session at OneLife, the Kif-Vesely'e connection.

"So you were there two years ago?"

"I was a mess, Emily, when I came back from LA. I've got bits and pieces. So, maybe. But, this guy's story, it's from when we were kids. It's his deal, not mine. I don't want to get sucked in."

"Thing happened to me once," says Emily. "Guy got fixated, became convinced I was his long-lost sister or something. He's researching me, tailing me. He amasses like evidence. Junior high shit, we worked at the same donut shop, our middle names both start with a *V*. But at a certain point, I start to get convinced. Like, wait. Maybe. Then my mom sets me right: I know how many times I fucking gave birth. Squeezing a kid out of you is not a thing that slips your mind. Your guy, the documentary guy, sounds like it's the same deal as my long-lost brother."

"Yeah, that's kind of where I ended up. The guy from my driveway is fixated on the video. If there are connections, that's how they link."

"What we should talk about is how you broke your word. How you were not supposed to be organizing encounters with this individual."

"I didn't organize—"

"Just so you know. I didn't fail to notice." She shakes her head. "In my experience when people start to mass, start to act all the same and head in the same direction, there's either money or revenge behind it."

"The Green Line, on game day."

"Money and revenge. I'm saying, I don't think this camp thing is anything— some kind of nonsense bouncing between them. This video of your boss's, though, that's a money angle. You know, I went back, watched it again a couple of times?"

"Shouldn't you be talking to your sponsor about this?"

"I'm not watching it like you watch porn, not like to get off. It's just—like why I did again is because I don't actually know what the fuck it is. Like the minute I figure it out, it's something else. So, for example, there's this actual celebrity sex tape, from a few years back."

"How many times have you watched it?"

Emily looks—for someone else you'd say sheepish, but for Emily, you'd have to say, she looks like how apologetic would look on a person who's decided they don't apologize. "Ten. I'd say ten times. To figure it out, though. Anyway, one thing is the bathroom lady video is the same, like identical, to the first thirty seconds of the sex tape. What does that mean? Is that art? I saw where someone said it was art."

I shrug. "Look, it's weird for me," I say. "Knowing what I can pursue, what I'm supposed to leave on the table. You know, I've basically stopped taking notes, and it feels like I let a bad dog out of its cage, and it's just wandering around sniffing things for now."

"You know who that bad dog is, don't you?" A real smile breaks on her face, and it feels good to make her look like that.

"I get all the therapy I need at the House. Don't shrink me. And also, stop watching sex tapes."

Emily releases a short bark, then looks around at the filling room. "Your friend in here, is she coming?"

I shrug. "Wait and see."

"I'll get us some coffee in the meantime." Emily goes over to the table with the sludge coffee. She knows a few of the inmates from her work in the courts and others who'd done stints outside before relapse and reoffense. I watch my shoes, think about the various scuffs on the leather and the fraying of the laces. A voice breaks over the loudspeaker, and inmates from the last block file in. I try to watch, and also not to look like I'm watching as they make their way to the rows behind us. There is a different way of walking in here, low slung hips and loose knees. There are fist bumps and occasional laughter, but as they pass the guards, their baseball-bat length wooden batons, their heads drop and I can't tell one from the other. Still, I remain aware of the bodies behind me, the shuffling and the nose-blowing and the muted chatter. Emily takes her seat at my side as the meeting begins.

"She here yet?"

"I still don't see her."

"Maybe you should talk today, make this trip count."

"And say what? My sobriety is really straining my budget? I'm worried my toddler might not get into an Ivy?"

"How about Monday, then? They'll shed tears for that shit in Brookline."

"I know," I say. "I know. Same rules for me as for everyone else."

"I can't let you keep sliding on it."

There is a rustling and a scraping of chairs, and a bone-thin woman in long, delicate dreadlocks stands up. "Good evening. This is the regular meeting of the

Framingham MCI sober club. I'm Serenna and I'm a drug addict and I'll be the secretary."

"You hear from the doctor?" someone whispers. I look up, but the question isn't for me.

"Yeah," says someone else. "But there's nothing he can do about it."

Emily joins in the recitation of the serenity prayer, and I mumble along after, dropping the *G-d* when I need to. I'm trying. I hope she can see that. I look along my row now, at Marisa, and Emily and the other women from Independence house; I take a sideview of the inmates behind me for whom the place I live would be a haven, and I know I can try more, work harder.

Obviously, this doesn't feel like my scene, but that's exceptional thinking again, that's my giving myself superpowers. I used an illegal substance. I took messed up risks. My half a college degree never really protected me from ending up here. It's luck, probably, and—a point Marisa's made—skin color that has protected me, and neither is anything to congratulate yourself about. It's nothing to act superior on.

Still, I'm keeping my eyes on my lap. I'm thinking it's an easy place to get accidentally in a fight for looking at someone the wrong way.

"Hi," I say. "My name is Mellie and I'm a drug addict." I take a breath. I raise my eyes from the floor to the level of laps. I see Marisa's broad tight waistband, the aqua butterfly ink visible at her hip. I go on. "I started using drugs when I was sixteen years old, and I've been sober for fifty-five days. I have every reason to stay this way, but it means I don't get to leave my life, and that's tricky to get used to."

I'm still not looking up much beyond the circle my shadow casts in the incandescent light, but I can feel Emily breathing beside me. She's surprised. I'm not spilling my guts, obviously, but even this small speech is more than she's used to hearing from me. I guess I'm getting practice in my daily sessions of art therapy, group therapy and normal therapy. Maybe even I can give some credit to the workbooks and guided meditation.

I am better.

A little bit.

Emily leans her shoulder momentarily into my shoulder. I take another breath, a deep one down into my lungs, and let it release slowly. And then we've reached the second row.

The women on either side of me turn, and I do as well. There's Niani, and Althea, Marisa, and the woman with the long scar. Around me, the women rustle and mutter small phrases of understanding, *One day at a time. Keep coming back.*

It works if you work it. They speak and they sweat and they wipe their noses and they ignore me.

Except for one. A skinny woman in a red bandana is watching me. She's bald beneath the head wrap, and which is why I had failed to recognize the woman who is not really my friend. It's Westie. She smiles at me, delighted. The forgery charge had been in LA. She and Lew shared a studio space, though there was more to it than that, and she'd been snared up in his legal troubles. I knew this because I'd been approached as a character witness, an opportunity I'd declined. Ultimately, her Massachusetts relatives had pulled some lawyer trick to have her serve in her home state. If I'd pictured her, in the intervening months, it had been in more of a country club facility, making crab apple jam with Martha Stewart and the other insider traders. If I'd pictured her, it had been as less broken by time.

When we have folded up the chairs and are circulating with our Styrofoam cups of coffee, Westie comes over to me.

"You got my message," I say. "You came."

"I'm not here to have Jesus get me clean."

Looking at her now, I can see that she still has the hair on her head, but it's cut short, and going gray. For so long, Westie looked half her age, and now suddenly she looks twice it. "How is it in here? Can you work at all?"

"Ink and paper. I draw people's kids on their arms so the tattoo artist can use them as a guide. But, you know, supply and demand. This is a place short on amusements. So, I appreciate your coming. Now, let me see if I can guess what brings you here."

"You made a video," I say.

"That is a very funny way of putting it. I made a few videos, but I imagine we're not discussing my entire artistic oeuvre. You seem a bit vague, Mellie. What's up?"

There's a buzzy feeling. "I am sorry," I say. "I feel like there's something you're expecting me to say. Is this about your lawyer, because, I should explain, when he contacted me, I wasn't in a position—"

She waves her hand as if clearing smoke. "I was who they had. I was the conviction they could get. It didn't come down to character." She glances at me again. "Listen, can you hustle up a cigarette for me? From one of your sober compadres over there? I don't want to shock you with how craven I've become, but the aunts cut me off. Delilah has Alzheimer's, so Beatrice keeps having to break it to her again what shame I've brought on the family. Can you imagine? I don't have enough in commissary for a fucking Jolly Rancher. I would kill for a smoke."

"Let me see what I can do."

I tap Emily on the shoulder and she gives me a look, like *you good over there?* I see how rough Westie seems, but I give Emily what I hope is a reassuring nod and bring Westie two cigarettes. She sniffs one, like it's a cigar, her nose all along the paper, then lights it. The tip brightens, deep orange on the inhalation, and then Westie lets out a stream of smoke. The whole process is completed in moments, the lighting itself done in a cupped hand, the matches or whatever invisible.

"Fuuuuuck. It's been like three weeks since I've had any tobacco. There's a ban on smoking going into effect like imminently. I'm going to be a husk, like human jerky, some freeze-dried piece of meat."

"So," I say. "This video," I say. "This woman, in her underwear."

Valerie begins to laugh. Her teeth are still rich-girl teeth, still straight and bleached despite the cigarettes. "This woman? That gorgeous creature is me."

"You?"

She studies me. For a moment, I see the old Westie, the venomous flirtation that was her MO. Then she smiles. "Shit, Mellie. You always kept it together. I did not understand how far things had gone. But you're like my aunt, now, aren't you? Like full on Alzheimer's. People still call it cloud sickness? That would be a terrific painting, I think. Cloud sick. Cloud sickness. What's it like?"

"You ate it. You know."

"I never got that taste of crazy like people do. But, I mean, I guess there's a bottom for each of us, some crappy outcome where we all end up, right? Look at Lew. Two years, and in Federal."

"I think you're working on bad information," I said. "Lew Cohen? He had a terrific legal team, those law enforcement connections. It was going to be time served and probation."

"You left in a hurry. Things shifted around. But, he's out now. I'm not trying to be cryptic. I thought you'd know all this."

"I'm piecing it together."

"Still—" She cracks another big, bitchy smile. "The worst tragedies of your life. People have to break them to you again and again. It's monstrous."

My stomach contracts, like it's absorbing a blow, like the feeling coming without the memory. "Break what to me?"

"You have no idea what it is, actually?"

"It's nothing," I say. "It's just a woman walking back and forth."

"That's my work you're talking about. Your work, too, for that matter." She inhales, blows out a big stream of smoke. "And it's not just one video. You should watch, maybe. It might give you a sense of how things went down in the end."

The first thirty seconds of a sex tape. The missing middle. I start to get itchy, the bug of writing it down burrowing into me. Someone had said something about it, me on the other side of the camera. Who had it been? Anywhere else in the world, you could get a piece of paper, but not here. *How things went down in the end.* The sense memory is of thirst, of an exhausted thirst, and of sand, sand stinging my skin. Of a weeping that lasted until I was as dry as dust. What led me there? Was it something I'd done to someone, or some stupid heartbreak because I loved someone who preferred someone else and left me?

"That's it," she says, studying my face. "You've got something. OK. I'm ready with my guess. This is my guess. It's about my lovely co-star—no? You don't even remember him? But you feel it, right? What does that feel like? You guilty? You mad? You want to get back at me? Look at where I am, Mellie. Look at where you are. Everything turned out pretty nice for you."

The speakers begin to crackle with their unintelligible code. *Eight forty-nine med call maintenance bay six front desk shift operator.*

She smiles. "God, Mellie. You'll see; you were right there with us. Everything vaporized; everything its own shadow burnt into the wall. The release date is coming; the thing is counting down. Even now, all those sweet numbers are being collected. It could hit a half a million, maybe, before those sleepers wake up. And you know what that translates into? Say it's just a hundred per user. Say it's twenty. It's going to be more than twenty. But nothing's going to happen until you do your part. You think it doesn't matter? You think it's none of your business? Check out my other works. I'm huge these days. I'm extremely popular. A question I'd wonder, if I were you. If I'd seen you at the end. How did you deserve to get plucked out of that mess and plopped down in this nice new life? How could you fail to pay that kind of favor back?"

Emily comes to me and puts a supportive arm around my shoulder. I resist.

"What about the end? What other works?"

Then, the two guards are opening the door, the speakers repeating whatever prose is the opposite of cloud speech. *All Call For Mod Seven. Procedure seven. Operation time clear.*

Emily steers me backward, and the inmates form a single file. The speaker continues to emit its nonsense. *All accounted for eight fifty front desk station nine.*

Then Westie, scratching at a patch of white, dried skin beneath the bandana, becomes indistinguishable from the other inmates.

On the two-hour van ride home, I wait while the conversation frays into silence. Around me, the Independence women drift into sleep. *Everything massing in the same direction.* Niani has fallen into my lap, her fingers loosening on her phone, and so I slip it out of her grasp and begin to tap. Now, when I search the headless woman video, there are hundreds of hits, people speculating. It's all a hoax; it's conceptual; it's exploitative; it's a scam; it's only a copy of the real thing. But it's Valerie I'm pursuing here, and after a few clicks, I land on the page of her gallery.

Gallery Schlegel-Heinfer, Los Angeles
Ruin Tape (2008–2010)
Director: Westie (Valerie Weston)
Producer: Lew Cohen

TRT 5 mins

In *Ruin Tape*, Westie interrogates a woman in her studio. The aesthetic makes explicit the editing process. Jump cuts and radical changes in angle highlight the framed nature of the conversation, its incompleteness. The subject of their exchange is a sex tape. At a certain point, the light shifts and the woman is alone, her back to the camera which may be hidden. She turns. In the final frames of the work, we see clearly the woman. Her eye sockets are swollen full; her mouth is a clown ring of raw red pucker. Her cheeks, puffed with fat, are indistinguishable from her chin. There is a buzzing noise, and she is engulfed in a fine peach-colored mist: vaporized.

Other Projects: *West 125* (June 1998), *Bright Big Future* (March 2010), *Found Footage* (release date: May 2010)

There are many reasons I choose not to play the video. The first is that being caught with another resident's possessions is grounds for terminating my stay. The second is that I am in a van of sleeping women who have just returned from a place they would prefer to never visit again. The last thing I want to do is wake them up with a video which may also be a sex tape. In the still image, I can see the woman as described in the gallery notes. She is horrific, inhuman, unrecognizable. I scrutinize the still image for as long as I can bear and then I drift off or I short out again because I am dreaming. I am thumbing through my paperback. The pages are thicker, sealed with old glue. There is something between, thin and hard with irregular edges. I slip my nail between the pages, and lift, but this is a mistake, a terrible mistake. My face begins to swell. My head is being stuffed full, like a laundry bag. The seams at my hairline are tearing.

I jolt up from the van seat. A woman is shaking me. It is ten thirty, eleven, and we've just pulled into the driveway at Quincy Independence. I am fine, my face is fine. I'm awake. I'm awake. I'm awake. We go to the nursery and collect our sleeping bundles, and when I hold Juni's sleeping warmth to my chest, I feel myself again. Juni is almost twenty pounds now, getting harder to carry. The weight in my arms is growing heavier. This is what's real, I think, this girl in my arms, and I let her anchor me, hold me in place until the feeling passes.

Nine

New York City
1993

What have I said already about the cause and frequency of cloud sickness? Most people think of it as a species of withdrawal, though certainly, you can be cloud sick while high. As well, the mechanism of the trigger is also different. It is not about receptors in the brain, not something that kicks in three days after you stop, and then gradually lessens until it's bearable. It's kin, if you will, to the LSD flashback, which is the capacity to reexperience a trip if the user has, for example, a sudden weight loss, chemicals stored in the fat reactivating weeks or years after the original high. It is the capacity of the user to experience hallucination without the ingestion. In cloud, it's not weight loss which sets off sickness, necessarily. In fact, we know very little about what initiates an episode at all. Maybe sex triggers it, or loneliness or exhaustion or experiences which are simply too vivid to be borne.

In cloud sickness, you occupy the initial state of disorientation typical of a high not for minutes, but for hours, or even days. Nothing during this time may be recognizable. Nothing may feel familiar. Words jumble. Even one's own body may feel strange. It may be likened to the state following concussion, wherein the injured party retains her muscle memory, the skills of life, but significance, the sense of history embedded in that knowledge, are missing. As the victim gradually emerges from the state, that significance returns, but imperfectly. It will feel, often, as though memories have been desequenced or that in certain cases a stranger's memories have replaced your own.

As I have discussed, many users take these features of the returned memory as a sign that the world has somehow slipped. Or, rather, that the user has slipped from one world into another, where slightly different things are true. In this view, cloud sickness may be seen as a kind of jet lag, the body metabolizing a new history as it moves from one existence to another. After a few hours or days, the body will integrate these strange memories in with the more familiar ones, until it is no longer possible to tell what we might call the originals from the impostors. Still, the sense of wrongness remains, the sense of terrible, inexplicable loss.

The first time I got cloud sick, I was twenty-one and I'd been clean for four weeks. After that, it was never totally clear. Was I cloud sick or just sickened, just sickened with the thing I was making of myself?

I have taken extension after extension on my residence in the dorms, but tonight campus security is finally kicking me out. I've scraped through my exams with time only to shove my belongings into Hefty bags. All along the hall, the doors hang open, the bare mattresses and full garbage cans gape at me from within. The guy from security keeps stopping on my floor, giving me a look. I'm sweaty and my fingernails are jagged, but I'm done.

Tonight is also Paul's opening. After a two-week delay, the curtain is going up on the revamped production, with Paul still in the lead role. Truth? I'm grateful to have the excuse to miss it, to miss the experience of crafting believable praise to deliver to the cast afterwards. Paul has said tomorrow, Friday, is the real event anyway, with Davos's people coming in, the cast party after. As the audience claps downtown, I struggle to the corner of Broadway with my two suitcases, my backpack and my garbage sacks. Paul delivers his first lines to a house of thirty-five relatives from Queens and Norwalk. I hail a cab to my sublet, a second-floor studio on 109th. It's 1,400 for the whole summer including the futon, a kitchen table, a set of chairs. I need two trips up the stairs to move in, my luggage temporarily stashed on the entryway's filthy hexagonal white tile that is the universal flooring of the Manhattan walkup. For dinner, I eat a Yankee Muffin and then listen to the passing traffic, the occasional pulse of a car horn. It's been four weeks since Paul arrived, I think. I am exhausted, but I want to write things. I want to note things down in the paperback I carry. I write sex → need → everything else → sex. As I drift off, pencil dropping to floor, I think, I have to get more of this down or I'll forget it.

I wake. I am lying on a bare mattress. The empty room fills with red flash. The red flash is gone. My chest aches, my throat. For minutes, I have absolutely no idea who I am, where I am. I am a round clown. I need a downtown. I wear a weed gown. I hurt loud. I feed proud. Clap greed. Power down. I heed crowns. I need cloud. I need cloud. I need cloud.

The sky lightens. The muezzin calls. I remember a person called Mellie. She is 3.05 GPA and she is 20/650 vision and she is West 109. She is not a person, really. She is not me. I am wearing parts of someone else, some of her toes and some of her elbows and we need cloud.

I feel along the wall for the unfamiliar light switches, find my keys in the artificial light. There are garbage bags but no garbage can, phone jacks but no phones, a door but no keys. I need cloud. Outside, it is suddenly cool, and the pavement is dark with rain. There has been a storm. The gutters run with brown water. Filth collects at the drains. I have a vague recollection of restraint, some period of trying not to do something, of struggling to resist my hunger. Why? There's nothing wrong with cloud; cloud washes everything clean.

The street is almost empty, except for a shadow slumped in a doorway, a vagrant or a pile of shirts. It shimmers, that pile, familiar and beckoning, but it is just rags and I need cloud. There is a fine gravel of glass and plastic caps littering the sidewalk, the crushed vials left by addict traffic. The guy running for mayor, I remember, wants to clean all of this up, wants to make New York into Disney. But no one can clean up New York; New York is filthy in all its cracks, is veined with dirt and debris.

I find a corner phone booth. The plastic receiver is unscrewed, but it still works. Nancy, I think. I should call Nancy. But where is she? She is drinking tequila in the Dean's office. She's on a train to California. She is coming to opening night. I can't make it make sense. A little cloud will put me right. I phone the number, and I get the pager on the first try. My cloud guy will call. All I have to do is wait. Light is coming and you can smell the bagels boiling on 125th Street. Soon, any minute, the city will wake from its slumber and begin to stir around me, but still, everything is quiet.

And then the pile of shirts stands. It is exactly like a child's nightmare, like what you imagine will happen if the shapes in your darkened room turn out to be alive. I think, it's true; I fell asleep and woke up somewhere else where clothing hides monsters. The phone begins to ring, but I am running.

I let my feet make the decisions, move on instinct, fast. The blocks between Broadway and CPW are deserted. Steps match my steps. They sound human, but

I am convinced it is a giant rat, a creature made of all the rats from rat rock, a creature escaped from *The Nutcracker*. I measure the shadow on the pavement beside me. Human size, rat-face. Where are the cars? Where are the people? Open the doors and look at all the steeples. Corner, now, the creature reaches me. It grabs my arm, wheels me around.

It is human, a human I know.

"You look afraid," says Mr. Boyfriend. "No need to be afraid." Something is wrong with his mouth.

"Wonder you allowing me," I say. "Act on some kind of spy?"

"Spying?" he asks. "I'm just trying to talk to you. I'm just waiting for you to ever call me the fuck back." I think of the knocking on my dorm door. I think of the missed telephone calls. I think of the piles of opened envelopes I found on his desk.

"Stop throwing me." I struggle, but he has me fast, presses my arm against my back with his one hand and holds tight to my free wrist. When will it be morning? Where is everyone?

There is new scar tissue where his lips join.

"Waddle over your face?" I say.

"This?" His eyes are shallow and green as a tornado sky. "What's weird is how you never asked much about my family."

"Four parents under grave," I said. "Should pain grapple—"

"I mean the rest of my family. The Jersey family. Big family, cousins and uncles all that shit. You never asked."

"Let me grow," I say. "I need to grow."

"I'm walking you. Where we headed? The B? You wanna visit your pansy fuck-buddy? That who you were waiting on at the phone?"

"Morning flower. Exchange vows later."

We have reached CPW, and Mr. Boyfriend pushes me up against an electrical box, his crotch shifted into me, my back grinding against the cool metal.

"You sound like one of those junkies," says Mr. Boyfriend. "Like a real junkie. Which is what they suggest about you, my family. You think they don't care about me, but they keep interested. In my financial well-being, in my 'am I leading a full and productive life'?"

"It's not like a pure sentiment. It's not entirely just fraternal feeling. Certain funds are meant to be reinvested. It happens at the accountant level. I don't concern myself with the details. But these other people do."

Mr. Boyfriend works his arm behind me and grasps my wrist then pulls it back and pins it painfully to my opposite hip.

"Gelt," I choke. "Gelt me."

Mr. Boyfriend pushes me in front of him, and we're walking. "This cousin of mine, I don't follow the family politics, but he came to see me last week, ostensibly over that factory in the Chernobyl exclusion zone." The scar on Mr. Boyfriend's mouth is fresh enough that it tears open as he grimaces, a little blood wetly swelling in the seam.

"Sasha—we're not close. He's into dogfighting, which although I may not be museum-cultured like you, not Pluto and Aristocraces, is not really my line. But he raises pits mean; teaches them to make their brothers into meat. He drives his Eldorado in to see me, and understand, Sasha hates the city, hates Manhattan people. Thinks I'm crazy to live here. The girls, for example, are tramps. But he brings his prize dog last weekend, for a visit. Because out of concern. In case I might be getting in over my head."

Now, I can see the outline of a jaw mark circling his entire mouth, as if the dog had gripped him in a tender kiss.

"It's not the cash, Mellie. Though that adds up. It adds up to just over eight grand, now you've given me time to do the math. In the scheme of things, that is not that much. Is an amount I could forgive you. I want to forgive you. But my family has a thing about respect, about self-respect. Getting taken by a girl who is fucking some faggot, that's hard to explain to my people. And, being honest here, it's hard to explain to myself. So, I'm interested in your opinion, Mellie. Do I tell my cousin about your new boyfriend? Is this information you'd like me to be sharing?"

He loosens his grip slightly, to lean back and assess my face. Far, far away, a single yellow cab speeds toward me, its light signaling available. I wait. I imagine I am a piece of scenery in a video production, that I am the studio on 125th. I wait until the moment sharpens, until I am on the edge of the razor, and then I wrench my hand free, hailing.

The cab swerves across the empty lanes.

"You bitch," says my boyfriend, says the man from whom I have stolen. "You fucking bitch, I'm coming after you."

But seeing the cabbie, a remarkably big Trinidadian man, my boyfriend hesitates, and I am gifted at time. My timing is perfect and I run, and the door opens and Mr. Boyfriend jerks into action too late and I am sucked into the sphere of dispatcher static and Hot 97, the safe smell of air freshener.

"Pull the door close," says Bill Johnson, medallion number 4567. "Where you heading, girl?"

"Round frown," I tell him. I shake my head to clear it, and the adrenaline, the passage of time, the mystery of cloud sickness, it passes. "Downtown. 4th between 2nd and Broadway."

"You like jazz?" asks Bill Johnson. "You listen to hip-hop?"

Mr. Boyfriend is a block away now, a block and a half. I imagine him scoring his own face, practicing the story. This is one trouble with cloud sickness, how you lose your grip on what's actual. But then I think of his black and white house, of his trouble with his gold painting, and I realize he doesn't have a lie in him, that the only kind of story he knows is one that's actually happened.

Ten

Roslindale
2010

After the encounter at MCI Framingham, I considered cancelling my trip to Roslindale. I explained it to my therapist like this: there were these two old junkies, used together for something like forty years. Opioids, in this case. One day, they got some bad stuff, or accidentally OD'd. They were on this street, this busy street, and they were dying. The woman was dying on the ground, knees bent, mouth open to the sidewalk, and some part of her, her thighs, were trying to keep her alive. They were twitching. That was all that was left of her will to live: a twitch in her thighs. The man, her partner of forty years, was hanging off the bench, drooping, then jerking awake, then drooping, until he too slid off and faceplanted. The thing is, to onlookers, it was funny. They were shooting it, on video, instead of calling the ambulance. They were uploading it for strangers to laugh at. The worst tragedy of these people's lives, and it would be viewed again and again. In the end, they both got clean. Separate facilities, a thousand miles apart. This is a true story, I told my therapist. This actually happened.

"Your point is humiliation?" she asked. "Mellie, you don't even know if the woman in *Ruin Tape* is you."

I shook my head. "My point is, they never saw each other again. The man and the woman survived forty years of junkie life together, but to get clean, they had to end it. This thing, Valerie's movie, it's technically two years old. Is it my actual face? The woman's so messed up you can't really tell, but I know that face. It might as well be mine. And not back then, in LA. It's me five weeks ago, licking dirty paper in my garage. I can't ever meet that woman again."

"That's cloud talking. That's why you took cloud, to leave yourself behind." She looked at me. "You don't really get to do that, in life."

"Listen," I said. "You want me to rely on my judgment, to remap. There are things worth pursuing, and things that turn into obsessions. I'm saying this is the latter territory."

"Acknowledged," said my shrink. "Like how you're staying off the computer, avoiding falling into that. I think that's healthy. But a place like Independence can be its own loop. Step out. You might be surprised, what you can handle. You might be underestimating yourself."

"And," I'd said. "You might be overestimating me."

Then, the morning of my release—this morning—something happened to change my mind. Now, all of a sudden, and completely, everything looks different, and so here I am in the Independence Van, heading home for the first time in five weeks. Emily's Focus is in the shop, and my car is still in my garage, so we're getting the guy to drive us. This is the season when the world becomes pink and white. Outside, it's a gorgeous spring day and we've cranked down the window and turned up the light rock. I'm smiling and for once I'm not faking.

The thing that happened this morning was I got the results of Juni's medical. The breathing issue was a consequence of lingering bronchitis. Now she's on liquid antibiotics and symptoms should clear up in a couple of days. She's OK. She's going to be OK. I get that this is not a ringing endorsement of my parenting, that the bronchitis is a condition I failed to treat, but she'll recover, and it's a reprieve I couldn't have earned, a commutation of a sentence I didn't know how to bear. I was standing there, with the medical report in my hand, and I couldn't believe it. Meanwhile, the day attendant was gushing at me. This new thing with sorting Juni was doing, how actually pretty advanced it was, how it was more of a three-year-old skill. Of course, sorting was what my forbears did in their sweatshops. It's not higher-level math or baby engineering, but still. I am not a mother used to hearing her child praised.

Juni is healthy. I have heard stories like this from other addicts. It's tangled up in the G-d stuff for them; they use the language of miracles. Emily has said, even if you don't believe, you're going to get socked with one. And here it is, miraculously. In recovery, they come, these things you don't dare to hope for. They come even for people like me. Suddenly, I can imagine us going home for good, just a mother and her healthy baby. Suddenly, I can begin to imagine life after. The smile is real.

Emily and I turn up the volume on the easy listening. The van guy is a former postman turned meth head who used to dump his mailbag in the woods behind his house in order to spend his shifts getting high and so he's cool with Emily smoking her New Hampshire cigarettes, doesn't care what we play on the radio, even if he is more of a metal guy. I'm a New Englander who hates winter, a freckled Jew who loves the sun, and Emily is a Dorchester blonde, and we all sing along. This glorious day, this dear friend, each breath my baby girl takes. Everything is miraculous.

The van driver pulls in front of my house. The garage door is stuck half-open, just as I left it. The pavement is littered with petals and everywhere but my own neglected lot, the neighborhood sparkles with the efforts of human industry. The driver cuts the engine, and hands me my dead phone and charger in a baggie, and begins to fill out the drop-off paperwork. In the sudden silence, something passes over Emily's face, and I recall she's nursing her own troubles.

"How's Leo?" I ask Emily.

She shrugs. "Shitty."

"You decide if you're testifying?"

Emily shakes her head. "You think I'm chickenshit?"

"No. I'm surprised, is all."

"It's not about backing down from a fight," she tells me. "I just can't ever be in a room with him again. Not ever."

"So? What do you think they'll do?"

"I don't know. They're deliberating."

"This very moment?"

She nods. "One of my contacts at the court says he lawyered up big time. Fucking Irish families. His dozen cousins chipped in, got him some 10,000-dollar barracuda."

"Holy shit."

"Yeah, shit is right. I don't know. They'd put an anklet on him; an alarm supposedly goes off if he's within a 1000 feet of me or Leo, but I'd rather him in prison. Don't you think crazy is a little bit like smart at the outer edges? My ex is no genius, and still, he always managed to hunt me down."

The van driver is waiting for us. When it's Emily's turn to sign, he says something low to her, and she gives him a faint smile. Then he pulls away, and we find ourselves among the shin-high weeds. Emily steps between the abandoned garbage cans which still block the garage.

"Help me get these in," she says. She holds out the keys she'd confiscated from me a month earlier.

I have not yet allowed myself to take in the house, and as I turn, I gaze at the uneven tufts of grass, the brown daffodil stems, and scatter of uncollected mail, something in my chest contracts.

"I get it," says Emily. "The garage is the addict mommy's refuge. When I was still with Leo's father, we had one, and I'd go out there with the baby monitor and eat cloud until I couldn't remember what street I lived on. I acknowledge your feelings, honey, now get over yourself and put some muscle into it."

I take the keys. Lawn sprinklers tick. Birds chirp and flutter. The garage door sticks, grinds, and then opens to allow us inside. A hundred years have passed in the last thirty days. So much life sleeps within; so many bad old habits could push in like a splinter.

"That woman I connected with at Framingham," I say. "She's no one I trust. I mean, she'd say whatever to get a reaction, but Emily, it's messing with me. I'm trying to stay put, but the current just gets stronger and stronger. Is this what it's going to be like? I'm just supposed to stand here and let it all rush around me?"

Emily hoists the last garbage can. "You know, I was the one put my Leo's dad in prison, right?"

I nod. I've heard Emily's story at meetings, and other bits have dribbled out in our sponsoring sessions, but I haven't dug into the details. Maybe I should have. Maybe I should make it my business to ask.

"My regret, right, my thing I was always wanting to go back and undo, was never that. Or, it was related, but not like regret for locking him up. Shit fucker deserved it. Deserves it still, lawyer notwithstanding. Naw, what gives me that aspirin thing, bitter, in my mouth, wishing I could go back and change it all, is that I waited too long. If I was going to do it anyway, get my own son's father sent up, file the protective order, go through all that, why not save Leo the scenes that came first, the times he found me bruised and hungover, the things his friends said when they saw me with a black eye, the times the man I loved and defended raised a hand to my sweet baby boy. That's my cross, you know? Those years, before I found my strength."

"Yeah," I say, thinking of Juni's cough, of my enormous luck.

"I didn't get clean instantly, after they put him behind bars. I stayed high for a while after. Loneliness, which I know you know about, was part of it, but there's a thing I need to tell you, Mellie. It happened one night. I was just high as Jesus after the Resurrection; I went into Leo's room and he wasn't there. It was another kid lying in his bed. No scar where he'd fallen on the smashed bottle. No indentation at the side of his head, where the doctor had to pull him with a forceps because I was too fucked up to push when he was born. Mellie, it was the son I would have had. If I'd done the right thing all along."

"Do you have any fucking clue? I like my Leo, my damaged Leo, the stupid little shit who curses too much, and won't do his homework, and screams at his nightmares, and fails his Paul Revere quiz. But. But. What it was like to see the whole story, laid out there, the impact of my own idiot choices. This perfect kid, how he would have been if I'd never gotten high. There are things we recognize, Mellie. We recognize them deeply, even if they are strange to us. Of course, I did what you do, what junkies do when they have too much feeling. I ate cloud. In the morning, it was regular old Leo, bottle scar, forceps head, bad fucking attitude and worse hygiene. My kid."

"I didn't know," I say.

"What's there to know? In normal terms, nothing happened. My point is, Mellie. Here's my point, the likely world, what we see on cloud—obviously, do what your shrink tells you. Do a curriculum, go on a field trip, remap the circuitry. Fine. What they do with you at Independence House, follow along—but maybe don't totally fucking buy into it. I'm sorry, I know it's the opposite of what I usually tell you, but Mellie, this is important."

I'm disconcerted by the sudden disclosures. Her ex is weighing on her, obviously. Which doesn't mean she isn't sincere.

"OK," I say. "Check."

"Mellie, that's how I got clean. For real. That perfect Leo lying in the bed. Did it actually happen? Did it not happen? That's not the point. It happened for me, and it's part of who I've become, how I've become who I've become."

"I hear you," I say. I'm trying to listen.

"There is truth there. That's the—shit—it's the only thing that makes my life more than a big ball of waste. That woman, the artist, she doesn't sound like a reliable witness. Take it with a grain. But these videos, I mean. That cloud woman in the tape? I think you should watch it. It could be like me, and my perfect Leo. We get truth back when we get sick, and being sober, honey, it helps you get the message."

For the first time since we've known each other, I can pierce the foil of her solid present and see clearly into her junkie past, can glimpse why she might have cornered the pathetic mom who was pushing a stroller endlessly around a block, why Emily might have been the one to drag that mother in to her very first meeting. She is shakier than I have seen her look, more wild.

"Hey," I say. "I'm here. If you need anything."

"You?" she says, but she smiles. "I know you are. And someday, when you're not falling into your own hole every second, maybe I will."

There's a moment, one which I will recall later, where we recognize something in each other. The thing of her sobriety, of her being my sponsor, drops away, and I feel like some other Mellie, one who could be leaned on, relied on, who occasionally could make things better instead of worse.

"Count on it," I say.

"I will. You're doing great. And Juni, seriously. She's grown about two sizes since you've moved in. You've got to be proud."

"I am," I say. And the weird intensity seems to lift; we are not natives to sentiment, and we dwell there only briefly before our Boston-bred aversion forces us to move along.

My lawn is shaggy, green shoots pressing through last fall's unraked leaves. As I step onto the sidewalk, the woman next door sticks her head out. I have been aware, as Emily and I have moved between the sidewalk and the garage, of a certain nosy rustling of curtains and breath-gathering on the neighbor window glass.

Emily secures the last garbage can. Lining my walk, there are rubber-banded circulars advertising faded pink Easter hams. Mail spills from my box. My neighbor emerges onto her stoop. She's in flannel pajama bottoms with what appears to cupcakes, has her hair in a hairnet. One hand holds a scrub brush.

"I thought that was you," she says.

"Here I am," I tell her. "Still myself."

"How was Aruba? I didn't think it was a big enough island to stay on more than a week. We thought you'd pulled a runner."

"Sorry. I'm so sorry."

"Death in the family," Emily stage-whispers as she secures the remaining trash bin. "Colon cancer."

"You know," says the neighbor. "Robbers case neighborhoods for houses like yours. All the neglect. It's like an invitation."

"I'll look into it," I say, which I've found is a catch-all.

"I have a brother-in-law. Does property management. You might not realize, but an uninhabited property, in a storm, what could happen is—"

Emily and I duck under the eaves of the porch to shelter from the volley of her suburban concerns.

"It takes a village," I call.

"Many hands move mountains," yells Emily.

We muffle our laughter as we gather up the envelopes from my steps.

"A raccoon has been trying to get into your cellar," the woman hollers, thereby proving she stays up all night just monitoring my house for fault. I am on the side of the raccoon. Though, of course, my neighbor is right. It's time to clear the downspouts, to plant the garden, to lay the mulch, but I have never been good for these things. I have never been the sort who ought to own a house, and yet I do. For years, I hid the money Lew paid me in shoeboxes. I know now you can't buy a home with shoebox cash. Lew had fixed it for me in some way I'd remained willfully ignorant of. Laundering was probably involved, perhaps the invention for me of a credit history. I've been mulling what Valerie said at the commitment, and I have to conclude I have my own missing middle. Something between the conversation I had with Lew while we watched his house burn, and my arrival back East, the towering pines where I'd dropped my bus ticket have been blurred by deliberate blindness. There had been bad people in LA, and we had been involved with bad things, and my idea, that Lew would wave a lawyer at it and everything would fix itself, is another example of junkie solipsism. There are distinct, particular questions I have not investigated. Something had happened, at the end. There is a sense memory of exhausted thirst, and of sand, sand stinging my skin. Of a weeping that lasted until I was as dry as dust. There was someone I'd left behind. Someone in particular. Then, I was beneath the tall pines. There is a mismatch here, how I'd been dropped into a better life while everyone else had stayed and paid the price. How could you fail to pay that kind of favor back?

I collect the bright red of the overdue envelopes, the third and fourth notices. It was possible, at Independence, to feel as though the world was on hold, but it hasn't stopped while I've been gone. At the end of the weekend—in three days' time—the countdown will run out. The *Found Footage* is due to drop. I had planned to wait it out, let it appear or not appear, but now I see that I may have a stake in the outcome, that I have a part in the missing middle. I had been picked up out of a bad place and dropped into one with a future. But there are pieces of the old life that follow me, and some I have left too long unattended. Deliberately avoided, my therapist would say. It is useful, sometimes, to push worries aside, but you must return to them in time. A woman with a home, a healthy little girl, she cannot hide out forever. I fish out my key over my neighbor's continued scoldings.

"You look scared," says Emily. "Are you scared?"

"Yes," I say and open the door.

"Listen," says Emily. "You know I'm here for support. I'm not going to scrub your tile or pay your electric bill, but if that thing trips you out. If you get nerves. I'm right here."

The neighbor, from her side of the fence, still tracks after us even as we move into the house. As I open windows against the mustiness that has gathered in my absence, I can hear her continuing to call. "It might not have been a raccoon," she says. "Your boyfriend? Meaty guy with the weird hands? Works out a lot? Is that your boyfriend? I've seen him here, too." Her head bobs along on the far side of her hedge.

Emily finds the sliding glass doors off the white-carpeted living room, looks out onto my little deck, its inviting Adirondack lounger. "I'll be on the patio," she says. "But just call."

I nod, watch her settle herself out back, and take out the flashcards she's made herself for the CPA exam. The red light on my landline blinks. There have been calls, a hundred and seven calls. I press *play*.

Blank, they're like blanks—empty audio with a diabetic huff at the back of them, a silence like a string of question marks and then—

"Hello? Mellie? I've had time to think, and—can't thank you enough—kind of a breakthrough—something I think I should—urgent, otherwise, I wouldn't call. Please call. I know I can't ask for you to—something you need to know." I scrawl a few lines and then stop. It's not the documentarian I'm afraid of. I delete the messages and head to the second floor.

Climbing the pale, carpeted stairs, I observe the stain of Juni's mishap, the dried dribble of regurgitated ketchup. I thought I was doing well, taking her on those long white-knuckle strolls, chewing the inside of my mouth, dying every second to get high. You tell yourself, she's only a baby; you tell yourself everyone screws up sometimes. But there are some mistakes that do not rub out. Still, it's not stains on the carpet that scare me.

Alone at home, with a small child, every rustle, every sudden wakening is a blow. Juni was just barely past a newborn when I took this place. I didn't have any childcare, and I didn't know how you got it, but the baby slept constantly and I thought I would work around her. I'd been alone so much of my life, it seemed I'd be less lonely with a drowsing baby than I'd been before, so I'd put her down and wait for word of the job I'd promised to do. Was I waiting on Lew? Now I return to that feeling, I find something else inside of it, something more like dread. There was much I might have noticed, then, that I did not attend to.

"So shoot me," Lew is fond of saying, and he's not kidding. He is a man who courts violence, who maybe prefers it to more ordinary forms of human interaction. "Come sit by me, Mellie," he'd tell me, patting the chair beside him with a greasy hand. "Come keep an old man company," and I would. He's like a father figure, like as in Darth Vader is a father figure or Fagin or, I don't know, from Plath. I thought, in those months I spent waiting, Lew was punishing me. But I can see now that that is loser thinking, deluded thinking.

I remember the endless journey in a Greyhound bus. I remember an interval beneath the pine trees, cabins in the distance. I had come to do a thing, but some warning, a red wall between me and it, had intervened, something had sent me here instead.

Through the upstairs window, I can see Emily settling herself into my red Adirondack chair, beginning to review the flashcards in advance of her CPA exam this week.

One criterion for a capital lease is that the term of the lease must equal a minimum percentage of the leased property's economic life at the inception of the lease. The minimum percentage is:

   A: *75%*
   B: *41%*
   C: *50%*
   D: *90%*

The sun is bright, the little walled space of my patio pleasant and private, and Emily must be trying to think her way into the future, to think about getting past the crap with Leo's dad and the encroaching exam and finally to a place where she might begin to acquire some of the good things I have here. She's not above it, a certain petty jealousy for all I've been given without deserving it. I am on the second floor where the air is sour, the standing water in the sinks, the forgotten garbage cans in the bathrooms with their rank human waste, the full diaper pails. But it is not the stink that scares me.

I try to hang onto the feeling from the van, singing and blossoms and the news about Juni but something grim has settled inside me. I remove my phone from its Ziploc and plug it in to charge. Text after text, lines and lines of question marks from the burner phone. As I enter the study, a sense of disturbance visits me. Here and there, a film cell, a theater ticket, a beeper number written in my adolescent hand, have drifted to the carpet. The scatter reminds me of cloud paper, the floor of my car, the mornings-after after mornings-after that had been my life for so many years. But it isn't cloud that scares me.

My paperback, where I have kept my life, is on my desk. It's a lunatic object, the kind of thing you'd recover from the serial bomber's cabin, its spine duct-taped, its pages lacquered with layers of glue. I think of the documentarian's map, of the drawer where Emily collects trinkets from another life. Maybe we all have them, these illegible keys to a past we'll never recover. Perhaps these repositories are not always keys, but are sometimes the locked vaults themselves, the things within meant to remain. As such, they fail. Things are always falling out. This scattering on the floor may be random. Some window may have been left open. Perhaps there really was a raccoon. Maybe nothing has yet escaped. These things might be true, but as I place my hand on the tattered cover, my sense of disturbance deepens.

Someone has been here, but it's not the stranger I'm afraid of.

I sit, tap a few keys on the keyboard, and the computer hums to life. There is a small object protruding from the hard drive, a new file sitting on the crowded desktop. For encryption purposes, Lew relied on a system of onion routing which ricocheted his data through volunteer servers, Azerbaijan to Cleveland to Quito to Dakar. Now, the signal begins to travel. Valerie Weston, her gorgeous body, begins to walk back and forth. *Don't talk to me like I'm some animal*, she says in her throaty smoker's voice. I let her pace, in the background. The nausea is there, fainter now, but more recognizable. I locate the shadow of the boom, momentarily appearing on a tile. I hear a muffled cough from off camera, observe the pantomime of the actress washing her hands in a dummy sink. Does it fascinate? I understand what Emily has been describing, that this is a film which changes as you look at it, is chimera. But it is too familiar, too intimate, to enrapture me. Some part of me knows what is coming next.

My fingers call up *Ruin Tape*. I have practiced deliberate blindness, but I think of Emily and her perfect Leo, the messages sent in our illness which our sobriety might allow us to read. There are things it is time to know, and this is what I'm afraid of.

Peach dust. She is different, in motion, from her still image: monstrous, but something else as well. I zoom in, absorb the bruises on her exposed skin, her stained clothes. This is a woman who has forgotten her body, whose body she drags around with her. In cloud, we are easy. She is not easy. For the first few frames, she faces away from the hidden camera. She makes tiny, precise gestures on the workbench. A brush stroke, the turning of a page. If you did not know what you were looking for, you would have no idea what these motions mean. But now I see her replace the cap on a pot of rubber cement. Carefully, carefully, she is sealing a tiny object between the pages of a book.

She turns. I must hold myself in place to look at her. Her face is not a human's face. The tissue beneath the surface is so inflamed that the skin at her hairline has begun to rupture. Under her glasses her eyes are like boiled eggs, but the slit that reveals the pupils gleams with purpose. She is me. It's no dream, no metaphor. Her mouth is a puncture in the risen dough of her face, but my mouth forms the same grim line. I know she is thinking about the thing she has sealed into the book. She is thinking she should have destroyed it, but that she lacked the strength. This thing, it tells the story of how she was ruined, and she cannot ruin that thing. So, instead, it must remain inside, always. This is the ending she has scripted. A woman destroyed, she holds her splitting self apart to make this argument. This thing will still exist, but it will never be released.

Data travels. Dakar links to Kuala Lumpur. Kuala Lumpur links to Brussels, Brussels to Bruges, Bruges to Ostend.

The peach dust rises, and slowly the woman fades into it. This is what cloud does to us. It lessens us, and lessens us, until we fade into a single dimension. She is detestable, but I find I do not detest her. I owe the feeling which surfaces in me to Emily, waiting below on the deck. I owe it to the driver of the van with his dumped postal sack, and to Niani and Althea and Marisa's five-year-old; I owe it to the Uno's crew and I owe it to Juni, her lungs filling with clean air: because of what I have absorbed from them, this unexpected feeling rises in me. It's a feeling like I have for the newcomers at the meeting, booze still on their breath, arms scabbed, stinking of their rising hunger. *You'll make it*, I think. *You'll make it.* The numbers aren't on anyone's side, but in the moment, I will believe it of them anyway.

So now I say it to the woman in the video. *You'll make* it, I tell myself. *Even if you can't see it now, someday, you'll be able to take this thing out again.* Now, it's up to me to steer this thing as best I can. My fingers find the sealed pages in my book. My fingernail slips in too easily. The pages barely crack as I open them. The thing is gone. Someone has removed it. Despair beckoning, I read its imprint—hard and small, the size and thickness of a penny. Right angles, or almost. On one side, I can see the impression of its circuitry, the toothed protrusions. And yet—something, something I've seen tells me it is not too late.

I shift my attention to the woman walking back and forth. The counter on the screen is still ticking down. Twenty-six hours, thirteen minutes.

The small protrusion from my hard drive. It's a chip reader. My intruder has left it behind. Why has it been left here? What does it mean?

Beneath the sea, the signal travels via fiber optic cable. Port of Boston. Dudley Square. The signal travels down my block. The new window on my desktop responds. They are speaking to each other, my machine and this video. They have found something in each other they know.

The open browser windows shift into alignment. The Valerie Weston video slides to the left side of the screen. The first thirty seconds. The beginning. A hand reaches for the waistband of the panties and the image stills.

The swollen woman appears to her right. What happened in the end.

Between them is a blank space. The missing middle.

Click yes to continue?

I tap a key.

There is just one frame more in the headless woman video before the malicious program begins to worm into my hard drive. The wrist, flicking upward as the waistband releases. The hand at the waistband, the hand at the SUV window: just a bit too girlish to be cool. He, Apollo Blue, is about to enter the frame. The man in the video, the man in my driveway. I make the match, and this time I do not resist it. Prince cigarette, his skin against my skin, his body gold in the light. My man, whenever he came from. Mine.

Between Apollo and the swollen woman, the title of the missing part inserts itself. *Found Footage.* The coming attraction. The countdown. How we got from there to here.

Something folds. Pixels collect, align. It is him I am waiting for, Apollo. I wait for him to step into the waiting frame, to tell me the terrible story. Colors flash. Vertical bars appear and stretch. For an instant, something almost materializes—a bed, two figures—and then it is decaying into digits. They seem to tumble and fall toward the edges of the window; the code sings to me, as in a cloud high. I know it. Not images but code.

The logic I am inside is the logic of trap, of things cinching in. I jog the mouse button. I give the monitor a slap.

The Seychelles portal opens. The link awaits, as before, but the instructions below have changed. *We're here. We've arrived. Where are you? And where is the thing you have?*

Panicked, I yank the card reader from the port, and perhaps just in time. My screen goes black.

From far away, I hear a phone ringing. Emily's voice lifts through the open window, a rising tone signaling concern. The slant acoustics, my fog, I receive her message as if it ricochets through Azerbaijan.

As if at a delay, my own phone begins to ring. The string of question mark texts lights up. The burner phone is calling. I pick up.

"Hello, Amelia." His voice is gummy; his throat rumbles with cough. I hear the exhalation of a cigarette smoke. "We have a problem we need to discuss."

"Apollo?" I say.

"Not yet, lady honey. Not quite. But you can help me with that."

"You were here," I say. "You saw the file."

"I thought that was it, lady honey. But it's just numbers on a screen."

"I know who has it," I say. "There's still time."

All the windows on the bottom floor are open, and I can hear Emily speaking. She says *verdict* and *release* and *Leo* and *home*.

"I can get a ride," she says. "Just don't let him out of your sight. Mellie? Are you there? I need a ride."

Over the line, there is a strange doubling. The sound of a car engine. It repeats.

"You know," says the man on the phone. "You know who has it. But do you know how to find him?"

Slow. I am slow as I descend the stairs, dazed. "I know who has it," I say. "But I'm not sure—"

"You've been there," he coaxes. "After it all went down."

Inside the garage, the light is dim, the air yellow through the dusty portals. I see Emily's head bobbing as she opens the gate from the patio and begins to move toward the front of the house.

"There are tall pines. There are tall pines, by a lake shore. Cabins in the distance."

"Mellie?" calls Emily again. "Mellie?"

"Right here," I say, or try to say. My voice is so slow, so low.

"I've got the map right here. That narrows it down," says the man. I hear the rustling of paper. "But still, I'm going to need insurance, lady honey. I think I'm going to have to take you with me."

A car pulls into the driveway. An SUV. A door slams.

The figure through the dusty glass might be anyone's, but his hand is the same. The feeling returns. Molasses and campfire. My armaments, all the weak wisdom I've collected, every little bundle I've made of desires—tremble. Then, as his gaze passes over the garage windows, his brow furrowed, his face flashing uncertainty, I realize he doesn't know my face either.

And now is when the bad thing begins. He turns away from me as Emily steps into the driveway.

She asks: "Where's the other guy? Where's the van?"

I am in motion. I fumble the garage door opener, then punch the button, but it glitches or I am doing it wrong, and the door doesn't lift. The gears grind and whine. I try again. I smell cigarette smoke. I press the button again.

My neighbor calls out. "It's him. He's come."

Inch by inch, the windows disappear into the garage roof, and then I can see underneath, the bottom of a black SUV, the plate not yet visible. I drop to the ground and begin to roll toward the maddening lift gate, its slow inches. Everything is going wrong. I see feet moving, Emily's and the man's, before they pass behind the high hedges. Four inches, five. It grinds. I push at the metal, and wedge myself beneath.

"Four lakes," he says. "Four campsites, four lakes. You think we can cover that in twenty-six hours?"

"What on earth are you talking about?" Emily stops in front of him.

"I'm done with you playing dumb," he says.

A fist closes around a handful of her shirt, her blue t-shirt. Emily folds into herself, shielding her face from some threat. It is a posture I can see she has learned well. In the sunlight now, I stand. He drags her toward the SUV.

"Help me," she calls. "For God's sake, help me."

"Somewhere in there, I know you know. I told you to dig. But it seems you need a little boost," he says and then he is stuffing paper into her mouth. Scraps drift around them.

"You're hurting her," shrieks my neighbor. "You're going to hurt her."

Emily's eyes find mine. I lunge as the door closes on her.

"No," I scream. "No. Let her go."

There is the screech of tires and the black vehicle careens into the street. I run after them. I make out what could be California plates. What could be a small white sticker. The man pulls a one-handed turn, coming abreast of the house on the driver's side. It's a marvelous piece of driving, confident and professional. The window is down. It is as before, everything on repeat. He pauses, and I watch his faceless face watch mine. One woman, turning into two.

"It's me you want," I say. "I'm the one."

Then the gears grind, the tires spin, and the car roars away.

"Oh, my God. Oh, my God. Oh, my God," my neighbor wails.

They are halfway down the street. They are turning and Emily is gone. There's her dropped purse on the sidewalk. On the ground around me lies the scattered remnants of a twofer of cloud, but Emily, my Emily, is gone.

Eleven

New York City
1993

I finally stop shaking from my encounter with Mr. Boyfriend when my taxi drops me in front of the St. Mark's Theater. It is too early for anyone to be awake, but the door is propped and I let myself in. The attic dormitory has the same apocalypse after-party aspect as it had on my first visit. The air smells of booze and weed. Someone has installed little art projects of melted spoons. In the bathroom, I find a garbage can full of the moist ashes of a burnt roll of toilet paper. I see the signs of a game of brutal honesty, a circle of chairs around a suitcase. Bodies, asleep, lie across the floor like a massacre. The director is among them with his fist around a hank of Nadine's hair. I find Paul on one of the iron beds, toe to head with Ned, the former lead, his nail-polished toes grazing Paul's cheek. Both boys are all still in stage makeup, their pillows smeared with the Turin shrouds of their faces. Paul wears the broken leather cuff I'd found in his messenger bag a few days earlier; it has been mended with electrical tape. The sling is back on him, too.

I crawl in beside Paul. Even with his new muscles, his skin is still smooth like a kid's. I shift him closer, and fold my softer limbs around his lean ones.

"Hey, Mellie," he says. He is groggy, but he swims through the fog of his hangover toward me. "Everything's OK now. We're all OK."

"I'm scared."

He struggles to wake for me, eyelids fluttering against the gum of sleep. "Mellie." He turns and puts his arms around my shoulders. My skin is cold, his warm.

"You know I'm in love with you, too, right?" he says. "Everything's OK."

And it is. It is the sop that absorbs the spill, that cleans the mess. And for him, too. I may not be the girl he would pick out of a yearbook, but I can feel him taking me through his skin, my love. It seeps into all of his empty places, all the parts made sick by the strange selfishness of the adults who were meant to protect him, my love finds the bruises and learns to reside there. He lets me. This is him sober and real; I close my eyes and he kisses my face until my skin is the same temperature as his mouth.

We slip off that day, go to Red Hook. A walk from the F under the BQE and beyond the vast and hopeless projects, you reach the water. Most of the warehouses along the docks are empty, but in one or two of the brick buildings, someone is welding. There's an Italian sandwich shop which has been there since the '60s and we get ourselves cold cuts with scoops of hot peppers. Later, we find our way back through Carroll Gardens, past Fulton and then toward the bridge. There is so much broken glass. It is as if the windows of all of the skyscrapers in Manhattan have fallen over Brooklyn, but in the sunlight it sparkles.

Halfway across, we stop and look at the water.

"Really?" I say. "Really? What do you love about me?"

"That's not a good question," he says. "What do you love about me?"

"I love your legs. I love the way your knees look when you bend them, how sharp and pointy they are."

He laughs. "I've never had a girlfriend that made me—" he pauses. "I didn't know you could be with someone and that would make your life better. I didn't know another person could do that."

We are halfway across the Brooklyn Bridge, and young enough to still believe that love can be its own reason, that its visitation can answer all challenges. Someday, people will fix locks here, to seal moments like these, make them tangible and marked. By then, Paul and I will have learned that being seized by love is not evidence, is something that can happen independent of right or wrong for each other. Those realizations are years from us now, like the craze for locks which will be snipped as soon as they are fixed.

Now, Paul smacks the back pocket of my jeans. There are people behind us, an art school girl, a couple of shirtless teenagers in trunks. I don't mind what they see of us. I smack him back, a little sting, and we start to move. Hello, New York. Hello Pearl Paint and Hello City Hall. Hello Little Italy and Lafayette and Court House. New York, here he is. The one I told you about. Now you know, New York. New York, I think he's meant for you, but somehow I'm the one who got him.

"There are these really spicy dumplings," he says. "And after, we should have gelato."

I have been living uptown for three years, and my mental map of the rest of Manhattan is about six streets wide. He's been here for a week, and already he can navigate, already he has graphed the city by its quadrants of best and cheapest food and now he leads me through them.

At four, we find ourselves in the thirties. It is still bright and hot, July a few days off.

"We should check in with Nancy," says Paul. "See if she's going to make it to the show."

I stop, unable to look at him. "Have you told her?" I ask.

"Have you?"

Maybe Nancy already knows, I tell Paul. Maybe we don't have to tell her at all.

It is time to head downtown. Tonight, it's the cast party at the theater, and to-morrow, assuming Ansel and Albert have stopped arguing, assuming Westie has cast a lead, we begin to shoot on 125th. I can't have Paul to myself. It is not going to be a cuddle-on-the-couch and container-garden-on-the-balcony kind of love affair, but until I release him, I will do what I can to fix a lock around him, to throw away the day's key. Before he goes, I want to extract everything inside of him, to have all his secrets. I remember what Nancy said, about collecting stories, how that's not the way to know someone, but she's wrong.

"What happened on your train, Paul? What happened in Siberia?"

"It's—I really don't remember. There was the game. We played for some hours; you couldn't tell how many. Time had become like that. It was my turn. Nadine and Ned were the only ones still awake, and Nadine asked could they have my bunk to sleep, and then Davos and I were alone. Sure, I told him. Sure, I'll still play and then it's all, all gummy. I lost the game. I've got the feeling of it. God, it's like right here, below my stomach. It was bad, I know. But, I have no sense of what happened. At some point, maybe, I started pulling things off the bunks, maybe people in sleeping bags. I threw something, maybe a shoe, at the window. I can see the glass shivering. The corridor. Holding myself up against the partitions. There are soldiers on the train, cars without seats, cars with just green duffels. It's cold. Your knuckles are cold, your feet. I want to keep going forever, but it's a train, right. It ends. It's the edge of the tundra. I find myself in a cargo car. I push through the last doorway, and something knocks into me from behind and I'm falling. There's this landscape of purple and golden flowers, and the train is disappearing, and I'm in pain."

"Someone pushed you?"

Paul shakes his head. "The train's moving like only fifteen or twenty miles per hour, and we're only it turns out like ten minutes outside of a station. But there was this interval when I thought I was being left behind. And now, I guess, it feels like some part of me is still out there, big nuclear fuckhole in the middle of the permafrost. In some life I forgot, I feel I'm still leaping from the train, still waiting to land."

"But they came back for me, or I caught up; so I wasn't eaten by an arctic wolf or a black bear; even still, there remained fifteen hours between there and Moscow, fifteen hours with a fractured arm and chunks of ice and nothing but Tylenol to relieve the pain. The crazy old guy who pushed the refreshments cart ended up sitting with me, telling me tall tales about the first cloud factory hidden in the shadows of the Chernobyl power plant. I ate a shitload of drugs because it sucked."

"What about the part? The change in the cast?"

"I don't know. I reach for it—but I can't recall it. Davos was trying to get a certain performance out of me, and I wasn't getting there. I couldn't let go. So, some kinds of directors will fuck with you a little bit. It's manipulative, and not maybe the best way to go about things, but if someone's really stuck, really just not opening up, then it can be worth it. I think it's worth it. Maybe I jumped. Maybe someone pushed me."

Paul has cast his face up to the afternoon sun, to the skyscrapers which loom so high above us, you have to flatten yourself to see their tops. Beneath his almost-brown skin, he is flushed with heat. He is anything but ice. He looks young, but a new kind of young from his high school self. He wears his body-knowledge like an easy garment on his shoulders. His hips lead him. I want to push inside.

I think of the actors from the audition on 125th street, the ones Ansel and Albert had rejected. I overlay them on Paul, imagine him among them. There's a thing about my boyfriend, a thing I think would work. In fact, now that I've thought of it, I have no choice. I need to give him something that big, something as big as his future. At the entrance to the theater, Paul hands me my ticket along with the remaining three spoons from his backpack. "I don't want to be tempted," he says. "I'm no good on it. It takes the razor out of the apple. You know?"

There is a throbbing in my chest, a beating at my rib cage.

He tucks the spoons into my handbag, and I walk him as far as the dressing room. I tell him to break a leg, but I've already become invisible, he's already been absorbed by the nervous static of the green room.

Twelve

New York City
1993

From the moment the lights come up, I know something has changed. Maybe seventeen people make up the audience on this, the second official night of the performance. The people seated in the third-floor black box are unused to downtown theater; the women wear dresses, the men ties. They know *Guys and Dolls* and *The Pajama Game*. They are carrying bouquets of flowers and fanning themselves with the programs. It's their kid backstage, or their college room-mate's kid. I think of my own mother, whom I have spoken to for the first time in weeks earlier in the day.

"I have to move a few things out of your room," she said. "So give me notice, all right?"

"Oh, mom. The internship runs through the summer."

"And what are you doing for money? Are you getting enough hours at the bakery? I can send you something, but the lawyers are still working out your grandmother's affairs. These things can take months."

"Sure, mom. That'd be great," I tell her. But she doesn't ask for my new contact information and I don't volunteer it.

"I've been learning about these flashpoints, you know, in the evolution of mankind, of humankind. Atlantis, obviously, the reign of Akhenaten, the Mosaic age, and each life, you know, has a timeline too—"

"Mom. I've got to go. The show is starting in a couple of minutes."

"Make sure I see you for a weekend. Amelia. Make sure you stay healthy—"

"I love you, Mom. I'll be in touch."

In the black box cabaret space upstairs at St. Mark's Theater, there is no air conditioning, no windows. A couple of rotating fans thrum in the doorway. Theater, Paul has told me, shuts down over the summer. People will see a Shakespeare in the Park or take a weekend at Williamstown, but no one wants to be inside in the dark when it's warm out. It's too much like a power outage.

Where is Nancy? As I watch the scant house collect, hear the painful small talk, I feel the crawl at the back of my throat that is my hunger for cloud.

"What's this, why does he play two parts?"

I slide my ticket between the pages of my paperback and begin to rehearse things I might say to them to the cast afterward. *The audience felt intimate*, I might say, though possibly that is too obviously backhanded. *People seemed really engaged. The dialogue was terrific. The pacing was very unusual.* Nancy could make this bearable. I think of a poetry reading we attended in Western Mass, how Nancy kept squeezing my hand to keep me from laughing out loud. I could use her here, but she must be drinking tequila in her mother's kitchen, or saving Andi from her bad boyfriend, or back on the farm because the late arrivals are being seated and the door is already closing. I think: I will not be able to sit through it. I will not be able to watch the whole thing. I will rush out at some point, unable to contain myself. I think of Paul's cloud in my bag.

So, but the lights come up, the music and Nadine is onstage. She is corseted and heavily made up, and she works in the part of the fortunate man's beautiful daughter. She stands to the left of a Scandinavian thatched cottage. The villagers in their bright knits leave little gifts at her feet. She's lonely, all alone, she sings.

"I am friend to the trees and I speak to the fox, but none oh none reply. I track the stag and I chase the hare, but neither will be caught."

Things transpire in the darkened patches of the stage. The missing set piece has been found, an arch which shimmers without light, and beyond it, the trolls lurch and wrestle and grunt. The lights dim, and the villagers take up the masks of woodland creatures and buckets of flake which they scatter and broom across the stage. And what is happening beyond the gate? What are the trolls doing? The fans lift the snowfall, and the stage whitens and everything is obscured except for Nadine. Beneath her hands, somehow, an ice form begins to materialize, a lump of gray solidifies into a human form. "If he could be real, I would give away all of my gifts."

I feel the audience squinting at the ice form. Can it be? Is there a person underneath her hands? That's when I realize: the show is working. Paul has appeared out of soap flakes onstage and when he moves, the audience gasps. Christ. It feels less like theater and more like magic, like black magic. Or something earthier and more crude: troll magic. We're rapt.

Another measure: the entire production, I'm riveted by a nasty bruise on Nadine's leg. Through her fishnets, I can see the large, blue mark on her upper thigh. It's in the exact spot as Linda Lovelace's wound in *Deep Throat*, the bruise Lovelace tries to cover in the scene by the swimming pool.

I saw *Deep Throat* with Paul and Nancy my senior year of high school. Paul worked at the Coolidge Corner Cinema, and so got us in during a festival of 1970s film, which showed *Klute* and *Cries and Whispers* and Lovelace. How I felt about watching porn is like I had to be pretty careful about what I did with my eyes and lips. It is hard to look regular while you are watching porn, like it is hard to look regularly at Nadine's bruise.

Through the fishnets, her bruise is not without its filthy aspect. It doesn't distract, but it colors my experience of the action, is a troubling subtext to my understanding of the narrative. Between scenes, when the hush falls, I wonder did someone do that to her? Did she have her own moment of falling off the train or did she receive it trying to fight someone else who was compelled to leap off the train into the permafrost? Did she inflict it on herself after Davos told her her rump was too big, that she was too thick-thighed?

The applause at the end is astonished. Everyone is sweat-sheened and ecstatic; no one in the audience is confused about whether we have just seen something great. It was great, is all I can say after. I am shining from it. It was great.

Nadine wears a micro-mini to the cast party after, and that's when I understand about Davos, that he's actually brilliant. Because Nadine does not have that bruise. Nadine's bruise was made in the Green Room.

The cast party packs out Blue and Gold Bar. There are easily eighty people there, spilling onto the street, running back and forth from the deli with packs of cigarettes. Davos regales the guests with stories of the Russian tour, which are somehow hilarious, claims they'd been being used to move contraband. Obviously, the bargoers haven't all seen the show. Obviously, they're not all there to celebrate the same thing. Someone's got a cake. They're singing in Russian and English. In the Russian song, a wizard comes on a blue helicopter and gives you one hundred ice creams. It's Davos's birthday, incidentally. The wizard song is a birthday song.

His being an actual genius doesn't make me like him more; to me, talented people who take advantage of others are like people who use any kind of power to mess with their inferiors. Before I disappointed her, Professor Mackin told me she thought a good measure of a human was how he treated his secretary. Mackin also wrote a book about sadomasochism in the American Congress, so it's not totally obvious what she meant by that, but to me, the director is not better than the assistant manager at Yankee Muffin, who is no better than Ansel and Albert. A boss who takes care, truly takes care of his people, is a rarity.

I ask the bartender to set me up a couple of shots, and watch the director fawning over Ned, the blond former lead, like the kid was Davos's own personal invention.

"This one," he says. "Brilliant. I wouldn't be surprised if they extended the show. But I'll have to work hard to hang onto this boy. Someone has already tried to snap him up, haven't they?"

"I got an audition. It's no big thing."

Davos beams. "They always do this to me. I pick them out, and train them up, and then they leave me."

Paul is at the edge of the circle, drinking hard and watching. He is particularly gorgeous tonight, but next to Ned he looks like the character part, the junkie, the street walker, the secret lover of the famous politician.

"The thing about the play is that there just aren't enough good roles. I wish I'd chosen something meatier, something like a *Lear* where all the parts are compelling."

Paul knocks back his whiskey and mutters something. The director turns.

"We have to be fair, don't we? We want to spread the love around." He laughs, claps a hand on Paul's shoulder, and moves off to introduce Ned to the owner of the St. Mark's theater.

Thirteen

Roslindale/ Quincy
2010

Outside, the neighbor woman is still shrieking, though her voice is trailing off from panic into something more like a moan. On the street beyond the mouth of the garage, seasonal flags flap with leftover Easter bunnies, piles of wet winter weeds await tomorrow's rake. Emily's purse lies in the driveway, my own on the garage floor. American cars gleam. There's a weeping pain at the base of my neck, a smoldering cigarette butt in the gutter. The man who was once my man is gone; he has done the violence he intended all along.

Upstairs, in my office, the screen is still dark, unresponsive.

Think, Mellie. Urgency grips me, and I seize what I can. I'm like a person arming myself, the paperback, the card reader, my dead phone, the two purses dropped in the driveway. I hesitate, and then I collect the dropped cloud paper. Some of it glistens.

My sober brain: a crime has occurred. I should get someone with credentials to help—my therapist, an expert, the cops.

Downstairs, I dial, from the landline. *Think—*

"911," says the operator. "Can you hold please?"

Police logic, Roslindale cop thinking, would peg this as a domestic situation. Emily's ex, obviously, the one just released. We run with a bad crowd, Emily and I, with junkies and ex-junkies and criminals and pornographers.

"Can you tell me your emergency?"

"Someone's been taken," I say.

"Can you describe the perpetrator?"

"I—it's a black SUV."

"Do you have the plate number?"

The things I know cannot help them. The oval sticker, numbers on a screen, the countdown, Emily's absence feels like an encroaching erasure; like she is becoming a missing thread in a sweater, pulled out from the hem. She will be an empty seat at the Monday meeting, an empty place at the microphone; a free parking spot on her street, an unoccupied desk at the courthouse. She will be gone, the way cloud people are gone, as if the world never held them. I think of Leo, out there in some schoolyard with no idea of the lurking threats, no mother to protect him. What I have is cloud logic, details with significance only if you've been in its fog.

"Are you able to speak?" says the operator. "We're tracing the call."

My eyes fall on the half-written message. *Something I think I should—kind of a breakthrough—something you need to know.* Cloud sickness teaches us, said Emily. Inside, said the documentarian, there is branching, possibility. Clarity comes, like a song, like Juni's song. Tall pines. I am vomiting by the side of a road. Four lakes, I think. Four campsites. Between the swollen woman, and mother I became, I had been there. My thinking is clear, like song, like Juni's song. I am in cloud, in its logic now. I will know how to find it.

"I made a mistake," I say. "Please forgive me."

I hang up and begin to drive. The neighbor woman is still screaming. The call is being traced. Let the cops run the procedural, I think. For now, I need to follow cloud.

I'm in rapid-fire traffic. Taillights and lanes, a hand's width between bumper and bumper. Morrissey Boulevard, two thirty. Channel 56 Ganett Corporation. IBEW. Ho Chi Minh on a water tower.

Fugue state. My brain singing. In the missing middle, I had become a woman with eggs for eyes. My man, a girlish hand, had transformed into Apollo. In the trough of my existence, I had known one thing: it must remain hidden. But somehow, substitution logic, a thing slipping into another thing, my object, the shape and thickness of a penny, but with right angles, had been the wrong thing, numbers decaying on a screen. Somewhere else, some other person holds it. *My part. Your part.* I discard irrelevant data. The weeping pain, the cigarette butt releasing its last curl of smoke: these are details that belong to some other version, and so they must wait for later, for never. It is about one lake among four, Emily and the man, and the twenty-six hours I have to find them.

Think. Think. Think.

Driving has become impossible. I take the familiar exit and park in the afternoon shadows. I am a block from Independence House, can see some kind of commotion underway. Althea and Marisa are hanging out the window, trying to get a better view. I should go inside, tell the counselor what has occurred. It's the likely action here, is the right and reasonable thing.

But cloud pulls me, the sense of revelation just out of view. A point so traveled through, it became erased. *Kif-Vesely'e*. It had been other things, an informal refugee camp, a warehouse for imports, a summer camp, a bungalow colony. Me. I owed my good life to a promise I had sworn not to fulfill and, in the torn place between those two vows, I had gone to the lake shore. There was a faded bus ticket with my name on it. New York. Something County. My phone barely holds a charge, but I scroll through. Allegheny, Chautauqua, Dutchess, Herkimer.

Think.

At this hour, naptime is ending, Juni unsticking her thumb from the roof of her mouth, rolling over on her mat. The caregiver is laying out the graham crackers and apple juice for afternoon snack. Everything is still locked into normalcy. For the moment, all that is about to occur still lies before me. Slowly, the sleepy children assemble in front of the nursery door. In the enclosed breezeway which links the nursery to the yard, the caregiver appears with a clipboard. She turns and faces her duckling line of children. In this long minute, each breath sustained, each bird song slowed, Juni is still mine. I must go to her. I will go to her, soon.

On the seat, as I have idled waiting for my phone to regain its charge, I have been pulling objects from my paperback, arranging them in a circle. Business card. Key card. Microchip. What was on the chip, code decaying on a screen, was not what the SUV man had wanted, but they need each other, the missing middle and the thing I had hidden in my paperback. The counter is over half a million. Sweet numbers being collected out of view. A hook being sunk into the fleshy secrets of individual lives. And these viewers, slack-jawed, mesmerized by some curious art, say yes, and yes, and yes. No crime has been committed. They have consented. But at some critical point, when the counter has reached its end, and the audience has reached capacity, my code could tug, reel them all in. It will not work alone, however. It needs its own medium, its own disguise. Half a million viewers are waiting on the missing middle and the man with the SUV is driving toward a blank space on a map to try to stop it. Data does not live in a physical location, not the way people do. It can be in two places at once, in a million. It can travel from Dakar to Roslindale in the space of a keystroke.

All of this has been set in motion years ago. What if the *Found Footage* is poised on some server? What if it uploads the moment the counter runs out? Then, a bank account suddenly emptied, critical data erased, secrets made visible; what will the SUV driver do to the woman he believes has failed him then? Twenty-six hours remain.

Think, Mellie.

Then I am rifling through the book. Bar napkin. Dried flower from a bouquet. Juni drawing. Even the borrowing card which has remained in the pocket all these long years, names hatched darkly out, a new one inked in. I stop. Is it a name? *Apollo*, it says. *Apollo Blue.* Detail. Detritus. I shake my head and return the item to its pocket.

Think, Mellie. Focus.

The children emerge, Juni toddling on her own behind Marisa's daughter. What does my slow heart say? There she is, her hair, and her soft belly and her baby Frankenstein lurch, each blessed and undeserved breath she draws in sweet. There is a way I should feel: I know. I know that a mother should know the color of her own baby's eyes, whether they are brown or green or violet, but at this distance, in the sunshine, you cannot tell, and I cannot be sure. Moments have passed, no time at all; the shadows of the trees outside of Independence House haven't moved.

A cop car turns onto the cul-de-sac, slows as it approaches Independence House, the call being traced, the neighbor's screams. A great bureaucratic system is grinding its gears into motion.

Still, I could slip in. Still there is a heartbeat before it all begins. Later, when I contend with myself, I don't want to make excuses. I have my chance. Outside my window, the children stand in a tidy line, awaiting instructions. The caregiver says something—*green light*—and they begin to run. There is order and safety there. *Red light.* They freeze instantly. Even Juni, Juni can understand these rules. As for me, I am safe for no one. I am no one who can be trusted.

My phone lights up. I shift my wallet and, beneath, find the muddied bus ticket. *Sullivan. Sullivan County.* I run the search. *Four lakes,* the man had said, *four campsites.*

Now, the cop car pulls into the Independence Drive. The women—my friends—lean out the window. The children look up from their game, expectant, and then I shift into drive. A spasm of longing seizes through me, but then I'm pulling onto the road. Something that occurs to me as I drive away: my therapist is going to be disappointed. If I get the chance, I'll give her the consolatory news. Her work has been a success, in this at least: my memory is improving.

Memory must be what tethers me, to this place and the tiny girl I am leaving. There is a process, a protocol, and it is already underway. First, they will pull my intake sheet. Under emergency contacts, I've listed first Emily and then my mother. Emily's phone is somewhere in the tall grass outside of my house and my mom's number rings at an internet café twenty miles through the jungle from her hacienda. I have done all this math already, had read it in the original documents I signed when I checked in. From the beginning, a junkie calculates for the worst-case scenario, because when you're a junkie, the worst case is eventually the case that comes to pass.

Interim custody goes to the house. They will give her cheese on a plate and spaghetti with ketchup, and in twenty-four hours, she will get filtered into the system. Next, a social worker with a heavy caseload, and a baby who speaks unintelligible babble, a lingering bronchitis and terrific sorting skills, Juni will be put in with strangers, or in a nursery with five other babies, where no one will touch her for hours at a time. Still: none of that begins for twenty-four hours, which is one hour more than I have before *Found Footage* is meant to go live, and whatever the man who has become Apollo believes, whatever value Emily may seem to have to him, will end.

I am thinking of the first time I left Juni at the sitter's. Walking away was miraculous: like weightlessness on earth, or the power of invisibility. I thought: I'm utterly unrecognizable. I could be anyone again. No one can tell I'm a mother. But when I reached into my pocket, I found a teether, still cool from the freezer. The Juni drawing resting on my seat is a real one, snot green, with slashes of red. I fold it up, and return it to my paperback. There are parts of you, maybe, that embed so deeply, you cannot cast them off. That's what I'm counting on.

The sense of insight which has held me in place in the interval since Emily was taken has now unmasked itself. The migrainous aura, the thing detaching from the base of my spine, the fruiting onset of inspiration: I am about to become cloud sick. I tell myself there's no such thing. But it's like telling myself that there's nothing to be afraid of when I'm alone on a dark street. Things do rise from the trash heaps.

Now, in the waning light of my awareness, I consider the satellite photo which has come up on my phone. Sullivan County: green, sparsely populated, and freckled everywhere with blue. There are dozens, maybe hundreds of bodies of water.

Fourteen

New York City
1993

I'm on the phone with Zarah who has mysteriously tracked me to the apartment on 109th, who had in fact been the first caller after I connected the line to the jack.

"The future," she says, "casts its shadows beforehand."

She continues to ring at strange hours. Paul and I are only up this early because *West 125th* begins shooting today. According to my friend the AD, relations between Westie and the brothers continue to be difficult, but I am rooting for the artist. She gave Paul the audition, then cast him in a small role. It's all happened beyond my view—I've been in Queens collecting properties and set design elements, so I haven't even glimpsed the difficult director, but I'm grateful to her all the same. Now, the morning of the first day of filming, Paul sits on the window, smoking and quizzing himself on his weird cues and I listen to Zarah.

"You are trying to give away what is precious. In this instance, my readings say, there is no profit."

The AD has the same advice as Zarah.

"Have you thought this through, Mellie?" he asked when I proposed the audition. "Because you're going to earn maybe one consideration, all summer long. I mean including invites to openings, including letters of recommendation. Albert is just beginning to distinguish you from the five other PAs. Ansel still thinks your name is Marlie. Is this how you want to burn the favor, on this friend of yours? On this bizarre script?"

On another note, I've been thinking about finances. An unexpected check in a strange denomination arrived from my mother yesterday: a hundred and thirty-six dollars. *Beware the gift.* I am waiting for it to clear. The check eases my mind, like a cool party I didn't expect to be invited to.

On another note, I'm getting fatter. I've put on at least five pounds since March break. Wanting cloud feels like being hungry and a thousand sugar calories consumed in the space of five minutes can sand the edge off. I think of Nancy, a phone call she'd made during the takeover. This was before she got kicked out of school and ran off to the farm. After a few days, they cut the phone line to the Dean's office, but for a while, she was making free calls from his desk. She was fasting, she said. It was half-diet and half-protest. She was high off it, the hunger.

"One of the guys they sent to represent the national organization is an alternate for the New York City ballet," she said. "I made them put on some music, and we all had a kind of a party. Do you know what that means?" She was laughing, manic, days of living out of an academic office. "I've danced with the New York ballet after all."

I didn't like her laughter. There was too much noise in it to read.

"Are any of them sick?" I asked. "The people who are in there with you?"

"Oh, Mellie. Everyone. Everyone is fucking dropping like flies." The hunger is a point of continuity, Nancy in the Dean's office, Andi fasting on the farm, the sick ballet dancer, and me, gorging myself. I shovel a turnover into my mouth. In my mind, Nancy's thinness and ballet thinness and the thinness of viral death all blur now into a single threat I can't comprehend.

I try to be vigilant. Traveling up Broadway to Westie's studio before dawn has fully broken seems a good way to dodge unwanted encounters. You have to love that about New York, that you can move five blocks and be in another world. But worlds also overlap. There is a handprint-shaped bruise on my shoulder which Paul refuses to notice. I don't want to cross paths with Mr. Boyfriend for my own sake, but with Paul beside me it feels especially important. Sipping our coffee, eating our Hungarian pastries, I am alert for animated piles of rags, for monsters who rise up in shadowed doorways. The future casts its shadow beforehand.

I stop Paul at the corner of 125th, like you do for a baby. The traffic is incongruously thick, coming around the construction at the exit from Henry Hudson. Paul is a bit dark below the eyes. I tilt his head back and try to dab on some foundation.

"Mellie," he says. "Seriously."

"You need to start to think of these things, Paul, develop your vanity. Show biz is not a merit system. It's not about the quality of your soul in there."

"Lucky thing," he says. He takes my wrist with one hand, then extracts the bottle of Visine from his messenger bag with the other and droppers his own eyeballs.

I'm afraid for him. It's one thing, at a cabaret. It's another on screen. I think of the little-brother actor I'd read with in the audition. Men with personal trainers and highlights in their hair. That is the world he is moving into. And he doesn't know yet how to use cover up. "And no cloud," I say. "Not until after."

"You're someone I fuck. Stop trying to mother me. I don't respond to it."

"OK," I say. "OK."

We take a few steps in silence while Paul blinks the tears out. "I'm nervous, Mellie."

"Well, it's just an art film. It's not Hollywood. The brothers got homeless people to act in one once."

"Terrific," he says.

I stop in front of the building. The block is momentarily empty, though I can feel the frenzy through the brick face. "We're here."

Paul looks at me and I'm as surprised as anyone when he captures me in a kiss, and then bounds up the stairs. I can hear him ahead, introducing himself, transforming into someone charming and loveable and full of confidence. Into someone who knows how handsome he is. I don't hold it against him, his having several selves. I have dozens; have been a Marshall scholar and a muffin slut, a thief and a clairvoyant and I am inventing new selves all the time, am who I am based on the audience exclusively.

Someone I fuck. Even that is OK, will do, as long as it lasts. For Paul, I am liquid. I will be whoever will keep him. I think about my extra five pounds as I climb the stairs. I think about how no other girl has ever woken him like I do. I am happy to be exceptional in some way, the latest if not the last.

Paul is talent, and even on a catch-can film set like Albert's and Ansel's, there's a tradition of insulating the talent from the crew. A PA appears as we walk through the door and leads Paul off to some curtained area where hair and makeup will go to work on his number four buzz and his three lingering adolescent pimples. Another girl is running to The Bread Shop to get more coffee, more pastries. He is out of my orbit.

The director, too, is talent, and the AD stands between her and the patter at the level of extension cords and what time the pizza will arrive, at the level of the blown fuse and the rising heat of the morning. They are calling her 'Westie.'

She wears boys' jeans slung around her hips with a worn leather belt, a wrinkled white button-down and a red lacy bit underneath. Her lipstick matches her bra. She weighs a hundred and five pounds, and probably a third of those are in her tits and her ass. She's got a slash of dark hair across her forehead and is the kind of woman the boys I like actually go for. I look away, look at the artist again. I realize we've met, after a fashion.

"Westie wants—" says the AD. "Westie needs you to . . ."

Which explains why I didn't know what was coming, why I didn't foresee it. Because I'd encountered her years before as Valerie Weston, an artist who worked in the medium of wax rather than film, whom I'd last seen sobbing behind closing elevator doors. She still smokes, I observe. She's still threateningly gorgeous.

"What?" I ask the AD.

"Westie needs the room to be cooler. We need all of you guys to go get your fans from your rooms. Can you get the PAs on the windows?"

He's displeased with me, but I am not attending to the AD anymore because Westie—Valerie Weston—has seen me, and is now walking across the studio in my direction. She recognizes me, and she is not smiling.

I recall my reaction to Westie's studio, to the pickled eggs labeled *Rat Poison* and the molar umbrella and now that I've connected this work to the maker of that long-ago wax penguin lamp, I understand my response better. The things she makes have cloud logic, are recognizable but alien, parts swapped out; they resemble in their incongruity a memory that has been returned to you from a mind not your own.

I reject what is happening; I reject the way Westie bores through the air between us, the way she projects her dominance through the space.

"I have enough," says Westie. "I don't want this one on set. Put her on something else."

I require being escorted out, the AD's hand on my shoulder. Of course it's bullshit, he agrees. A stupid prank, a long time ago, but Westie is talent, and I am bottom-rung crew, and the AD's sorry—he's actually sorry—but I'm going to have to leave. There is a faint trace of "I told you so," but also a kindness in his disappointment and I wonder, what if there are men like him all along the parallel tracks of my life, if I just keep missing them for some reason, just keep failing to catch onto whatever they are offering?

I wasn't completely lying to Mr. Boyfriend when I told him I was working as an EMT. I'd gone through the training, nine months of extra classes so I could sign onto CAVA, the volunteer ambulance that serves campus and Morningside Heights. Almost everyone else who did the training was Pre-Med, was thinking about getting into graduate school. I had begun to feel like something important was missing from me, that I did not quite react to things with my native intensity anymore. For example, I could sometimes forget for days that my grandmother had passed away. For an ambulance driver, however, being imperturbable was a virtue. And maybe, I thought, a few knife wounds would wake up in me whatever had gone dormant. But I never went on a single run. There turned out to be a drug test which I knew I wouldn't pass. Still, along the way I did learn about the physiology of cloud, that clinically, cloud overdose is impossible because of how quickly the body metabolizes it.

You sweat cloud out almost as fast as you take it in, cannot die of it no matter how much you eat. On the other hand, this doesn't mean there aren't consequences, outcomes from too much cloud over a life. You consume enough and things happen—the recognition troubles, the meaty deposits, the confusion and the sickness. You give away your mind that many times, you dismantle yourself on that many occasions, and eventually, you can no longer put yourself back together. They may not call it an overdose, but it amounts to the same thing.

The second night of filming *West 125*, Paul comes home smelling of craft services, boursin sandwiches and donuts. "You still have that cloud?"

There's one spoon left from the Avenue D excursion. I've been doling them out to Paul since he'd given me the stash to hold on opening night, but this last one, I've unthinkingly secreted in one of my old hiding places, and Paul watches as I extract it from the back of a drawer.

"Sorry," I say. The hoarding is still instinctive with me, is the addict's reflex which getting clean hasn't left behind.

Paul dangles the spoon from his lips. He's always at his best, his kindest, just before the cloud hits. "You're so stark, Mellie. You have the moral compass of a nine-year-old. You've got to shed that good person/bad person mindset. Out here in the oxygen, up here on the top of Manhattan, I forgive you. I forgive whatever is making you look at me that way."

Paul's window fronts on the fire escape. He sits next to his ashtray, his burning cigarette perched on the edge for when the cloud vacates his mouth. Technically, the apartment is nonsmoking, but I don't care, really. It's Paul who seems hip to things like security deposits. It has surprised me about him, his areas of pickiness, his little specializations in the country of worry. For example, getting back security deposits, sneakers as cool or not cool, what the weather report predicts. I want this quality to translate into awareness of things like the bruise on my shoulder, things like whether anyone is lurking suspiciously on the street below, or where we are getting the money for our groceries. Paul watches the action on 109, the junkies, the shooting of junk, but he doesn't see anything.

"What did you even film today?" I ask.

"There's only one scene," says Paul. "One long scene, broken into five shots."

"Well, what's it about?"

"What everything's about, Mellie. How small and petty we all are inside. How our lofty ambitions for ourselves and how the bullshit myths that we make evaporate when a tiny little treasure is offered to us. The elaborate narrative we make to justify our own basic selfishness, our animal minds. All the things that make more sense than 'good' or 'bad.'"

The spoon drops from his lips.

—*pop*—

I watch the depth and meaning drain from him; I watch the little sparks reignite within; I wait for the evidence that I am still in there somewhere.

"I'm entirely out of socks," he says. "Everything's still downtown. I don't want to go downtown."

The news from the East Village is terrific. Other publications have released reviews, and the owner of the St. Mark's is considering moving the revamped production to the main stage. But still, they don't call Paul.

"Borrow mine," I say, and pull laundry-gray tube socks onto the feet of my cloud-compliant boyfriend. "Come to bed."

The next day, the AD calls for Paul in the morning, and tells me I can come down to the set after they wrap for the day; there's some location work that needs to be done. To kill time, I go to the library and look up Westie in *Art Forum*. The critics argue over her graduate thesis video, if it's about lynching or vegetarianism or evil. In various interviews, she claims her next production will be an animated comedy about genocide, will be an exact replica of her last film, will document a lover's breakdown in real time. "Actually, though," Valerie is quoted as saying, "I abhor documentary. You know those films where everything was incredibly fucked up between the crew and the talent and everyone's crying in their trailers every night and there's a civil war thirty miles away, but it's still a musical? That's my kind of movie."

Valerie Weston—Westie—Video Artist—Filmmaker—Sculptor—Painter.

See: —20 C women American artists–Realism, Anti-realism, surrealism

b. 1965 Brookline Massachusetts. Daughter of Pierce Weston, Industrialist and Mamie Weston, 1981 Director of Membership Junior League Boston. Major Works:

—*Boy Girl Tree Meadow*

—Wax Zoology

—*Several Originals*

— (Found) Objects

—The Dentist's Apprentice

I look up Mr. Boyfriend's family name, the real estate holding company in New Jersey, and turn up the accidental, single-car crash that killed his parents on a sunny afternoon as well as a guy with his same last name in Philadelphia who testified at a trial, then ended up impaled on a bridge. There's an image of some post-Communist factory exploding. Also, there is a photograph of pit bulls being seized from a breeder.

I exit blinkingly into the afternoon. It's still too early, too early to be expecting Paul. I think of his socks, consider washing the gray pair he'd left on my floor, but somehow it seems easier to take the train down to the theater. I'm skittish on the subway. Little scraps of movement keep attracting my eye, but when I turn, I find that corner of the car empty. It's hot and I'm feeling disgusting.

The girl at the box office, the one who'd taken all the free lattes, ignores me, or pretends to ignore me when I wave from the front door.

"I'm here to pick up a bag?" I say, tapping on the glass in the doorway. The girl nods me to the empty upstairs. I see none of Paul's things. The bed where he'd been sleeping appears to have been taken over by someone else. Eventually, Nadine appears, having returned from church. She startles to see me, showing something in her gaze which she masks with a smile.

"He left his backpack here? Are you sure?"

I shrug. "What he told me."

"Why didn't he come down himself? Is it because he missed rehearsal yesterday?"

I shrug. I find you get the most information when you act as if you already know, as if you don't need to be told.

"Or has someone told him? I knew Ned was going to tell him."

With Nadine's help, I manage to find Paul's frame pack, with the bullshit Maple Leaf patch he's worn since the Gulf War.

"Listen, you know and I know that Paul's the best actor among them. It's bull crap, the casting. But, also, honestly, it's a theater *company*. There have to be consequences. If you go off message."

"Because of the review, still?" I ask.

Nadine shrugs. "It probably seems petty to you from the outside. But it's like showboating, like Paul isn't always doing what's best for the group. You know the concept of stealing the scene?"

"I think," I say.

"Well, so, it's not just an outcome of being better than the other players. It's like, a stylistic choice. A choice to act in a way that commands attention. When you notice the acting, then it takes you out of the play."

"So—" I'm trying to put all the pieces together.

"So, that's why he is going to be cut from the mainstage production. It's still not official, but we all know. It was only ever an experiment anyway, Paul in the lead, but Davos could have kept him as a villager. That's the part I disagree with."

My initial response is an ugly delight. It's disloyal, I know. But it feels like a victory, like I've won him from them, somehow. I say some girl-to-girl thing to Nadine. Like, you really deserve better than these guys, or another empty exit line. I want to be alone on the subway, rocking back and forth. *New York,* I say, *it's out of my control. Things are starting to spin and I don't know why or where they're going or what to do about it. Keep me awake, New York. I don't want to miss it.*

I haven't eaten all day. My lips are puckered with dehydration, but I don't feel hungry. I ride the subway in a daze of starvation and paranoia. I get to my stop, but I have that recognition problem where I don't know where I am and then I have to walk back from 125th. Some of the crew is outside the studio smoking, but no one makes eye contact as I pass, so I can't gauge how much my shakiness is visible on the outside. In my apartment, sorting through Paul's clothes, the delusion develops. They don't seem like his things. They seem like things from some other Paul, someone I've never known. I want cloud, but Paul's eaten the last spoon and I can't remember how you get it, how I get it. I know I'm waiting for a phone call, for a page from the AD saying I can come back, but it's past whatever hour I was supposed to hear and now time is putty, stretching to infinite thinness, articulating into strands. Darkness begins to fall, and it's one long scene.

I jump when the phone rings.

"Amelia." It is not Paul, not the AD calling to say I can come. It's my mother's psychic goon. "I'm concerned you may have misunderstood. This reading is going to be free of charge. I personally am getting nothing out of it, do you hear me? This is something your sister asked of me before she left, and I am doing it out of my continued regard. Even and despite, with no benefit to me. Your danger is elevated. There is a very dear person to you who may be at great risk."

"Sister?" I say.

"Are you still eating the unusual foods? Have you recently changed your diet or are you about to? This is very important," she says.

"Sorry," I say. "Who told you to call me?"

And then, it is like something has been swapped in for something else. I hear a PA system announcing departures in the background, and it's as if she's calling from Nancy, like Zarah has been switched with Nancy.

"Your sister is coming for you. She sees the danger, and she's coming to get you."

I hang up. It is time. I push aside the cloud hunger, the crawling sensation of being followed, and start walking toward the studio on West 125th.

Fifteen

New York
1993

In Manhattan's protracted evening, the substitution art of Westie's 125th Street studio is somewhat less unbalancing than when it had been full daylight. Something has shifted in the arrangement of the objects; objects have been placed between other objects, so that the viewer can follow a sort of logic. Pickled eggs and bird's nest, for example, knucklebone dice and tooth umbrella. On this visit, I can be pretty confident the molars *are* actual molars, enamel and calcium, rather than some wax facsimile. I can see a few fillings and the dark discoloration of old cavities.

It is not fully dark because it is never fully dark in Manhattan. The light pollution, street lamp and passing car and all-night deli, invades an interior in even the deepest night. After sundown, city dwellers enter a kind of non-time or extended twilight which perhaps explains why the bars stay open until four and why a daytime party feels so transgressive. Westie's art works in Manhattan, the shelving dissolving in the perpetual magic hour of the city. I hear rather than see someone entering the studio behind me.

"She collected those, you know," says the voice in the muted light. It's my AD. "Fucked up, right? She posted ads at like shelters and places poor people would take their kids, social service agencies, certain neighborhood parks and select schools. This is in Boston, not New York—back where she's from. And it's more sick because she is actually rich, was born to money. Has never worked at anything but making this stuff. So, anyway, in the ads, she's like, let me be your tooth fairy. Basically, it's offensive."

"Ali?" I say to the shape moving through the gloom of the darkened studio.

He comes into the light, smiling. "You can never remember my name. And I'm beginning to think you will never go to coffee with me."

"You said you wanted me for set work?"

"Yeah, but they're still shooting up there. We're not going to get to it today. Anyway, it's stupid. She wants us to do this stop-motion thing with the cubbies: film, empty certain ones, film again, until the whole configuration is different. She's drawn this map, but no one can follow it."

At this point in my life, I have not yet seen *Boy Girl Meadow Tree*, the student film which had so won over Ansel and Albert, but I've heard about it, and the idea for the shelving sequence is similar in a way, a very slow transformation from routine to atrocity. Valerie Weston's genius, her special quality, came from her absolute willingness, her enthusiasm for doing the things that appalled other people. At a certain point in our lives, this will make us well suited for one another, but the person I am about to become will not begin for a few more minutes. For the moment, I'm still capable of qualms, of being shocked or repulsed.

Valerie Weston is watching this Mellie, even now. I hear her, behind me, in the studio's murk. I turn, expecting one of the brothers, expecting Paul, but I'm wrong. It's her, her own white, privately educated teeth a disembodied smile in the dimness.

She's laughing at me. "You thought you'd dodged me, huh? Well, you're here. Come on up. You're supposed to have a good eye. We could use another opinion."

Light isn't perpetual up here. On the roof, there are twenty minutes left before darkness, even accounting for the ambient light of window squares and Kansas Fried Chicken and the McDonald's at the corner. Albert is in cut-off shorts and a white men's t-shirt. Ansel is chewing out the script supervisor who fans herself with the continuity photos. The AD extracts them from her hands and shows them to me. A breeze has picked up. Even though it's been a hot day, here in the air, after dark, my skin cools. I don't pick out Paul right away and then I locate him.

He is seated, wrapped in a green cotton blanket, and sipping a coffee. We wave, far away from each other. I think: he looks spaced out. Not high, not like he's on cloud, but like he did that night I collected him from the St. Mark's Theater.

"Everyone nice and rested?" Westie asks. She has the kind of voice which always carries, which others listen to. "Everyone ready to roll?"

I glance over the rooftop, the water tanks and the thinning of buildings toward the Hudson, the density to the north and east, the purple clouds against the indigo horizon. I take in the chicken coop three roofs over, the tile details on the building that fronts LaSalle. This isn't a set, precisely, but Valerie has purposefully done violence to the sense of the normal world. The objects hanging from the clotheslines are not clothing, for example, but loose pieces of yarn roughly strung together. For another example, there are train tracks running along the asphalt roof tile, a berth that appears to have come from a vintage sleeping car. Still: the familiar world seeps in. New York is vast and doesn't want to be squeezed into a costume to suit one woman's whims. A horn, for example, honks its irritation at the intersection with Broadway. The moon, its benign presence rising over the scene, inserts time into the piece, suggests an ending and relief. "Get rid of it," I say.

I can tell Ansel and Albert think I'm a nut, but Valerie Weston consults with the AD and looks through the DP's lens. She makes minor adjustments, calls the properties master, and in a few minutes, someone shifts the yarn clothesline and the moon disappears.

Westie peers through the lens again, nods to herself, and then favors me with a look. "That's it," she says. There is much in this phrase, acknowledgement, recognition of mutual skills. When later, in Los Angeles, she hunts me down to work for her and I in turn introduce her to my employer Lew Cohen, it will be because of the moon and not what is about to happen with Paul.

"OK," I agree.

"Places, everyone," calls the AD. Ansel and Albert fall silent.

Paul stands. He's dressed in boxers and a t-shirt. Another man, the main actor, takes a place on the lower bunk of the berth. He is wearing a bandana, smoking a cigarette. He is not tall. One of the PAs places a backpack on a pale chalk X very near the actor.

Paul approaches. Beneath the thin clothes he wears, his is shadowed against the corrected sky, against the vista that I have made right for him. Paul kneels on the backpack. The man on the bunk is not Davos, but could pass, could pass for Paul's director. The crew wait for the elevated subway to come, to transfer its noise to the scene. The tiny treasures, Paul had said, what cruel things we talk ourselves into.

"When were you last afraid?" asks the actor.

I can see that it doesn't matter about Paul's acting, after all, that he doesn't need to act for this part.

Of the film, it will eventually be said that Westie wanted to shoot confessions; she wanted to stage and manipulate content so that something secret, or even unconscious, emerged into this universal space. She wasn't trying to make a statement about public, or private, though as the technology emerged over the following decade, her work would be read that way, would be part of how people talked about blogging and social media and the diaristic mode of the early twenty-first century. She would tell interviewers, rather, that she was performing an experiment. The will to fame or the will to privacy? Which essentially American desire would win? But of course, it was like everything she did, like bad cloud. She didn't want one thing to win over the other. She wanted the mismatch, the alien invading the familiar, the raw pain as material for a dispassionate artistic eye.

How the actors felt, what it meant to the humans on the rooftop was part of Valerie's medium, was like the yarn on the clothesline to her. I can't offer an opinion as to outcome of the experiment. I have never been able to watch *W 125*, Westie's first professional film. It is said to be good, I guess.

I will keep it in my brain for years, until cloud sucks it, like so much, away. Paul, the visible erection, in the reenactment of his most terrible moment, while all of Manhattan watches. The breath is sucked out of me. Beneath my skin, a dozen species of jealousy crawl like exotic parasites. I want that confession for my own, to be his love token, but now I can see that this is not the way he is mine, not privately, not absolutely. There are things, I see now, that he wants much more than he wants a life with me and I realize I've been lying to myself: I can't stand to have just a part of Paul, to be the second or fourth choice. On this night without moon, a small portion seems all I can hope for.

———

Here is what I think the director told Paul on the train, in the Siberian game of brutal honesty. Here is what I think the Oblako swallowed: (Paul is beautiful, and the director might have acknowledged it. Paul is talented, and the director might have granted this, too.) *But you are slim, my dear, and it is not a man's beauty you have. This is why you will always be typecast. You will always play gay.*

That is what would not play in the states, Paul as a straight man. How he 'got thrown' off the train. Paul and men. There are things in the country of sex which never get unraveled between couples, and this part of him would be something I never totally understood. Still, I have guesses. I have made inroads. I would never learn anything more about that incident with Davos, what kind of pleasure he might have taken, whether it would have been willingly or unwillingly given.

I am told certain insights emerge in Valerie's movie, but even if I could have stood to watch it, her work was never the kind that revealed truth. For her, truth was only a mercury from inside of which a subject emerged into something beautiful or poisoned or sometimes both.

I must have left the studio, traveled the blocks to 109th, but I was in my own mercury already, already becoming the thing the night had made of me.

Sixteen

Longwood Towers
2010

There are places we fall into, like a crevice or a trough. We can be drawn there, into alignment with their polarity. These places may not be geographically linked, but lines run through them, again and again. It may be possible to meet strangers there, to exchange with strangers. At a certain point, you must step inside, and with the proper sacrifice, you may be able to exit at will.

I am trying to find Emily. In geography of satellites and kilometers, there are a hundred lakes, but there is a shadow geography, in which years and lives may collapse, may exchange. I am looking for another map and cloud has led me here.

The crenelated towers, the mouth of the garage. I descend into the darkness, find a half parking spot between a pillar and an Escalade. Paranoia whispers to me like a wise older sister, and I slip the battery from the back of my phone and drop it on the seat cushion. My blood sings with the advancing sickness.

I'm coming, Emily.

Inside of cloud sickness, there is a branching. The woman reflected in the elevator brass is a soft-core girl, has eggs for eyes, is a faceless face through the dusty window glass. The door opens on the second floor of tower C. I have been here before. I know the way. Details. Everything is enriched in the sunset of my sickness.

The light below 2f spills into the hallway, a blurred square summoning me. I pick out details: a mezuzah by the door, scrape marks by the lock, and splinters in the wood. There is a memory of violence here, of ancient fire and it layers over, a voice saying *help me, for God's sake, help me.* Everything blurs and brightens.

Enemy. I am coming.

I slide the key card in. The lock clicks and the door swings open. The smell of stale smoke assaults me, molasses, campfire. Through here, I think. Right through here. There is a shattered brightness within, everything sparkling. A tuft of blond hair emerging from under a sofa cushion. There is bleached blond hair through the dusty glass.

There was a map here, but the map has been stolen.

Lady? Lady honey? I'm coming.

As through the wrong end of a telescope, I scan the apartment around me, books knocked from shelves, the glass coffee table smashed. On the screen of the monitor, a woman in her underpants is frozen mid-stride, cigarette butts mashed into the cup beside. Poking from beneath the couch cushion is the artificial hair of a dirty naked doll. From the shelves, decayed film spills from rusted canisters. *Audition (Probe), Dayan Roza, W 125.*

Things branch out and out and out, and endlessly out. Which to choose? How to go?

A voice: *you're so close. It doesn't have to be this hard.*

A magic trick, my hand filled with glistening scraps of paper (confetti on grass that I gather up). The scent of lemon rises. A small sacrifice. The small sacrifice to find the way. Inside the mouth, a sobbing that wants to be a sucking. Ease beckons. A small sacrifice.

Then, gently at first, but with a terrible insistence, something, a voice or a presence, stays me. It is a kind of song, but without sound. Dry with longing, with a weeping that has lasted for days. A sacrifice, it says, is not ease. The song becomes a woman. She moves terribly close to me, and I can smell her own lemon on her; her eyes have been eggs, her mouth punched dough. Sacrifice, she says, is right here. She touches me at the base of my breast bone, and I feel something enormously tender leave me.

Darkness has fallen. Dim light from the street falls through the tower window.

I'm holding a recording device in my hand and listening to a woman speak. The woman is me. *It's someone else. You confused me for someone else.*

The light picks out details, the sparkling of shattered glass. Beneath, a photograph still in its smashed frame. I peer closely. Boys in athletic shorts smile joylessly. Bunk *vv, Kif-Vesely'e.* I cannot make out all the faces, but behind them, there are the towering pines, the cabins in the distance, and there is a lake. I have been there before, and cloud will lead me back.

No, says the voice of Judah Cohen through the device's imperfect speakers. *You come to me, too. That night, at the Fens.*

And so I stand, and I follow.

Seventeen

New York City
1993

In the health class of my dreams, women tell girls about love, and girls pay attention. When you are young, the women will say, and you love, you will let love go inside you and replace everything that was there before. Living with love instead of organs makes you ravenous. You will try to eat things like glass and small animals in order to survive. When love goes away—and it will, girls, it will—you yourself will become the hunger. And when hunger has a mind it can destroy everything. Later, you will be a hundred and six, dementia-ravaged. You will be three husbands into your life, and still you'll be able to prod the suffering from that time like the gap of a pulled tooth. There, the women will tell the girls. Now we have prepared you for love.

Back in the sublet, my beeper explodes. 487 7285 487 7285 487 7285 487 7285. I turn it off, and the telephone rings. On the answering machine tape, Paul is drunk. He's drunk and angry. He calls me and he pages me. He pages me a couple times, then he leaves more messages on the machine. He's sorry he said he was mad. Everyone's having fun and I should totally come out and he's fucking serious about it. He's not kidding around. I lie on the futon, smelling his scent, and listen to his distorted voice over the speaker. He's at the West End shooting pool. He's going for pizza. He's back to do a couple more shots. He's just got to—unstick the wrap from this spoon and he wants to talk to me. He just wants to talk to me, but

I can't. I see him on the rooftop, hard for a man I don't even know, and telling the world the secrets he claims he can't remember. I don't answer the phone.

Maybe I'll go out to the Night Café, somewhere Paul won't be, and pick someone up. Someone disgusting and fat, or some foreign guy from School of International Affairs. I find one of my heels and sharpen my eyeliner. It is runny with the heat and I look like I've already been out all night, like someone you've already taken home and woken beside the next morning. I tie up my sweaty hair in a hairband, and wiggle into my shortest skirt.

The machine goes on again. Paul's voice is gummy with confusion. I don't know if it's drink or cloud or my nine-dollar phone. "Mellie. You reread the entire suite before anyone else solves the crew. I thought you knew how graphite and full of acts it was. I am just so wired of being tight cast."

I stand there, balanced on my one bare foot, craning to hear. Misery, like addiction, is solipsistic. It convinces you that no one can be hurt like you can, that you suffer uniquely. But misery is full of shit. Right now, this very instant, your dear ones are suffering on your behalf. In the depths of misery, you are like any addict. You are a victim, but you are also an abuser.

I can hear Paul's voice cracking over the line, the static. I can hear his anguish. ". . . And then how are you going to no sorry. It's the bouncer line at the gallery. My precious privacy lip—Mellie, I thought you wanted me to. I thought—" He's speaking in cloud, but it gets through to me. He's saying, he thought I knew. I think of his silence in the previous two days, the smoking and the glowering. He's saying, he thought I'd wanted him to play this part, that I'd understood what I'd signed him up for. That it's my fault, his shadow silhouette against the uptown sky.

Something happens. I hear what sounds like the grunt of a sucker punch, a scuffle through the machine. Maybe it's only a drunken fall, but there is something wet and gagging in the sound. Then it fades. There is street noise, traffic and car alarms, and it blends with the sounds through my open window. He's not far away.

I pick up the phone. "Paul? Paul?"

No one answers.

I have eyeliner on one eye, blush on the opposite cheek. I am wearing two different black pumps, but I hobble down the steps and out to the street.

I calculate the distribution of pay phones in the area, cross to the west side of Broadway and begin to scan at 110th. A girl in a transparent rain slicker and pink skirt lies across a park bench gazing at the sky; a cop lolls against a car, looking up and out at the river. A pair of teenagers pause, chopsticks hovering over their takeout containers, tilt their chins to the clouds. The street is unusually crowded. There is light where it isn't expected; there are distant explosions. I focus on the shadows. My eyes scan the dark spaces. I call on my powers of recognition.

At the end of the block, there's a payphone but it's broken. I double back. There's a booth in front of the West End. The receiver dangles. I double back again toward Yankee Muffin, my old dorm, rat rock.

The rats on rat rock squeal.

Overhead, the sky bursts with light and color and an instant later a boom echoes.

There is sudden, violent movement by the fence which encloses the rats. Two large forms and a smaller one have cornered someone. I think of bears, of a mama bear and papa bear and baby bear. I think of bearbaiting, of grizzly attacks. I begin to review my bear lore in my head. You punch a polar bear in the nose. Brown bears are vegetarians. The thick pelt of a bear protects it from bee stings. I try to remember if you can kick a bear.

The cornered man is Paul. I see his face in the starburst of light from above and the baby bear is not a cub. It is one of those white dogs with pointy faces and not enough fur. A prize dog, I think, who knows how to make its brothers into meat. It strains at its collar, baring its teeth and the chain links rattle as Paul scrambles uselessly backwards.

Boom Boom Boom Boom.

The rats are in frenzy, and it is not because of the flashing the sky. I understand now why the streets are full of people, what the explosions going off in the night sky are, why everyone is looking up. It's the Fourth of July. It's Independence Day.

In the raining green light, I examine the men with the dog. Yes, the one whose face is visible has the heavy jaw and crew cut I associate with Mr. Boyfriend's New Jersey relatives.

"Whatever you want," says Paul. "I could write you any size check you want."

The men from New Jersey do not want a check.

There should be a lock on the fence that encloses rat rock, but now the gate is opening. The second figure emerges into the street light, the almost-healed bite marks around his mouth. Mr. Boyfriend has a chain and a padlock in his hand. I see that he has planned all of this, the cut lock on rat rock, the dog. It is my flaw to underestimate people, but Mr. Boyfriend is not stupid, can be determined when he needs to.

"What's it worth to you?" says Mr. Boyfriend. "Are you just going to sit there?"

"Jesus," says Paul. "We're not even serious."

The dog strains. Mr. Boyfriend gives a few lazy kicks in Paul's direction and he scuttles back through the open gate. I cannot see the shadows of the rats, but I can tell where they are by the movement of Paul's feet, by the dance he is doing. The dog barks. Mr. Boyfriend locks the gate.

"Jesus Christ," screams Paul. "Jesus Christ. Let me go."

Paul is clinging to the fence, trying to get higher. Me, I'm in mercury time, waiting the slow seconds while Mr. Boyfriend and his cousin walk toward Morningside Park, dragging his dog, like they're just out to watch the sky.

It is the finale. The sky cracks and splinters. There is a silence between explosions. The rats squeal. I should go to him. But there is a hitch in my love. There's a piece of me that wants to gaze at the sky with the rest of the crowd and wait till the noise is over. It's a nanosecond, or it's a full minute, and then I waken back to myself and I am running. Paul calls to me. He has crawled up the fence, six, seven feet in the air, and now I can see the fence is writhing.

"It's OK," I say. "It's OK."

"Help me," he screams.

I shake the lock, but there's no give.

"Can you go over?"

There are rings of barbed wire at the top, but as I glance up, I also see something else.

"Hold on," I say.

"Don't go. Don't leave."

I still have the keys to Yankee Muffin. I unlock the gate, slide it up, open the bolt on the glass door. The shop smells of ammonia and powdered sugar, is dark but the faint red of the emergency exit lighting. *Boom.* The sky flashes again. Paul is screaming and the rats are squealing. I drag the step stool from the utility closet and boost myself up to transom height. I punch open the window. *Boom.*

The mind. The insanity of our thoughts. I think to myself: maybe I could have been an assistant manager here. Maybe I should have stuck it out at Yankee Muffin. Maybe I'll do it in the fall.

As if I'm coming back to school. As if a normal course is still available.

"Paul," I call. I can see his face, now. He's been beaten up pretty bad. But worse are his ankles. Things are there. Animal things hanging from him. Paul spider crawls across the fence, toward me, and I take his hands guide them to the transom. He shakes himself, like a fishing line that has picked up an excess of seaweed. I reach for a hold—his belt buckle—and I pull and he pulls and the sky explodes with color.

Eighteen

The Village Fens Apartments
2010

I am sitting in the living room of a refurbished townhouse. The air smells of fresh paint, and fluorescent bulbs glow in all the fixtures. An old woman pours me tea.

"So you are friend who bring picture? Camp friend from Andi?"

Midnight nears; my journey from Longwood Towers had traced a confused march through the Fens, the sickness leaving me in stages, my destination clarifying slowly. My hands are sliced with razor grass, my shoes soaked in dark mud, water darkening my cuffs. Judah leans against the wall, watching me and Mrs. Auslander. His face is—a face. Lined, weary, beneath his shaven head, but still handsome. The face of the lead guy in the nostalgia act, leaving his two kids behind to go on the reunion tour. Me, though, I always went for the keyboardist, stupid jaw, bad hair.

When I had hammered on the door, I had seen him. Judah: shirtless, the faded tattoo legible on his chest. The faded tattoo I recognize from Dickinson now I see it whole: *If I can stop one heart from breaking, I shall not live in vain*. I had said his name. I was still sick and slightly raving, and he hesitated to admit me, but his name in my mouth had shaken him. Then, the old woman in the hallway behind him had stepped forward, insisted he let me in, and then taken my arm and led me inside.

"Myself, I have stood outside locked door. And also, my child. I think, what if someone had let her in?"

Now she sits beside me, her hands clutching the photograph of the soaking wet girl who is her daughter. She runs a finger over the color-saturated image of the child saved from drowning.

"Everything was lost during the time she spent in the nursing home," Judah explains. "There was a storage unit, but no one was keeping up with the payments."

"No nursing, at that home," says Mrs. Auslander. She looks at Judah. "He gets me out of that place, brings me back home."

"But it's the same," I say. There are doilies on the television set, a bright afghan. The mushroom curtains hang in the window. "It's like I remember."

"He tried," says the old woman. She is dressed differently from the last time I saw her. The ratty house coat, and gray slippers are gone. In their place, she wears a velour track suit and white sneakers. "For make me feel at home."

"So," Judah says. "So it's the only photograph we have of her." He looks at me.

Still, I glance around, and I can't help the impression that things have been shifted, time collapsing and collaging itself into something not quite continuous with what has come before.

"Do not," says the woman. "Do not begin with the branching and the connections. The friend needs finding. This is what is important."

I glance at the clock. Hours are missing, lost.

"I still think you should go to the police," says Judah.

"Police," says the old woman. "With Andi. I go to police. I try police. They do nothing."

Each time, you come down from the sickness, when you reassemble yourself, there are things are returned to you, things not your own. Now, as I sit in the living room, I find something of this man inside my thoughts. He was not a man yet, but he became a man, and was standing with the girl on the train platform. It was old between them, and she was sick with it, but she could not do what she needed to do without him. He said no. Still, it was fifty-fifty he would follow her. It was fifty-fifty for a wedding in California. Seaside, hymns, cake and dancing. There is more I remember. Or it is not cloud, but these mushroom curtains, the fanciful buildings crumbling back into the Fens, the old woman with her ancient sorrow.

Also, each time, each fugue, you lose something. The thing I've lost is right there at my breast bone, breath on my skin, but the feeling that should accompany it is gone. Don't misunderstand. I remember her like you remember a car accident, the blank shock of exposed bone and sinew, of the mangled metal and the beginning smoke. I can hear her crying as if she were right here, each breath and sob, but it is all attached to me like a prosthetic limb. It dangles from me.

Nothing rises, no yearning. Which is only right, because I have left her, have done the one thing I could not do, and I have always known I would.

The old woman stands and tries to lift the tea things, but her hand shakes, and Judah steadies her. He is not a son, but I see between them that feeling. He is like a son, he is as if a son, with grief instead of blood between them. The girl with the red hair had never arrived at the place where she was headed. I remember that now, too.

"Get map," says the old woman. "You show her."

"There is no map," he reminds her. "The man took the map."

"Computer map," she says. "GSP."

"There's the field compass, but it's—I don't know. It might work, but—here, come with me."

"Wait," says the woman. Then, she is handing me a piece of rye bread, wrapped in a paper napkin. I look from one to the other for an explanation.

"You never heard that?" asks Judah. "Cloud sickness and rye?"

"You're making that up," I say.

"Try it and see."

The field compass he used to navigate to Kif-Vesely'e only charges in his battered car. I follow him out while he begins to attach the wires to the decommissioned radio. Now, he taps in coordinates to a field compass. The screen clears, and a map of Sullivan county comes up. The area on the screen is roughly a pentagon, transected by three minor routes into six parts.

"This guy," says Judah. "You think he was the one who broke into my apartment"

"Looking for your father. He had a map. Your map, I think. But there were only four lakes on it."

"Give me a minute," he says. "Something like this?"

"Something you marked off," I say. "A portion? A circle?"

"Four lakes, you said?" He zooms in on the screen, taps one of the wedges. It enlarges.

"That's only two," I say. "Or—what's that?"

There's a dark mass at the center, kidney-shaped, two circles conjoined.

"A glitch," he says. "Bad satellite coverage? It always registers like that. Kif-Vesely'e, and yeah, there's a lake inside . . . maybe a little pond as well, but Mellie—"

"I have to take it," I say.

"Mellie, listen. Your daughter, she's what? How old? I've only ever seen her in the stroller."

I close my eyes. "Judah, what are you doing? I can't. Please. Not now."

"Not two? Not quite two years? I have something to say. Something I need to tell you. I did the math, with your bus ticket. You would have been close, when you went there. You were about to have the baby."

"All right," I say. "So?"

"So, I went back," he says. "After you gave me the photograph. Maybe the picture, or talking to you. Something had changed for me. I went—right there." He points to the dark mass on the field compass. "I found it. But Mellie, it's not what I thought. The cabins, the mess hall. Look, whatever that place was, polarity, trough. It's all gone. There was—I don't know what to call it—a kind of nest there, as if someone had waited, camped out for some time."

"You're saying, me?"

He shakes his head. "Even my father. I can't see him sending a pregnant woman to a ruin. What I thought was—forgive me, I know this sounds crazed—but it was as though the thing inside, it had been wiped out. Like the place that was there had become the blank. The possibilities vanished."

"But that's you," I tell him. "For me, it doesn't have to be the right place. It doesn't matter about Kif-Vesely'e, or the camp. Or what I can see, or if it was some different thing before. It just matters where Emily is going, and the place she's going is on your map."

"Of course," he says. "I see that. But, you know my father has diabetes? He was in the jungles of Laos, but that was a long time ago. I can't see him hanging around there either."

There's some outcome, some eventuality, where this matters. I am returning from my sickness, my thinking regulating itself. I can almost see it, but I can't quite grasp the significance. I chew on my bread. It's helping. Maybe it's helping.

I hold out my keys. "So, can I take your car? Mine is in your old spot at Longwood."

He shakes his head. "I have a failure of judgment, where you're concerned. I kept calling, and calling. There was a way I was going after you, Mellie. And I had to stop, to talk myself out of it. Because, I said, it isn't right. Pushing someone. To get something. It's how I made my mistakes, by fixating. Kif-Vesely'e, you and the baby carriage. It's how I've made every mistake. It wasn't the right track, but I didn't just hop off. I am a person who has to have rules for myself, but the people who have to have rules for themselves are also the kind of people whose brains are always finding sneaky ways of breaking them."

"What kind of rules?"

"Woman rules," he says. "Intimacy rules. Rules like, not, phoning someone thirty times who doesn't want to talk to me."

"You called me thirty times?"

"Here's what I want to say, Mellie. I can tell about you. That you're breaking your own rules, too."

The old woman—Andi's mother—has come to the porch and is listening in. "Are you doing branches again? Empty place? Friend is in trouble. You give car."

He rubs his head, then hands me the keys. "If you do find my father—" he pauses. "You know, I was raised on that stuff, the stuff he makes. This is what I thought was love. It's not just you, and Emily. A lot of people get caught in those gears. I hope he isn't there. I hope he's nowhere near."

"I have to go," I tell him.

The clock is chiming. Hours have gone and, in the morning, Emily will have outlived her value. The kidney on the compass throbs, shifting slightly and I begin to drive toward whatever is inside.

Nineteen

New York City
1993

At St. Luke's ER, they treat Paul's black eye and put an ice pack on his stomach bruise, but they can find no rodent bites, no visible leg abrasions at all.

"Violence," Paul says. "I need to make violence."

"What kinds of drugs have you taken," they ask, flashlights strobing. "How much have you had tonight?"

He is shaking. "If you don't make violence, they make it to you. You need to learn violence."

I use my EMT training to try to command some authority. "He's in shock."

"Who's this woman?" they ask Paul of me.

When he and I have been together for longer, when we've seen enough crises to make this one seem minor, I will have built the reflex to claim *sister*. Later, our America will become one anxious enough about color that my paleness against his darker skin will no longer disqualify me as a relative. But now, ringless and white, the nurses do not believe I am anyone to him. I am ejected to the waiting room to pace with the other illegits, the gang members and the rent boys and the assailants.

The 700 Club is on the television. The hours elongate toward morning.

It's not far from St. Luke's to my apartment, and I think of collecting his dirty clothes and laundering them into a neat bundle. I think of having for him this small offering when he is released. Five in the morning is a good time to slip in, I reason. I'm wearing Paul's hoodie, and I pull it down over my face and make the walk down Amsterdam. I turn the corner. I get about a third of the way down the block before something shifts in the shadowed doorway across the street from my sublet. I flinch. I pause, pretend to be confused, and then wheel around. I manage not to look back; I manage to keep my pace steady until I make the corner. I can live without the things in that sublet. I can live without my books and the three-hundred-dollar tennis bracelet from my paternal grandmother. What I can't live without is Paul. I will take whatever small thing is offered.

A miracle: the check from my mother has finally cleared. I withdraw the first twenty and wait for the orderlies to return Paul to me. On the a.m. news, a group of protestors, gorgeous in evening dress or bone-thin with illness file through a line of cops, hands on their heads. I think of Nancy's ballet dancer friend. The protestors look dirty and defeated on the small screen above the waiting room.

Paul, too. He's been given some Neosporin and a Band-Aid for what they insist is a healed wound several days old, but at least there is less gray beneath his skin. I wrap his hoodie over his shoulders. On the walk to the subway, he keeps stopping, bending down, rubbing at his ankles. It is morning, very early morning.

"Where should we go now?" he asks me. "I should go to the theater. I missed rehearsal. I should at least explain."

"Should you?" It's in my head, how I will tell him about getting cut, about his being dropped from the cast of the extended production, but I can see that he's somehow worked it out—or has always known—the news. "You don't owe them anything."

He shakes his head. "Naw, I guess not."

He rubs his ankle again. I slip a token into the slot and guide him through the turnstile. My mind is like something brittle, cracking. It is trying to hold onto thoughts, but they keep falling apart. One thought is, last night. Is, did he see me? Is, when he was sobbing and clinging to the fence, then, did he see how long I hesitated, how many coward's seconds I waited before I came to his rescue? We played a game, once, Paul and I, and Nancy and some other people, called Dilemma, which basically broke down to if you had to choose between x and y, which would you go for? A lot of the questions were like, sex with Paulina Porizkova for a gut shot at close range or a million dollars for letting someone crap in your mouth. In love, I think, we often end up asking ourselves at what point would I deny him? The Jews and the Christians have all sorts of stories along these lines. The martyrs dying by lion, Mordechai refusing to bow before Haman. In love, you might ask, what price my betrayal? I know now. I wouldn't lay down my life for him. But OK, we're even there. Given the chance, we sold each other out to survive. Paul and I, that's our kind of love, one that wouldn't risk its own skin for the other. I am trying to hold onto this, at the same time as I'm wishing I could excise it. It's too much to know about each other, the hard boundaries at the border of our feelings. My brain is shedding things; thoughts are curling off me. I am sick. I am cloud sick. Why I have been abstaining is one thing I can't remember. Why not cloud. It's the early morning after a holiday and the platforms are empty. I put my arm around Paul, my cold skin touching his cold skin in the warming July morning.

"Let's go to Avenue D," I say.

"Yes," he says. "Mellie, yes. You and I. Together. We need to eat cloud until it comes out of our pores."

It is something we can do entirely, entirely together. We can eat all the cloud in the world.

Twenty

New York City
1993

—pop—

Our mouths are sharp with lemon. He pushes me; I push him; he pushes back; we kiss. I touch his arm, as if in tenderness, but his muscles resist me. I don't recall why we've come to this particular gallery, but here we are, being warmed by the light through the tall barred windows. There are no mistakes that cannot be undone.

Paul slumps against the marble wall and I drop a quarter into the payphone and tell the operator it's collect from Mellie.

"I should get up," Paul is saying. "I should help you."

My mother answers. Her voice sounds groggy and I picture her in the ragged pink robe she got from a boyfriend ten years ago. She thinks it's sexy. She thinks it makes her look elegant.

Paul says, "I could use a cigarette."

"Mom." I am surprised to hear the sob rising in my own throat. What can it be about? I'm so happy.

"I know," my mother says. "Don't worry. It's going to be OK."

"I can't stay here," I say, smiling and crying.

"Listen: I understand. Nancy said she'd sent you some kind of message, or warning, but that you didn't receive it."

"An elevated danger," I say. "A great risk. Mom. Mom."

"She called me. We've got it arranged. She'll pick you up soon."

"Nancy?"

"Sweetheart," she says. "We've been so worried."

For an instant, my mom is as tall as the Statue of Liberty; she is marking safe harbor for me. Mothers: what is missed in all your psychology is also their super powers to heal, is how a mother's love is a port after a shipwreck. Sails tattered, mast split, it's where you drift when all the instruments fail.

"Stay where you are," my mother says. "Nancy is coming to you, because of your friend in California. You're going to be OK."

"What friend?" I say. "Who is in California?"

But when I look in my paperback, I find a note from myself, written weeks ago: *Wedding in California. Fifty fifty.* Between that page and the next, wedged into the spine, is a photograph of a man and a girl at a lake shore. Are these the bride and groom? I crouch beside Paul on the gallery floor and show him the photograph.

"She looks too little to get married."

Paul shakes his head. "That was before," he says.

"Anyway," I tell him, "it sounds like a nice plan."

I pull Paul to his feet and we emerge onto the steps of the gallery.

It had been I, and not my mother, who had gone to my grandmother's funeral in New Jersey. I'd taken the train, a Thursday because our law says you cannot wait on convenience before you put your dead in the earth. My grandmother had lived her life, the second half of her life, in the shadow world of mid-century Jewish wealth, JCC and country clubs and gated complexes and charity auctions. In all ways but the intervals of matzoh and menorah, fasting and feasting, noisemaking and shiva sitting, these institutions were like exactly the institutions of goyim, striving and bland and monochrome. But something had happened, late in my grandmother's life. Her assimilated friends had died off, moved to Florida, or she'd lost them in temple feuds. They were all gone, these golfing and dinner-party friends. There was a whispered intimation she'd picked up an atheist boyfriend. She'd bought her first blue jeans, and given her library card a workout. And then, she left a disconcertingly large gift, not to Combined Jewish Philanthropies or Temple Beth-El, but to Workmen's Circle labor relief fund. Her service was held in a funeral parlor rather than a synagogue and the guests, whether from an earlier life or acquaintances of the secret boyfriend's, were not who I expected, were not the pearls and prime rib crowd. They were union organizers and bookshop owners and the Catskill bungalow colony neighbors. A tiny wizened man, so bent he came up to my elbow, rose on his cane and made his way to the front of the room.

"She was always a friend to the workers. She was in solidarity with the people until her last breath," he said. Then he winked at me, and I understood that this person, his wild white hair and his crooked spine, had been my grandmother's last love.

"You know," he told me afterwards, when I introduced myself, "it isn't true that I'm an atheist. I believe in the tsaddik. You know tsaddik? The righteous men? Sometimes, they are ladies, too. They appear, at times of great peril, and they provide just exactly what is needed, and then they vanish. Sometimes, they don't even seem like nice people—they have to be hidden. Like a superhero. That's the deal. Even a wealthy grandmother could be a tsaddik. Check in the mail, college tuition. I don't believe in G-d and we're not about the afterlife, so much. But I do think that: the perfect person for a particular moment who appears at the perfect time."

It seemed, sitting there in that New Jersey funeral parlor, that who we were was just a function of where a spinning dial landed as any given time, and that my grandmother's number had come up on a day when she was a Trotskyite. She had been a JCC chairwoman and a country club member and a closet red and a tsaddik. We all had them, all of us, secret identities we occupied. We could intersect any one of them at any time.

Sullivan County, New York
2010

I drive west at eighty miles per hour toward the dark spot on the field compass, the engine of Judah's ancient car whining. Once, I pass a cop car lurking in the shadows. Its flashers signal, as I hit the curve, but when I emerge in the straightway, it does not pursue. Here, tonight, I make it through. I have had the sensation, sometimes, when I return from the sickness, that I have entered some other timeline, that I have left another version of me behind. Perhaps other Mellie gets caught in the speed trap, never makes it where she's going. But, if so, there's also a version of me where I arrive, where I find Emily in time. I have seen all kinds of addicts, inmates, lawyers, moms nursing their babies on junk, and I have come to believe it even of them, that there is still a possible version of them where the best outcome is possible, and so also, reluctantly, I have to believe it of myself. Even the least of me, the most weak and hungering version, she could muster herself for Emily.

And here, in the actual world, I am not alone. Emily is still out there, high maybe, wounded perhaps. But high and hurt, Emily is still stronger than anyone I know. If nothing else, this knowledge spurs me on.

Twenty-One

Santa Clara, California
JULY 1993

Nancy slugs on her Coke. "The thing is, I know exactly what Zarah would say. Certain trajectories, you can't pull away from them. Certain fates call us. But then, isn't that just a trick you play on yourself afterwards? Like, this spring, when I was in the dean's office, I thought here is my glorious destiny, the thing I'd been moving toward all my life, but it was just like the farm, like all of Zarah's so-called healing: everything gets fucked up in the end." She catches my eye in the mirror, and shakes her head, as if I've disagreed with her. "It's not because we were students. It's not because we clogged the toilets of a mediocre state school in the Pioneer Valley that we failed. It's because of who's sick. Because it's poor people, and junkies, and criminals, and hookers and queers. Because to them, it's just another dead body. What I'm saying, what happened in California, same thing. Not fate, and not because we didn't try."

Paul looks at her. "Someone died?"

"During your protest?" I ask. "Or are we still talking about Andi?"

Nancy swerves. "Whoops! Who needs a coffee? I need like a gallon of coffee. I need to burn my tongue on a gallon of coffee."

Nancy has always been a great driver, but a day into the trip, she's becoming erratic. She drinks full-sugar Cokes, ripping them out of the plastic six-pack, tossing the empty cans out of the window. Periodically, she'll swerve around nothing then be like, "Oh, shit, that was close." The only way to make it in time is to drive straight through.

There will not be a wedding, after all.

Nancy won't trust either of us with the driving, except for her to take brief naps. I'm trying not to be uptight about it. After all, she basically saved us, me and Paul. She swooped in and saved us.

Judah had sprung Andi from the health farm, but it hadn't had the same outcome.

"Does anyone know how it happened?" Paul asks. "Do you know what happened to her?"

"They found her in the water," says Nancy. "You know, Judah saved her from drowning, when they were kids? That's how it all got started. So, I don't know. Maybe that means something."

Nancy fiddles with the dials until the weird Christian radio is on full blast. Nancy drinks Cokes and ashes in the empty cans.

"Look," she says. "I'm sad as shit. OK?"

When did they first sleep together? Say, she was sixteen and he was twenty-four. Say, it wasn't sex, but just moving together on the sofa, bodies warming, until one of them pulled back, dismayed. Say it was he who pulled back. Say that happened twice. Five times. Twenty. What if she desired him, but was also scared by him? What do we ask of him, then? Say she was thirteen. What parameters make us comfortable? Is there some point at which we give him a pass? Or do we determine culpability based on the outcome? Does it only matter where she washed up in the end? At what age do we confer on a girl her own autonomous desire?

She is eighteen when she calls him in the middle of the night. She is thinner than he remembers, gaunt even. She wears a nightgown, is barefoot in the grass. Her one eye twitches.

"I can't do it," she says. "I tried, but I can't."

"It's OK," he tells her. Finally, she looks like a woman. "It's OK. I'll get you through this."

He puts her on a train. He is going to follow her, right behind her. They might be married.

We're putting states between us and New York, but I don't feel like we've really left until we reach the edge of the American West. Colorado. The earth reddens as we approach the sunset. The mountains dwarf the modest peaks (Monadnock, Moriah, Katahdin) of our childhoods. Nancy's engine grinds as we slope up in first gear on the interminable forty-five-degree angle at the boundary between the green, flat world and the water-starved land of our future. There is an animal we cannot identify, large, rangy, deer-like. None of us has ever been this far from home. Naming the animals: we had presumed our knowledge of the world was fixed, that new things would no longer open to us, but here it is, the weird, shaggy beast, chewing cud in a field of tiny white flowers beneath a glacial white peak.

A set of train tracks climb up the mountain at a distance.

"Maybe she went right past here," says Nancy.

It isn't only the terrible things which can surprise you.

We skirt Nevada, defunct vastness with out-of-order signs affixed to peeling paint truck stops, and enter the weird outlands of California. Everything about the Inland Empire says *not California: not water. Not bikinis. Not blond. Not movies.* It is dry, and hot and brown, or irrigated into flat green squares.

Now that we're nearing our destination, Nancy has become concerned about the dress code. She pulls off the highway into a ditch and begins tossing items from the hatchback into the passenger seat. Sitting next to me in the backseat, her rear facing forward while she strips to her bra and some kind of black girdle thing, she tries to squeeze into a satin cocktail dress.

"It's so fucking cold where we're from. Seriously. After this fuckstorm, I need to be at the edge of the continent. I'm going to dangle my feet off the Santa Monica pier, and eat a skein of cotton candy and roast in the sun until I blister."

"No," I say.

"Yes," says Paul.

"I need everything to be shallow, and warm, and I need to stuff my face with spun sugar," she says.

Nancy is, I notice, thinner. Much thinner. She has almost the same tits and ass as in high school but her waist is cinched in, and her cheekbones have sharpened. She's suffered defeat, I think, but it hasn't broken her. Also, she looks hot in the dress. She slides back into the driver's seat.

"I'm going to sit on the pier, and then I'm going to get rich. Either rich people have to start dying, or people like us have to get rich. That's the only way."

"Yes," says Paul.

"No," I say.

"What is with you guys, anyway?" says Nancy. "Are you guys like sleeping together?"

There is a silence, which we blurt into nonsensically as we exit, follow the ramp, U on the divided boulevard, and then pull into the parking lot of a funeral parlor. Nancy lets us babble all the way through it, expressionless, eyes on the road until eventually we both peter out. Then she half turns so she's facing Paul in the back and me in the front at the same time, just exactly like a mother dealing with squabbling children.

"From my perspective," she says, "it's basically gross. You guys, to me, are basically siblings. But if you can get past the genetic-level physical revulsion each of you must inspire in the other, I offer my blessing." She pulls the key from the ignition, shrugs back into her parka, and steps out of the car.

I go, "Are you sure we should go in? We weren't that close."

Nancy slams the door hard. "We all knew her." Then she looks at me. "We're not going for Andi, Mellie. We're going for the mom."

The mother is in the front row, seated next to Judah. Everyone else sits a few rows back. Nancy makes a beeline for the empty chair beside her, and takes the mother's hand. The mother, Andi's mother, holds Nancy's hand to her face and presses in so hard it looks as though it hurts. Judah takes her other hand.

The other friends come in an assortment of Manic Panic, tattoo and leather boots. Judah's family has paid for the event, and apart from Andi's mom, the softcore pornographer and his wife are the only ones in actual funeral attire.

The closest thing to Jewish the venue can muster is *Rock of Ages,* which only mentions a cross once, and which they play twice, before the funeral director reads from a script. Then, unsteadily, Andi's mother rises.

"It is not fault," she says. She is looking at Judah and Nancy. "It begins a long time ago. The loss is difficult. Sometimes, help is possible. Help comes and it is right. Sometimes, help is not possible. Sometimes, there is no recovery."

In accordance with her tradition, the funeral director announces, she will be buried immediately and privately, but the family of Andi's friend invites the mourners to attend a small gathering at the Ramada across the road.

The casket is pink, covered in satin. I think of her neckties skirt, her boxes overflowing with fabric. It's the only actual thing I can recall about her. They play *Rock of Ages* again; the cleft in the savior's side, the sin that can be washed, and the only thing that belongs here is the water and the blood.

I sit at the bar with the father while Paul sneaks off with Nancy to smoke a clove of remembrance. I can see them, through the window. Nancy hunches to the ground, and it's pretty clear she's crying. I'm trying to make myself feel something, but nothing will come. The soft-core pornographer offers me a drink.

He's a big man, ex-military, and he's drinking plain tonic water and lime.

"Prediabetes," he says, sticking out a hand. "I'm Lew." He indicates a small woman wearing heavy jewelry beside him. "My wife, Trudi."

"Hi," I say.

"How long will you be in California?" he asks me.

"I haven't seen the ocean yet," I tell him.

"If you want to see the ocean," he says. "You can just go out back. It's right there."

"And you?" I ask him. "Are you sticking around?"

"I live here," he says. "I'm in movies."

For a moment, we watch the other mourners kick their studded boots against the bar.

"Excuse me for saying so," says Lew. "But you don't look like you belong with this crew."

Nancy's mascara is runny when she returns and she's inexplicably changed into her red dress. "Were you seriously sucking up to Judah's dad? Do you get the level of slime of that guy? Plus, what's there to gain? It's like compulsive with you."

We've come into the bathroom to fix our makeup and now we lean up against the sink and swab at our eyes.

"No one else was talking to him. I was being polite."

"Seriously: it's obsessional. You're always nosing for the biggest ass to kiss."

"That's my basic problem?"

"Parent. Teacher. Boss. Whatever. You have an upsetting passion to be direct-ed. What I think, I think you just can't bear the fact that you have to run your own life. Which, hello, you do."

"At least I'm not trying to run everyone else's."

"Here's the thing I've come to," she says. I can see her eyes redden again. "You can make a person get on a train. Maybe. But even if you do, you've got no control over where they get off."

I look at her in the mirror. It's a bad day, in a bad month, in a bad year, but still: she looks so pretty. "We can see the ocean," I say. "It's right out back."

We aren't the only ones spilling out onto the patio. There's a pastel wedding party emerging from a tent, and the Manic Panic crew has begun to spill from the bar. Paul's talking to one of the punks.

"Would you like to know my diagnosis of your apparent boyfriend?" she asks.

"I'm in love. We're in love, I think."

"Ew." She swipes a half-full cocktail from an abandoned table, and begins to walk toward the edge of the embankment. "You need to be the favorite. I need to be the answer. And Paul just wants to be popular."

The ocean comes into view. The sky at its edge is purple with the last light, and the water already dark. "That's how Andi was different, I think. She didn't win. I mean, she maybe was never going to win, but she fought it anyway. She didn't just give into herself."

I am pretty shitfaced by the time Judah approaches me. The pastel crowd and the Manic Panic crowd have begun to overlap, the tattoos and the tulle starting to sway in the way that suggests dancing might follow.

"Hey," Judah says. "Thanks for coming. It means a ton to have people here who knew us before."

I have packed a little cloud into my gums, and everything that drifts toward me is buffeted. Still. I laugh and he looks uncomfortable.

"Way back when," I say. "Back in the day." This accident, of where we started, is what has to pass for value, for worth; we carry some citizenship of an amorphous homeland, and that makes us all kin, no matter our sins. It's a blanket amnesty. I don't know what I'm even thinking about. I can barely remember this guy, anyway, and the hostility that rises up, suddenly, washes away.

"Because of how it started. People think that's why—" he waves his hand to indicate the inebriated crowd. "They think I don't know. But I know all that, Mellie. All that stuff years ago—"

"Totally," I say. "Thanks for inviting us."

The pain that flickers across his face momentarily startles me. Then, it fuzzes out. I can't see him anymore. Paul comes to my side and takes my hand. We're not perfect, I know. We've still got things to fix, but it could be us, maybe, cutting the sheet cake in the low-end hotel. It's not impossible. We kiss.

"Gross," says Nancy, who has begun flirting with one of the groomsmen. "Seriously," she says, in the nicest way possible. "You guys give me hives." Then she's dragging her groomsman out onto the patio, and I'm realizing she gets to go to her wedding after all. By the end of the song, everyone's joined them.

Nancy was always that kind, who could get a bad party started, who could turn a rough night good. Paul takes my hand and we dance too.

Interlude

Good Samaritan Hospital, Westlake, California
2008

The nurse is helping me pull on my pants and then she hands me a clipboard. "Just your name, honey. We just need you to write your name."

"Misty," I say. I shake my head. "No. Wait."

"Can you try again?" says the nurse.

"Amelia," I tell her. "Everyone calls me Mellie."

In the room, there's another presence, sharp-edged, perfumed, by the window. I hear the jingle of heavy jewelry.

"Honestly," says the nurse—she is not talking to me but to the person by the window. "Honestly. You can still see the swelling in her eyes. It's honestly criminal to release her in this state."

I nod. She is tiny, the woman at the window, ageless with surgery and injections and a life spent avoiding the sun. In another life, I think, she'd been shot at, seen people die. She has a survivor's pitilessness for the weak.

"You don't feel very good right now," says Trudi. "The doctors and nurses here understand that. They could send you home with medication for your symptoms. There are a number of good options to help with the disorientation and the nausea, and to ease the cravings somewhat, but because of your condition, they are refusing to prescribe at present."

"My condition?—oh, yes. The baby."

"We've always taken care of her," the woman says to the nurse. "That's my husband and I. She's like a daughter to us. Isn't that right, honey?"

"Where is—why isn't he—"

The nurse pinches her lips. "She's been like this. I think she's looking for the father, but she won't give us any information."

The presence shifts. "There's no father." Her English is lightly accented, careful and correct.

The nurse raises her eyebrows, and speaks past the woman to me. "My job, Mellie, is not to be kind. My job is to help you see the situation from a medical perspective. I need to detail some of the risks you've run, some of the outcomes our initial screening indicates you are facing. These conditions, these fetal conditions a baby might have, appear untreatable."

"Are you listening?" says the woman. "Please open your eyes, Mellie."

There is wetness on my face. The woman leans in with a tissue and dabs at my cheeks.

"Can you give us a minute?"

The nurse, reluctantly, leaves.

"Listen to me very carefully," she says. "We've always taken care of you. Lew and I. We will take care of you now, too. Do you understand?"

"You and Lew."

"We're like parents to you. You're like our child."

"You've always taken care of me."

"Always," she says. "And what you've done, the bad place you've put us in, it doesn't matter. We will shield you, and we're the only people you can count on, and this is why you must pay attention."

The nurse taps on the door.

"Quickly now. Listen to me. I need you to listen very carefully. There is something I believe you have."

"I might have forgotten," I say. "I'm sorry."

"Don't play stupid with me. There's footage. You're on tape, hiding it away. I already know you have it."

"I'm sorry," I say again. "Do you want it back?"

The woman releases a short, cheerless bark of laughter. "Currently, I am under a certain amount of observation. I am subject to search, at this particular moment. Not to mention other threats. And, Mellie, these threats could land at your feet, too. Who is to blame? There's a real way of thinking that could put it on you. So, wake up. Listen very closely. There is also the possibility of correction. Let me remind you of certain things you want, that we can do for you. Of promises, specific promises, you have made. Can we still count on you?"

"I promised," I say.

"And then the house, everything you wanted, all that can still happen, too. That life. We are the ones who can take care."

"You take care of me."

"We are your family, Mellie. You have no one else. You have to promise."

"I do," I say. "I promise."

"There's a safe place. You take what you have, and you bring it to this place, and you can rest and recover, let us clean up the mess. You'll be safe, and everything will be nice."

"I'll be alone?"

"A couple of days. We're coming. Just wait for us." She hands me a bus ticket. "Where should I put this, Mellie, that you won't lose it? Is this good?" She is riffling through pages of a book on my nightstand.

The nurse leans in, now. "All set?" she asks.

"It's very hard to do things alone, Mellie," says the woman.

The nurse appraises us, and then moves close to my bedside, muscling the woman out of the way. She has the manner of a school principal talking to a repeat offender. She leans in. "I want to be clear about what we are already looking at with regard to normal development: the outcomes may be mild, but they range to conditions which are extremely painful. There is the real possibility of a potential child's physical suffering and early death. In light of that, as well as your own comfort, you may want to consider options with regard to bringing the baby to term."

"There are options," says Trudi. "But some are worse options."

"If you choose not to terminate, I want to be clear on the kind of responsibility you are facing. Even someone equipped, even someone fully equipped might falter before such a commitment. We are talking about the potential for a very vulnerable being."

I know what they want me to say, and it might even be right, but I shake my head. "No," I say. "I'm not considering any options."

part three:

this must be the place

One

Los Angeles, California

2008

Paul and I share an apartment in a two-story building in Carson City. It has Spanish-style architecture, SoCal pastels, a few potted palms in the courtyard. To a recent arrival from the East Coast, the place might look posh, but I've lived in Los Angeles for fifteen years and I know the signs of cheap housing. Shirtless men smoke on the open-air walkways, ashing over the railing. Between the units, the walls are so thin, you can hear the whine of the neighbor's caged dog and when you turn out the lights, large insects begin to move across the Formica countertops. This is what you can afford when you work in a cash business, when your credit history looks like you've spent your twenties under incarceration.

Now it is evening, and he's been gone for fourteen hours. I stand at the kitchen counter, chopping vegetables for salad and trying to sit with the anxious static of my thoughts. When I called into his voicemail today, seeking any reassurances that he was safely through the checkpoint, any clues as to the hour of his return, there were only three calls: a hang-up from a buyer, a message from the club regarding a missed training session, and then there was one from the woman.

"You're perfect," said the woman's voice, which is a thing we've never been for each other, Paul and I. Never perfect.

We had cloud, for a while. Back when Paul was still getting some auditions, and I was working the production end for Lew, we'd come together at the end of a dry, hot day, pour ourselves giant glasses of lemonade or beer, point the window fan at our faces and eat cloud. Very occasionally, cloud produces hallucinogenic properties, typically for new users or after a dry spell. Paul got into being a gourmet about it, started to chase the hallucinations with herbal additives, etc. that his guy at the gym got him. Then, abruptly, Paul quit cutting in the cloud altogether. For the past nine months, even during our shared evenings, we are residents of separate chemical countries, speak only across the border in untranslatable languages.

What happens, I write in my old paperback, *when you love someone for many years, and you disappoint each other for many years. What happens when every day makes you both smaller and angrier but never enough to leave?*

Paul has evolved this routine in the nine months since he started dealing. He'll bulk up, get puffy and forgetful, then he'll go on a starvation diet. I know when he reaches the hungry limit of the cycle and it will seem like the secret thing he's holding is just about to surface. What we both know: this cannot go on forever. There are not old people who live like we do. Last night, he was there, at the malnourished edge of his cycle. *Say it,* I thought. *Tell me. Make me tell you.*

Instead, in the morning, the Lexus was gone and I knew he'd left on yet another run for incendario.

Paul's point is that a little slackening of enthusiasm in a long-term relationship is natural, is just to be expected. There's this plateau, now, and if he hits it, he can't orgasm unless he pulls out and I tell him variations on this one particular story in which he is being held under water by a woman who isn't me.

There is a dopey side-effect to the drug, a slackening in his speech, that doesn't entirely lift when he comes down. He's only half himself as he travels back from Ensenada Sur with the incendario tucked in the hollow of his dashboard. Paul at the border, Paul in a dumpster, Paul with another woman. There are ways, and ways, and ways he could leave, and for the past nine months, I've felt it closing in.

You're perfect, she said, and I could not tell if it was a role or a romance she had in mind, acting or action. In the background, there was ambient noise; the sense was muffled. Still, I caught the mood. The mood said, soon talk won't be enough; soon, steps will have to be taken.

I have my own secrets to share, my own things cracking out of me. Today, I called Lew and told him I was ready to move on our arrangement. I am at my limit. My chicken is uncooked, my vegetables only half-chopped, but I have held off as long as I possibly can, have pushed myself until I am ravenous. I open the lid of my bureau, move aside the birth certificate, the unused ticket to Belize, and the three shoeboxes where I keep my future. From beneath, I extract a Lucite box of cloud.

Most junkies eat through their restraint two years into a serious habit. But me, I've got it still. Nearly twenty years after I started using, I still sustain the hunger.

Mornings, when I'm in the classes Trudi pays for, I dole out my fixes like some-one who is trying to dose down. Getting high isn't hard. It's not getting high; it's coasting from hit to hit, always at the edge of craving, that ruins me.

But it's why I'm not dead. It's why I have a job and a union card and a couple of friends. And Paul, of course. Paul needs someone who can pay for things, will always need a girl to take care of things, but I'm aware, even as his hair thins, and his face develops lines, that it does not necessarily have to be me.

Nine months ago, we were at the cusp of a different ending. Paul wouldn't tell me the details, but there was an audition. It wasn't for something small. Twice, he took phone calls outside, curling sides left beside the sofa. A few days after, he left the house in a borrowed business suit, muttering cues to himself. As the callbacks approached, he entered a state of tamped frenzy. Paul from those days: not eating, still spending hours at the gym. In my own world, things teetered. In the previous year, Lew had banked seven and a half million on a pay-per-use model, then lost twice that on a subscriber interface. In the interval, one of Lew's actresses, a woman named Caty, had gone missing, and there were intimations that he was responsible.

This, then, was the climate in which I decided to board a plane to Belize. My mother had taken up with a man from Al-Anon, and together, they'd been duped into buying a hacienda in the jungle. The place was twenty miles from the nearest internet and, it turned out, already inhabited by squatters who could not be evict-ed. A problem that wasn't mine appealed to me, maybe, or my instinct was more for flight. As it turned out, I'd overestimated my capacity for even the gutless getaway. In Houston, I dumped out of the airport to score more cloud and missed my connecting on a three-day bender. When I emerged, I was in an American sedan, at the edge of a city, flat, dry palms poking into the wide sky.

In my absence, for Paul, there was a period of dwindling hope, followed by a terrible bleakness. What the casting director told him by way of rejection: he looked too different from his headshot and should consider getting a more recent one done. The path from that phone call to the Medicaid ward at Dignity Health ran through his gym drugs and a sudden decision to quit cloud. They called it an apparent overdose, but I don't think that describes it, fully. He was withdrawing, as much as anything. Withdrawing from cloud, and from a possibility which had been dangled in front of him, and then cruelly rescinded.

When I finally got back to the house, Paul had already been released. Three-day-old cereal was drying in a bowl, and the rooms smelled of neglect and sick-ness, and every screen in the room glowed with pictures of my boyfriend. He was studying himself, as if some secret was contained in those flickering images. Then, he looked at me, and he saw how I had been.

"What should we do?" he asked me.

We were just kind of freaked out and staring at each other, and then, without really discussing it, we got in the car and started driving south. Nancy had been living in this weird desert town on the cliffs past Ensenada Sur, some guru lodge/bullshit factory. In her emails, she was alternately the filthy-mouthed teenager of our memories, and a self-help alien. Still, there were natural hot springs in the cliffs overlooking the sea and these magical stones which were supposed to fix everything; Mexican natural resource law required they be open to the public, so between the hours of three and five in the morning anyone could go and bathe in the living waters. Nancy implied, without being explicit, that the compound ran a sideline in truly excellent and diverse substances, but it had taken the failed audition and the weirdness on Lew's sets to get us to finally make our way down the peninsula.

Los Angeles had made a driver out of Paul, but we maintained the practice from when he was still learning that if it was both of us, I took the wheel. It was leased, the car. Lew knew a man who knew a man, who'd gotten us the credit despite the lack of history. Paul said, you couldn't show up to auditions in a beater, so I mostly drove the Corolla and gave him the Lexus, even though they were both in my name.

When we reached the border guard, Paul got the usual brownish person pat-down, then we drove along the twisty coastal roads and across the desert talking.

"I'm the king of second-guessing," said Paul. "Which is the opposite of acting."

"The problem is not with your acting, Paul."

"Then what is it?" he asked. "Because I would do it. Whatever it was. I would cut off my fingers."

Fact, we weren't twenty-five anymore. Even Nancy had left her commune for better digs. It was fine, easy to be charming and righteous about poverty, about not racking up the accouterments of adulthood, kids and mortgages and retirements savings, until a certain point. Then you became sad or mentally ill.

"Honey," Paul said. The endearment surprised me. And then he said it again. "Honey. I've had an idea. Maybe we should leave California."

"Finish college, register to vote," I told him. "Live in a yurt in a national park."

"Work in a pet store selling tropical fish."

"Show up for jury duty. Mow the lawn."

This was the filthiest fantasy we could contrive: that someday, in some life, we'd get clean. Out there in the darkness, under the clear desert sky, it felt like we were the only people in the universe, that we would make whatever choices we wanted and nothing practical or trivial could constrain us.

"Teaching certificates," I said. "Nonprofits."

"Get married," he said. Which was a joke. Which was only a joke.

At the edge of the blackened desert, there was a beer shop and we stopped for cold Tecates. It was the middle of the night, but there was this family, kids and all, in bright polyester clothes selling large unfamiliar fruit from baskets. We stopped talking about our difficult lives for a stretch after that, and just watched the rutted road in the headlights.

The landmarks for the route to Nancy's were natural rock formations and ruined churches. Paul and I had fallen silent, and in the air between us, I thought I felt a weighing of possibilities. I thought we were really thinking about living some other life. The night was wide and empty.

We arrived at OneLife at three thirty in the morning. The gates of the compound were made of the large, local stone which appeared like dried sand formations, but which was metallic and cold to the touch. There was a pervasive mineral smell. A mist collected around the place, the drift-off from the springs. Nude bikers and Wiccan girls with piercings and non-American white people passed us looking stoned or strung out. *Nancy's around, man. She'll find you. Relax. Dig the vibe.*

It took the better part of an hour, wandering the narrow camp trails between the villas. I was disconcerted by the apparent luxury, the screened-in yoga studios, the tiled fountains and the white-graveled paths set with torches. The parking lot was full of Mercedes with leopard seat covers and Tibetan prayer beads dangling from the rearviews. Finally, we found Nancy running a stone therapy table down by the big cold pool. Even from a distance I could see she'd been eating better. She wasn't back to the double Ds of her Brookline days, but she had a little tummy again. A couple was just finishing up their treatments, and they were audibly enthusing to Nancy while she stacked a dozen or so palm-sized, flat rocks beside the benches.

"There can be something like a high," she said. "After an enversion. Think of this as a kind of preview, of where you'll arrive after you complete the program. For now, you must take it gradually. The results, after the present state wears off, will be subtle for the present."

"If it was up to me, I'd be back for more tomorrow."

"Two weeks, minimum, before your next treatment. If we move too quickly, there can be a kind of disorientation."

"You warned us," said the woman. "You can't become a new person overnight."

"Or if you can, it wouldn't necessarily be a good idea."

The couple retreated respectfully when they saw us coming down the path, still cooing. Nancy nodded at us, like everything was just what she expected.

"Finally," she said. "I thought I'd have to go up and drag you here myself." She threw an arm around each of us. We weren't, Paul and I, traditionally huggers. Touch—this was a Boston legacy that had traveled with us—made us awkward unless it was leading directly to sex, but Nancy, all the years she'd spent around earth nuts, had figured out how to be good at it.

"Let go," said Paul, pulling away from the embrace. For a brief moment, I saw his failed audition face, a spasm of self-loathing, but Nancy wouldn't release him until he hugged her back. I could see we'd been right to come. We stood there hand in hand while she looked us over and waited for her to make her assessment of the fucked-up place we'd landed.

After a moment, she shrugged. "This thing with you two still makes me retch, a little." Then, she signaled for us to follow her toward the pools.

The OneLife compound was enormous, but as we moved from space to space, each one felt serendipitous, nestled into trees, or a circle of the stone benches, or at the edge of a cliff outcropping. You'd catch a whiff of something in certain spaces, see someone scurrying out of sight as you approached, the hint of a secret life to the place, but the surface was still more or less seamless.

"This place is impressive," I told her.

She smiled. "I think it's moving toward its potential. There's more to be realized, of course."

May I say, for a girl who works in porn, I pretty much detest being naked around strangers? I don't mind their nudity, but with my clothes off, I always feel flabby and misshapen, and can never chill out enough about it to enjoy myself. So, among the Hell's Angels and the Mexicans and the Israeli kids slipping into and out of the pools that night, I was the only one who wore a bathing suit. But we were in natural rock springs set at the edge of the world, the ocean far below us, cliffs hanging into the night, and I made cracks about my clothing, and this one Swedish couple thought I was funny, and Nancy hooked us up with some herbal ice tea at just the right moment, and it was like being high for a little while, like being high and clean at the same time. Obviously, drugs were being done out of sight, the famous Ensenada Sur dope, but Paul and I weren't moved to join them for once. His hand found mine through the water. I thought, maybe I've eaten my last cloud. The terrible days behind us seemed like they belonged to another continent. Maybe the future was as easy as that.

It was almost sunrise, almost time for the pools to go private again. Daytime, all we vagabonds were supposed to leave so the drivers of the Mercedes in the parking lot could reclaim their waters.

Nancy crouched down beside us in the dwindling crowd of bathers. "You want to try enversion therapy?"

Paul did his audition face again.

"Don't worry," said Nancy. "I don't have to touch you. It's just heated rocks."

"What does it do?" I asked.

"People call it memory work. It unblocks you. Anyway, nothing bad."

Paul and I looked at each other, then shrugged. Maybe we'd picked up a mild case of hippie from the backpackers in the springs.

"One at a time," Nancy said.

I wasn't worrying about him and Nancy for some reason. She didn't give the impression of wanting anything, I guess. I mean, nothing in the world. From us or from her shitty parents or from a guy or even G-d. I marveled at it.

Nancy set me up in one of the pavilions to wait while she did the thing with Paul. There wasn't a roof, so I lay on one of the cedar benches, watching the stars disappear as the sky turned pink. At some point, a girl appeared and started sorting through a bag of rocks. It made a strange rhythmic sound which soothed. Some more time passed. Paul had surpassed my expectations for his attention span. I sat up to ask the girl whether it was five yet. I could tell even in the early light, she'd been through some rough things. She was bone thin, like an anorexia patient or a refugee.

"Caty?" I said. For a moment, I thought it was the missing girl from Lew's set. She startled, looked up at me, a weird panic lighting her face. Then Nancy was returning, shaking her head.

"She's on a vow of silence," Nancy said sitting beside me. "She's one of our—I guess you'd say, interns. We call them acolytes, but that language is a holdover from when this place was more of a scam. It's like work-study, but for people who need to heal."

"Is she from LA? She's the spitting image of this girl—"

Nancy put her hand on my arm. "I don't mean to sound judgmental. It's the last thing I want. But you still use cloud?"

"From time to time," I told her.

"Some people, you know, after a more intense episode, they have those recognition troubles."

I didn't say anything for a moment. I didn't like to talk about cloud, but tonight I felt easy. I felt easy with her.

"I guess maybe," I said, stealing a last look at the girl. It really did look like Caty, but so skinny and altered, I couldn't be certain, and then she was gone before I could really reach a conclusion. Still, it made me recognize something about the place that situated Nancy in it in a way that felt less confusing. There were people who might not be rich, who might need to hide, and some of them had found shelter here. Following Nancy toward the cliffs, I passed this kind of campground area as we traveled through the trees, camp fire, tents, a parked RV. It was over a fence, but you could tell somehow that it was a satellite of this place, at a different price point.

Then, we were back among the scrubby trees, the ocean air and the sulfur from the springs and the woody perfume somehow wonderful together. Nancy was carrying what appeared to be a backgammon case.

"What a place," I echoed myself. "It's really spectacular."

"It's a work in progress. The current management are kind of fuckers and there's a kind of gross breed of white lady who show up here looking for Mexican boyfriends—no offense. The locals don't see the kind of benefit they could. It's no wonder the narcos find so much support in the area. Still, there is something to the stones. It's not even really drug-like. It's more, stuff the body produces already—like a supplement or a hormone."

I shrugged. I'd heard of incendario then, but I didn't know all the lore—that its qualities were dependent on being processed through special volcanic rocks, that it was filtering it in this way which stimulated production in the male body of some hormone or substance—all I knew was that it supposedly led to better workouts.

"I don't want to bulk up," I said.

"Most people just hold the stones, or they wear them in this headset. Ingesting is what produces the physical results."

In a clearing, there was a circle of large stones big enough to lie on. I thought of Nancy's Western Mass guru, Zarah, the one she'd sicced on me in an earlier intervention. OneLife was a different animal, less about panic and control, more about perception and acceptance. By coincidence, my mother had been following some of the OneLife teachings—by audio disc, via mail, which was a practice that felt outmoded by ten years. Although I didn't make the connection at the time, these audio discs also referenced the local stones, which according to my mother, were meant to allow you to penetrate inaccessible possibilities. Unfulfilled hopes, for example, abandoned ambitions, might live in certain blind spots, if only we could get inside them. The example my mother gave was of herself as a teacher. She'd done a teaching degree, dated teachers, teacherliness recurred in her life, but for some reason, this theme had never actualized. There was an origin point, where you'd veered away, and the stones allowed you to enter it. It wasn't necessarily simple from there. Only through practice might you actually begin to move toward what had been lost. From where I stood in the cedar glen, I was open to OneLife having some substance, to its not being total bull crap. Nancy sat and I took a place beside her.

"You can lie on the rocks, but I think the headset is really the best way to experience it. The box keeps it warm." She withdrew the headset from the flat, wooden box and placed it at my temples.

"Is this what you did with Paul?" I asked.

"He's at a different phase," she said. "It's a personalized process."

I lay down.

I was cold and the warmth of the headset felt like something I couldn't pull away from. I heard a sound. It was a mantra or a song, and I couldn't tell where it was coming from, or even precisely if it was a human voice or something like wind through the rock formations. The sound of the sea wasn't far. The voice, if it was a voice, was yearning, full of feeling, and it called up a compassion in me, an understanding for this alien, unexpected pain. It didn't feel like it had to do with me, but I felt like I could sit at its bedside and hold its hand and keep it company for a while. *Ay yi yai ya.*

"The OneLife therapy suggests that we each operate in our own idiosyncratic realities. A daily commute, a walk along the cliffs, flipping the pages of a photo album. We will attend to certain things—faces, places, objects, and others will vanish. Let us say this is an external representation of our limitations. What we are going to do is walk backwards, revisit what has been missed. There are things of significance there, and if we focus on the right one, then new directions open."

"That woman you were working with, though. She said a new person."

"A trained practitioner makes sure that is not the case. That's why we move slowly. Rush, and there can be mistaken recognitions, calling to yourself something that does not belong to you."

"Who's we?" I asked. "Do you have like a leader?"

"I know," said Nancy. "I'd be skeptical too."

"I'm not laughing," I said. I was thinking of my drive with Paul, how much

I would like to already have lived that life. Spent my twenties in AmeriCorps instead of coasting from high to high. What if all your impossible fantasies were simply signs? I heard the yearning sound again. Was this unlived life so lonely? Or was it yearning for me, for me to simply return to it?

"You remember when you lived in that shitty apartment in Brookline, with all the bugs and your grades taped to the fridge? How you were going to be a politician?"

"I don't want to be a politician," I said.

Nancy shook her head. "It doesn't work like that. It's not about actually being a ballerina or in Commedia, or whatever. You remember when your mom regressed me? I know this sounds insane, but there was a place I went to, a desert at the edge of an ocean. And I saw you there—but it was a better you, and so you were going to some place better, some place you always could have gone, if you hadn't kept circling back. In this place nearby, you're a—"

Brush cracked nearby. A flashlight wavered in the trees. What I thought Nancy had said was "you're another—" which didn't mean anything to me.

"What?" I said. "I'm a what?"

Then Paul drifted through the brush. I say *drifted*: there was a way about his body, hovering and partially deflated, like a helium balloon the morning after the party. So, Nancy's message, whatever it had been, was put aside for the moment.

"Paul?" she asked.

"Apollo," he said, and his voice was like something leaking out of him. "I'm Apollo Blue and I'm so empty, you could fit another me inside me. I'm not even inside me anymore."

It was a name I knew, the one he used in his more questionable projects or when he was working non union, and I didn't give any particular credence to his words. I should have, but at the time I just assumed he had gotten his hands on some bad cloud, and so I took him back to Nancy's dorm and put him to bed.

When I emerged in the morning, Paul was back to himself, seemingly, chatting up some local boys while the three of them peered at the passenger dash of the Lexus. Nancy was AWOL, already off on some motorcycle adventure with a hot guy.

"Something wrong with the car?" I asked.

One of the local kids leaned into the car to wedge a chisel into a crack near the side view mirror and jimmied the lever back and forth.

"That's a leased car," I said. When the kid turned, I could see that he'd lost an eye, that whatever clinic had treated him had left a bad, dark scar where his eye socket had been. He and the normal dude looked at me, like *who the fuck is she,* then went back to removing the dashboard cover. It cracked off. That was when I noticed a taped bundle on the seat beside him. I could make out a collection of paper packets through the bubble wrap and tape, some brown volcanic rock. The two men nodded at Paul, slapped hands, and then took off.

"That's not cloud," I said.

Paul grinned, a teenaged boy who'd discovered a way to leap levels in the video game. "That is Nancy's pure, rock-filtered incendario. It makes you into a fucking machine."

Look, I'd fallen for it. Nancy's transformation in the cedar circle, the truer life you'd already lived, inversion, whatever. And it sounds dumb, but it also meant something to me that Nancy had wanted me to come, that she'd missed me, that she'd reserved a private moment for me, away from Paul. Now I saw that I was the sucker, lying in the pavilion while Paul and Nancy jumped the compound fence to visit the drug lords in the neighboring encampment. My whole idea, that this trip was a prelude to Paul's and my escape, had been delusional. We'd been doing a drug run, with the magic stones and the friendship and the scheming for our future as a cover.

A peasant-looking girl was seated in our back seat. She was a teenager, fifteen, sixteen, wore cast-off OneLife pajamas and it transpired we were meant to give her a ride on top of everything else.

"Try not to be so uptight, Mellie," said Paul.

"You don't need it," I said. "Fifteen years, Paul. We're not teenagers."

Paul returned to jimmying the dash. "It's not for us, for *personal use.*"

And I shut up, because I'm always getting confused about virility v. fertility v. potency and for all I knew, incendario was about aging man things like leaking urine and chin wattle. It wasn't for sex, for us *personally,* and it wasn't any coincidence that he was making this run now. It was because of the big audition, the one he had gotten so close on. When we'd arrived in LA, fifteen years before, it was a shock: the banality of perfection, how your barista looked like a Ken doll and your checker like Sean Cassidy. It was a currency more valued here, beauty— typical, anglo beauty—than talent. There was a kind of freedom for me, congenitally pale, large-mouthed and bespectacled, because no surgery in the universe would put me among their ranks. Paul came closer. In New York, in the light of a downtown dive bar or a non-Equity theater, he could unhinge you. Here, he could chase the standard, but age was running right along beside him.

In the nine months since, his body has changed. On the weight floor, he joined a cohort of pro-lifters and B-movie hopefuls, veins popping, skin taut over their muscles. Make no mistake: these men suffer to look the way they do. They sustain injury and starve themselves and they pump their veins full of whatever they believe will make them grow. They do not make small talk between sets, or eye contact with one another. Instead, they watch themselves in the mirror looking for the most part angry—with their bodies and their lot and their suffering. But there are substances other than incendario that can make you big. And Paul has changed in ways other than his size. I think, as I have watched him transform, of Nancy's words. There are things in our lives we have glossed over. They have been right here, but for our own reasons, we have failed to see them. Paul himself has become harder to notice. He speaks less, as if his native verbal gifts have been rescinded in this warm climate, as if he is fading himself out. It occurs to me that these very side effects, more even than the physical promises, might have been what called Paul to OneLife that night, what converted him to the mineral life of incendario.

Already, as we drove back toward the border, I could feel a new distance between us in the powdery odor gathering in the car. It was to that same Tecate stand we delivered the girl from the back seat, where that same fruit-seller family awaited, the mama and the papa and the two younger kids. At the sound of our car, the mama stood and the girl in our back seat began to hammer on the window and we were still moving when the daughter tumbled out and fell into the mom's arms. The whole family were crying and striking each other's faces and kneeling and wailing things at each other. And I knew there was a whole part of the story I wouldn't understand, but I saw that Nancy had put that child in our car deliberately. Somewhere else, I realized, in the place that was keening for me, I was *a mother*. In this future that Nancy had seen when we were sixteen, I was a mother. I thought we could slip into that life like a cliffside pool, but LA had scripted something else for us, for Paul and for me, and that was what we returned to.

Lew and his driver were waiting for me when I arrived. I'd left without word four days before, been halfway to Belize, to Mexico and back, and I'd been missed.

From his seat beside the driver, Lew leaned over the seat back to give me a fleshy, damp hug. "We have been, to understate, worried, Mellie. I take it no one died during your vacation? There was no national emergency or volcano? Little sun do you good? A little sand in your shoes?"

"I'm sorry," I told him. Neither Lew nor the driver replied as we climbed into the hills above Lew's house.

"Here is what I understand. You are a smart girl, according to you, and I do not disagree. According to you, what we do together, what you and I collaborate on, it's smalltime. Here, too, I have to confess I concur on one level. We are not nurses or social workers. No one is going to think you're a brave, good soul because you make movies with fucking. And yet, this is our livelihood, which is a thing about which I care very deeply. Maybe you want something else. You want to go to cosmetology school? Go back to wearing parkas and riding the T? You want six babies and a house in the suburbs? Wanting is fine, but you do not walk out on me without a word."

"I don't know what I should say," I told him. "Tell me what I should say."

"You vanished. And an opportunity came, and I made a shitty picture, and I lost a fuckton of money."

"I understand."

"A fuckton," he said, his voice rising. "I keep this little ledger. It tells me how much I've paid you over the years. Cash. Hard to operate in cash, right? But you want something, you ask Lew. Lew fixes it. All you ever had to do was ask, Mellie. There are always ways of smoothing. Always, things can be arranged."

From below, from his bungalow, smoke curled. He was not a man who liked to spell out a threat, but he wasn't a person who let you misunderstand it, either.

"This business—even for us—doors are closing, sure. But how you did, in the middle. It will not happen again."

It was a threat, but it was an offer, too. I knew I couldn't get there with a headset, but this, I thought, made sense to me, so I agreed to take the classes Trudi had found for me, and I made the arrangement Lew had suggested. And in another way, since Ensenada Sur, I have been throwing the dice for a better future. The first morning after we returned, I woke up early and cleaned the apartment. I washed the cereal bowl, and I scrubbed the bathroom until the smell of Paul's health crisis had been banished by ammonia. Then, before he rose, and every morning after, I popped my daily Ortho Tri-Cyclen out of its foil and flushed it down the toilet. *To the future! To motherhood! To happiness!*

The pills are gone, just as if I've swallowed them, but at some point, I will discover that I have been pregnant all along, that I must not have been taking them after all. Paul, too, is remaking himself for some unlikely and inadvisable future. His muscles have grown, but the muscles are not the point; the muscles are for something, or perhaps someone. At some point, for example, I realized he'd thrown away the last of the things he moved here with. None of it fit anymore, he said, but it wasn't only clothing he threw away. He is divesting himself, and of course I think about it. If he's divesting himself of me.

Nine months, when you use, can slip away like water. So much of a user's time goes unregistered. It feels like last week, we were making our plans, driving down the coast. But things have happened in the interim, both of us moving along our own tracks.

You're perfect, she said. *You're perfect for it.* In the background, there was ambient noise; the sense was muffled. Still, I caught the mood. The mood said, soon talk won't be enough; soon, steps will have to be taken.

I have been too passive. The voice on the phone, the frequency of the runs, the clothes in the trash. The last window of opportunity is closing. Now, it is evening, Paul fifteen hours gone on his incendario run. I carefully replace the lid on the bureau, wipe my face and check myself in the mirror. The peppers in the pan are just starting to sizzle. When he returns, I am going to tell him what Lew and I have planned, and finish the conversation we began on that drive. I am going to ask him to leave with me.

—pop—

Where I am when I hear his key: at the stove, just plating the dinner. He is standing at the threshold, the drifting balloon quality of the incendario still upon him. For all that fear drives me with Paul, he still calls up such tenderness in me. I guide him into the house and then I place my head on his chest. His arms hover for a moment, at his side. In one hand, he holds the warming case from Nancy's compound. It's a joke, he says. It's not like he buys into it. Still, he is careful as he sets down the case, takes his time before he wraps me in his arms. That way, wrapped together, we hold each other until the stutter in his breath calms.

During dinner, he pushes his food around on his plate, nibbles when he catches me looking.

He looks like he always does when he gets back from a run, like his whole body is having an allergic reaction. He is imposing, now, fills up door frames, but the drugs from Ensenada puff out his face, hide his eyes, still twice, he takes out his phone surreptitiously under the table, and by that I know he has returned to himself.

I set down my glass. "I called your father," I say. "He got that offer he's been talking about."

The conversation about Frank's three-story brownstone has been ongoing between us. When we go back East, for whatever, often a medium-level Jewish holiday, we stay with his dad. He's gotten, if anything, more erratic since the days of kicking Paul out over custody disputes. There is a hole in the bathroom, for example, where he tried to take on a plumbing project, and you can see into the tenant's unit below. They've stopped paying rent, and Paul's father claims to shower at the Y, but by the facecloth and soap in the kitchen, the stepstool by the sink, I suspect him of relying on sponge baths instead.

Frank, the hole in the bathroom being just one sign, needs taking care of, but it has been hard to imagine ourselves as caretakers.

Now, Paul pushes aside his uneaten dinner, glances at his phone again, and sighs. "He'll never take it. He'll never sell the building."

"I don't know," I said. "He spoke to his lawyer. There's paperwork being drawn up."

"Fine, then," said Paul. "One less thing on our plates." But his voice did not sound fine.

"His lawyer tells him it's a good offer, but they're not lunatics. There are all kinds of conditions before they'll close, things inspected and fixed."

"He could do it. Contact it all out."

He means, *contract.* That he is using too much incendario is an urgent conversation, right beneath this one, but I have my own indulgences, and there is the whisper of *soon* and *perfect,* so this is my last, best offer.

"I told him maybe we could take it over."

"As in, buy it? Are you crazy? We can't even get approved for a credit card."

"Come here," I say. "There's something I have to show you."

I lift the lid on my bureau. Paul and I salvaged this dresser from the trash. After we'd wrestled it up the flight of stairs and into the bedroom, after he'd gone off to the gym, I discovered it had a secret. If you flip the top, underneath you find a thin, plastic-covered pad with little kitsch ducks and a vinyl strap to hold a baby down while you change him. Here is where I have kept my secrets since. Now, I push aside the papers and the cloud, and stack the three boxes in my arms. Paul is silent, regarding me. I set the boxes on the bed, and open them.

"That's real?" he says.

I dump one of the boxes on the bed. The sight of that much cash is disconcerting, I know. It turns money back into paper, filthy paper.

"It's a down payment. A good one."

I can see thoughts moving beneath the surface of his skin, faint signs whose meaning eludes me. Perhaps he is thinking of all the things he might have bought along the way, voice coaching and five-hundred-dollar t-shirts, the little luxuries which might have altered the outcome of his auditions. Perhaps he is deciding what it means that my love is the kind that can keep this much from him. But I am not the only one. We keep things from each other.

Then, at last he smiles, though it is still a smile with things behind it.

He shakes his head. "There's always some point where you stop being what you wanted to grow up to be, isn't there? It happens even to—what's the word? Astronauts, football players. People who get what they wanted?"

"Success?"

"It happens even to successful people. They begin to ache, to slow. Mathematicians pass their prime. Maybe some people are relieved when they get there. Maybe some people think, thank God. I'll never have to hear applause again."

"Paul," I tell him. "I'm just getting so tired. It's like it accumulates; at some point, it's going to be unbearable."

Paul finds my eyes. G-d, he's still so beautiful. And I'll admit it, as much as I hate the incendario bloating around his face, I do love the hard muscles. What a strange delight for a thirty-six-year-old to suddenly find herself beside.

He takes my hand. "I'm not an idiot, Mellie. I know what we're doing to ourselves. I know you don't retire from lives like ours. I know you don't start getting work at thirty-five. No one leaves this life for a sweet old age."

"But?" I say.

He shakes his head. "I don't know how to feel that way about applause."

I sit beside him on the bed. The money is still there, the filthy metallic smell of handled bills nestled between us like a Labrador or a toddler. I feel the weight of his arm around me, the thump of his adrenalized pulse in my ear.

"Yes or no?" I say.

"Lady," he says. "Honey. Give me a day. Just let me think."

And then, at once, both our phones are ringing. He picks his up, says hello, and then steps out onto our balcony. Mine is from Lew, and it's an emergency.

Paul may still be aiming for perfection, but I cling to the smaller hopes. That no one else will want a brownstone without a toilet, that we can learn to sand and sheetrock and rewire doorbells to prevent total collapse, that Paul will say yes to me instead of to the woman who calls.

Lew is still talking to me. "Do you hear me, Mellie? We've found what we needed. Get in the car. Come to me. Everything begins now."

Two

Sullivan County, New York
2010

The compass pings faintly as I near the place where Judah had found Kif-Ve-sely'e. It directs me down county highway, rural route, and into abandoned farmland with clots of purple flowers pushing up through last year's gray ragwort. The woods are dense. Dawn is still an hour or so off, and the gathering clouds blot the moon. The two lakes come into view, and at the edge of the screen, the dark kidney shape appears. As I grow nearer, I slow. Occasionally, the trees leap and sway. Probably, these are only animals, but how am I to know?

Any one of them could be Emily. Any one of them could be the man.

I am good at details, can pick a bright thing out where others only see a dark landscape. This has always been my talent. But, too, it has betrayed me. I have missed things, or confused one thing for another; I have read significance where none exists. For the final miles, I have been trying to think of the man from my driveway—not my response, the rush of recognition, the certainty, but the data. For example, the way his speech gapped into silences, as if the words that might have been there no longer existed. It had not only been my confusion, I think to myself now. It had not only been that I was trying to make the man match the longing inside me. As a person, he'd been more blank than filled in. What any of this will help me, as the dawn approaches, and my journey ends, I can't say.

I reach the first lake. It is denuded of forest, and I circle, peering into the shadows. The instinct is to speed, but I force myself to take my time. I find the campsite, a few tents, a station wagon, an RV. There is nothing like a cabin visible and the few trees are leafier, squatter than in my memory. There might be movement beyond my field of vision, things across the water. And now what? At Independence, I have been learning how to tell the difference between what I should pursue, what I must release. I have been trying to remap the circuitry, so that new, rich links will form. But this is a slow way, a hard way. Anyway, it is too late to take time, so I follow something older, stranger that tells me this is not the place.

And what of the man from my driveway? Is something similar pulling him, too? Or is it only the map he follows, Judah's mark?

The second body of water is a dammed reservoir, elevated and fenced. I cruise the neighboring roads, find a VW Bug abandoned in the trees and startle a deer. I smell pines; above the line deciduous growth, the pointed silhouettes of conifers thicken, and some sense, some small force begins to pull. I am not there, but I am moving closer. There's a thickening. It's akin to returning somewhere after a long absence, but richer even, as if I have returned here this way again, and perhaps again. As if my returning has intersected with other returns. I turn back onto the road, and the impression intensifies as the dark spot on the field compass grows larger. I cross some invisible barrier, and now the entire screen goes dark.

Then, the world. The headlights blink out. I am hurtling into darkness, the woods beyond shapeless and colorless and I might be in deep space or under the sea or might have slipped out of time.

My journey back east, two years ago: I am wearing my hospital bracelet, carrying a bag I know I have not packed. I am standing in line at the bus station, a woman urging me forward from behind. Focus, she says. As we reach the front of the line, she hands me a pharmacy bag which rattles with pills. I am pliant, unresisting. My body is slack, the effort too great, but I shuffle up the steps anyway. Then, there is an endless interval of highway, toilet smell, the sticky floor. I lurch up suddenly to vomit. Mountain after mountain, billboard, desert, industrial sprawl, cornfield, sex shop, forest. At last, after an eon of pain and sickness and drugged sleep, I am descending into a parking lot. I am large. I have grown large, but I refuse to look down at myself, to see what is happening to me. Still later, I am on foot, moving through a place which smells of pine and leaf mold and algae.

The headlights illuminate again. Trees rush toward me. I pull on the steering wheel and swerve into a field and the compass pings my arrival. The smell through the windows is the same, is the same as every time I've been here.

Occurrences, my mother once said, can leave ghosts of themselves in the landscape. Judah says, cloud is mapped into the world like a scar. We can fall into these places, quarries in the landscape; we are drawn to them as if guided by a faulty compass. These points are points of inversion.

I navigate my car into the tall grass of the clearing. Light is coming, delayed by cloud cover, but the shapes refuse still to emerge from the darkness. Nothing is around. There are no landmarks, no signs.

Somewhere near here, I had dropped a bus ticket. How had I gotten from the station, if even it is the same place? I could not have walked in that condition.

A stranger, a kindness, red truck slowing on the road between the bus depot and this place. "Your boyfriend ditch you?" The driver clasps a thermos of coffee between her legs. "People go camping in these parts, don't know what to expect. I'm always finding lost backpackers."

"City people. You a city person? They think it's all rolling hills and sound of music out here. But people cook meth; bad stuff happens. You sure? This is the place?"

This is the place.

"I'm meeting my—" *they would always take care of me;* I have instructions, where to go and what to do; there is a thing I have promised to do, and sworn never to.

"Father? Mother?"

"Family."

"They did a drug bust here, back in the eighties. Big one. Made the news. And then they turned it into a summer camp. Isn't that funny? Same place. Drug den. Cub scouts."

Still, I climbed from the truck, walked into the trees alone. Beyond, a lake shore. Towering pines. A nest where I curled up. And what next?

A red wall, and a voice. What I remember cannot be so, but still it comes. It's a boy, and he's telling me to get up, to turn around. Then I am in the pickup truck again, beside the woman.

"Christ," she says. "Christ almighty. I should have known. I knew better. How could I not know?" She leans over, puts a hand on my stomach. "I'd like to get my hands on that boyfriend."

"There's no boyfriend," I say.

The interval between plays like a night of broken sleep, though it is longer, a circle that goes around and around, that keeps sliding into a blank place. The rattle of the pill bottle, the twist of the cap. The smell of animal droppings, the collapsed eaves of a building, drinking muddy water from an old Coke can. No one comes. And eventually I know that no one is coming. A sense of fading, time lengthening, hunger I cannot move to sate, thirst I cannot slake.

The red place. The boy. The boy had gotten me up.

Perhaps that is the thing which pulls me now. The car makes it maybe forty feet into the unmown meadow, and then it's done. I pocket the chip reader, my keys, place the book in my purse, my purse on my shoulder, then fling open the door and launch myself into the knee-height grass. Creatures scatter, as from gunshot. Black shapes lift from the trees. Into the overcast sky, gray swarms of insects lift and then veer oddly. The coming rain has darkened the sky, and I am coming down hard off a cloud high. I am sleepless and exhausted. But I am as certain of my feet as I am one of the ghosts that inhabit this place. *The future casts its shadow beforehand.* I push through the memories like cobwebs.

All that matters is speed. Light is coming, and there are two lakes left, and I may already be too late. I have a sense of moving toward something, something in particular. I do—I recall my body, how it felt when it was pregnant and drugged. Another body, younger, light and afraid. As I near the tree line, I make out some incongruity in the movement of the wind in the grass. My older sense falters as, ahead, the trees part to form a track—wide enough for a car. A few more feet, and I see it, a double black parabola burnt into the meadow. Tire tracks, fresh.

I let the specters leave me, and I follow the hard evidence. The first drops of water fall from the sky. I stumble as I hit a downward slope in the land—a new sound—the rain landing on the surface of the water. Shapes in the darkness, textures and angles, a gathering of deciduous crowns. Before me, a lake. Rain drums on the leaves overhead, on the wooden roofs. And yet, there is no perfect recognition, no final piece locking in to complete the picture. The lake is not a lake, but a pond. It is like, yes. But imperfect. An imperfect match. And where is Emily? It must be here. This must be it.

Then, to the left, something tiny sparks.

In the space around the flare, I pick out the clean curves and dense blackness of a vehicle. The spark, within, comes again, metal against metal in the electric air. I approach, keeping low, hear a branch crack, still. Then, after a silence, I take the last few feet toward the car. Black SUV. I lift my face to the window and peer in.

The vehicle is like a rodent's nest, bunched clothes, soda cans, indecipherable shapes crowd against the glass. Mud-spattered. It is a vehicle that has been lived in. I find an eyehole: nothing, darkness. Then the thing sparks once more and illuminates the contorted body of a woman who has fought like holy hell. Two bloodied fists, pant leg slashed open, skidded flesh beneath. Her face, under her filthy bleached-blond hair, is fixed.

Maybe it's because she's still high, but she doesn't startle when I slide into the car.

She only says, "Easy does it. He's coming back. Any minute." In her bound hands, there's a key. It's a house key, not a car key, but she is working it into the lock.

"Oh, Emily," I say, beginning to try for the knot. She pushes me away with her elbows.

"Don't. Don't you fuckin' get sentimental." There's another spark and she swears. "I used to could hotwire anything. But these new fuckers. You gotta get into the steering column."

"Come on," I say. "Let's go. There's a car, not far."

She looks at her leg. "I can't, Mellie. Don't you think I'd be gone by now? I can't fuckin' do it." Something happens to her voice, a thickening.

The way she looks at me, even cloud could not denature what it means. There is no forgiveness. Not possible. Not in this lifetime, not in a dozen dozen dozen steps. There will be no amends.

"I had five years, Mellie. Five years like you can't imagine. Now I have one day. And you saw it happen. You just watched it. And Leo—fuckin' Leo—"

"Emily," I say.

She stabs the key into the lock, and the alarm flares. The night strobes. Sound pulses. And between, the break of branches, a man's voice. There is no room for guilt, or for apology. I bend, and gently, quickly, slip my shoulder under her good arm. The skin of her legs, one of her arms, is pulped raw, a mess of graveled flesh. There is no touch light enough that it doesn't make her seize, and I must grip her to hold her.

"Emily," I say. "Emily, you can. I think you can. Emily, you can."

The man breaks into the clearing. I haul her across me. I hear her grunt of pain, but then she's on the seat beside me, opening the door. I press the keys into her hand.

"Follow the road," I say.

He nears the car, a faceless man who has become the size of two men. I count to myself as he steps forward, as Emily's uneven and lurching footsteps fade into the sound of the rain, and then, as he comes even with the driver's side door, I lift the handle, release the hinges and slam the door into him with the full strength of my body.

Three

Los Angeles, California
2008

The Los Angeles night is so clear, you can almost see the stars, but the switch-back roads that lead high into the hills afford scant visibility. It is not until we see the cars crowding the circular driveway that I recall Lew is throwing a party. It's not a minor party, not an inexpensive one, but like everything in porn, there is something cheap and shitty bordering the decadent center. The house, dried leaves collected in the corners of the unused rooms, smog dust grayly embedded in the white shag carpeting, isn't actually Lew's, because his place is undergoing construction from the fire damage. The actual owner is doing time for something which may or may not be relevant to Lew's urgent call this evening.

The muscle at the door is packing, but plays like he's just there to take coats. Paul offers up his messenger bag but I hang onto my oversized purse which is scuffed and unfashionable. Lew's in the study, the door guy tells me, so Paul and I separate at the entrance to the patio, him heading for his gym guys and me for the stairs. The music from the poolside is a Latin mix, favoring Brazilian. Through the window, I can see the usual early dance floor of actresses and hair stylists. Paul, in the designer t-shirt he'd swiped from the gym, blends.

Lew looks up from his phone as I enter. "Mellie," he says. He stands from behind the too-small desk, his belly straining against the buttons of his tropical shirt. He gestures toward the window, the goings-on below. "I know you hate this shit as much as I do, Mellie. Thank you for coming."

"You plan to hide out here all evening?"

"I wish," he says. "Trudi would have my head." Tonight's event, whether the people below know it or not, inaugurates a new venture, one which has been in the works for just over nine months, and which will never appear in the books.

"So there's a new tape?" I say, sitting. "You think it's the thing?"

"It's going to be just like with that *Baywatch* girl's video." He picks up his phone, which is one of those new ones where you can watch a video if you're patient for it to download. He shows me the image on the screen, a still of a woman, head and feet cropped out of the frame. "Like that, only bigger, because this pop star is bigger. Ninety-nine percent of internet searches in the next thirty days will be for this sex tape. Meanwhile, the pop star is getting injunctions, is lawyering all the ISPs and search engines, and so the tape's coming down almost as fast as it's shared. Trust me, we are not the only ones paying attention. Bangkok is already making a version with Thai hookers. We're in a race, Mellie. It's a race, not to remind you of unpleasantness, we lost last time we had the chance."

He does not need to remind me. After the house fire, he'd sat me down in the screening room to do forensics. On screen, the actress's vagina was the size of an elephant. At that scale, and hairless as a newborn rat, the human pussy looks totally sci fi, a probe's photo of a Martian sea. Lew ate greasy popcorn and sucked on a lime rickey, commenting on the lighting and the angle. The question we were discussing was whether it was leaked on purpose.

"How you know the whole thing is premeditated: the high angles, the washed lighting. In normal hotel fluorescents, a woman like that would look like Baba Yaga."

"It's produced," I said, "of course. You're right. But imagine the vanity entailed here; these people aren't going to make private tapes that look like shit either."

"My theory: the is-it-or-isn't-it question isn't one you want to resolve. The uncertainty, for the audience, is key." Lew fast-forwarded through a few scenes. "They stay tuned in exactly just because they're trying to figure it out."

"That's trickier to manipulate than simple arousal, though."

"Simple arousal?" says Lew. "Are you aware that it's almost impossible to make money on prostitution anymore? It's too easy to get laid without paying a hooker. The johns now, they're all repressed foreigners, or guys with some kind of real kink or deficit. We traffic in sex in a world where sex is too cheap to sell."

Tonight, in his criminal-buddy's study, Lew taps the screen of his phone. The loading icon appears. "The tech assistants, even now, they're mapping all the broken links. In seventy-two hours, we get the film in the can, and when Iggy from Indiana searches for the pop star sex tape, he gets ours. And the genius thing is, the providers and the Googles, they permit all this activity because they want the traffic through their browsers; they want what we provide which is the content without the lawsuit."

"You think we can pull it off? Make a clone, or whatever, which is convincing enough?"

"Convincing is not the point, Mellie. I've said it before. You screen the original. Map us the tension points. Think in terms of uncertainty, of putting the audience on edge."

"Tonight?"

"It's all on the chip. If I had my way, we'd have started shooting *before* she leaked the damn thing. If it was her who leaked it. If it was even leaked. Point being, tomorrow, you are in the editing booth as we film."

On Lew's screen, the video is still loading. "Fucking guy. Who fucking owned this place? Wrote the program you are holding. You'd think, technical wizard, all that shit, he'd have a faster connection." He puts down the phone on the desk. "I'll have my guy burn a copy to disc."

"Good," I say.

"Good?" he says. "I don't have to remind you how important this project is."

Lew says, the internet has accelerated porn-making into some other physics. Everything is over the instant it is made. This is why embed approach has become crucial. Even porn as a delivery mechanism may be in decline. It's in the code now, he says, the tease, the delay, the final payoff.

"So," he says.

"So?"

"So, you're finally leaving me?" He says it in a friendly way, but with Lew, tone is never to be trusted. In Laos, he ran interrogations, and he still wears cyanide around his neck, still gives the impression he might use it. Tonight, however, nothing he says feels as urgent as the whispering of *perfect* and *soon*.

"I can still work for you from Boston. These days, telecommuting. Everything's electronic—"

"Mellie," he says. "Mellie. Do I have to spell it out for you? This thing is not such a thing as you carry on your merry way afterwards. We have a deal, you and I. I believe your recompense is more than adequate, but you have to be clear that this is not the usual project. Parties involved, and parties uninvolved, will be genocidally displeased. But before the shit hits the fan, there's a window. When it does, I will not be sitting at my known address and waiting for that outcome, understood?"

"Right," I say.

"What I am doing for you, you will be protected. So, you understand. You're ready with the payment?"

I lift my giant bag, remove my wallet and keys, and slide it across the desk.

Lew takes a look inside and thumbs quickly through the stacks. "Now, be sure. You sure about this? This represents a lot of trust."

I nod.

He stands and opens the safe behind him. There are a few manila envelopes within, and the butt of a gun, which I recognize as Trudi's. "Good. The guy at the bank, in Brookline. So, according to him, this transaction doesn't exist. On the other hand, I am making you an identical-sized gift into your new account." He writes out a receipt which I tuck next to seven similar receipts, then he places my purse in the safe on top of the gun and locks it. When he turns around again, he is holding a small, red chip reader. "I trust you, too," he says, and hands me the object. "This is the program. All the magic, it's right in there. I'm counting on you to get it right. Now, let's go, whatever. Mingle."

For fifteen years, I took pride in my work—which I get is a weird thing to say about porn. In the video rental era, most of what we made were mainstream film knockoffs, *Night of the Headhunter*, that kind of thing. I had a skill in managing what you might call tone. You'd reference the original, which made it funny, fun, but it couldn't be a kind of humor that took you out of the libidinous high, funny but not farce. Lew worked with other people, at first. At first, I was contract. But I was the best, which mattered to me, and then he refused to work with anyone else. The fine points of my craftsmanship, you might imagine, do not entirely apply to the amphetamine-fast era of modern porn, click-throughs, peer-to-peer, and camgirls, but I can see, if only in rough outline, how this new project might require my personal skills.

I talk tech, thanks to the classes Trudi pays for. We've done our best to evolve, but it's already obvious the future belongs to the man who wrote the program on the red chip, not to the woman who discerns the subtle tumescent moment between the tug of the zipper and the emergence of flesh.

It belongs to the money men picking hors d'oeuvres from the tray as I make my way through the bikini-clad bodies at the party, to the conspicuous bodyguards, and the insectile assistants peering down at their phones. There is a mood in the air—and part of it comes from this new thing of phones you can watch, of people's interacting in the light of a screen. Lew may talk to crew as if this project were a baton-passing, but I know him to be a man who would not step down lightly from anything. It rankles him, that he has been turned into a middle man, while the real money, the retire-to-an-island money, is being made somewhere above. For this project, there are aspects of my assignment which aren't meant to be visible to the new partners. And there are things, I believe, he is withholding from me. Lew, whose affective spectrum runs from sardonic to sadistic, has been nervous. And there are other variables. On the outer perimeter of the party, a Dodge Charger, in inconspicuous black, circles the block.

The mood of the woman on the phone had said, *soon,* and this seems to be the tenor of the entire evening, the money men, and Lew, and the new video. It is my mood, too. Paul is poolside, talking to Valerie Weston's latest boyfriend, who, like all her men, is under twenty-five and has limited English. As I said, my boyfriend can look as if he belongs in a scene like this one, but as I pass, he touches my arm and gives me a private nod. The East Coast nod, you might call it. The acknowledgment we've landed on an alien planet and that at any moment, we're going to be unmasked. I do not cling, on a night like tonight. I do not act the jealous girlfriend. I know how to play cool but that doesn't mean I'm not watching for signs. I have my own *soon.*

For the time being, there are rounds to be made, mingling to be done. From the other side of the pool, I am being waved over by the only other brunettes at the party.

Westie and Trudi have ensconced themselves in a little grotto, out of the way of the hard bodies and blondes. The artist is already good and sauced, while Lew's wife gets funky on the red dye in maraschino cherries. Lew has emerged from his study as well, to join Paul and Westie's boyfriend by the diving board. He places an arm on each man's shoulder and shows them the thing on the phone.

Paul nods his head at the video, laughs. His voice carries over the water. "It's fucking uncanny."

Westie's boyfriend, incidentally, is not smiling.

"Lew should give me a producer credit," Valerie says.

Trudi nods at the grouping, then turns in her lounge chair toward me. "It was Val who found it for us. The pop star piece."

"Is it any good?" I ask.

Trudi shrugs. "Not my taste."

"It's supposed to be awful," Westie says. "The woman gives head for thirty-seven minutes—single shot, one camera, real time. My tonsils ache just thinking about it."

Trudi shrugs. "People will watch it because it's awful. Like a car wreck."

"I don't know," says Valerie. "That's not why I watched it."

Now, a couple of the insectile boys appear beside Lew and Paul, and then everyone's got screens in their hands, is shaking their heads—'amazing.' Valerie Weston's boyfriend is crowded out of the circle. He marches past us sulkily, sheds his robe and jackknifes into the pool.

"You know why Giovanni's angry?" asks Westie. "It's lunatic. He thinks she looks like me, the woman in the dirty video, and now he's convinced I'm sleeping with someone else."

"It isn't actually you, right? Lew said it was some pop star."

"That's what so nutty," says Westie. She draws hard on her cigarette, exhales. "The woman is famous. He *knows* it's not me, but seeing her film made him imagine it could be me, so he's having a jealous fit. Gio—" she stands, and waves to her latest lover.

"It's that one from the 1980s," says Trudi.

"The super-famous one, or the one that wore those crazy dresses?"

"For legal reasons, Lew is calling her pop star for the duration."

I look at Westie. "I guess I can see it."

"If you still imagine her the way she was in her heyday, a blonde, trashy, showing her lingerie, it's a stretch. But she wears her hair like mine now, and she's had a lot of work, and somehow she ended up with my face."

Giovanni emerges from the pool in his tiny Speedo. He steps into a towel which magically appears on the arm of a nearly equally handsome pool boy. A funny thing about Los Angeles is how much of real life seems to have been scripted by a pornographer. Westie stretches a lean freckled leg through the slit of her white skirt. "Let's make up," she says. "Come here."

"Even if it wasn't you," says Giovanni. "I hear you on the telephone. You have conversations with other men. You want to fuck them."

"You're the one I'm taking to Cartagena," Valerie soothes.

Giovanni crawls across the deck and places his head against Westie's legs, gazing up like a pet at her. "They have nice beaches," he says from her lap. "It is not dangerous like in *Romancing the Stone*."

"Go find your guitar, honey," says Westie, "and get the party planner to shut off the sound system. I want to hear you play."

Gio beams at her, thrilled.

"He's actually really good," she says. "Hilariously, he plays only Hawaiian music. He found out I used to like it when I was in my twenties. Plus, Barack Obama.

Giovanni thinks all things Hawaiian are radical now. Oh, my God, it fucks me up to hear him sing Aloha Oe."

"I'm afraid I'm going to have to miss it," says Trudi. "We all have an early start."

They lean in and plant dry kisses on one another's cheeks, and then Giovanni is calling some question to Valerie and she pads off after him.

Trudi snaps shut her two thousand-dollar purse and looks down at me. "Lew is going to miss you. But things are changing. I think this is right, your going."

"Thanks," I say.

"So, this piece. Are you up for it?"

"Why wouldn't I be?" I say.

Trudi holds my gaze for just a moment. There's some unspoken message she's trying to communicate, but I am not receiving. More and more I have this impression lately, that people are expecting me to pick up on hints, or read expressions and I just can't see what they expect me to see.

"Don't worry," I say.

She nods, leans in for goodbyes, and then she's making her way across the party just as Valerie returns. "Amplifier," says the artist. "Somebody's looking for the amplifier."

Valerie lights a cigarette and I take out my lip gloss container full of cloud. Trudi still lingers on the outer edge of the party.

"Have you ever made one?" Valerie asks. And when I don't register her meaning, she adds, "a sex tape."

"Me?" I laugh and shake my head. "There's every fetish in the world, you know. People who fantasize about being eaten, about having a carrot stuffed in their asses and being trussed up like turkeys. But no one wants to watch me get it on, including me."

Valerie shrugs. "I don't have the mindset to evaluate that," she says. "For me, whether it arouses or not is boring, is a boring question. I'm interested in the dynamics. How does what happens off the set transform what happens on? I'd like to cast divorcing people; the victim of a crime and the criminal. I'd like to lock everyone in a basement for a week with only crackers and water, and then start shooting."

Everything Westie does is like a Milgram experiment, is an unethical test to see how terrible other humans can be made to behave. For example, she had this recent project in which she produced really top-notch quality forgeries with like tiny images sketched into the corner, and then exposed the idiots who bought them from her. Her art is this way, obviously, but so are just like her interactions with others, the shit she pulls on her men, her way of being friends with me. Her life is a longitudinal study in which she does harm and records the impact.

Now, Valerie watches me staring at my boyfriend who has just been drawn into conversation with one of Lew's new actresses.

Valerie says: "You almost want him to step out on you, you think about it so much. It's like you're willing it to happen."

I know she's picturing it, me naked in some film of hers, being humiliated in some way.

She smiles, extracts herself from the lounge chair. "Some morning, you're going to wake up and wonder what you ever saw in him."

"You're kind of a bad person, Valerie. You're just actually not good."

"I'm not, like the rest of the world, on some long desperate quest to be loved."

"I know," I say. "If you weren't sleeping with an underpants model, I'd find you sad."

"Not sad," she says. "I'm never sad." Then, she stands and pads after her boy-friend. She's curious, a curious person I guess. When I met her in New York, I know, it wasn't the first time, but whatever the initial meeting had been, the memory has been a casualty of my adult habits. Maybe there'd be some insight if I could recall it, but with Valerie it's probably best not to look too deeply.

Now, the music cuts out and the speakers amplify the static of a guitar being plugged in. The party's attention shifts and the doorman is handing something to Lew. He looks for me, scanning across the heads of the party-goers, signaling with the DVD sleeve in his hand. This is his level of tech, something which at least has in common with film canisters a shape. The thing on the red memory stick, he distrusts, which is what he has me for. Now, the first strains of a song lift over the crowd, and Valerie, looking smug, reaches her lover's side, but my leisure time is over. It's time to get to work.

But first, I detour to my boyfriend. The actress, sensing my approach, fades into the crowd. I think about whether she's Paul's type, or just another of Lew's heart-land girls, too bucktoothed or damaged to make it in legitimate film. Paul, apart from the crowd for a moment, looks—unlike himself. Maybe it's just the drinks, or the recent incendario run. The puffiness is off him now, and here is where he looks his best. Maybe that is all I am reading, but in the pool light, I realize, he stands taller. It is as if the wariness, that he has carried on his back since the failed audition, has lifted.

"I have to go," I say. "Come with me?"

"I might stay. Just for a bit."

"You used to hate these parties."

Paul smiles at me. It's there again, the thing. Like he's less knotted up. "I mean, they're horrible, too, but I don't have the same disdain. I bet some of these guys are terrific actors."

"Acting is not what the medium calls for, chiefly."

"No," he says. "I mean, hear me out. You've got basically two veins of great performers. There's the genius, and he's a guy who just cracks open his chest, and there's his inner life. But this other type is kind of the opposite. Blank slate. These guys, I've seen them get roles, who are just so—so—"

A group of men has crowded onto the diving board. They hold shot glasses, and have begun to chant—*Go. Go. Go.*—drowning out the island music. The blonde actress—or is it another girl?—claps. The spring break portion of the evening is commencing.

"Being an actor doesn't require you to be a Neanderthal," I say.

Paul sips at his drink. "It's not that. All right. You go on. I promise I won't stay too late. And yes, I'm still thinking about it—Coolidge Corner, drywall, whatever."

So I hand him the keys and catch a ride with Lew. This isn't the first night Paul and I have left separately, and the blonde is bucktoothed, and so far, all this time, he's still come home to me. I lean against the window and let the cool glass salve me against the crawling cloud hunger. Vegetation. The prickly green and dry sweep of palms above, the periodic pulse of a lit driveway between the gated estates and the vagaries of the twisting road. Above, the night is light-pollution orange. *Perfect,* she whispers. Paul, at the party, the months of desperation lifted from him. My head against Paul's chest, listening as the stutter leaves his body.

Lew holds open my door and reviews the instructions before he hands me the disc. "One, tonight: make the changes to the code, screen the original. Tomorrow, two: we shoot, you do simultaneous post. Three, we upload. If you did your job right, those little codes plant themselves in hard drives."

"How much trouble can we get in, Lew?"

"That's the genius of this new program," he says. "Everything up until a certain point is above board. Step four, is trickier. For step four, I'd feel safer in a place without an extradition treaty. I'll explain step four after we shoot."

"Got it," I say. I try to climb out, but Lew's got me blocked. There's something else.

"Don't be upset with me," he says. "I couldn't stand that."

I sense what he's going to say, but gut-sense it. I don't know the meaning of the coming news, but I start to feel the constriction in my chest, the acidic ache where my ribs meet. The lip gloss case is warm in my pocket.

"Paul—don't be shocked. I'm putting him on this one. There's a part his look is perfect for."

"Paul agreed?" Things fly out of me at panicked angles.

"Look, Mellie. I've been clear that this project would not be like our previous projects. That some discomfort, some crossing of lines might be involved. And you said—"

"I know what I said."

"Mellie?" says Lew. "Don't worry. It's nothing too perverted, nothing too obscene. The industry has changed; the world. This is not like the shit we did in '03. Haven't I always looked out for you? Like, the real estate thing. I'm looking out for you bigtime."

Lew has been in interrogations; in Indochina; he'd been assigned to Psy-Ops. Which is why he always has leverage before he comes to a negotiation. This is how my understanding of the night shifts, the exchange in the safe, the way the information has unfolded.

"Watch the video," he says. "You'll see why it has to be Paul."

He closes the door and the driver pulls out. I try Paul, but he isn't picking up. I punch the code for his voicemail. There's a new message from the whisperer. In the background, music plays. *You're perfect for it.* Whoever made the call, whoever she was, it was this, some shitty copy of a leaked tape, that she though Paul was perfect for and he'd agreed.

It is time for another confession. It wasn't only yesterday that I listened to his voicemail. And it isn't only his messages that I spy on. Sometimes, when he is at the gym, or on a run to Ensenada Sur, I enter his closets, feel around the bottom of his drawers, review his browser history. The video I found during one of these episodes was called *Teen Ass*. It was one of Lew's, one with the missing girl Caty. When I edit, I skate lightly over the content. The taste of cloud, in my mouth, slowly dissolving, allows me to avoid thinking about things like the women we film, about what it might be like for them. But that day, I don't know. I really watched. I paused at certain points, and put my hand over Caty's mouth. If you do that, with a picture, sometimes you can see things in the eyes that the smile or the moan masks. What I saw in Caty's eyes was not good. *Teen Ass*, I thought. I thought: maybe I should buy some better pants.

Now, I slide Lew's disc into the machine, and begin to map the tension points, and I dip, at last, into my supply of cloud. The lesson I took from *Teen Ass* was that porn was different for men, although had I not so badly wanted reassurance, there were other things to be gleaned, other insights I ignored. For example, watching a film is not the same as being in a film. For example, I had never put my hands over the mouths of the actors.

—*pop*—

Now the key is in the lock, and Paul's shining face returns from Lew's party. I hear his pocket change jingle, his feet as he steps around my work on the living room floor—Lew's disc, the red chip reader. Then, he is standing by the hiding place, and lifting the lid, to take a gander of our future which I have already bargained away.

"All of it?" he says.

I'm half-asleep, and the code from the chip reader has been running over my eyes for hours. Vicious code, just a little beyond my skill set, but nonetheless troubling. I'm still high. "What do you mean?"

"Oh, Mellie," says Paul. "You're supposed to be smart at this kind of stuff. Judgment. Isn't that right?"

At last, I understand he is referring to my arrangement with Lew. "He gave me receipts. He has a banker. Look, I don't like this thing of you on the shoot either. I won't let him insist. I'll go through headshots. There have to be a dozen guys."

"You misunderstand," he says. "It's not myself I'm worried about."

"I've been doing this for fifteen years, Paul. But there are risks. I mean, physically. You should think it through."

Paul shakes his head, as if the pain were a given, or irrelevant, or even welcome. "I'm not delicate, Mellie. Anyway, if it's weird, I can do it as Apollo," he says.

There is something drifty about him. Something vague. Maybe he's just high, but I think of Ensenada Sur. The cliffside Apollo.

"Don't make me explain it to you." He turns to me, and comes to sit beside me on the bed. "Or let me say it this way: this is part of how I have to leave this place."

"So, are you? Are we?"

He places his hands on my shoulders. "Do I love living off you? Do I want to go back to my father's on a giant pile of your cash? More than a decade, Mellie. I have nothing to show for it. Maybe it's not the Actor's Group. Maybe it's not going to make my page in IMDb, but it won't be easy, right? It's something to me. And anyway, I don't have any other offers."

Why don't I fight harder? I tongue into him, taste his night. There's something unfamiliar, some seasoning I can't identify, but he's still mine. I don't fight harder because his offering is fragile, can still be retracted, and that's the thing I decide to push for.

"Tomorrow," I say. "Before we got to the set. I want you to call your father tomorrow."

"OK," he says. "All right. I promise."

He drops his shirt on the floor, and I see the new lines of him. He prepares a needle, his bedtime dose of incendario. He squeezes his eyes shut, and I can read like slowed frames of a film, the shadows he is trying to banish, and then he depresses the syringe.

He speaks next when he is lying beside me. "Should I be scared?" he asks.

"Of which?" I want to know. "Of what?"

But sleep and incendario have taken him before he can answer.

Four

Toward Kif-Vesely'e
2010

Apollo, the god, was a wrestler. He defeated Ares in combat, and he is the oracular god. He is, therefore, also a Jacob figure. The struggle through which one comes to know the mystery.

In the rainy dawn, as Emily flees, the man and I grapple at the side the black SUV. We fight teeth and muscle and neither of us concedes.

We are not only fighting each other, as we fight. He fights to break something out of me, aiming for my head, pummeling down. Whatever remains in me, he must force it out. I fight to even the score, aiming for his soft parts. I hit him in the place on his chest where a child would rest, and I shove my fist into his mouth like a handful of cloud. I scratch and I bite and I kick and I kick and I kick. I don't need to win, only to distract long enough. There are years in our fight, a tonnage of things unsaid, of hurts we held in secret, of battles we were to weak or afraid to launch.

We are not only fighting, as we fight. Our faces are strange to each other, but our bodies are known. His muscles, his patches of fat, his jaw—alien and beloved. He lifts me, pushes me against the car. He is stronger than me, much stronger, but when my hand finds his skin, the curve from his waist to his spine, he shudders. Disgust? Arousal? I use the advantage.

Slippery with rain, I slide along the car body toward the open door of the vehicle and fall inside. He stumbles. Knees, then on his feet, he throws his weight on top of me. Forearm, elbow, sternum, stomach, fist, fist, fist. The car alarm silences, and silence after such an intensity of noise shocks. In the distance, I hear an ancient engine catch. Emily. My chest, and the man's chest heave against each other, but we remain gripped on the uneven floor of the vehicle. The gear shift digs into my back. My face on the car floor has come to rest against a familiar nylon. An odor, tinged with plastic, holds a bodily mustard to it I recognize, a slight yeast.

The stolen bag. My face is pressed into Juni's diaper bag.

Far away, a church bell rings the morning. Light is breaking and I am four hours from home. Back in Quincy, Juni will be waking from sleep, expecting the usual weekend routine, a private breakfast meal of frozen waffles in our efficiency, then cartoons while the mothers do church and chores and prepare the Sunday dinner. She will wake in the wrong place, the routine broken. Instead of me, there will be the caregiver's support stockings, the nursery smells of tempera paints, Lysol, and spit-up. The social worker will be waiting already, the paperwork being signed. Twenty-four hours. The process will begin by which my rights and responsibilities as a parent are suspended, by which Juni's mother is replaced by a flawed and merciless bureaucracy.

I can feel my baby's distant body pull away from me as if we are attached by an impossibly long, slender cord. There is the beige pocketbook of the woman who has come to take her away. There is the battered car seat into which she is strapped, the distracted reassurance from the front seat.

In some geography, this place leads to that place. There, time does not matter, but the spot at my breast bone which might allow me to leap has gone cold. The thing which links us becomes thinner, and thinner and then it snaps.

Through the SUV window, morning has picked out shapes, a collection of rude dwellings, the frame of a swing set, the white crater of an ancient pool. The rain pours through splintered roofs. Here, where I am, is not the place of my childhood, but some earlier echo. It could have been a bungalow colony, the houses for families rather than children alone.

Children alone. My grief will not come. My missing heart remains a monstrous blank. I release a sound into the man's chest, the man with whom I have wrestled, my breath sobbing into his clothes. His skin finds my skin, and I shudder, too. It waits for me, the old feeling, the familiar feeling. It beckons me to fall into it. *Here you belong,* it says. *Here you have always belonged.*

It is light enough to see one another, the person with whom each of us has wrestled. We turn our heads. Light to lens to optic nerve; signals travel a million fibers, a branching and rebranching. Looking at him is like falling into sickness, layer over layer over layer. Things flicker and vanish. Me, too. I am flickering.

He considers me for a second, two, three. Then he leans back. "You get it now,

I think," he says. "You understand. Before, you wanted to go back. Undo, redo. Whatever. You thought you could get yourself into some nice life, hang some pictures on the wall? Live there?"

"But why not?" I say. I reach for my paperback. "I feel like, if I could just hold on, it would appear. It always felt so close. But things keep falling out."

He looks at me, and the looking is strange because we see each other but cannot see each other. "I don't know, lady honey. Maybe no one really has that," he says. "But even if they do, it's not for people like us. There's only one way, when you've been where we've been. You've got to get rid of it; every last thing."

From the paperback, the borrower's card, crowded with names, protrudes. He tugs at it. He's no longer a reader, but he has the muscle memory of an afterschool library regular. He turns it over, blinks, and then hands it back to me.

"There's nothing there. There's nothing back there." His voice is rich with molasses, with campfire, and I want to listen to it. I want it to tell me everything it knows.

"Where was that? Where have you been?"

He looks at me, at what stands for me for him. "Let me tell you where I come from. There's this place, like a crack in the rocks. Outside, it looks like nothing, but you slip in and everything is there. You can go anywhere. You only have to choose. Maybe you've already been inside, Amelia. Maybe where we are, it's where you chose to go. Inside is the desert, and the ocean, and the inside of the earth, and the sky and nowhere. And when I came out, I took nothing with me, and I was perfect. Oh, God. To bring nothing with you. That's perfection. But the world is tricky, does not like nothing. You have to destroy it all, every little thing. Or else things follow you."

He jimmies the cover on the dash, slips his hand beneath the plastic, and extracts a roll of felt. He unwraps it on his lap. The sharp point of a needle gleams. Granules shift in a glass vial.

He dribbles a little water into the vial, sloshes it around. "Look at my face," he says. "I'm nothing, right?"

"It's not nothing. You're not nothing."

The smell of mineral rises from the moistened substance.

"When we were driving around, when I first found you. That was something wasn't it? I love to listen to music. I love driving. Why not? Because there is still this one thing, Amelia. And it doesn't want to release us. Here's easy: we can get high. Then you and me, we drive off and we can stay high for as long as we want. Nothing will follow us. Even that face you try to wear. It doesn't have to stay."

It feels possible, what he says. We will be two people without faces. This is the perfect place for that to begin, a place of ruin with nothing left inside of it.

He glances at the time. "You got a little left?"

I nod.

"I don't have to force it. You see things, Amelia. You've got this thing. It's in the videos, right? So many people watching them, when there's nothing there? That's the problem, see? It wants to copy itself, to be everywhere, and then how will I stop it? But, it's the solution, too. I know you can get me there. We have three hours left. There's one more lake."

I am so exhausted, so bruised and spent. Parts of me throb. Inside parts. It almost doesn't matter that I know he's lying to me. There is nothing at the fourth lake. So, there will be no driving and listening to music. I have no special talent that will fix this. He's in a different geography, where this place can get us through to where he wants to go.

"It's almost done. The last of it, Amelia. It's not too late to end it."

He turns the key in the lock and the engine starts. He leans back against the seat. "It felt like something was close. Something in this place." With his free hand, he ties off. "I thought we had it. But I couldn't quite get across."

He pushes the needle into his arm. For a moment, the shadows lift from his face. I think, it all begins when we are so young. There is no unwinding it. There is only going forward.

He pulls a beautiful turn, backing almost into one of the listing buildings, and then veering back onto the road behind us.

"Something I do remember," he said. "I was bad at it. I guess you were, too. But we also took care of each other. You and I, how we could. We took care of each other, until we couldn't."

We lurch down the road, rain sheeting the windshield.

"Which way?" He says. "You know."

I know where the ghosts want to take me, and I know I want him to have what he wants. We reach the place in the road where my mind forks. "There," I say. "Just there."

"I think this is it, Amelia," he says.

The only sign from the road is an incongruous thinning in the tree cover, a place where branches have grown into an arch, but our wheels find the memory of a route; we careen in saplings, bounce as we hit rocks. And then, an entry or gate, rusted ironwork, barred entrance hanging on hinges. As we near it, I make out a six-pointed star at the apex. *Kif-Vesely'e*. Around us, the unmistakable topography of summer camp: a cluster of cabins, flag circle, playing field with netless, sagging goals. A circle of towering pines. In the distance, a lake. The right lake, all of it deserted. He brakes, and we both survey the scene. A mob of birds shrieks alarm and otherwise everything is still. It is as Judah had said. The place has become a blank, overmapped until it has emptied. Nothing and no one remains.

"This is as far as I can go," I say. "I don't think we can get there."

I look at him. I can't read his expression, but determination is carried elsewhere in the body. He has it in his posture, in his grip on the wheel, in the tension of his musculature. Pack up, go home, live with the consequences. Leave the bad dog to wander in its own direction: these things are not possible for him. One way, or another, this day will see an ending.

"I'll tell you something else I remember," says the man, and now he is reaching into my bag, extracting a tab of cloud. Fresh, it glistens with moisture. He places it on my fingertip. "Something I'm sure of. You were a genius of this stuff. It loved you."

Lemon and sharpness. My throat opens. Through the rain, I make out an unnatural color between the towering pines. Pink, I think, but once red. It stretches around the camp, a barrier or a wall.

"It loved you," he says again. "And you love it more than you ever loved anyone." He moves his hand to beneath my hand, and begins to lift. There is such tenderness in his gesture. I think of the old couple, the ones dying on the park bench. This is who we might become. I just need another moment to decide, and as I shift away from him, I brush against the diaper bag, its mustard and yeast.

Some will is left in me, some me still in me, a filament pulling at the base of my breast bone; *Mama*. It isn't true, I think. It isn't true. There's one person. There are two.

Now, reflexively, I shift my weight toward him. Startled, he releases the brake, and then I bring my foot down on the gas.

We are accelerating. I think of my baby, the tiny filament. I think of Emily, loping into the woods. Ahead of us is the red wall. I hold my foot on the gas. Faster, and faster. There is a crash, a splintering, the scrape of metal. Impact. The man beside me collides with the windshield. I see the imprint of blood, his body going still as my door flies open and I am thrown from the car, my glasses lost on impact. Stunned, I lie before the gap in the red wall. Everything is blurry. From the other side, two figures approach.

Five

Los Angeles, California
2008

Even in love, there are whole lives you live apart, entire narratives you miss. Paul for a time hid his needle marks between his toes, but eventually the veins there gave out, and the strange bruises began to migrate up his body. Nine months on, Paul's incendario ritual is no longer furtive. I wake on what will turn out to be our last morning together, and through my blurry, uncorrected vision, I mistake the tilt of his head for another kind of concentration, think he is already calling Frank, already beginning the next part of our lives. But then I put on my glasses. Bare-chested, he sits in front of the mirror with his eyes closed. He wears the OneLife headset, and on the edge of the ashtray rests a syringe, its plunger depressed, a dab of blood visible on the needle tip. His skin is waxen, his expression molded—neither flat nor fixed. I understand this as some form of preparation, like a vocal exercise or visualization, for Lew's shoot today, some deliberate thing that he is doing. But that understanding doesn't render this vision of Paul any less alien. I close my eyes and pretend to sleep until I hear him replace the headset in the warming case and begin to move about. Then, I move conspicuously and reach for the already-ringing phone.

So Shoot Me, Lew's production company, is housed in a down-market studio between Silver Lake and Northeast Los Angeles. The empty sets are pool party, sophisticated loft, high-rise apartment, and nightclub. But these narrative films are already a thing of the past. No one wants fiction anymore. They want teenagers, shot through the window of the family SUV. They want college girls getting gangbanged by fraternity brothers, your slutty ex's masturbation selfie. Lew's recent hits have all been productions that don't look like productions.

As we cross the parking lot, Paul's father still rants on the phone, the crookedness of contractors, the unrealistic expectations of buyers on the Brookline markets. Making his offer, Paul had favored euphemisms, and I'm still not entirely sure Frank understands, but it's good enough for now.

"As-is," says Frank, "means as-is."

"We know," says Paul.

"Forty-eight hours," he says. "Then, I'm taking the other offer."

Paul disconnects, and looks at me.

"We could do this," he says.

"We are doing this," I tell him.

And then, for some reason, we're smiling at each other; our smiles are scratch-ticket smiles, the smiles of the bump-up to first class, of the unexpected celebrity sighting. It's like we've walked accidentally into one of those parallel worlds where everything turns out right. The feeling comforts me, banks me against the strange vision of the morning, and the anxieties about the day to come. If the feeling falters, well, then, I have cloud. Cloud will see me through.

At the door to the studio, Lew meets us, followed by the muscular doorman from the previous night and a PA with a clipboard.

"You got the chip?" he asks.

I pat my pocket. He points to one of the cameras, from which a similar device emerges.

"You'll watch from the editing suite on the live feed," he says to me. "The angles will be different, but it'll give you the sense. Then, we'll run you the chip as we finish each one. If we're going to get this in the can before our competitors, we have to do simultaneous post and production."

For just an instant, the incendario look crosses Paul's face, a blinkering out.

"Mr. Greene?" says the PA. "You're with me."

Then he shakes it off and follows after the girl.

"And PS," Lew tells me, grabbing my arm. "You're in lockdown. Even for you, my rule holds. No wives on the set. There's pressure, here. I need no variables."

"I'm not his wife," I say.

"I am well aware, Mellie. It's a term of courtesy. It's an honorific. You are wife-like."

Paul, when I look for him, has vanished, absorbed into the human noise of a production about to go live.

Muscle trails us as we walk the length of the hangar, but Lew lopes along at my side.

I had made it through only a portion of the first scene last night, the pop star's headless torso pacing in a condominium bathroom, before the video cut to static. Whoever Paul was to play, he hadn't appeared. The husband, Guy DeLauris, was in it, obviously, behind the camera, his hand occasionally straying into the frame. From the tabloids, I had him as a villain-type, South-of-France tan, with a perpetual brushstroke of facial hair. He was too Anglo, too old, to be played by Paul. I imagined some pizza boy cameo for my boyfriend, later, the walk-on for the neighbor. The rest of the night, between my departure from the party and Paul's return, I'd spent investigating the code on the microchip. The modifications Lew had wanted were a simple cut-and-paste job, one routing number for another, but the work required precision and exactness. Even a tiny error might sink the whole project. The classes Trudi had paid for gave me a focused skill set, enough that I could admire the trickiness of this new program, but never replicate it. Of the pop star's video, I'd formed less of an impression.

On one sound stage, the carpenters are putting the final touches on a bland bedroom with a familiar painting. It's one of Westie's, I realize, her Kitten Rothko. To the left is a finished set which I recognize as the bathroom from last night's corrupted file. Several cameras are already in position as one of the assistants hangs a shower curtain.

"Do you know," says Lew, "fucking Westie pulled down a bigger profit than I did last quarter?"

"So, you're switching to fine art?"

"She doesn't make money on the paintings. It's all on the mystique, the little origamis and the souvenirs and the licensing. That's how Disney does it, too. It's all on aftermarket shit, on princess merchandising."

"Action figures," I say.

"Moneywise," says Lew, "legality-wise, what has limited us in the past is basically a problem of infrastructure. You need a certain infrastructure to hide the trail, or you need the time to get yourself to a place where the trail goes cold. The infrastructure, I lack. But on this project, I get time." Lew is rich for a reason. This plan of his, I'm sure, will make him a pile. I look up. Somehow, Paul's gotten ahead of us, and I see him, flanked by Legal and Makeup, stepping into the dressing room. Muscle's walkie crackles behind us and he falls back to confer with Lew.

The two men in front of Paul's door close ranks, as if guarding.

"Hey," says Makeup. "The girl's in there with him."

"I have a new scent," a female voice can be heard to say. "It's pretty masculine. Close to sandalwood, but with a kind of bright note at the back of it?"

The girl is the enema girl, I realize. She's famous, among us, for her expert cleansing skills. Her services are coveted, like those of an excellent hairdresser.

Legal leans into me: "Do you know how recently he's updated his testing?"

"Breathe out," says the girl.

On the other side of the wall, Paul yelps in surprise or pain. There is a scent, which is not masculine, not sandalwood, and the sound of rubber gloves snapping. The actresses I have known say you get used to it, but I think of Caty's face, when I covered her mouth in the video. *Yes,* I say, though the moment has passed. *Yes, this is a thing to be scared of.*

Lew and Muscle have caught up to me.

"That's not the set," I say. "I'm not interfering."

"Everything is the set. We start filming in forty minutes."

"Just, it's a small role, right?"

"The actress does all the work. I could do the boy part, even with my diabetes. But I doubt casting would approve."

"Right," I say.

"You, of all people. Have been in this business for fifteen years. It's a little late to get prudish."

Lew peels off, to deal with whatever's come over the walkie, but Muscle sticks with me. When we get close to the editing suite, I decide to ditch. I send him to get me a coffee and then I duck through the hidden door beneath stairs.

The editing booth and Lew's office sit on the second story at the far end of the hangar. Beneath, there is plywood wall painted a peculiar shade of dusky purple. This is Valerie Weston's studio, which Lew lets to her rent-free. Lew likes her work, is a fan, and she'll step in as camera operator in a pinch. Still, there's more in it for him than the occasional collaboration and an infrequent wall decoration. Having a working artist provides cover at the level of just how interested or basically bored the cops feel about this particular edifice. Lew and Westie's work, their traffic in weird copies, is simpatico, of course, and Lew and Valerie both enjoy a certain defiance where the letter of the law is concerned.

On the other side of the door, Valerie is wielding a small implement with a rapidly oscillating spring called an EpiLady which is designed to pull multiple body hairs out at their roots. Westie is covered in a fine layer of peach paint dust. Behind her, the vast windows are partially covered. No great loss: the view shows a vast parking lot with nothing in it but an idling Dodge. Two images are projected on the walls. I recognize them as stills from the pop star video.

"Lew's assigned me a minder so I don't talk to Paul."

I hoist myself onto a countertop, pull out six Lucite boxes. For me, too, Valerie's studio provides me cover because, obviously, she knows I use, and she lets me retreat here when the need comes on.

"He's on Pop Star?" she says, nodding at the stills. "You want to pull him off? Interesting."

"Paul wants to do it. But, look."

"You've seen the film?"

I shake my head.

"It's amazing." She nods her head at the two slides. "That's her in minute one. She's perfect, right? A doll of herself, totally her own creation. That's minute thirty-seven. I think it's utter, the destruction. Everything from that first shot is gone. So, now we know: thirty-seven minutes of oral sex is how you take a person apart."

"You think it was forced?"

Valerie shakes her head. "By vanity, maybe. By the camera. Anyway, it rivets me. I feel a total kinship with it. But you were saying, about Paul."

"He's been shaky. I don't know. I'm nervous."

Valerie smiles. "Don't you have something you take for that?"

"One, maybe," I say. "I'll just take one." The burring of the epilator silences. Valerie stands back from her canvas to consider, then she walks to the studio door.

Valerie's forgery project has been her artistic focus for several years now. She's an amazing technician, a craftsperson of staggering skill, but after the work is meticulously copied, period canvases, authentic pigments, she does the thing where she fucks it up by sketching in some bit of modern kitsch—the internet cat, the talking vegetable. There's a web site, a virtual environment where users can collect cryptic clues about the originals and fakes, which all accrue toward some unclear goal. Now, apparently, she is making Romantic portraits of shitty home video stars. It's a fuzzy set, with her, scam and joke and art.

Paul, for the record, has an interesting online existence, too. He did a dub, several years ago, of a fairly bawdy Japanese import animation. That's where Apollo Blue came in, the name assigned him in the credits. Eventually, it transpired that this was a generic pseudonym that film people use when they're dodging Equity, or when a project isn't going to appear on their resume. Anyway, the series has rabid fans, and Paul's voice was deemed a poor substitute for the original actor. Some lunatic fangirl developed a wiki dedicated to documenting and mocking all of the pseudonym's work. The funny thing, though, is that since the name was so widely used, they misattributed a fairly impressive body of work to Paul's alter ego—he is a collage of a dozen men—and as Apollo, he's a success. I will catch him looking at images of these other men, these men who are not him, studying them.

One. I wedge a tab into my cheek, then on second thought, add second and then a third for good measure. I slide off the counter.

"Also: Lew wanted me to tell you he's using your name with that Christian supplier; he claims you're doing a documentary."

"I hate documentary," says Valerie. "There's so much wasted effort in it, waiting for your subject to tell you a story. I prefer it when the drama is induced, like how rich ladies have babies when they don't want to ruin their snatches."

I swallow.

—pop—

A light blinks at me from the wall. Projected on either side of it are images of a woman, one in ecstasy and one in some combination of horror and suffering. It is the same woman, the same bed, but in the second slide, she is utterly transformed. And then, she is alive, standing at the sink, vigorously washing her hands. It is not the pop star. It is Valerie Weston.

The light is blinking on the wall, and next to it, a lens glints. "Are you filming?" I ask Valerie. "Are you filming me?"

"Sorry," she says, shaking her wet hands and turning off the faucet. "Forgot about that." She drops the straps of her overalls, steps out of them, and then, standing in her underpants, approaches the camera.

"You know what would never happen in a documentary?" she asks me.

"Turn off the camera, Valerie. I hate being filmed."

"I'm just saying I like contrivance." She nods to the square of uncovered window, where there is nothing but a black Dodge. "Surveillance," she says, "is the opposite of documentary." Then, she depresses the button on the camera and extinguishes the light.

Someone knocks at the studio door.

"That'll be for you," says Valerie.

I pack full my lip gloss case, and return the Lucite boxes to the drawer. Then I deposit the little sticky tabs of paper into the garbage, place a balled piece of paper on top to hide the evidence. To be a dedicated and secret user like myself requires a constant, sure supply, a handful of allies and a vigilant mind.

"Thank you," I tell Valerie. "And help yourself, obviously."

"I would," she says, "if you ever left me any."

"There's plenty," I say.

"Then I'll expect another visit."

It is nearly ten in the morning. Trudi's forearm grips my arm; her hip is locked against my hip and she steers me between a teamster with a two-by-four and a stylist with a flatiron toward the post-production suite. Muscle follows along behind us, clipboard under one arm.

"Me," Trudi is saying, "I try to hole up for even one minute and it's impossible. But you know all the little hiding spots, don't you? You are a hard girl to find."

I can see from Muscle's scowl that he's been chewed out for losing me, for forcing Trudi to get involved at all.

We climb the stairs past the actor's dressing rooms to the editing booths. I am supposed to screen the original sex tape in Lew's office, a space of wood panel and Marshall McLuhan hardcovers he'd had carted over entire from a defunct B-Studio. There is a bank of monitors which show, in small slices, the security feed of the studio below. Everything is being surveilled. Trudi watches one for a moment, the money men arriving through the studio door, Lew moving to intercept them. She signals for Muscle to take a place on the bench outside the office, then shoos me over the threshold.

I see that somehow she's managed to extract my purse from me in the process of the transaction. Now, she reaches into it and withdraws my lip gloss case. "I thought we made clear our expectations."

"It's not—" I say.

"Yours?" Says Trudi. "What I think? My position, Mellie, is that we're in the middle of a shoot which has implications that aren't visible to you. My position is that this is not something we can resolve today." She closes her hand over the bundle of needles. "What you do at home, what you and Paul do, it can't interfere here. So, tell me now, if there's anything I need to know."

"It's under control," I begin, again.

"Is that what you think? You think you're pulling it off?"

"Trudi," I tell her. "Listen—" I shake my head. "I'm not getting high. It's for— weight loss. I'm trying to lose weight."

She holds my gaze for a moment. "Be at your best today, and not so sloppy, not—what's the word—erratic—like you have been."

And she opens the door, whispers briefly to muscle. "Focus," she says to me, pressing play on the video. "And stay off the set. Very important."

And then I am being locked in the editing suite, and Trudi is walking away with my cloud.

I try. For an hour or more, coasting the earlier hits of cloud, I avoid thinking about Paul. The distant burr of anxiety rises occasionally from the studio below, a white noise, but I tune it out. I press play and rewind and watch the pop star strip and unstrip, flirt and unflirt, and kiss and unkiss her husband.

Sloppy, says Trudi again in my mind. *Erratic.*

I can feel the edge approaching. A woman in underpants, her head and feet cut out of the frame, paces the bathroom. I freeze the image, press play. The husband of the pop star, invisible behind the camera, reaches for the waistband of her panties and snaps. Snap. Rewind. Snap. I look at the code again. Here is where I would dip into my cloud case, but instead I lick the pockets of my cheeks, hoping for a little lingering flavor. The need crawls up.

I glance at the call list, and it's puzzling. Paul, the first scene, he's listed in every shot, but it's just the woman, walking back and forth, her husband's hand occasionally entering the shot. Where is Paul in this?

I hear the PM call for Greene, for Greene on set one.

I turn to search the live feed. I am maybe closer to my need point than I realized. I should be able to go five hours, six. But probably, it's been a while since I tested that. The screens seem to pulse and then my vision clarifies. Where is he?

On the first security feed, two assistants lead a man toward the set. His back toward me, the man shuffles, rather than walks, like a patient coming out of sedation. He could be sick, could be mistaken for sick. I catch glances from the crew, quizzical maybe. Maybe concerned. The camera drops him, as he walks through the door onto the active set. On the next feed, the crew are checking equipment, swapping out battery packs, taping X's into the floor. The lights are already fixed; everything is poised and the man, the man who looks like a patient, steps onto the tile.

His back straightens. His face tilts toward the camera. The anxious observers relax. He squares his shoulders. He is the spitting image of Guy DeLauris.

You're perfect for it, the whispering voice said. And now, the glow of the lights upon him, his bruises vanished under the makeup brush, his hair slicked, it is true. Now, at last, I can see the resemblance.

The minor roles for which I've scripted him, the guy who brings room service and joins in, the bellhop, the maître d', I'm prepared; but of course, they don't use the enema girl for the bellhop. They don't get hair and makeup to work on your track marks if you just bring room service.

"I look exactly like him," says Paul-the-actor, as he is guided to his place, someone dabbing from his lip a drop of saliva. "I'm perfect."

A smirk settles on his face, Guy's famous smirk. It's Paul, of course. I know it, but he has done something to himself, altered himself at some strange cost I cannot yet understand.

Someone steps onto the screen in the pop star's bra and panties. At first, I see only her body. And it is like, very like, the pop star's. Then the actress steps forward, into the frame, and I recognize her. *Perfect,* she had said. There had been music in the background, tropical guitar. Which is why, scrubbed of the peach dust, her painter's weeds shed for expensive underwear, Valerie Weston is now onscreen with the actor, being encoded into the tiny microchip of the single camera.

I think of the silences which have been dropping between us, Paul and me, since our visit to Ensenada Sur. I think of the boxes he has thrown away. I think of the half-promises he'd made to his father this morning.

The actor onscreen kisses the woman, and the kiss is marital. Comfortable, boring, a little contrived and full of real affection. It is not a kiss I will ever have with him.

"You're my husband," Westie says to the man who won't marry me. Valerie looks up—and I know she's looking for me in particular. She's not sorry. Sorry isn't Valerie's thing. But she is curious, curious how the movie is going to end. Maybe, she looks pleased with herself, like she's done me a favor.

Leaked Celebrity Sex Tape
A Screenplay

*Handheld camera, ECU: a shoulder. A hip. An elbow.
A breast. It takes a moment to orient, then . . .*

*For an instant, the frame is empty, then a tor-
so and trunk begin to pace between the camera and
mirror. POP STAR wears black underwear (new, tag
visible above the waistband). There are two light
sources in the room, an overhead compact fluorescent and the array of incandescent bulbs around
the vanity. One of the bulbs is gray and dead. POP
STAR mutters indistinctly. DELAURIS laughs. He is
the cameraman and he films from his perch on the
rim on the bathtub while POP STAR gets ready. The
setting is the bathroom of a new condominium.*

POP STAR
Of course. You're my husband. You're supposed to.

DeLauris
Tell us what you're doing, you beautiful beast.

POP STAR
You're like obsessed. You always film me.

DeLauris
[indistinct] to the same stupid [indistinct] again.

POP STAR
It's Wednesday. It's standard.

DeLauris grabs POP STAR's hand as she walks past.
She pulls out of his grasp and he catches her
again, this time by the tag at the back of her
panties. SNAP. He snaps her waistband.

```
                    DeLauris
    I can smell your [indistinct] I can smell
    [indistinct] leaking out of you.


                    POP STAR
    Don't talk to me like I'm some animal.

    POP STAR pulls down her panties, granting us a
    brief view of the hairless skin below.


                    POP STAR
    You're supposed to talk nice to your wife.
```

What do I feel? Stomach-sliced. Monstrously alive. The throb of it, sharp like cloud, cuts through all the worries. It is a kind of feeling so rare, it's almost pleasure.

I freeze the frame, transfer the code from one chip to the other. At some point, someone has entered the room behind me and inserted the chip in the editing apparatus. The first scene is in the can. I watch Valerie approach the actor who is Paul on the monitor, knowing it has already happened.

It's over, I think. Almost. Soon everything will be over.

Time splinters into three: Valerie's first scene loops. On the live feed, the gruesome final scene begins, and running five minutes ahead, the pop star original speeds toward its conclusion. Thirty-two minutes. Twenty-seven minutes. Now. I shift my attention between monitors.

In the pop star's version, the camera is perched on the bedside table, positioned to capture her extended congress with Guy Delauris. It is a single, sustained shot, without breaks or cuts. I am coasting from need to peak. Something about this shot has me troubled.

I squint at the original as the scene approaches its climax. Guy, the husband, pulls out. Pornography has to end this way, with the money shot. I read a paper about it in college, how necessary it is, how it provides visual evidence to the viewer that the sex on screen is real. I freeze the frame. The pop star's face is like something melting, like a melting thing I saw once long ago. If I had some cloud, I could see it. I run my hands along Lew's bookshelves, feel around his drawers. Nothing.

The little puzzle, a thing not right.

Outside, Muscle is moving, some chatter or anxiety reaching him from the

322 | *The Likely World*

studio floor. Bottom drawer of Lew's desk, left side: I find a keyring. I'm thinking of cloud, of the Lucite boxes still in Valerie's studio. Silence in the hallway. I try first one key, and then another, and finally the lock turns.

At the other end of the hangar, the final minutes of the last scene are being encoded. *34:58 34:59 35:00 35:01.* Shadows move at the edges of the set, tension rising. Even now, as the actor-husband's face contorts with effort, he inhabits the role. It is extraordinary, an extraordinary performance, but something is off. Something is wrong about his body.

In Valerie's studio, I unearth the last box of cloud. Staggeringly famous paintings surround me, but they, too are wrong, the dopy zucchini waving his gloved hand from the scene of the execution. Valerie delights in failure, the melting penguin, the kitten in the copy, the boy so eager he throws himself from a train. Everything she makes ruins itself. The cloud is on my fingertip, my mouth already open when I realize what has been troubling me about the final scene: Paul is not equal to the requirements. He cannot perform the money shot.

On the perimeter of the pop star's bedroom, a clipboard drops to the ground.

"Now, Goddamnit," screams Lew.

I drop my hands, and begin to run, weaving through disused sets, pool party, cowboy ranch, apartment, drug den. He cannot do it anymore, unless—in my head, as I close the distance between us, I start to tell him the one story. It is the story which is the only way he can get off anymore. *There is a woman. She is holding your head under water. You try to surface*—I am the only one who can tell it to him.

Because isn't this love? The place where we keep each other's terrible secrets, the dark patches which will never find closure or resolution or healing? The evil things about us we can't change? So what if he's vain, if he's mean to me, if he doesn't really think I'm pretty, if he won't give me a baby or a ring, so what if loving him means I always live here on this coast among these shallow and hard humans? So what? Who has it any better?

The husband pumps, five times, ten, again. Valerie sits up, not acting, not the pop star, but herself, radiant with art and attention. The scene is magnificent, a perfect facsimile. Then, the husband stops. He opens his fist and reveals the terrible soft part of himself. It looks pale, like one person's organ grafted onto another body. People shrink, as from a maniac or an explosive. Then, limp in front of the twenty-person crew, the husband plucks his silk robe off a chair and strides, still naked, toward the hangar's exit. I call his name. Between us, crew step backwards, hands going involuntarily to mouths and in their wake, Lew pushes through, followed by a clump of men.

At the door, the husband-actor turns, seeking something. Our gazes intersect. I wait for pleading, for need. I am the only one who knows the story, so he is mine. I wait only for him to recognize it. We know each other. But it is not need he shows me. It is perfection. Naked, soft, he throws his shoulders back and steps into the punishing sunlight. Then, Lew and the other men close between us.

Hands grab and restrain me. Things go white, blur closing in. There is a floating quality to everything now, all that was verge becoming. I struggle and struggle and then I am released. I burst onto the parking lot. Only Lew remains, staring at a black smear on the pavement, dark and glistening. My boss wipes some organic matter onto his Chino pants. Distantly, a radio crackles to life, an incident being phoned in from the surveillance vehicle. Within the hazy interval, the naked man has vanished.

———

If you use cloud long enough, it is said, you will begin to intersect yourself. Your toothbrush replaced with one very like. The keys on your ring will no longer fit your lock. You will ask certain questions, such as where is my father? And find you do not know the answer. Some people call these things memory problems or problems of recognition, but there are things these explanations fail to account for.

Six

Kif-Vesely'e
1986/2008/2010

I am lying before the faded red wall.

Lightning cracks; the world splits and another sky opens. The color of the wall resaturates, darkens and deepens.

It is the middle of the night, and I am twelve years old. I'm in the woods. I'm looking for my friend who has snuck out of the cabin to be with the teenagers. We're not supposed to be out of the cabin, but I'm turned around or I took the wrong path because the way back has vanished. From far away, there's a splash, and a cry of alarm as a little girl dives into the iced-over water, but I am here, following the only light in the woods toward the wall. I'm out of bounds, and you can get in trouble for being out of bounds, but everything else is dark, and so I stretch out my hands and move slowly forward.

Lightning cracks again. On the dock, the teenagers begin to scream, but I am too far away to be part of that story. I take another step toward the wall and then, my foot trips on a root and I am smashing into a barrier, my chin knocked into my skull, my neck bent back. My glasses go flying. I'm lying on the ground and I can't see. I don't know where I am, and I'm alone in the woods, and I'm lost.

"Who's there?" Someone is near. It's a boy. It is his light I have been following and now he sweeps the beam of his flashlight over the leaf-covered ground.

I lift my head, and I see him, folded against the wall. Even close, he is blurry. He balances, cigarette in one hand, flashlight in the other, a book resting on his knees. Even blurry, I can tell how beautiful he is.

"I'm lost," I blurt. "I lost my glasses." And then I'm crying, like a little baby. In front of this boy who already smokes.

"Hold my book," he says. I can't see the title of the book in the darkness, but as I watch the boy's flashlight and cigarette coal move along the wall, I touch its pages. It's a paperback, a library book. When he hands me my glasses, I see his name on the borrower's card, written again, and again. Then I look up and I see his face.

"This is the worst camp," he says. "I hate this camp."

He's scared, too. He is also lost.

"Let's go back," he says. "It'll be easier together."

Lightning cracks again.

It is daylight. I am weak with thirst and exhaustion, my adult body heavy with another creature's weight. I have been here for days, in these woods. I reach the wall, the red wall.

There's a boy. A beautiful boy. I know him.

"Not yet," he says. "You have to go back."

There was once a beautiful boy in a forest. It was cold, and the grownups were gone, and we had only each other in darkness. In a moment, and for a lifetime, we would be wrapped again in our crueler disguises—we would wear the thick skin which would seem better than being hurt—but for that moment, briefly, we sliced ourselves open and were afraid together. That moment has persisted, through my highs, through my all of my losses. A point of inversion.

I might have stepped into it, in the hangar—he was naked and open, but I could not reach him. Then I was in the parking lot, and there was only a dark smear on the pavement.

Lightning, and after a moment, thunder. I am lying on the ground, stunned beside the wrecked SUV. It is daylight, but the sky is dark with rain. *Get up. Get up. Fucking get up*, a voice urges, and it has in it the voice the boy in the woods, of Emily, of Leo with his forceps scars, of the Monday meeting crew, the Independence women, the perfect man in the hangar. *Get up*, I tell myself in my own voice, which carries all of them, *get up and stay sharp. You have to stay sharp.*

Something has begun to worm its way into my circuitry. It is like a virus. *Paul Greene. Paul Greene.* His name, over and over again, inside a library book.

"Get up," says a voice.

And another adds, "Come on, Mellie. Get on up. It's time to come through."

The two figures move toward me, come to either side. She is small, powerful, and she is holding something like a shadow in her hand. He is larger, and weak, but she steadies him, and together they are reaching for me now. Trudi and Lew. She gives him the object in her hand, and I am close enough now to see it is a gun.

She begins to touch me intimately, as though feeling for bruises. But it's not that. Her hands slip in my pocket, and she nods at her husband.

"She's got it with her," says Trudi.

Stay sharp.

"Oh, kid," says Lew, and there is family feeling in his voice, real relief. "Kiddo. It's all going to be OK."

"We're with you. We've got you. Take it easy," says Trudi. She hands me my mangled glasses.

I stand, and I see the collision point of the wall. The impact has splintered it, but on the far side the wooden supports were already listing. Crumpled, the hood of the SUV has accordioned into the trunk of a pine. Its driver is motionless beyond the red smear on the glass, but I see his boy face in the darkness, and his name, *Paul Greene*, branches out and out and out.

Trudi opens the SUV door and nudges the man behind the wheel. There's no response.

"Leave him," says Lew. I resist, struggle to reach the driver of the car, but in the end, the nose of Trudi's gun wins the argument.

My companions lead me toward a formerly white building. Trees press in on the foundation, but someone has made an attempt to maintain it. Together, we step into a vast and largely empty room which once served as the director's residence for the summer camp. Inside, there is a faint human smell, like sickness and salt. A few rusted canisters of film still sit on shelves, from the time it served as a warehouse for contraband skin flicks. Now, it is a miserly sanctuary. Lew transfers his weight to a chair back, leaning painfully, his exposed veins beneath his wrinkled shorts throbbing. There are new discolorations on his face, a patch of blue by one ear. Trudi takes the weapon back from him and moves toward a pre-War ceramic stove. Her hair is longer, and almost entirely gray. They've been arguing—the crackle of the conflict is still in the air—and now Lew looks at her. I know that look, because he's given it to me in tricky circumstances. The look asks, *how are we going to play this?*

Trudi sets down the gun on the stovetop, and lights the burner under a sauce pan, pours in water from a plastic jug.

"Didn't I tell you?" Lew says to Trudi. "Didn't I say?"

"Huh," says Trudi. Then, she is placing three mugs on the table and shaking into them instant coffee powder. They feel just like family, but I know they are something else. There is a tiny, tender force inside me which reminds me I must keep sharp.

"You don't look good," says Lew. "Are you back on that stuff?"

The Cohens have been traveling. There is a battered set of Louis Vuitton luggage which appears stuffed mainly with paperwork and evening dresses. Through my scratched lenses and bent frames, I make out the source of the smell. It's a kind of nest—bedding, an unrolled sleeping bag, a mildewed pillow that has been picked at by animals. A glimpse of orange which might be an empty pill bottle, a rusted Coke can. I have been in this place before.

"How much time do we have?" Trudi asks.

"Enough," says Lew. "She might be injured. Let her drink a coffee, for Pete's sake."

There's a laptop on the table, and they sit me down before it and slide the chip reader in. "Just look, kiddo. Let me show you how good you are, when you want to be."

He opens the laptop and inserts my chip reader. I do, I see its beauty. And my fingers want to respond. They want to do the work.

"You're great at this stuff," he says. "No one else can do it like you do it."

Finally, I speak. "There's a video."

"Of course," says Lew. He taps his chest. Around his neck, where he used to wear the cyanide capsule, dangles a plastic case. "It's funny, right? Unless it's contraband, they can only keep seized property in evidence hold until the end of the trial. Turns out, there's nothing illegal about making a dirty picture. That's maybe part of the problem now. Back in the 1970s, when I started bringing in foreign films, the money leapt into your hand."

My head throbs. The screen, too, is throbbing.

"Code, that's the hot item now. That's what everyone is after," says Lew.

Trudi pours the hot water over our coffee grounds. "Drink up. You have to get to work."

I used to take sugar, when I ate cloud. My mouth tissue was so damaged, I couldn't tell the difference between coffee and water unless I sweetened it excessively. When I got clean, I realized it was terrible, not just the sweetness but the kinds of coffee I'd been willing to drink, burnt convenience store sludge from a filthy percolator. Lew and Trudi, we were the same for each other, the sweet that hid the bitter.

Lew sips, then winces at the taste. "Instant," says Lew. "Everyone wants instant."

"This is the same problem with the porn business." Trudi pours water from a jug into the empty pot and replaces it on the lit burner. "Amateurs, free content, piracy. Quality programming cannot compete with the ceaseless supply."

Lew shakes his head. "When I got started in this business, there was so little product that anything would sell. Slutty Svetlana! The ladies of Leningrad! I was importing these Russian blackmarket jobs, iron curtain girls in blue eyeshadow. You could get rich off subtitle porn. This was a business I thought was recession-proof. People have been looking at tits and ass since the dawn of the cave man."

"Turns out, there's no such thing as permanent profitability," says Trudi.

"You adapt," says Lew. "We did a spell helping people come to America. They call it trafficking now, but what we did was good work. This was right after I got back from Indochina. We started with boat people, then we branched into the Soviet Union. That was another line I thought wasn't going to dry up. Then, end of the decade, so many visas get issued, you can't make money from people. So we got into the chemicals. Great business until people figure how to cook their own. Now the same thing is happening with domestic porn."

Lew taps the screen. "This is where the money is now," he says. "Only, I'm too old for it. This is not stuff I can make on my own."

I've begun to move through the code. It isn't mine, isn't something I could have written, but I can see the insertions I've made, and I recognize them as routing numbers. It is as if the name which has been returned to me, Paul's name, has begun tentatively to find other things in me, as if the name itself is a branching through which I am still traveling to a place more whole than before.

"You need the infrastructure," I say, remembering. "You need the infrastructure or you need time."

Lew nods. "You listen, Mellie. You learn. What's happened so far is nothing."

"Everything aboveboard," I say.

"You pirate a video ever?" Lew asks. "Half of those fakes dump some shit into your hard drive. Do the feds show up? Are police knocking down your door? No. It rises to the level of nuisance. Nuisance is how I want it to be until I am wheels up, general aviation, from a lesser airfield in the Catskills."

"And then?" I ask.

"And then we're in stage four."

I think of the code from the headless woman video that has already hooked the data from three quarters of a million hard drives. There is an interval to prepare, to get yourself on a plane to an island somewhere. Here is the code that will collect it, siphon it, deliver it to Lew.

"The account, the one for the routing number you entered, it's still sitting there," he says. "We have taken care of you, kiddo. We will keep looking out for you. Everything nice and easy. Like it should have been two years ago."

There's a pause, in which I'm clearly meant to be saying something, but I'm watching the elegant code on my screen. Trudi scrutinizes me. "It's that junk. That's what I'm telling you. She doesn't even remember enough to be grateful."

"It was a messy time," says Lew. "A debt situation developed, and you, Mellie, were not incidental to all of those losses. These are the circumstances under which we became entangled with the foreign actors. They kept us afloat, and how it was fixed, also most of the profit."

"A bad deal is still a deal," says Trudi. "Only, one aspect of it was that Lew and I, and our people, were meant to shoulder less of the risk. Police surveillance is not less of the risk."

"So this is the point at which the cost-benefit begins to shift. From the beginning, the profit situation was uneven, but now we're being surveilled. If there's a legal threat, it only seems fair that the compensation shift in our favor. There would have been a justice to it, Trudi and me on a plane with all those motherfuckers left in Los Angeles." Now, Lew swaps out the chip reader, and inserts the other chip.

"You ready for the video?" asks Trudi. She has moved out of my field of vision, and so it is only Lew I can see now, but I hear her going for something. There's a click. The conversation, thus far, has had the quality of a negotiation, but I know that's not what it's really been.

"Wait," I say.

Trudi clicks her tongue. "You can't 'wait'. You don't get to delay anymore."

"I can't," I say. "I can't look at it."

"Be a professional," says Trudi. "Be a professional person."

"You have a good life," says Lew. "Thanks to us. You and Juni." This is how he means my daughter's name: as a thrust to the heart. He thinks he knows me, what I live for. He thinks he can make me behave. He thinks that what is inside me is weakness, but it's something else.

"This could all have been handled," says Trudi. "You're on a plane to Boston. We had our tickets. When the code wakes, it's an instant, then it's wheels up, in the air, gone. That was the plan."

"Even after it went south," says Lew. "We looked out."

"You remember how we left things?" asks Trudi from behind me. "The movie is worthless. Cops, crawling all over the studio. It's unsalvageable. But we got you out anyway."

"I waited for you," I say. "You never came."

"You know why," says Trudi. "Lew did time. Two years. At any point, he could have given you up. You were the one who had what they wanted."

"But then you would have been involved," says Lew. "The state you were in. We insulated you. We tried to insulate you."

Details, I think. I am good at details. On the stove, the second pot of water has begun to boil, Trudi moving just out of view. "There's also the money," I say.

"Well, of course there's the money. Private sex. A monumentally famous woman. Two years ago, this was the holy grail. But a couple of circuits around the sun, and even this is now boring. People make money electrocuting themselves; you can watch a live beheading if you know the right channel, and my actresses, the women that used to work for me, you know what they do for cash these days? Sit in front of a camera and take direction from some basement amateur. But you know what the view count is for our picture in sixty days' time? You want me to speculate why? I think Weston saw it coming. Misery is the only turn-on left, the only thing that gets through. The best porn is the ruin of a life. Anyway, I'm not interested in analysis. I'm interested in hits. We've got this chance to make it right. And it's your money, too. Yours and Juni's. You could use it, right?"

"And then what?" I ask. "Do I vanish too?"

"Whatever you want, Mellie."

"We're almost out of time," says Trudi. She shifts again, so I cannot quite see her, but I catch the blackness of her gun's nose as I swivel in my chair.

"How I want this to go," Lew says. "Is that you do this for us, and then we've got you. But Trudi and I disagree. Even if you pull it off, in her opinion, there are still outstanding accounts. What she's not clear on is, why didn't you warn us? I say, the outcome's the same, maybe better. But, she points out that time in a prison cell has not been excellent for my health. She points out, if it weren't for the unfortunate occurrence on the set, this would all have been done. Not to be intimate. But of all people, you would have known. Wouldn't you?"

Now, the video opens. The counter at the bottom reads thirty-seven minutes. The still shot reveals a bed, two bodies which have just pulled apart. In the frame, the man's hand blocks his nakedness, but you can see his face. I see his face. It is the face of the man in the car, of the boy in the woods, of the person I loved so badly for so many years, that this was how it had to end. It is Paul's face.

The things that return are terrible, a naked man moving across the hangar, a smear of organic matter on the pavement, but I steady myself and then I stand. "He was the one I should have warned," I say. My hand goes to the chip reader.

"You want to blame us?"

"You hurt him," I say.

"I was angry, sure," says Lew. "My people were very, understandably, angry. But you think we what?"

"You did something to him. You hurt him."

"What we did was we arranged things. For his continued safety, Mellie. There were people he had over the border, I understand. That's where we left him. It was exactly what he wanted."

"I can see why you'd tell yourself that," says Trudi. "The state we found you in. Filthy, Mellie. I mean, infections, not to mention that stuff you were putting inside you. Inside Juni. What kind of man would leave a girl that way? You'd rather think he was dead, wouldn't you?"

"You want to go outside, tend to him? Cry over his body? You feel loyal to him now, after everything he's done? Even if he didn't love you—"

"Love," says Trudi. "It's not sacred. You can leave a person you love."

"Even if he didn't still have feelings, shouldn't he have helped you, for the sake of the baby?"

"It's on him, too. What you put inside yourself. Maybe not equally, but the dad counts, too."

"Mellie, it's this simple. He left you, and we were the ones who showed up. It's not even about debt, about owing. It's about who has been there."

Lew is right. He has been there. He's a pornographer, a psycho who made his money off young people and trafficked in misery and has done harm upon harm. People have disappeared from his set. What he's offering, forgiveness, security, may be real, but I have taken such bargains all my life, and it has made me small.

I pull the chip from the drive, and I turn. It is their surprise that gives me the moment I need to reach the lit burner and drop the tiny object into the flames. Too late, Trudi fires her weapon.

Seven

Los Angeles, California and Baja California, Mexico

2008

When I return from the studio to Carson City, enter my apartment, an alien presence is everywhere, Paul completely absent. The roaches skittering across the counter are not my roaches. The dampness on my pillowcase is not my pillowcase. A cat, smoky gray, suns on the sofa. I do not own a cat. Paul and I detest cats. I am afraid of the cat, of what it might mean. Sometimes, when I come off a cloud high, there is a sensation like this, like a stranger's life has been swapped with yours. But then, logically, it is also possible that one day you might get lucky. All the bad decisions unmade, the life you might have had. From the back of the freezer, from behind the frozen peas, I extract a box of cloud and shovel a couple of tabs in my mouth.

—pop—

The cat meows.

At the gym, they're not sure. Maybe Paolo? Could that be who I mean? None of his guys he dealt to will speak to me. When I call Brookline, a contractor answers. The owner is selling, is what he heard, not that it's any of his business. From my phone, I send an email to Ensenada Sur. On the way home, I stop by my guy in Koreatown and score a one-off of cloud. Is there someone I normally come here with, I ask him? Please. Can you tell me? Something about the way I ask must scare my dealer, because he is backing away, closing the door. Sure, he says. Of course. Big guy, muscles, like something out of a beach movie. I come here with him all the time.

—*pop*—

The cat is crying as I open the door to the apartment.

Online, I search for old videos of Paul's, the hate sites from his dirty anime—I listen to the audio and it's not his voice. I find dozens of Paul Greenes, his PhD namesakes, a chef and a Canadian soccer star, but none of them is my Paul. It is as if, piece by piece, all evidence of him is being extracted from my life. I eat another tab.

—*pop*—

The cat kneads at my pant leg.

I let her out, and I follow after. It's night—nine, maybe. I wander into the Best Buy at the end of my street looking for a soda pop cooler. Televisions surround me and a perky nineteen-year-old commentator discusses what's going viral, what's trending, what's so last week. Then the show cuts to a clip. I recognize the kitten Rothko. I recognize Valerie Weston, her dark bangs and massacre eyes. She's about to go down on an actor. I squint at him. I watch carefully. He's on every screen in the store, magnified and multiplied, and it's not Paul. It's Westie and some man I've never seen before in my life. Some weird Paul replica and Valerie Weston about to go at it like porn stars. *Spicy!* says the commentator. *Next up, this superstar teen went on a Malibu joyride, and we've got it all on tape!* I puke on a gaming console, and then pop a square of cloud to wash out the taste.

—*pop*—

The cat slips between my legs as I open the door. In the apartment, male evidence is everywhere, but even the clothes are brand new and scented with the mineral odor of incendario. I rove the rooms looking for proof. Underneath the sofa, I find three pages of an old audition script. CRAIG: *Male. 28. All-American type. Newly arrived in the city, his whole life before him. ACT I Scene A.* I pop the lid on the Koreatown cloud, but it's already empty, the freezer, too. Then I'm in the bedroom with the fucking cat, opening the lid on the secret hiding place, pushing aside the cracked boxes. I pick up the long-overdue library book. Ten-year-old receipts stick in the spine. In the margins, I have scrawled incomprehensible messages to myself. *Bed frame, Tomato sauce from scratch, softball girl?* Why this book? I can no longer recall. When did I begin? So much has dissolved like lemon in my mouth.

Even the library book where I have tried to keep a record: every time I open it, something falls out. Tonight, it's the borrowing card. Squinting in the light, I make out the stamped due dates. 1 Jun 1986 20 Jun 1986 14 Jul 1986. The names should appear beside, but at some point—today? Twenty years ago?—someone has blacked out the letters in angry ballpoint impasto. My hands shake. Shadows swim in from the edges. It feels so like cloud, so like the way cloud steals things from me. And yet, something of the flavor is wrong; there is something about it too crude, too deliberate. Cloud, when it takes, takes completely and suddenly—

I would do it, Paul had said, the night we took this road together. *Whatever it was. I would cut off my fingers.* The window is open, the cat sitting on the ledge, and then she leaps away. I take in the details. I tilt the borrowing card toward the pool of ambient street light, and I make out faint letters scrawled between the scratched-out name of the original borrower. The writing is crabbed scrawl, written as if wrong-handed, or palm gripped around wrist to still a tremoring hand. *Apollo*, the new letters read. *Apollo Blue.* The name that was once here has been replaced.

He was perfect, and he wasn't sorry. It was what he'd intended all along. Some night, long ago, now smeared with the Vaseline of cloud memory, I took cloud to stop wanting so badly. Was there something in particular I had wanted to stop wanting? It's no longer relevant. But, perhaps, for Paul, it has been the opposite. He has fed his life to the want itself. Slowly, over time, Paul has been erasing himself, until he became only that single desire. Act I. His whole life before him. Something vital. He has erased himself even from me.

There's a logic here I recognize, because it is ancient and universal. To achieve the impossible thing (save the doomed city; defeat the immortal monster; win the unwinnable war) the sacrifice of a loved one is required, but which of us has made the sacrifice?

———

I find myself back at the studio, close to midnight. I let myself in with Lew's keys.

In the ambient street light, I read the blank squares in the sawdust surrounding the abandoned set. The cameras, with whatever they have recorded, are gone. An overturned sawhorse, the glitter of shattered lens attest to some incident. The back door hangs open onto the night. Skid marks, if I cared to read them, have written the opening of a chase scene into the parking lot beyond. The lights, when I flip them, don't respond. Still, I find my way to Lew's office and let myself in. The chip reader is no longer in the port. I drop to my knees, fingertips moving beneath the desk, sifting through the pocket scatter and hole punch confetti, the penny, the sticky plastic spoon, until at last I encounter a toothed piece of plastic the size of a penny. The chip. On its own, as an object, the things onto which data are recorded reveal nothing of their contents. The film canister, the video cassette, the floppy disc, the chip: no sweat, no color, no taste of their contents passes from the contents to the medium. A snuff film resembles a holiday cartoon. A newsreel looks like a melodrama. Even if the actual footage could burn me alive, encoded, it might as well be tax records. I hold the chip in the palm of my hand, waiting for some ancient essence to seep through, some flash of recognition to come, but it is only material, I can't bear to watch it even one more time. Still, I hold onto it. Because if it is what I think it is, no one else should watch it either.

But first, I take the Epilady and grind Valerie's canvases to a fine, white powder. What's each of these worth these days? Five thousand? Twenty? All this money around me is dust. This is how you ruin, I tell her blinking camera. This is what you do when you destroy. Then I open my paperback, and press in the chip, and glue the adjoining pages. I will forget. I will forget. I will forget about it altogether.

As I set my raw, burned hands on the steering wheel, the phone is already ringing, an international number. Nancy, on the other end, sounds concerned and ethereal at the same time.

"I have news, Mel."

"What kind of news?" I ask.

"You know what. He's in Mexico."

I want her to say his name, to have anyone acknowledge him other than me, but I am afraid to break the fragile spell between us.

"I've thought it over, and I think you can do good," says Nancy. "But there's one thing. It's very important. You can't eat cloud until you arrive."

"It's like nine hours," I tell her.

"Mellie, this is nonnegotiable. You've got to."

"All right," I tell her.

I've been so high so long I don't know what my body will do if I deny it now, and I'm not sure I should be driving deserted Mexican highways alone in any condition, but the story of the sacrifice, I realize, is also told in reverse. If you can follow the prohibition (seeds you must not eat, a candle you must not light, a turn of the head you must resist) then you can bring the loved one back, and so I agree.

———

I am greasy-haired, unshowered, rank and sour. My skin in the rearview has a gray pallor. I'm fattening beneath the chin and on my finger pads. I listen to right wing radio because music and NPR make me nod off. *Now*, says Glenn Beck, *now I get sent about a hundred books a month, books people tell me I've got to read. And from these I maybe select ten to put on my bedside table, and I'll tell you the truth. When* Prayer Spiral *came out what was it? Two, three years ago, it passed me by. But then this friend of mine—have you ever prayed with Rafael Cruz?—well it was Rafe Cruz and he said I had to, just had to read it. You know people who when they pray you just know they are* intimate *with God? And you think to yourself, I pray, but I'm not—anyway, Rafael, he's got that thing. A prayerful, an intimate knowing. Well,* Prayer Spiral *turns out to be about that. Moving inward, with prayer. Locating the center. Along the way, those things that interfere, your sense of humor? Your pride? How busy you are? It has to be discarded. You is your soul in connection with God. The rest is in the way.*

San Diego. The funnel of the border. Homeland Security drowses over his automatic weapon. The floodlights are the only thing awake. Tijuana. Ensenada. And then the vastness of the desert. I am headed toward the border between Baja California and Baja California Sur, where a road breaks off from Highway One and heads for the OneLife compound. I have about three hours to go before the turnoff, before the road gets truly hairy, before I do the final miles in absolute darkness, on broken paving and sand. The cloud need is crawling all over me. I've got beetles under my skin and I'm blinking hard and gripping the steering wheel. The radio is mariachi static, the landscape Martian and unchanging. I blink, shake my arms, blink again.

Suddenly, a single headlight appears in the darkness. It's a motorcycle, and it accelerating toward me at a terrific speed.

I try to swerve on the narrow road. It swerves, too. I try again; it mirrors me.

Ten seconds.

Five seconds.

Four seconds.

I yank on the wheel and veer into the sand beside the highway. Scrub growth and night. The motorcycle, piloted by a helmeted figure with long dark hair, slows. She flashes me twice, and, instead of stopping, revs again until she's back up to ninety. I watch the taillights for maybe thirty seconds, listen to the engine, and then both are gone.

Leaving me—nowhere. In the well of light around my car, I can make out the bulbous organic forms of the cacti. Nopale. Saguaro. Chain-link Cholla. Beyond, the horizon has a touch of orange from the cloud-hidden moon, but otherwise the earth and the sky are a uniform color. About thirty miles back, I had passed the lit Tecate stand, where Paul and I had brought the girl from Nancy's compound back to her family—tin roof, stucco walls, a man within slumped against his cash drawer. Then, maybe fifteen miles later, I'd passed a group of five on foot, filthy water bottles strung from rods over their shoulders, trailing a barefoot kid at the back of the group. But now, I am in a dark geometry, shape barely differentiable from shape. It might be mirage, but I think I can make out a cook fire somewhere in the brush. It can't be so far that they aren't aware of my plight. Who would live here, and how? Are there springs in the desert? Are these traffickers, camping the night, or some family who has chosen this stretch of scrub and sand to live? I turn the key. The wheels of the Lexus spin and whine, but I stay put. I think of a story I heard, this couple Paul knew from his gym contacts. Before him, they said, they used to do their own incendario runs through the desert. This one night, middle of BFE, they'd seen a girl by the side of the road. "Little thing," the woman said. "All alone."

"We didn't stop," said the man. "But we slowed, to see what was what."

Then, out of nowhere, swarming, two ancient pickups had barreled toward them. It was an ambush. The man of the couple had floored it, one door flapping open, and the first pickup had thundered past, searing the metal off at the hinge and giving the woman a burn on her shoulder she showed us in the light of the bar.

"What happened next?" I'd asked.

"I drive a BMW," the man said, knocking back the rest of his cocktail. "They were in pickups that still took leaded."

His wife or whatever, bleached-blonde, showing cleavage, placed her big diamond on top of his hand. "We outran them."

The fire seems to waver in the desert. Is it moving? Is it coming toward me? And the land around me is not depopulated. It rustles, as with wildlife. The sand spatters against my windshield. Even though the night is windless, it is moving. I try the car again. No luck.

There's a thing I remember my mother used to do, in the snow, back east, sliding a piece of cardboard under each tire. If you can just get a little traction, the power of the motor will take over and you can get out of a snow bank. I launch myself over the back seat and begin to root around amid the fast food papers and the soda bottles I've tossed over my shoulder. My hands are shaking. Damnit. Damnit. Damnit.

My foot knocks against the dashboard, and dislodges it. There, in the hiding place, is a single forgotten box of cloud. I don't think. I open the box and unstick a tab. Nancy's going to set conditions? She's going to tell me if it's right to come? Screw that.

—pop—

—ease comes, emptiness. There is a fire moving toward me, accompanied by shadowy figures that bob in the scrub. I turn the key. The Lexus loves me. She spins once and then pulls back onto the highway. In the rearview, I watch the fire disappear behind me, until I remember to look ahead at the road. I am in darkness again with only my own reflection to look at. G-d, what a mess I am. Before I reach my destination, I decide, I will have to take a mascara break.

I could write an autobiography of the sordid places I have squintingly tried to pull myself together: gas station bathroom before visiting my father's mother to beg for money as a child; in a pay toilet, as a teenager, before I really got it about having my period, and after I'd bled through a purple silk skirt; off Avenue D, to put on more lipstick over a fresh mouth of cloud, in the So Shoot Me Hangar. Tonight, I am parked in the tropical flora at the side of the sand and gravel road, dome light bright, occasional VW van passing behind me to take the last turnoff for OneLife. It's late at night; the pools are open to the public.

I braid a kind of hippie thing into the front of my hair, smooth my flyaways with my fingers. I layer on the eyeliner and the lipstick and brush bronzer over my cheeks and brow line. Extra mascara. I pop a crusty tic tac from the bottom of my purse, and I rub a little coconut lotion under my arms and into the fabric of my underpants. A bug the size of my fist is crawling across the windshield. A rubber tree branch stirs in a light breeze. The undergrowth is alive with sound. In the mirror, the little portions of myself I can see at a time, I look attractive for a corpse. I am counting on the night to cover for me.

I'm not high, probably, but I'm not sober either, and I've got adrenaline so bad I am rocking, tapping the wheel with my fingers. I'm exhausted and I know better than to trust my brain, so I don't prepare what I'm going to say to him or wonder how I'll feel. I needed to come to him. The next part is just the next part. I back out onto the route and then pull a K-turn up onto the road that leads to Nancy's retreat center. I park in the first lot and ascend into the hush of the wee hours. It's changed since I came nine months ago, but in some way too subtle or intangible to define. There are Jags in place of the Mercedes; the mindfulness messages along the footpaths have vanished. There is more wind, more sea and sulfur in the air. From the inky shadows, a blue creature emerges who turns out to be Nancy.

She hands me a glass of water and puts her arm around my shoulder. I drink steadily. Then we step apart. We look at each other. It's been almost a year since I've seen my friend, but the main sign of time is that her hair is shorter. There's something else, maybe grooming, those blond streaks exclusive hairdressers put in their clients' hair, weight loss—but she resembles, more than I recall, her rich-lady clients. She carries herself with that sort of assurance and authority. I know the months have not been as kind to me, but I am unprepared for the scrutiny I'm getting from Nancy.

"I look like shit," I say. "I'm fatter."

"You don't know?" Nancy tells me. "Seriously?"

"What?" I touch my face, suddenly convinced I've sprouted a mole or a port wine stain.

She smiles and touches my stomach. "You're carrying," she says. "You're pregnant."

"Fuck you," I tell her. "Since when does being a massage therapist make you a midwife? How the fuck would you know?" And yet, even as I say it, I feel a little thrill inside, a little something flip over in my heart. I think of all the little caplets of Ortho Tri-Cyclen I've introduced into the sewage system, all the days unprotected.

"Massage therapist," Nancy says. "You sound like my mother." She puts her arm around my shoulder and begins to lead me. She isn't in the dorms anymore, some sort of promotion to do with the new outlet venture—she's got her own tasteful building, set apart from the others in a protected grove. Nancy pauses at the entryway to her house, and turns to me.

"Did you do as I asked?" Nancy asks.

"Yeah, but I didn't really see the point." I say. I follow her over the threshold, across the warm brown tile and through to the courtyard in back "So, how is he?"

As we pass by the kitchen, she takes my water glass from me and puts it on the counter. "Listen, there's a thing I should prepare you for, a thing maybe you're not totally aware of. When he's been coming here, it hasn't just been for business."

"You're saying there was what? A girl? Was it you?"

"Snap out of it, Mellie. I'm saying, I know you don't have much confidence in the work we do here—"

"My boyfriend doesn't even like to hug, OK? And then, I wake up one morning and he's got rocks on his head. How does that happen? Someone had to convince him."

"Obviously, I bear responsibility. His interest in the work flattered me, and I thought it could help him. I was sad."

"I'm fucking sad," I say. "But I guess you didn't think I needed a better life."

"Look, be pissed at me. Just, save it until after."

We find the rear entrance, and then we begin a climb up a narrow path which cannot be heavily trafficked.

To the left, as we curve upward and toward the sea, the mutter of the midnight bathers is audible.

"Where are you taking me?"

"This place, the OneLife center, has been here for a long time. It's been other things, before it became what it is. And there are holdovers from before, and also people at the fringes who are kind of attracted here. They've been kicked out. They return. And the legality of it, of their encampment, is a little tricky. Anyway, these are people with very few other options, and I've always thought it was kinder to let them stay. Sometimes, they come into our orbit, and that tends to justify it. But also, it happens the other way around. He got involved."

We've left the public part of the compound now. The paths are narrower, kept up by foot traffic rather than gardener's shears, and so I have to walk behind Nancy. Not every word she says is perfectly clear. I can see steam rising from the springs, but we skirt around the cliff edges, and keep to the rocky trail.

"When did he leave you?" she asks. "What kind of shape was he in?"

I don't say anything, but I can see the organic matter on Lew's clothes, the smear on the pavement.

"Mellie?"

"He didn't leave me," I say. "He got hurt. I guess I let him get involved with some bad people, too."

Nancy waits, and when I reach her, she puts her arm around me. I stay stiff, and after a few moments, she releases me.

"How long ago was this?"

"A day, I think."

A fence of bleached driftwood and barbed wire marks some boundary. Beyond, there are flattened beer cans and snack bags caught in the scrub.

"Are you sure?" She shakes her head. "I think it may have been longer. Four days ago, I heard this rumor of this pocho hitchhiking south. I tried to intersect him, but it wasn't possible. The whole balance, between the villages and the Center, it goes through phases, and recently, something having nothing to do with either of you, I overstepped. I was able to ensure he got this far."

We have reached a reach a break in the wire fence.

"So, wait—you haven't seen him? How do you know he's OK?"

"He's alive. That's the point. The point is, it's not some other life this is about now. It's life. We're trying to keep him alive."

Before I can respond, Nancy reaches back a hand and gestures for me to stop. A man approaches the opening, and he and Nancy have a whispered exchange. In the trees, I make out the encampment that I had noticed on my previous visit, but it's larger than my earlier impression suggested, six or seven trailers, a few shanties put together from plastic rain barrels and corrugated roofing, the triangular lines of nylon tent flaps bisecting the space between trees. The man at the fence is shaking his head. Nancy accedes with a little gesture of her hands and steps back toward me.

"Listen, Mellie. The long and short of it is, I can't go in there. Which means, it's on you now."

"It seems like you're not telling me something, like there's something you're avoiding saying."

"Later. Ask me anything," she says. "But now you have to hurry." Then she hands me a headset. "There's a lot in you, Mellie. There always has been. He's been lucky to have you."

The encampment is shadows and impressions in the firelight. There are coolers carefully marked in permanent marker, as for a school field trip, and also something that appears to be a skinned animal hanging over the fire. A length of chain encircles a tree. Children's underwear dries on a line. No one is about, but a pipe set in a dish releases curls of smoke. Shadows pass behind tent flaps and a sleeping bag rustles out of sight. The man I follow has not introduced himself, and does not give me time to observe his face. The trees fade behind us, and then we have come to a rockier area. I can hear the sea, more loudly, but as if underneath me. It should be to my left, I think, but the sound seems to come from the outcropping of stone ahead.

The man says something. "Where they quarry it," I think, but maybe it's "incendario." And then I realize there is a gap in the rock face ahead. An opening. Behind me, the man has retreated. The disorienting sense of the ocean below me returns, growing louder and more distinct as I step across the threshold into the cave-like fissure in the stone.

It smells of wood smoke within, and of creatures. Something—a syringe—cracks beneath my feet. Then, ahead, in a shaft of light, I make out a figure hunched under a blanket. Shadows the color of bruises or bruises as big as shadows darken his exposed skin, and he holds himself bent in a way that suggests deep damage in intimate places, organs and worse. It is more terrible, I think, because of the size of him. He is so big, he should be invincible, but he's been hurt, and not just once, and not just by one person. The pain seems to shimmer off him, but as I draw nearer, I see that his shimmer is physiological, is a kind of tremor or spasm. Twenty feet away, I stop.

His back is toward me, and he wears a head set.

He is speaking indistinctly. "I can go anywhere," he says. "Here is the point where everything passes through."

"Paul," I call. "Paul." He is maybe twenty feet away from me now, rocking a little bit. Some dirt or loose rocks scatter before him, and I hear them plummet. This is when I realize the source of the ocean sound. As I've followed the twist of the passageway, I have again approached the ocean, and now I see that we're on some sort of promontory, and there, not far from his feet, the rocks open again onto a cliff. "Paul, it's me."

"Hey, lady," he says. He taps his headset. "You have to put yours on. Otherwise you can't hear it."

I put the headset on. The warmth enters my temples, but I don't feel compelled by it. There's nothing different here from a waning cloud high, and since that's where I'm at, the feeling is hardly magic. "What am I listening for?"

"How about a joke? It's not that funny. You OK with that?"

"Sure," I say. "OK. Go ahead."

"So there's this guy, right? And he's in love with a horse. Crazy about this horse. He tries everything. Love songs, gifts. People tell him, that's a horse. A horse can't love you, but he won't listen. He's like, nope. If I love this horse hard enough, someday, it's gonna love me in return. *I love you,* he screams at the horse.

But the horse doesn't say anything. After years and years, he dies still pleading with the horse."

"Yeah," I say. "That's not a funny joke."

"Wait," he says. "That's not the punchline. It's the guy's funeral. Everyone's crying around the gravesite, flowers, hymns, all that shit, and then the horse wanders up wearing a widow's veil. People are like, how dare you show your face? And the horse goes, *Lo siento. No hablo ingles.*"

"Paul," I say. I've edged forward, am maybe fifteen feet away. The headset feels uncomfortable against my skin. "We can take time. You can explain it to me."

There's some place I've missed along the way, failed to look at properly. We can walk back, take eons to talk it through. Nothing and no one will press on us. We will reassess each terrible betrayal, calculate the damages to the fraction of a cent; there can be payouts and generous compensation packages. There can be reparations.

"It's not too late," I say. "We can be new."

He coughs, or is it a pained laugh? "Is that so, lady? So how come I still smell it on you?"

"It was just a little bit," I tell him, slipping a little as I move closer. I right myself. "I do it all the time; I can handle it."

"Your way keeps looping around, back again. Different animal at the gravesite. Different way to die."

"I'm the horse?" I say. "I thought I was the man."

"Oh, now," he says. "Oh, now. Lady. Honey. That's the point. You're not the widow; you're not giving advice; you're not the man and you're not the fucking saddle. The joke is not about you."

"This is the great wisdom the man in the cave has for me? That I'm selfish?"

"It's not my wisdom," he says. "I'm just a grunt." He taps the headset again. "Listen."

I try to listen. The sounds of the world are louder, the sea below, the moist drip of the cave. I remember the yearning song, the familiar voice, the strange heat I'd felt when I'd worn the stones before. But the stones have gone cold.

"Everything is in there," he says, "but you can't receive it. You aren't getting any of it. You've put too much other junk inside you. The end is coming in on a live feed, but you can't even hear it."

"What did I do?" I ask. "What should I do?"

"Time's up," he says. "Do you know yet?" He takes a little step.

"It's a question," I say, stalling as I lurch forward. "You want to ask me a question."

He shakes his head.

"I'm supposed to give you something. There's something I have, that you want."

"That's closer. You're on the right track." He lets out another little cough and steps forward toward the cliff edge. I've come within touching distance, but even in the moonlight, his face is still shrouded.

"I can give it to you," I say. "Whatever you need. We still have enough," but it's a lie, because anyone who uses knows that loving someone on cloud is like drunk driving. It is good enough, it is always good enough, until you smash yourselves to bits.

His feet kick at the earth, and a handful of rocks skitter forward toward the edge, followed by a long disappearing sequence of pings. The sound of the sea swallows it.

"Christ," I say. "Step back from there. You're pretty close to the edge."

"Last chance," he says. "Which way are we going to exit?"

"Happily ever after," I say. "A baby. Our baby."

He pauses, as if considering it, chin down. If he would just look up. If he would just see me. But then, his body makes a little jolt of dismissal. "I'm not too sure I work that way anymore, lady honey."

He takes just one step. There is a version of this story which is perfect, in which he falls. He plummets down. It is the completion of the fall he's been making his whole life, slipping on Nancy's roof in the middle of the winter, arcing from the train on a clear artic day, his hands releasing from the chain link onto the furry rock below, or under Lew's blows.

But instead, I pull him back. I have him, skin and meat and bone and ache. He is in my arms. I pull him toward me, turning his face toward my face. "Paul," I say.

The man before me is gray. His skin has the peculiar puffinesss and pallor of a longtime-user. Otherwise, he is blank. I cannot see his face.

"What have you done to yourself?" I say. "Oh, G-d. What have I done?"

"Now she gets it," he says. "Here's the punchline. Paul's already gone."

I remember reaching the edge of the cliff. Dawn had come. It was not a lovely view. The camp people had dumped carts and trash bags full of diapers and husks of squash and bright aluminum cans over the edge, and the objects caught in tenacious cacti that clung to the slope, caught in the matted brush. I could see a path, such as a falling body might cut as it made its way to the rocks below. A gray blanket moved slightly in the wind, but there was nothing beneath it. I picked up a handful of rocks and put them in my mouth.

Now, someone comes to stand beside me. She puts an arm over my shoulder.

"What do you need?" she asks. "How can I help?"

"I've lost something," I say. My chest aches. My ribs feel like they've been cracked open. "But I can't recall what it is."

"Do you want me to help you remember?"

I shake my head. "I want to be better," I say. "I want to figure out a way to feel better."

She pulls me into her, her free hand straying to my belly. "I think you can. I really think you can, but it's not going to be quick or easy. Real stuff never is."

Eight

Sullivan County
2010

I want my story to be that I got off cloud with an epiphany. I had a growing child inside me, and she changed me. But that is not what happened. The hospital detoxed me, because I was asleep most of the time and because I was incapacitated so the incoherent time during which I would have sawn off my arm for more cloud I was prevented from doing it. When I was released into Trudi's care, I allowed her to feed me sleeping pills which were not authorized by the obstetrician. I took the bottle with me when she put me on the bus east to dull the trembling and the hunger that would still arise. Even so I had between five and twenty relapses, depending on whether you counted the episodes as distinct, or as sustained benders. I ate cloud while I was pregnant. I ate cloud while I nursed. I was so high one night, I dropped my baby on the stairs and she bled because of my negligence. I would get clean, and then I would eat again. It wasn't easy, and I didn't do it right, but I have two months sober, and I am headed home. I wish I had more to bring to the fight that lies ahead.

It is Monday morning and I am on a bus again, making the journey back to Boston. The burns on my hands are salved with a particularly rich-smelling ointment, and the bandages themselves are made of torn cotton towel. My purse is gone—ID, cash, and also my paperback. The borrower's card I discovered in my pocket when I shed my clothes to shower and treat my wounds. On the reverse of the card I can read Paul's name still, and I think I will hang onto it, this one scrap. If I can make my way back to Juni, I will need to figure out what kind of story to tell her about this person, and I know the boy with the library book who found me in the woods is the best part of it.

I thrust my hand into the fire, and I held it there, flames leaping up my sleeves. Trudi lifted her weapon behind me. The plastic casing on the tiny chip bubbled and melted—the thing was gone. Trudi shot again. I felt the bullet shoot by me and then there was no sound, only the throb of the *bang*. Deafened, I waved my arm wildly, and Trudi leapt away from the flames. I fell to the ground, rolling toward the window. Pain sparked through me. The fire jumped from my arm to the nest of bedding in the corner. I beat my arm against my body, and the flame leapt, like something alive. By now, the bedding had caught, and spread to a stage curtain pulled to one side of the room. Trudi took another shot, and now I was throwing myself against the glass of the window. It shattered, the glass driving into me and I leapt. Bleeding, I ran for the nearest shelter—there was a shed—and I managed to get myself inside of it before Trudi and Lew emerged.

The structure was old and the plywood siding had warped away in a corner, and it afforded me a partial view of what was still unfolding outside. The fire had not been contained. Smoke was leaking from the broken window panes. Trudi and Lew stopped and scanned the landscape. Just as they turned toward my hidden position, someone leaned on a horn. Trudi raised her weapon and pointed it toward the site of the car crash, and shot again before Lew unexpectedly reached out and restrained her weapon hand. Of the two of them, he still must have had the better hearing because he'd heard the approaching fire engines. Then, with barely another moment's hesitation, they made for the rental sedan. By the time the trucks arrived, both the SUV and the rented white sedan had escaped.

What I thought when I emerged from the shed: this is the sunburn hour, when good mothers slather their infants in sunscreen, pull hats over their tender scalps. Juni was no longer an infant, had at last a head of wispy hair, but who would protect her skin? Who would be there, for whom would the day's heat spark the instinct to cover her? There was room for very little else in my mind but going forward. The first of the fire trucks arrived, and I began to wave.

I like to think Paul had leaned on the horn on purpose to draw my pursuers' attention away from me. If that's so, then maybe it's less disconcerting that he has the only record I've kept of our life together. It feels strange to have it gone. But I know, I understand, that that man and I don't owe each other anything anymore.

I was sitting in the cab of the fire truck, headed back for the fancy resort town where the bus station was, when I asked to borrow one of the firefighters' phones.

The countdown on the page for Bright Big Future had run out, and the links, one of the links when I tried to click through, was already broken. We'd paid our debts to each other, and what happened after wasn't something I was going to get to know.

But what of Juni? What of what she deserves? A better mother, a stronger one. But as it happens, she has only me. There will be for her still those moments when she will show her true face. *Here I am*, she will say. Even if all I have inside me is a lump, I will have to be there then.

Anyway, the fire department's medic cleaned me up and put me in one of the Sullivan County FD t-shirts. The burns, though painful, ran only to mild blistering on my hand and arm. The cuts from my leap through the window were worse, but their guy had picked out the glass, and the bleeding had stopped.

"You sure you don't want to ride in the ambulance?" the firefighter asked me again.

"I have someone there who can help me," I said, showing him the address on the device.

"Family?" he said.

"Yeah," I told him, which turned out to be true.

"Hi," said the counter-girl, "welcome to OneLife." She wore a nose piercing and a stack of leather bracelets. She'd had some reconstructive surgery: there were delicate scars at her hairline and nose, but the work was excellent and you hardly would have known.

I gave her my name, and she typed it into the computer. The girl betrayed barely a flicker of surprise at my bloodshot eyes, my oversized shirt, the medic's bandages which had begun to soak through. Behind her, there was a little altar set with cacti and succulents, a photograph of Nancy. She stared straight at the camera; her little tummy and her big tits undisguised by posture or trickery, daring you to call bullshit. At these places, they treat her with the reverence usually reserved for the sainted or the dead, though Nancy is apparently neither. It is said, among her adherents, that she has 'gone into retreat,' which is code for an unresolved financial matter which makes Mexico friendlier territory for the moment.

With a muted beep, the computer returned my file and whatever my status, it impressed.

"Oh," sighed the girl, her skin coloring, the scars darkening momentarily with the blush. "You're a level twelve."

I used to think it was tits, the difference between Nancy and me, but you could also call it grace. Something leapt her from one way of being to another, some spark; Nancy would probably have it that it was something in those stones. Me, the only thing that ever really felt like a leap was cloud. Maybe the problem was in a mindset. Fundamentally, I am a New Englander. I expect to pay for my sins eventually, even if cloud let me flee for longer than most. But Nancy could allow for a concept of total rehabilitation, somewhere between therapy and redemption. Nancy was committed to the radically humane idea that even your worst mistakes, you might not have to be punished for.

Me, standing at the OneLife counter: I'd been crawling for so long, and I was trying to crawl still, but the way seemed unclear. I didn't need grace or saving, but I needed something, a little shock to push me in whatever direction I needed to go and I was ready to call down a bit of secular magic. I was ready to do something Emily might call praying, if it got me there.

"It says in your preferences you usually do a video session?" The girl asked.

"That's right," I answered. "And if I could, I'd love to borrow a scissors."

She led me to my private pod. At the entrance, she cast me a furtive look. "Did you know her? Like, personally?" she asked. "She inspired me in more ways, you know? Anyway, sorry—" she consulted her device. "I'll patch you through as soon as we get someone on the line. It's our busy season. I'm afraid we might not have a fully certified—oh, oh, wow. You're in for a real treat." She smiled again, then opened the ionizer cabinet next to my private cubby. "Here's your stone set, whenever you feel primed for enversion."

"That's new," I said. Rather than a headset, the stones were attached to a slender cord, like a necklace.

"We stopped using the temple stones; they reminded people too much of earbuds, too much of a form of distraction. May I?"

I had already climbed inside my cubby, but I leaned my head out again and allowed her to place the cord around my neck. The stones fell right on Juni's spot at my breast bone. There was a pleasant sensation, if only slight, when the warm stones touched. Maybe, even there was some kind of pulse which entered me, which didn't convert me; the entire ritual was complete horseshit.

The pull-down mirror reflected back my frazzled hair and the deep hollows of sleeplessness and grief below my eyes, the beige stones at my chest. Then, the screen descended in front of it and played the introductory video about the glory of OneLife.

They did good work, I had to admit, along with all of their crackpot self-improvement. *The primary pillar of OneLife tells us that no benefit can come to a person which does not also visit another.* OneLife was at the women's shelter, and the Center for Exploited Children, and the Organization against Human Trafficking.

I clicked through.

Nancy had invented a vehicle for impelling rich people to help poor people. A place like OneLife doesn't list prices, but a rough estimate told me that to reach the private pod level would cost approximately $50,000.00. To some extent, the fees redistribute wealth, if for no one other than the cute counter girls who bear the marks of their rough adolescences. I know this has always kind of been Nancy's life goal: to take country club money and transform it into health advocacy for Latin American sex workers. Still, it has to be said that this is an imperfect mechanism. There are hairdressers running up credit cards at these places; there are people like Judah, who think a stone can soak the past out of them, can free them from what they must carry.

A voice said—and it did not sound recorded; it sounded precisely like the voice of the scarred counter girl—"I'm going to patch you in now."

Nancy appeared, smiling, in her black crop top, a stone set around her neck. "Hello, friend," she said. "Power and strength to you. Inspiration and whatever."

"Whatever to you, too," I answered.

She held herself with a sense of purpose, of certainty which wasn't so much new as newly visible to me. Between '06 and '08, she'd been gathering wealthy benefactors, managing local factions, and priming the former directors of the OneLife compound such that when things faltered with the retreat, she was positioned to take it over. Now that I recalled my time at the compound, I realized she had operated with a kind of command, was already running things, but I hadn't seen it—she had still been fuck-up Nancy to me.

The first OneLife franchises had been in friendly territory, Telluride and Ashville, in Eugene and Taos, in Killington and Provincetown, college towns like Ann Arbor and the one here in the Catskills. Then the storefronts had spread. She'd made money, lots of money, but I would never believe she used it for personal enrichment.

"Are you my private counselor?" I asked, keeping my eye on the towel, which I had begun to cut into strips. "Or is someone more objective going to minister to me?" I was for some reason unsurprised that they were piping Nancy into my cubicle. It was much less strange than my friend's being the mastermind of a new age empire.

Among her current followers, at the several dozen OneLife centers in North America, it was widely held that Nancy had made her retreat at the original site of Ensenada Sur, from which location she sent north vague guidance that would arrive to avert crisis at mystically perfect moments. There were accusations, embezzling, that OneLife was a cult, that they harbored fugitives, that they had some sort of agreement in place with the narcos. Someone snuck onto the compound not long ago and filmed an exposé, but then he retracted it. Anyway, I wasn't there to get worked up about the ethics of her organization. I thought of my Nancy, my fifteen-year-old friend with the weed in her Altoids tin and the diaphragm jelly in her pocketbook, and I saw her easy smile from the screen in front of me, and I wished for that ending for each and every young girl on the planet. For each boy, too. Why be sexist about it? I wished for the hideout and the beach and the money to do what you believe is right.

"What kind of work would you like to do today?" asked Nancy.

"Honestly, Nance. I've pretty much had all the memory fucking I can take."

"You never called me Nance when we were young," she said. "Remember that phase I went through when I wanted to change my name to Nana? And you guys were like, but that's a grandmother's name? Different life, honey, different world. I could be an actual grandmother by now. Women in their mid-thirties are, without its even necessarily being a scandal."

She twinkled at me. In the background, now, I could see she was walking through the dry, hard country on the promontory above the OneLife center. It had been allowed to go to seed when I'd been there, that time before I left Los Angeles. There were things that occurred during that visit, probably, that would never return to me with any clarity, but it was clear to me finally that he had survived. Whatever had happened to him in that dark place, he'd emerged, but the person who had returned to this world had no longer been Paul. Anyway, this part of the compound had been covered with trash and abandoned machinery then. I remembered the morning, looking over the cliffs, and Nancy's approaching me.

On the OneLife screen, the dry scrub appeared transformed, had been converted into a working ranch. Before me, Nancy climbed the sandy path, palms and other hardy arid plants flanking her. A handsome horse whinnied. Distantly there was the sound of manual labor. The workers were nearly all girls, young and newly strong, as if they'd been growing their muscles for a very short time. There was also a cohort of lean, feminine boys flirting with one another over the barbed wire. Steel buckets clanged; gates were opened and closed. Two high-pitched voices called to one another in Spanish.

"When we were kids," I said, "*you* never twinkled."

"Do you remember what you said to me, back in school? How the problem was that each person assumed everyone was just like her? It's a kind of delusion, or projection. People just act, so often, just lash out for animal reasons, and we're all kind of like paranoiacs; we assume that if it hurt us, it was intended to."

"I said that?" I was paying attention to Nancy, sure. She was speaking to me from a more enlightened state, which I respected, but I was also taking advantage of the lavender salve, rubbing it into my burns, and I'd begun to wrap strips of towel around my hands. "I was wrong, obviously. I think the basic problem is that the world is full of fuckers."

"I'm not sure," says Nancy. "Take the end of a relationship. One person leaves. The other person tries to make a coherent story out of it, a cause for the effect."

"Great point," I say.

A girl in braids who looked somewhere between fourteen and sixteen appeared at Nancy's side. She was a brilliant redhead, pale and seemingly Anglo, but when she asked her question, it was Spanish she spoke. Something about *el cerdo gordo*. Nancy laughed, and then the girl laughed, and then she ran off, braids flying. There was in her limbs total possession of her body, the confidence to leap rocks and tree roots. Wherever she came from, whatever she escaped, it would appear she got out in time.

"Sometimes, we don't intend to leave. Sometimes, we don't know why we've left. The world is always more chaotic and nonsensical than we tend to assume."

"Or crueler," I told her. I dipped my fingers in some of the cucumber water, splashed it on my face, and prepared to get moving.

Nancy brushed her hair out of her face. There was a slight breeze. The stones at her neck clicked. I realized she'd let her long curls become threaded with gray. Nancy had broken through the trees and I could see now that we'd reached the scar of an old stone quarry. There was a little house there, empty but maintained.

"Who are all those kids there with you there, Nance?" I asked.

"People I've tried to help. But it doesn't always work."

"I know," I told her. "Believe me, I know."

"Shall we begin?" Nancy asked.

My eyes were sticky. "Mmm," I said. The stones' warmth permeated my chest, seemed to spread.

The lights dim. Soft music gains in volume, something you can almost dance to, but which instead aligns with your heartbeat. The warm stones on your chest seem heavier, more gravitational. You resist. You have urgent business elsewhere. There are fires burning in the brush land and there are survivors in the rubble, and you cannot stop and listen. You are listening. A man's yearning voice begins to call. The song is familiar, the singer. But you must rush on. Everything is collapsing, and only you have the tool which will stall disaster. *Ay yi yai ya.* You know this voice. You know this singer. The song is alien, but utterly familiar: Oh, love, it calls to you. Oh, love. Listen to me. *Ay yi yai ya. Ay yi yai ya.* Remember the day—*ay yi yai ya*—you hid my token beneath that prickly tree—*ay yi yai ya. Ay yi yai ya.* Now all the prickly trees have grown and which one shelters me? *Ay yi yai ya.*

Something stirs. You feel yourself brush against an ancient worry, a childhood panic. The song carries with it some knowledge, some terrible knowledge. *Ay yi yai ya.* Find the token you have lost beneath the prickly tree; the knowledge is not new; it is something you knew before but lost or it is something you refused to know, because you did not think you could bear it, but now it is returning and you can no longer fight it.

I, Mellie. Say, *I.*

I could not bear it. *I* could not bear to know it. It cannot be undone, that fragile thing we once were. It cannot be returned to.

"It's going to hurt," said Nancy. "Being alive is going to hurt."

The stones on my chest pressed down and down and down, as if Nancy were reaching out of the screen and touching me just there.

—pop—

The knot in my chest at the Juni place loosened. And then there was something, small and terrible, a dense point of pain just where my ribs met and I felt her, right there at my breastbone for an interminable instant. The grief returned like a cloud blackout, like a fire, and it hurt, but I knew it was the fire that would drive me through the end.

"You'll be needing your refund," said the counter girl, on my way out, and she handed me a couple of bills. "Sorry for the overcharge." Maybe there was a wink there, but it might have been the scarring. Anyway, it was enough to get me my bus ticket home.

Nine

Brookline and Environs
2010

The bus pulls into South Station on Monday morning. I take the T to Long-wood, and on foot, I follow a car into the Towers' garage. Judah's spot is empty, the car Emily had escaped in not returned, but this doesn't necessarily mean anything bad. My own hatchback is where I left it, in the Cohens' secret space by the pillar, the door open and the key in the lock. Otherwise, it appears undisturbed. I ease the car forward, readjust the mirror, and I roll. I'm already on 93, crawling through traffic, when I acknowledge the object poking into my back. It's my phone battery. I find the device on the floor, plug into the car char-ger, and follow the flow of commuters onto the exit ramp.

School's out and the day is warm. Flag Day, Patriot's Day, some quirk of the school calendar. The kids are gathered in front of Quincy Independence, waiting their turns to jump in the sprinkler. Marisa's girl, the overweight one, is dangling an unfamiliar toddler's toes in the spray. Her boy is showing someone something he's been awarded, a certificate of being awesome at hallway behavior, a commen-dation for sportsmanship, whatever.

The minder with the support hose counts her kids. There is no child in her arms, no one grasping at her knees. She calls the small ones back in, ticking off their names on her clipboard list. The spot on my chest where my daughter be-longs throbs. I want to hold her in my arms and fall asleep with her breathing next to me and know everything is over, but I don't get that. Juni is not among them. That deadline passed with me in the front seat of the black SUV, pounding my fists into the driver's chest. I see the slog ahead, what it's going to take to fight for my daughter. To the system, I am a woman who abandoned her child. I have no job, and little money left to pay a lawyer. Even with the best luck, there are no guarantees of anything except a long, hard climb out of the pit I've dug into. I make the small incantation that I can, for good hands, like the ones I've fallen into from time to time, the hands of Nancy, and Marisa, and Emily, for those to be the arms she's held by until I get her back. I am just like Noreen now, a child-less mother. I've come to believe in ordinary loss, its grinding and mundane evil. How you lose what you love: by loving other things, bad things, more.

I'm no longer welcome on the premises and while I wait for my phone to charge, they send out a woman with my things. The new resident—black bangs, knuckle tattoos—isn't someone I recognize. I can see she's curious, that she's eying me for lessons or warnings or just gossip, but she keeps her distance as she hands the shopping bag through the window. She's got her program, and she's fought too hard to get my spot to let my bad fortune contaminate her future.

At the far end of the parking lot, I see the van idling, ready to take the Quincy Women to their commitment, and for a tenth of an instant I try to recall where we're headed this week, which basement, which community room, which treat-ment facility. Like I still have a place among them. Like I'm ever going to be rid-ing in that van again.

But it's almost noon on a Monday, and there is somewhere I have to be.

I pull into an illegal parking spot. I'm just in time for the Monday meeting. Al-ready, most of the regulars have headed inside. Only a few desperate smokers still stand in the circular drive, sucking down the butts of their generic cigarettes before the bell tower chimes. I recognize the pink-haired rehab enthusiast from two months ago. I'm surprised, but then you can never tell who's going to make it back, who will wind up overdosed in an alley. She's flirting with a boy about her age in new white sneakers. They've both got their problems. The girl expertly push-pulls a janky baby stroller with a sagging fabric seat, periodically checking in on the little one bundled within. The boy pauses in his conversation to kneel in front of an older woman in a wheel chair. He dabs at her knee with gauze. She's been through hell, but her hair is a perfect, Dorchester blonde. I begin to run.

Oh, G-d, I think. Emily. Relief floods me. She's alive. She's safe.

I want so much for her to be fine, annoyed that I'm behind schedule, ready with a program platitude. The world wobbles. Her back is to me and Leo makes careful, minute ministrations, concentrating very hard. My legs are weak, as after illness or extraordinary exertion. As I near, I see her leg. It is propped on one of the elevated footrests. The skin on her outer thigh and shin, from the thigh to nearly the ankle, is covered in bandages, but there is bleed-through, and Leo lifts away the gauze. The skin has been sheared away entirely.

Leo timidly applies some kind of ointment to the raw mess, and I can see from the rigidity of Emily's spine, the controlled wince, that it hurts. No fucking duh, Nancy would have said. No fucking duh.

"Just let me," says Emily.

"I can do it," says Leo.

"You're all fidgety and nervous."

"I don't want to hurt you."

"That's why I should do it. Anyway, Britney someone needs to walk her inside."

"Would you?" asks the pink-haired girl with the baby stroller. "It's dumb, but it feels, like, awkward alone."

Leo pauses, and I take advantage of the opening to step forward.

"Hi," I say.

As I move in, the child in the stroller reveals herself.

"OK Mama all day Mama make way." It is my waking child, raising her tousled head. There is the afternoon sun through the arch of the bell tower; a kid across the street strikes a pop-it on the pavement; the smell from a pizza delivery bike drifts past, and I am beside myself. *Juni.*

Leo unbuckles my daughter from the borrowed stroller and gingerly sets her on the uninjured half of his mother.

"Mama," Juni says, reaching for me. "Mamamamamamamama."

"Well," says Emily, finally meeting my eye, "one of us is in a forgiving mood."

I step forward, everything in me seizing, then Leo turns and steps between us.

"Ma," he says. "Ma, she showed her face. Look who showed her frickin' face."

Emily raises a hand. "Stand down, big man. Since when have I needed you to protect me?"

During my muteness, Britney shifts from one foot to the other; Emily gestures to her and Leo relaxes his stance. The pink-haired girl is more interesting to Leo than whatever is unfolding between the adults. He only hesitates another moment before walking her inside.

I lean forward to take my sweet Juni in my arms, but Emily holds her tight. I can't believe what I am seeing.

"There's a caseworker, Mellie. A docket number. I do not have to release her to you. I'm within my rights."

"Oh, Jesus, Emily. No."

"I'm five years sober." She lights a cigarette, blows the smoke away from Juni and me. "My ex is coming for my kid. He's circling my fucking block, and no one can find Leo. You stood there gaping like some dumb animal while this phantom with a pocketful of cloud shoves me in his car. Honestly, it was like you were high again."

There are excuses I could make, explanations I could offer, how the door stuck, how the cloud sickness overtook me, but what she says is also true. That I was chasing cloud, what it offered, the whole time.

"You know how I find Leo, when I get back yesterday? His daddy's car parked out front of the house, and the kid is leaning in the window. I swear, Mellie, I have had nightmares this exact scenario. Leo's dad comes back, all the sweet talk I know he can do, and then it's all over, because I can fight the daddy, but I can't fight them both together. Mellie. I felt it. That—whatever—the crack or the pop when you pass through from one thing to another—like here it is, one of those instances when everything breaks apart. The hitting, the blacking out, everything's going to start again, and this time we won't get free. Then Leo sees me; he sees the blood running down my leg. And by the time I reach him, he's so totally perfect. He's—" she pauses, her throat caught, swallows.

"I can hear him. He's standing like you do before a fight, filling more space, man-sized space. And he's saying to his daddy, to his shithead daddy, *don't you ever come around again.* He's like, *you hurt us. You don't get to be family anymore.*" Her grip around Juni is gentle, but there is rigidness elsewhere in her body. "And Mellie, that boy, that is why I can't do apology time with you. I have to be at least half as strong as a smelly eighth grade boy."

I don't know what to say to that. She's right. It's fair. "He's OK, though?"

"Seems to be. I don't know. I believe in that flaky crap. Maybe this is how it had to go down to get us through the crisis. Anyway, yeah, he's back in now, my ex. Parole violation plus all the judges in Middlesex know me. Plus, there was some press too, so now every teenaged girl in Metro Boston seems to think Leo is a tragic celebrity, like Twilight or some shit."

She nods at the door through which Leo and Britney have disappeared.

"You, though, you are lucky as shit. It was my courtroom they brought Juni to. I'm on your emergency list, with your signature and everything, so it was legit enough, but if I hadn't known everyone in that room when they called her name, she'd be in some state-run nursery now, twenty babies in a room."

"There were some near misses," I say.

"And some direct hits, Mellie. I don't doubt how you feel about her. And it's worth something that you came back. There's some other you out there who's headed for California, headed for the next high."

Emily begins to dab at her wound again, even as the bandage on her skin shows a bright, new blotch of red. I watch how delicately my toddler plays in this injured woman's lap, the terrible evidence of her instinct to be careful around broken things. Everything is so vivid, like the taste of sugar after your mouth heals, like that terrible sweetness. This is the pain you live inside.

"I stayed clean," I say.

"Yeah, Mellie. You have the worst sixty-two days I've ever seen, and I've seen some bad sobriety. But, it's still sixty-two days."

She relinquishes my child and I reach for her.

Juni feels heavier, and the same, and she smells of unfamiliar bath products, but she rests her mouth near where my necklace falls on my collarbone, and breathes into my skin. Then I hear it again, her clear words.

"Mama. Mama."

I look at Emily for confirmation.

"Yeah. She said it. She said your name."

The hour begins to chime.

"Get your ass in there," says Emily. "You need to find yourself a new sponsor."

Maybe only at the DMV, but not even there because really marginal people let their registrations lapse, or get their cars repo'd, so actually only at an addiction recovery meeting, do you meet such a cross-section of humanity. Gathered today, there are lawyers, and there are homeless, and there are sanitation workers and there are college kids. People are brown and white and straight and trans, and they are sixteen and they are sixty and they are Jehovah's Witnesses and Baha'i. Some, like Emily and I, used to be friends. In this room, you might meet your ex-stepbrother from the side that got the money, or a boyfriend who doesn't make his support payments; Paul could walk through the door; even Lew. There's no immunity from personal bitterness just because you're sober, but still, we all hold hands when the time comes. It's not so different from cloud in that: here, your mistakes do not condemn you. It's amazing.

The van from Independence pulls in a few moments after the meeting begins and then Marisa and the gang file in the room, along with the woman who took my place. All of them coo over Juni, pass her around, and then they turn to me. Marisa chucks me on the shoulder, hard, and tells me I can go fuck myself. They call me *Wellesley, junkie*, and a new one, based on my internet activities, *porn star*. Even so, I have to run a gantlet of perfumed hugs before I take my seat. There's N and Noreen and all the rest of the Monday usuals, none of them very surprised at the revelation of my daughter. There are new folks, too.

"Keep coming back," I say to the young woman with the black eye. I can tell she thinks she doesn't belong here, that she's got some other ticket to a better life, but there's no direct route—we zigzag in and out of redemption.

Everything around me seems too colorized, bright with significance and meaning and right next to me, there is an empty seat, and I see a million shadows of a million people who might be there, but missed their chance. Then, someone is sliding in to take the chair. Judah looks at me.

There's an awkward thing where we go to hug, and then stop.

"Give me thirty or so years," he says.

"Count on it," I say.

Juni fidgets and babbles in my lap. A woman rabbi takes the mike and begins to talk about a Bat Mitzvah she had presided over while high.

"You are not really supposed to freestyle the Torah," she says. "But there do turn out to be a lot of great words that rhyme with Yaweh."

Without Emily, there's no one to push me to talk. It's me against me, like it always was and I know I have to stand up anyway. Which doesn't mean it's easy. Which doesn't mean I wouldn't like a tab or two of cloud to get me through the sweaty-palmed nerves. I rehearse in my head: my name is Mellie, and I've been sober for sixty-two days, and sometimes my life doesn't feel like my life. Sometimes I feel like I veered into some other universe where I am in a life I am unable to bear. There is vertigo. And I could tip backwards, to the moment when I raised my hand for my thirty-day chip, to any of dozens of moments when despair seemed my path. Too often, the ones we love suffer without mercy. Too often, the actual villains go free. But this is the world we're given, where we must make our way.

The Rabbi is finishing up. "In our faith, we believe there are thirty-six Tsaddikim Nistarim. These are hidden people, righteous people who appear at critical moments, and save the rest of us idiots from ourselves," she says. "We can never know who they are, or that they've touched us, and once they do their good, they put back on their disguises and become secret again. And yet, I believe I must have met each and every one of them to make it here today."

Who knows? I think and hand my baby into Marisa's lap, and stand to tell my story, but they might not be here among us now? Leo pushes the wheelchair to the front of the room as I take the stage. Emily nods at me. Judah leans forward. A magic stone around my neck, a boy in a dark forest, a woman in a red pickup. Who knows, but that they might have been here all along? Even my enemies have, in moments, reached out a hand. There have been irrecoverable losses, but also in the cruelest hours of my life, I have been visited by something like the Tsaddik-im. Perhaps others, even, have been visited by them through me. I am not strong enough on my own, and yet I have ended up here anyway, and so, I decide I can believe in this one irrational thing: a secret tribe of saviors who surround us, me and Juni, here in the actual world.

Acknowledgments

This book would not exist without the intervention of my own tribe of people who appeared at critical moments. First, my mentors, whose assistance long outlived my time in their classrooms—Peter Ho Davies, Elizabeth McCracken, Chang Rae Lee. My readers, some of whom have pored over as many versions of this book as there are worlds within it, Jen Savran Kelly and Bob Proehl most especially. This manuscript was also read by Charles King and Sonya Posmentier, the latter of whom is also my lifeline and my external moral compass and my favorite person to meet at a hotel bar. I've had the good fortune to encounter some terrific writers during my directorship of the Trias Residency for Writers, most especially Mary Gaitskill who told me about the bruise on Linda Lovelace's leg and agreed to read my book. Julie Remold, my friend since 1983, gave me permission. This book was found and shaped by Bill Clegg of the Clegg agency and Kate Gale and the talented team at Red Hen Press. It could not have been luckier.

I have been supported for many years by my academic home and my inspirational department at Hobart and William Smith Colleges, where I had the particular great luck to encounter Tina Smaldone and Deborah Tall. Over the years, I've done work at the Constance Saltonstall Foundation, UCROSS, and the New York Mills residency, for which respite and inspiration I am grateful. The Tompkins County Public Library also often served as my informal retreat, backup bookshelf, and occasional babysitter. When I worry about the world, the fact of libraries' continued service is an absolute comfort.

My participation in the Trampoline story slams taught me incredible things about how nonfiction works and doesn't work, and I'm indebted to its organizers and participants.

My dear, dear family. None of them ever suggested I should be anything other than a writer. My mother, Lynne Conroy, raised me to think art was important. My father, Joshua Goldman, has read everything I've ever written, no matter how weird. My stepparents, Marcia Landa and Bob Colford, not only believe in books, but also taught me how to be a stepparent with their graceful navigation of the family ecosystem. My sister, Arielle Goldman, read part of my book and additionally provided useful insight into the world of recovery. My brother, Evan Goldman, is the person I know in the world who is living best, and when I am not, I have taken inspiration from his path. Also, sorry about forgetting birthdays.

I have three grandmothers, Barbara Cameron, Eleanor Landa, and Harriet Teller. They're all in here, a little bit, are the book's angels.

Although in my tradition, we are not supposed to brag about our children, mine make this avoidance impossible. My daughter, Coco Hamilton, and stepdaughters Clio and Dorothy Hamilton are brilliant and gorgeous and powerfully their own people, and their light continues to sustain me. This book was born beside my love for my husband, Charles Hamilton. There were days we had that transcribed themselves right into these pages. All the good parts, my love, are yours.

Some parts of this book are collaged from other texts. These texts are fictionalized, and altered freely from the original, but I'd like to acknowledge my sources here. *SpongeBob SquarePants* Season One. Created by Hillenburg, Stephen and Jennings, Nicholas. Written by Hillenburg, Stephen, Drymon, Derek, Hill, Tim, Tibbett, Paul, Burns, Peter, Fonti, Steve and Mitchell, Chris. Nickelodeon, April 30, 1999–April 8, 2000. *1 Night in Paris*. Directed by Saloman, Rick. Red Light District Video. 2004. *The Glenn Beck Program,* Premiere Radio Networks, Philadelphia, Pennsylvania 2007–2013. I have also drawn on my own diaries. Additionally, this text owes a debt to *Reality Hunger: A Manifesto* (Shields, David. Vintage, 2011). I was intrigued, in reading this book, by the presumed organic link between reality-based art and the genre of nonfiction, and the question of what would happen to a fictional text created through similar processes as those discussed in this work. Lastly, I would like to acknowledge two artworks which are used in a more traditional fashion in this text, "This Must be the Place (Naïve Melody)". Talking Heads. *Speaking in Tongues*. 1983, used by permission. The cover art was provided by permission, as well: Cao, Yang. *Liminal IV.* Oil on Canvas.

Biographical Note

Melanie Conroy-Goldman is a professor of creative writing at Hobart and William Smith Colleges where she was a founding director of the Trias Residency for Writers, which has hosted such notables as Mary Gaitskill, Lidia Yuknavitch, and Jeff VanderMeer. Her fiction has been published in journals such as *Southern Review* and *StoryQuarterly*, in anthologies from Morrow and St. Martin's, and online at venues such as *McSweeney's*. She also volunteers at a maximum security men's prison with the Cornell Prison Education Program. Her work is represented by Bill Clegg at the Clegg Agency. She lives in Ithaca, New York, with her husband, daughter, and stepdaughters.